HUNTING THE
HORNETS

In memory of my father

Alfred Edward Bartlett
(1911–1987)

who loved a good action story

Crumps Barn Studio
No.2 The Waterloo, Cirencester GL7 2PZ
www.crumpsbarnstudio.co.uk

Text copyright © Michael Bartlett 2023

Cover design by Lorna Gray

Printed in the UK by Severn, Gloucester on responsibly sourced paper

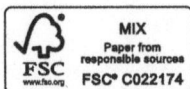

MIX
Paper from
responsible sources
FSC
www.fsc.org   FSC® C022174

CARBON NEUTRAL

ISBN 978-1-915067-32-6

MICHAEL BARTLETT

HUNTING THE HORNETS

Crumps Barn Studio

PART 1

NOW

CLAPHAM

GATEWAY TO THE SOUTH

MOST RETIRED PEOPLE don't expect to have to shoot six men – and kill three of them – before lunch, but sometimes things just turn out that way. She'd always known her retirement was only temporary so she never stopped taking the practical precautions that had kept her alive over the years. Of course, she did have one big advantage. Apart from the members of her team and a couple of others, everyone else believed she was dead.

The fact that she wasn't was mainly due to her constant vigilance. She never dropped her guard so, when her doorbell rang one Tuesday morning and she glanced up at the monitor which covered the front doorstep, she knew at once retirement was over. She recognised the two men who stood there immediately, not as individuals of course, but she knew precisely where they came from.

However, when she opened the door she gave no sign of recognition. The two men were faced with the puzzled face of an ordinary housewife, a middle aged woman dressed in fawn slacks and a dark green sweatshirt with a picture of Rudolph the Red-Nosed Reindeer printed on the front.

"Yes?" she said, "can I help you?"

The men smiled expansively, mouth smiles, no eyes, she

noted. They looked quite incongruous standing there, one big, one small, wearing identical black suits. They reminded her of Laurel and Hardy.

It was 'Laurel' who spoke. "Good morning, we are come to see Mister Peregrine Cracken."

For a moment she was thrown off balance. She had unfinished business with a number of people but not Perry, Perry was dead. For a moment anger flamed within her – it was people like this who'd caused his death – but then her professional instincts recovered and she shook her head. "There's no Mr Cracken here. I'm sorry". She made to close the door but the man already had his foot against the jamb.

"We think he is, so we come in."

"No, you won't." She made to push him backwards but he caught her arm and thrust her back into the house.

"I think so, yes."

This time she responded in what she always thought of as her 'little woman mode'. "What d'you think you're doing? Let go of me."

He released her arm but by then they were all in the hall and 'Hardy' closed the door behind them.

"Please do not make fuss. We just want Mister Cracken."

"There's no one else here. I told you."

Laurel gave a jerk of his head and Hardy disappeared into the living room, then the dining room and finally the kitchen from which he emerged a few moments later shaking his head.

"Up." Hardy disappeared upstairs while she stood there, outwardly fuming but inwardly patient.

She heard the steps moving through the rooms above, then the sound of the loft hatch being slid aside. A pause then Hardy returned with another shake of the head.

"So, we are alone. But Mister Cracken, he return soon, yes?"

"I don't know any Mister Cracken."

"Oh, but that is not true. We are given this address most exactly."

"Well, I don't know why. There's no one else here." She turned to Hardy. "Did you see any signs that a man lives here? Clothes, razor, dressing gown?"

His brow furrowed then he shook his head.

"There you are then. Your Mister Cracken must live somewhere else."

Laurel regarded her, his lips pursed. "It is very strange. Please, lady, be sensible. Tell us where he is or we need to persuade you." He nodded towards Hardy. "My friend is very good at persuading."

Hardy reached inside his jacket and produced a long-bladed knife. He smiled, a slow anticipatory smile, and slid his finger along the blade.

"You're ... you're frightening me."

"Maybe we cut off your fingers one by one. It is not long before you tell us where Mister Cracken is, I think."

She began to shiver. She had long ago developed simulated shivering down to a fine art. "Who are you? Go away. I'm going to call the police."

As she began to move he immediately blocked her way and suddenly there was a gun in his hand.

She looked at it in horror and moved into the next stage of her little woman mode. "There's been some mistake. Please go away." She moved the shivering performance up a notch. "I feel faint. I need a drink."

Laurel glanced towards the kitchen. "Is okay. Get drink."

He gestured with the gun and she stumbled through to the kitchen with the two men following close behind her.

"I don't understand what you want."

"We want Mister Cracken. He is bad man. He has

9

something that belongs to us. We will get it and he will be punished. If you do not wish for punishment too, then be good if your memory improves. Better for your health, I think."

"All right, please don't hurt me." Her voice was still tremulous as she moved towards the kitchen sink. She sensed, rather than saw, the men behind her relax. Just a little middle-aged English woman getting herself a drink of water, perfectly normal. She picked up a glass and then, shielding the movement with her body, she reached under the worktop and found one of her guns in its little holster. No time for half measures, she removed it, turned and shot Laurel right between the eyes.

As Laurel dropped like a stone she leapt across the room and before he could move she kicked Hardy ferociously between his legs. He went down screaming and she stood above him, her gun pointing at his head.

"That's for Perry," she said.

He lay there, moaning, looking up at her in bewilderment. "Who ... who are you?"

She sighed. "They call me 'The Hunter'."

MEANWHILE ...

THE HUNTER'S DAY may have gone belly up but elsewhere across the UK there were five other people who at this precise moment were quite relaxed, getting on with their day-to-day lives. As yet they had no idea that their world was about to explode again.

And what would be the trigger for that explosion? Nothing more than the unmistakable *Ping!* when a mobile phone announces that it wants attention.

CLAPHAM

GATEWAY TO THE SOUTH

HARDY, LYING ON the floor beside the dead body of his partner, was visibly shaking.

"Hunter? You're not Hunter?"

"Why not?"

"But they have told us Hunter is dead."

"Well, that's a slight exaggeration. Your friend here on the other hand …"

She poked at him with her foot. "Yup, not much doubt about him. Now, let's get this over with, shall we? Turn over, face down."

"Ty suka …"

"No, I'm not a bitch, just a woman."

He glared at her but a gesture with the gun made him obey.

She knelt on his back and patted him down. She found a gun in a shoulder holster and another long knife in a sheath strapped to his leg. She removed them, then stood up and edged backwards, watching him all the time.

"Good. Don't move."

As she opened the cupboard and reached for a roll of gaffer tape she heard a scrape on the floor. She turned and fired one shot into the wall just above Hardy's head and he immediately froze.

"Good boy."

She knelt on his back again, pulled his hands behind him and strapped his wrists together with a long strip of tape, then another length round his head covering his mouth.

Then she turned and looked at Laurel's dead body on the floor. The hole in his head was oozing blood so she grabbed some towels and wrapped them round the wound to staunch it before filling a bucket with water and sloshing it over the kitchen floor. It didn't exactly clean it up, but it did make it less obvious. Not that it mattered, her time here had clearly come to an end.

She shook her head. This was all very irritating.

Long before she'd been forced to retire, she had made her preparations. When her Muswell Hill flat was no longer safe she'd had the choice of five other properties, all in different parts of the country, all bought in different names and all regularly maintained.

She'd chosen to retire to the terraced house in a back street of Clapham in South London. Apart from its anonymity, its biggest advantage was it had a cellar. She heaved Hardy to his feet and, with her gun tight against his head, forced him down the cellar steps where she handcuffed him securely to the water pipes. Then she went back upstairs and unceremoniously heaved the dead body of Laurel after him.

She'd always been prepared for this moment. She took out her mobile phone – the work one with two SIM cards. She entered her main password and then another one which took her to the second SIM. She found the list of five names, all encrypted. She selected "*All*" and hit the send button. She hesitated for a moment then selected one name and hit the send button again.

The time had obviously come for them to finish the unfinished job and for that she needed her team on full alert.

THE BARBICAN

RISEN FROM THE ASHES

THE GYM AT the Barbican was always very busy first thing and again from late afternoon into the evening. However, towards the end of the morning it was often empty and that was the time he preferred.

He worked out there every day. His physical fitness was almost a religion for him. Even after the chaos of their last job and the immediate, inevitable tedium of temporary retirement, he had known their work was not finished and he was determined to be in shape when he was needed again.

He was a tall man and all muscle. The special forces he had once worked for may have thought he was past his sell-by date but he knew he could still give any one of them a run for their money. As he finished his session and headed for the shower his phone gave a particular ping – an incoming message. He stiffened. That was the summons for the team. He hadn't heard that sound for a long time. Even as he paused there was a second ping, a different one. With a surge of excitement, he recognised his personal signal. It meant that the Hunter needed him and needed him now.

No time for a shower. Moving fast he threw on his clothes and headed out the door, calculating how fast he could get to Clapham. The Defender was answering his summons.

CLAPHAM

GATEWAY TO THE SOUTH

SHE STOOD IN her kitchen contemplating the mess staining the tiles with mild irritation. She'd cleaned that floor only yesterday, some people had no consideration. Still it didn't really matter, she wouldn't be here much longer. She could be out of this house for good in less than ten minutes but she was pretty sure there were going to be other visitors and it would be better to deal with them first.

It was about twenty minutes later when there was a loud banging on the front door.

Here we go, she thought. *Round two.*

She picked up her gun, put a tea towel over her arm to cover it and went to open the door. Once again she was faced with two men who she recognised in principle, if not in person, but these two were not smiling. They didn't waste time talking either, the one in front pushed a gun right into Rudolph's Red Nose and they shoved her back into the house, kicking the door shut behind them.

Again she played the frightened card. "Who are you? Is that a gun? I ... I've never seen one up close before."

The first man looked at her contemptuously. "Jesus, you bloody Brits. Weak livered bunch of losers."

He grabbed hold of her and pushed her into the

16

front room.

"Okay, bitch, where is he?"

"Please don't point that thing at me. What do you want?"

"Cut the crap, lady. We've come for Cracken. We know he lives here so don't try to hide him."

"I'm not hiding anyone."

"Don't get smart with us. If Cracken's not here, tell us where he is or you'll be in deep shit."

"I don't think so."

He laughed. "Don't bet on it. We don't do chivalry. We just want results."

"Oh, good, so do I. Don't we, Perry?" She let her eyes slide sideways towards the door as though talking to someone and instinctively the man followed her gaze.

In one swift motion she dropped the tea towel and shot him in the knee. He went down screaming as the other man leapt backwards pulling out a gun as he went. Her second shot took him in the wrist and he added his screams to the cacophony.

She went swiftly across the room and picked up both guns. The man on the floor was incoherent with pain but his partner, nursing his wrist, was more vocal.

"For Christ's sake, what you doing?"

Her brow furrowed in apparent puzzlement. "Well, disabling you, of course, with this gun thing which apparently I've miraculously learnt how to use. You're lucky I didn't kill you like the last one."

"Lucky …" His voice trailed off as the meaning of her words dawned on him. "What last one?"

"A couple of Russian hoods. One's dead, the other's been secured."

"Russians?"

"Yup. They beat you to it but I thought the CIA wouldn't

be far behind."

"How do you know …"

She sighed. "Oh, grow up. A blind man could spot a CIA man from a hundred paces. Now why don't you be a good little bunny and use this tape to bind your friend's wrists together."

"No way, lady."

"Okay, then I'll do your knees as well. Choice is yours."

"Who the hell are you?"

Once again she sighed. "I'm known as The Hunter."

"Crap. The Hunter's dead and anyway you're a …"

"Woman. Yes, I know. Luckily for me, but less luckily for you, I'm not quite dead yet."

DORSET

A PLACE FOR OLD FOSSILS

THE TRAVELLING FAIR was doing good business. The crowds were thronging around the various stalls, cries of mixed fear and pleasure were coming from the big dipper, kids were rushing round clutching huge mounds of candy floss. The smell of diesel mixing with that of steam engines, sweat and barbecued sausages.

The rifle range was also doing well. The hopefuls, mostly young men, paid their money, picked up a rifle and squinted at the line of moving ducks. Ten shots a go, knock down five ducks to win a prize, knock down ten and the giant teddy bear sitting to one side was yours to keep. A few shooters managed five ducks and wandered off, smirking, with an ashtray or a box of chocolates. No one managed all ten though the showman, unsurprisingly, kept urging them to try.

At one point when the crowd had thinned out a bit, the showman noticed a mousey looking woman eying his stall doubtfully. She looked about forty, quite trim but rather dowdily dressed in slacks and an anorak that had seen better days – having a wander round while the kids, or maybe the grandkids, were enjoying themselves, is what he reckoned. In a sudden spirit of natural showmanship, he waved to her.

"How about it, love? Want to have a go?"

For a moment she hesitated then with a quiet smile came forward. "Okay. Why not?"

He handed her a rifle, explained what to do and stood back. For a moment she contemplated the gun then leaned forward, aimed, fired and missed. Nine more times she did the same. She caught the showman's eye and smiled ruefully.

"Ah, well."

"Want to try again?"

Again she hesitated, then nodded. He took her gun, reloaded it and handed it back.

She stood for a moment as though readying herself then without seeming to move she fired ten shots in rapid succession. To the showman's amazement he saw that all ten ducks had been knocked down. He caught the woman's eye and she smiled ruefully.

"Sorry."

"How the hell did you do that?"

"Not difficult. The sights on these guns are always set badly, fair enough, but all I need do is fire a few sighting shots, work out the layoff and then it's quite straightforward."

The showman scratched his nose. "Well, I hope there aren't many like you around. Hang on, I'll get you the teddy bear."

"Keep it. I don't need a teddy bear. I was just tempted by the chance to shoot again."

"Used to do a lot of shooting, did you?"

"Yes, once upon a time," said the Armourer and at that moment her mobile phone went *ping!*

CLAPHAM

GATEWAY TO THE SOUTH

THE TWO CIA men were neatly trussed and their moaning had started to get on her nerves.

"For Christ's sake, lady. We need a doctor."

"No chance."

"We could bleed to death here."

"So? Not my problem."

"Jesus, you're a heartless bitch."

"No, I'm efficient, that's all. You threatened me. I dealt with it. Why on earth would I help you?"

"When I get out of here you'd wish you'd never been born."

"You wouldn't believe how often I've heard that, yet I'm still here."

They continued to rant but by now she was bored so she gagged them, dragged them into the kitchen and dropped them down the stairs into the cellar.

Back in the living room she straightened the rug, then realised it had blood stains on it so rolled it up and dumped it behind the sofa. Another job for the clean-up squad. So far she'd acted instinctively but now she began to think about the implications.

She'd always known the past would catch up with her but

why were the Russians and the Americans both apparently looking for Perry? Back in the day when she'd been told Perry was dead she'd believed it, but now doubt was creeping in. What if, like her, being dead in the eyes of the world had been the safest course of action for him?

But if that was the case, what had changed?

Then another thought struck her. When Perry died, access to the Minnie Ha-Ha process had died with him but if he really was still alive, then that danger was also back in the frame.

One thing was clear. If the Russians and the Americans had found her then it was a safe bet that the Senator's hired guns would do so too. This was no longer a safe place to be. As though on cue she heard a faint ting, like an oven timer going off which told her that something or someone had triggered the light sensor across her backyard.

She picked up her gun and silently slipped up the stairs onto the landing. There was silence for a moment then, although she'd heard no sound, a man appeared in the kitchen doorway. He paused, glanced into the two downstairs rooms then called softly.

"Ground floor clear." The words were whispered but he was clearly American.

A second man entered, they were both dressed in black with balaclavas over their heads.

"Any sound?"

"Nah. But you saw that load of shit on the floor back there. Something's been going on."

"Maybe he's upstairs."

"Yeah, maybe. We'll wait."

The two men stood silently in the hallway. The Hunter stood silently round the corner on the half landing.

Five minutes passed and then one of the men said, "Guess

no one's at home."

"Yeah. Best check though."

They moved to the stairs and began to climb. The Hunter let them get a little way up then stepped round the corner and shot them both. One she hit in the belly and he fell screaming down the stairs, knocking the other one down as he did so. He rolled over and got one shot off which seriously reduced the second-hand value of the mirror on the landing but that was his last attempt. The Hunter's next shot hit him in the head and he rolled over and lay still. Drastic action, but she recognised shoot first, talk later thugs when she saw them.

The first man was still screaming, clutching his belly. She went down the stairs, kicked their guns out of reach then one by one heaved them across the floor and dropped them down the cellar steps. She followed them, dragging the wounded man to one side and securing his wrists with another pair of handcuffs. It was a sensible precaution though she didn't think he'd live for much longer.

She knew she didn't have long now but in spite of herself she felt a quick glow of adrenaline. She and her team were about to go hunting again.

AVIEMORE

A HAVEN IN THE CAIRNGORMS

THE DAY HAD started well, as they so often did since he had finally begun living his wildlife dream. As he walked along the riverbank at first light, he reached into the pocket of his waxed jacket for a tube of his favourite fruit gums. When he reached the tall conifer about a mile from the road he was rewarded by the sight of a male osprey bringing a fish back to its nest. That pleased him, not only for the suggestion it had chicks in the nest, but because he knew that when he brought his clients back here later in the day they'd probably see the osprey too – one of the specific things they'd asked about.

"Sure we can try," he had said, "it's always worth a punt but birds don't offer guarantees."

"What about a golden eagle?" the man had asked.

"Same answer. I can take you to a place where they're often seen but in the end it all comes down to luck."

Later in the day, when they'd seen the osprey, he took them up the Findhorn Valley. On the drive up the winding road they saw red deer, mountain goats and a dipper underneath one of the bridges so his clients were very happy when he parked the Land Rover and they got out. As always he revelled in the harsh beauty of the scenery and his heart sang.

"Is this the golden eagle place?" asked the woman.

"I have seen them here," he answered. "But who knows?"

At that moment a golden eagle appeared as if by arrangement, spiralling up into the sky from behind the hill.

"Oh …" The man and the woman stood there in rapture until it disappeared below the horizon.

"Oh, that was magnificent. Thank you so much."

He shrugged. "We got lucky."

Later back at the hotel the man said, "It's been a great day. Thank you." He hesitated then added. "D'you happen to know anyone who could take a look at my car tomorrow? There was a kind of rattle on the way up here that I didn't like the sound of."

"Sure, Angus at Crombie Motors will do that. I'll give him a bell, get him to pick the car up first thing tomorrow. Anything else you need?"

The woman said, "Well, I did say I'd take some single malt back for Dad. Where's the best place to get that?"

"Up at the distillery. We could pop in there tomorrow afternoon." He winked. "Might even be able to wangle you a small discount."

The man looked at his wife and they both smiled.

"We're very glad we chose you as our guide for this holiday. Is there anything you can't fix?"

The Fixer gave a wry grin. "Not a lot."

Then his grin vanished as his mobile phone went *ping*.

CLAPHAM

GATEWAY TO THE SOUTH

ALL HER INSTINCTS told her it would be sensible to go now but she was pretty sure the list of visitors was not yet complete. Better not leave any loose ends.

She glanced round the kitchen and gave a wry grin. She had planned to make a cake that morning, a process which meant creating a lot of mess, she'd never been a good cook. Well, there was certainly a mess now, though a very different one. When they sent a forensic team in with the clean-up squad they'd have a field day.

She closed the cellar door, checked her gun, reloaded it, then slid silently out of the back door and into the little shed which was just outside.

She crouched there in the dark, waiting. She was sure her visitors for the day were not done but, if she was right, it would be better if she didn't shoot the next lot, tempting though the thought was.

CAMBRIDGE

TECHNICAL BRILLIANCE (NOT ALL AUTHORISED)

H E WAS SITTING in his workroom surrounded by the technical gear he loved so much when one of his phones rang. He sighed and pushed aside a half-eaten tuna sandwich and wiped his fingers on his jumper. He didn't have to look at the display to know who was calling.

"Hallo, Mother, how are you?"

"Oh, I'm so glad you're at home, dear …"

"Mother, this is a mobile phone. I could be anywhere."

"Yes, dear. But if you weren't at home you couldn't have answered it, could you?"

This was a regular conversational opening and it always infuriated him, but he'd learned that whatever he said, however much he tried to explain, it was water off a duck's back.

His mother went on. "Now then, dear, have you had your hair cut yet? You looked very shabby last time I saw you."

He gave the easy and untruthful answer. "Yes, I have, Mother. Now what can I do for you?"

"Well, dear, my email thing has gone all peculiar. The little box where you write a message seems to have vanished and it keeps making pinging noises whenever I try and use it."

"You've been playing with the settings menu again,

haven't you?"

"Oh, no, dear … Well, perhaps just a little. It's just that Mrs Collins down the road has these pretty flowers all round her email messages. I thought it looked really nice so I tried to do the same."

"Pretty flowers?"

"Yes, in a sort of border. So much nicer than just boring bits of typing, don't you think?"

"Okay, pretty flowers. Are you sitting at your computer now?"

"Yes, dear."

"Okay, well, don't touch the keyboard. I'll take control from here and sort it out."

"You wouldn't like to come over and do it for me, would you? It would be nice to see you."

"That's not really very practical, mother. You're in Exeter and I'm in Cambridge. Now just sit back and let me sort this."

He moved across the room to another computer, sat down and clicked on the icon that gave him access to his mother's machine.

"Oh, look at that. The little flashy thing's dancing all over the screen."

"That's me doing that. Don't worry about it and don't touch anything."

A few more moments and then she gave another squeak. "Oh, that looks better, oh, and there are the flowers."

"Happy now?"

"Oh, yes, that's lovely, dear. Thank you so much. You are clever. Is there anything about these computer things that you don't know?"

"I doubt it," said The Python.

And, as though to confirm that statement, his work phone

chose that moment to give a special *ping*.

CLAPHAM

GATEWAY TO THE SOUTH

THE BRITISH ARE always late, but they always come. These two came exactly as she had expected. They made a classic approach, one of them went up to the front door – she heard the loud knock – while the other one crept across the back garden. She watched him try the kitchen door which was unlocked and after a moment he stepped into the house leaving the door open behind him.

She slipped across the garden and paused. She heard the front door being opened and then both men were inside the house. The garden man said, "Doesn't seem to be anyone here, but there's a hell of a mess on the kitchen floor."

"Best have a look round then."

She heard them go into the living room so she stepped into the house, her gun now hidden in the pocket of her jeans. She crossed the kitchen and stood in the living room doorway.

"Good afternoon, gentlemen," she said. "Can I help you?"

They were calm, she could say that for them. It was the first one who spoke.

"I'm sorry, we did knock. We're looking for Mr Hunter."

"Are you? Well, in a manner of speaking, you've found him."

There was a long pause then the second man said, "You mean, you're the Hunter?"

"That's me."

"But you're a ..."

"Woman?" She sighed, "I get very bored with people saying that."

The two men exchanged glances. "Well, we were just told to come here and speak to the Hunter."

"Then go ahead. At least you didn't think I was dead."

The man smiled slightly. "Most people think you are, but we were told specifically that you're very much alive."

"As you can see. Now what do you want?"

Instead of answering he gestured backwards. "I couldn't help noticing the state of your kitchen. Would I be right in thinking some" – a small hesitation – "some other people have already been here today?"

"You could say that."

"Were they looking for Perry Cracken by any chance?"

"Now why would you think that?"

"He seems to be flavour of the month. We'd like to find him too."

"I understood he was dead."

"A lot of people believe you're dead."

"Both events slightly exaggerated then."

"We need to find him. He has something that belongs to us."

"I think you're telling porkies. What he has is something you would like to belong to you, but in fact it doesn't, any more than it belongs to the others who'd like to claim it."

"What others?"

"Well, for starters there are two Russians, a pair of CIA guys and what I take to be a couple of private hit men down in my cellar. Some of them are still alive."

"You're joking."

"I don't joke. So you want Perry but you don't know where he is."

The two men glanced at each other. "No, but apparently he sent you a message. Something to do with parrots. It's pretty pointless."

"Let me be the judge of that."

"If you like. The message reads: *The parakeets are still squawking but without any passion*. Told you. It's nonsense."

"Ah." She registered the little nugget of information which obviously meant nothing to them. "So what happens now?"

The taller of the two men smiled but there was no warmth in it.

"You're to come with us. Whatever you may say, our masters think you know where Cracken is."

"What if I don't want to come?"

"You don't have a choice. There are two of us, and we're bigger than you. We don't want to hurt you so why not be sensible?"

"I see your language and thinking are still rooted in the school playground. But you've got it the wrong way round. It's me who doesn't want to hurt you."

One of the men laughed. "That's very kind of you."

"Yes, it is, isn't it? But there's no need for anyone to get hurt. After all we are, technically, on the same side."

"I'm glad you see it our way."

"Oh, but I don't. I see it my way, so I'm not coming with you. I have business elsewhere."

The smile vanished. "You will come with us now."

"Or what?"

"Or we will make you, and if you get hurt it'll be your fault."

"Good line. Might use it sometime." Behind them she

saw a tall figure appear silently in the doorway.

"Come on now, Hunter, be sensible. You're outnumbered."

"Not strictly speaking true. Okay, I'll take the left one."

"What the—" but the man's words were cut short as an arm went round his throat and at the same moment she stepped forward, grabbed the other's man's wrist and flipped him face down on the floor.

"Hallo, Defender," she said to the tall man.

"Hallo to you too, Hunter," said the Defender.

SWINDON

ONE TIME RAILWAY TOWN

IT WAS HIS money moving day and as usual he arrived in the office very early. He took off his jacket and carefully put it on its hanger, rolled up the sleeves of his white shirt so they wouldn't get dirty then sat down at his desk to fire up his laptop and check there hadn't been any security breaches.

Once he was satisfied the system was clean he began accessing the various accounts around the world, paying some people, accepting payments from others, keeping the money moving so the account activity looked normal.

None of the people or companies on this list actually existed but they all had a traceable record which would certainly satisfy casual investigation and even though the team had ceased to function over six months ago he still meticulously kept the various accounts alive and active.

The junior partner in his accounting practice knew nothing of this dark web of accounts. She knew that he didn't really need to work anymore and she'd always assumed he kept the practice going to alleviate boredom. She didn't mind. She was given most of the interesting work and she made no comment when he used to disappear for several days at a time without telling her where he was going.

The final stage of his money managing process was to

compile what he called in his mind his 'casual cashbook'. This listed all the funds the team had spent, together with any money that had flowed in. The whole operation might function in a very grey area, but the accounting and financial reporting was flawless.

He checked the final entry and was about to close the laptop when his mobile phone gave a very distinctive *ping*. The Housekeeper sat very still. So it had come at last. The summons. The team was being reactivated.

CLAPHAM

GATEWAY TO THE SOUTH

IN THE LIVING room of the Clapham house the two intruders were now handcuffed and lying on the floor. The Defender glanced down at the rapidly congealing pools of blood.

"Looks like you've been a bit busy, Hunter."

"You could say that?"

"So, I guess we're back in business."

"Looks that way."

For a moment her mind drifted back to that final team meeting when she'd been forced to stand her team down. It had been a sombre gathering, she and the Fixer were still nursing their wounds and the mood was grim. As far as the outside world was concerned she was officially dead and the others had to return to their normal lives. However, they had known it wasn't job completed but only job put on hold.

"If we need to get in touch we can use Python's encrypted network," she had said.

And now she had used it to put her team on standby. She didn't know what the future held but perhaps this time they could finish the job once and for all.

She thought of them all. The Defender standing beside

her, the Fixer, the Armourer, the Python and the Housekeeper. It would be good to see them again. They had come a long way together since that far off day when she had first been recruited.

PART 2

THREE YEARS
EARLIER

WILLESDEN GREEN

ALWAYS CAUTIOUS SHE arrived an hour earlier than the time she'd been given. She was dressed in jeans and a denim jacket with a baseball cap perched on top of her brown cropped hair. She wasn't really slim but there was a sense of power in her, the way she stood, the way she held herself.

The road in this ordinary London suburb was lined with parked cars, some had clearly been there a long time judging by the windscreen deposits from the lime trees along the street. She stood further down the road on the opposite side, watching and waiting. A few cars passed but always different ones. A few people were walking along the road but no one was loitering, she didn't see the same person twice and everything seemed normal. Of course she knew that any good watcher would be very hard to spot but her instincts were not warning her of any danger.

When the appointed time came, she crossed the road, walked along to the address she'd been given and rang the bell. She hadn't known what to expect but this little nondescript terrace house was definitely not it. If the house was a surprise, the man who answered the door was even more so. He was around sixty, dressed in corduroy trousers and an old cardigan. For a moment she wondered if she'd come to the right place but then he gave her a quiet smile and stood back to let her enter.

"Right on time, that's good. Just go through there." He indicated a door and she went into a bare room with flowery wallpaper and brown paint. It had an unlived-in feel. There was very little furniture, just two office chairs on castors and a small table with a tray of tea things. He noticed her slight surprise and smiled.

"Yes, I know. In all the best spy novels we'd be doing this in a gentleman's club in St. James over a glass of brandy, except of course you wouldn't be allowed into a real gentleman's club, not even in this enlightened day and age."

She matched his tone. "Not a problem. Anyway I don't like brandy."

"No, you prefer a single malt, Laphroaig of choice."

"I see. What else do you know about me?"

"We'll come to that. Now, please, have a seat. I hope you didn't get too cold waiting out there."

So her precautions had been noticed – or perhaps just assumed. She didn't remove her jacket, but pushed her cap slightly further back on her head. They sat down, her chair slid slightly backwards and she pulled it forward again. Without asking, the man leant forward and poured two cups of tea. He took a few sips, she ignored hers.

"I had a message to say there might be a job for me."

"Indeed there might."

"One that – I think I'm quoting accurately – would make full use of my specialist talents."

"You are quoting accurately."

She glanced round the room. "Well, I guess you're not looking for a housekeeper."

He smiled but said nothing.

"First question, am I meant to call you 'sir'?"

"Most certainly not. Our relationship, should it develop beyond today, will be a lot more informal than that."

"But you're not going to give me your name."

"No, and I won't be using yours. Now I'd like to check a

41

few facts. Are you all right with that?"

"Try me. I'll let you know if I'm not."

"Good." He took another sip of tea. "Stop me if I get anything wrong. Back in the day, you were a leading light in your university gun club, part of their match team for three years running. After university you joined the army, rising to the rank of captain but then you decided to leave. The implication was that you were a little too independent for army life."

A brief smile crossed her lips. "Something like that."

"Of course, beating up a senior officer can't have helped."

"I'm not willing to discuss that."

"You don't have to. You found him trying to bully the wife of a junior officer into going to bed with him, and dealt with it in your own way."

She regarded him thoughtfully for a moment then said, "How would you know that?"

"No matter. After that you joined the police and you had a real aptitude for that job, in fact you became a Detective Sergeant. Do you want to tell me why you left?"

"No."

"That's fine. You left because of a toxic work environment, plus the fact that one of your colleagues was taking bribes but it couldn't be proved and no one believed you when you brought it to light."

Her face remained impassive.

"Then you went to work for IGS as a personal protection officer, a job you were very good at. So why did you leave them?"

"No comment."

"Perhaps it was when you discovered that one of the people you were protecting was running an extortion racket and providing teenage girls for sex. Well, that was until he suddenly disappeared. They never did find him, did they?"

She smiled faintly but said nothing. The man went on. "Then of course there's the question of your affair with Perry Cracken."

Her smile vanished and she went very still. Perry Cracken was someone she had tried very hard to forget, but had never been able to.

A NIGHT IN A GARDEN IN SPAIN

S HE REMEMBERED THE last time she'd seen Perry, lying in bed in the small hotel in that tiny village on the north coast of Spain. She was sitting on the side of the bed pulling on her boots when he reached out and touched her arm.

"Well, that was great. but I guess you're going now, yeah?"

"Yes."

"And you're not going to tell me your name."

"No." She stood up and glanced round the room for any stray possessions.

"I'm guessing the guy you're with ain't your husband."

"You guess right."

"Or partner."

"Only in a professional sense."

"Ah. So what do you guys do when you're not rescuing passing Americans?"

"We're probably rescuing someone else. We ... well, let's just say we sort out problems. Now I must go."

As she turned to the door Perry pushed himself up from the bed she'd just left. "Well, you certainly sorted my problem." She laughed and he went on. "I meant thanks for getting me out of a tight spot, of course ..."

"You're welcome." She paused then added with deliberate ambiguity. "I enjoyed it."

"You wouldn't like to hang around a mite longer?"

"Not a good idea."

"Maybe not. Guess that's it then. Adios, though I'm kinda

hoping it's really only au revoir."

She hesitated. Through the window she could see the hotel garden, a circular rose bed, a green hedge and beyond that the sea. Parakeets squeaked and squawked in the trees outside, a picture of peace. Peace. Something she had very rarely known.

She looked down at the man in the bed. In another world, a parallel universe, he might well be the kind of man she could have fallen for. For the fraction of a second a fantasy flashed through her mind. She and Perry sitting in a garden somewhere, Sussex perhaps, glass of wine in hand, two children playing on the lawn, the sun setting over the elms.

The thought vanished as fast as it had come. She'd decided long ago that a life like that was not for her and anyway all the elms were dead. Death held no fear for her but just occasionally she felt an urge to live without constantly being on guard. Only very occasionally though.

It was as though he'd read her thoughts. "Passion and parakeets. Tempting isn't it, but I'm guessing not quite enough."

"Not quite."

"If this were a movie, now'd be the moment to bring in "*Nights In The Garden Of Spain*" on the soundtrack."

She laughed. "We're a long way from Granada."

"We're a long way from Ocean City, New Jersey but should you ever find yourself round there, just you come right along in and say howdy."

"And you'd be there, would you? Not sniffing around the backstreets in some other foreign town?"

"I might be. Worth a roll of the dice."

She shook her head. "Cheers, Perry."

"So long, mystery lady."

She lifted a hand in farewell and left the room.

WILLESDEN GREEN

"**I** DID NOT HAVE an affair with Perry Cracken."

"But part of you wishes you had."

"That's none of your business."

"Oh, I'm not judging you. Perfectly understandable. You and your IGS colleague saved him from a nasty beating. I'm sure he was grateful, and you, well, these things happen."

Her voice was cold. "But he probably deserved the beating, didn't he? We didn't know it was the bloody CIA all over him."

There was a long pause then the man said gently. "I'd really like to know a bit more about that particular incident."

"Would you indeed? Is that really why I'm here?"

"Not entirely. However, the way you acted back then, what you did, why you did it, could be very relevant to the job I want to offer you."

For a moment they regarded each other silently then she nodded. "Very well." She took a deep breath. "When we saw the fight we thought it was a violent mugging, three against one. It looked like it wasn't going to end well for the guy being mugged – so my colleague and I decided to intervene. We dealt with what we assumed were the baddies, grabbed Perry, heaved him into our car and got the hell out of there."

"But you didn't report the mugging to the police."

"Perry asked us not to and, to be frank, that suited us fine. The job we'd just completed had been … well … a little sticky. All we wanted was to get the hell out of there as fast as we could."

"Was Perry badly hurt?"

"Bruised. Shaken up. We decided to take him with us, then drop him off somewhere before we crossed the French border. He was quite happy with that."

"But you began to have second thoughts."

"Once the excitement had died down I felt something wasn't quite right. It all looked very up front at the time. When we asked Perry what had happened he said they didn't ask for his watch or his wallet. He thought they were Basque terrorists trying to kidnap a foreigner for ransom."

"It happens."

"Sure, but Basque terrorists don't often swear in English."

"Ah."

"It was all … oh, I don't know … too neat. The guys who were attacking him were pretty nasty and extremely rough …"

"Not as nasty and rough as you were."

"We did what had to be done."

"As you saw it at the time."

"That's all any of us can do."

"True." The man paused for a moment. "So then you …"

"We headed north. We'd already said we'd take Perry with us for the first part of the journey and I thought that'd give me a chance to have a poke around a bit, as it were."

"You were suspicious?"

"Not really suspicious – more curious. Something was going on and I didn't know what. I don't like not knowing, it can be dangerous."

"So you decided to investigate by going to bed with him."

"That wasn't Plan A. It just happened. We were all very tired and needed an overnight stop. And it did have the benefit of making him relax?" She coloured slightly. "Actually it turned out to be quite enjoyable. He was really rather sweet."

"I didn't have you down as a 'sweet' person."

"I'm not, but sometimes … well, you know."

"Okay, so after the … er … interlude … you searched his belongings while he was asleep."

"He was travelling light but there was nothing out of the ordinary until I found two bars of soap in his toilet bag. Why two? When I picked them up one was heavier than the other."

"So you cut it open."

"Didn't need cutting, came apart easily. It had been hollowed out and there was a USB flash drive inside."

"Which you purloined."

"Which I liberated."

"Did you examine the contents?"

"Not then. Later. When we were well into France I plugged it into my laptop. It had a long list of names and contact numbers for people all over Europe. I had no idea what they were but I guessed it wasn't his Christmas card list. Anyway it was interesting. Hiding stuff in a bar of soap didn't seem like the behaviour of a casual American tourist."

"Is that what Perry Cracken claimed he was?"

"It's what I thought he was when we first rescued him."

"And now,"

"Now I think he was probably a very naughty boy, but whose naughty boy I don't know."

"What did you do with the flash drive?"

"I suspect you know exactly what I did with it. I handed it over to the British authorities."

The man nodded. "You did very well. Would it surprise you to learn that it contained a list of contacts for a drugs distribution ring based in the States? It was mostly details of European officials who'd been bribed into turning a blind eye."

"I guessed it must be something like that."

"I imagine Perry's ardour must have cooled quite rapidly when he found it had gone."

"I imagine it did."

"And the CIA was very upset."

"I'm sure. We gave their guys quite a clobbering."

The man leaned forward, picked up his cup and took another sip.

"Did you ever try and find out what happened to Perry?"

Suddenly she was impatient. "Look, okay, I fancied Perry Cracken something rotten and just for one night I indulged myself. But I'm a professional. The pleasure was secondary to the job. Okay?"

"Of course, but I need to know if you have any regrets."

"What for? The job or the man?"

"I was thinking of the man."

"No. Maybe in another time, another life, but in the circumstances it was never an option. Now for God's sake can we cut to the chase?"

"More tea? Oh, you haven't finished that one. Never mind. Well, all right then. You're here because I – we – want to offer you a job, an unusual job. If you say yes then we can move on to the next stage."

"And if I say no?"

"Then we part company. You go back to whatever it is you are currently doing …"

"Which, as I'm sure you know perfectly well, is bugger all."

"Quite so. Well, you can go back to bugger all, though I would have thought retirement in your forties is neither a good idea nor what you really want, but it's your choice. You can leave now and we'll forget we ever met."

She let her gaze drift round the dingy room. "And let me guess. If I come back here in a week's time this house will either be owned by someone else or be on the market or something like that."

"Something like that, yes."

She finally reached for her tea. "All right then, what's the job?"

"A bit of background first. You're an intelligent person so I suspect you'll agree with me that the concept of justice is all very well and good but it's an uncertain quality. In theory available to all, in practice rather less than that."

"Assume I agree."

"And democracy is a lovely idea but doesn't really function as it should."

"It's better than the alternatives."

"Most certainly, but even so."

"Can I ask a question?"

"Please."

"Are you from the Firm? Is this an intelligence job we're talking about?"

"That's two questions but with the same answer. No. I am not part of the intelligence services, though sometimes there are links between them and the people I work with."

"So what sort of work are we talking about?"

"Off the record work. There are certain situations which in a truly just world would be dealt with but which, in practice, are beyond the normal processes of law."

"Such as?"

"Let's take a hypothetical example. There might be a man, let's call him Jones, very rich, very powerful, very successful in business. However, behind his legitimate businesses he has a number of money laundering operations. He's been arrested three times, but the evidence has always mysteriously vanished and any charges, if they were made at all, were dismissed. The next stage is for very expensive lawyers to start claiming police harassment so in effect he has now become untouchable. There are a number of people who don't like that."

"What sort of people?"

"I'll come to that. The point is that Mr Jones is just one example. There are always some cases where guilt is certain but the law can't act. Sad to say Justice and the Law do not always go hand in hand."

"They never did."

"True. Do you know the Russian proverb *'Laws catch flies but let hornets go free'*?"

She gave a half-smile. "I see. So where do I come in?"

"We want you to catch the hornets. If you accept this job your first task will be to form a small team. It must be small and it must be completely independent, it will not be part of any larger set-up so it will need to be self-contained."

"And will you and your ... associates ... want to approve this team?"

"On the contrary. We don't even want to know who they are. Only you will know them. In the same way your only contact will be me."

"Cut outs right down the line."

"Exactly."

She took another sip of tea, grimaced and put the cup back onto the saucer. "So I form this team and then, taking your hypothetical money launderer scenario, what do we do? Kill Mr Jones?"

"Good God, no. We're not asking you to lead an assassination squad. We're looking for something with more imagination, something to show, whoever it is, that they may be able to manipulate the law but they're not above justice. We want them to know they're not untouchable, make them realise there are worse punishments than death."

Silence for a moment, then she said, "Well, that's a

tall order."

"It is, and each case will be different."

"Who makes the decision that guilt is certain? Or, to put it another way, who would tell us what we had to do?"

"In the sense you mean, no one. A suggestion, and I use that word deliberately, would come from above, it would filter down through the various cut-outs until it reaches me. At any stage down that chain it might, for a variety of reasons, be abandoned."

"And if it isn't?"

"Then I pass it on to you, but not as an order, as a suggestion. I will give you the facts, any background material we have and then the final decision is for you and your team. If you feel it's wrong, then you don't do it."

"So this isn't just a case of the government, or whoever, by-passing the process of law and acting as judge and executioner."

"No, that's the whole point. If you want to be slightly frivolous you could argue that the various stages, ending with you and your team, is rather like the jury process. If everyone in the chain thinks action should be taken, then action is taken. If there are any doubts along the way then nothing is done."

She was silent for a while then said, "It's an interesting idea."

"And one which would enable you to combine your natural skills with your independence."

"What about the practical stuff? Money, resources, come back."

"Let's deal with those one at a time. Money. First you pick your team and you let me know how many of you, no real names, just work names."

"Okay."

"One of your team needs to be in charge of all practical details. He or she will set up an encrypted email account. Send me the details and I'll give you the financial information to gain access to certain bank accounts in different parts of the world. It would be prudent to move the money around from time to time but you would always have funds to draw on."

"Okay."

"Resources. Well, if you are absolutely desperate then you would need to come to me and make a case. However, if you pick your team carefully, you should be self-sufficient."

"And deniable."

"Of course."

"How about back-up documentation? Suppose we needed passports, driving licences, credit cards, stuff like that?"

"You need to bear that in mind when you're picking your team." He paused then went on. "Which brings us to come back. There is no safety-net here. If you get into trouble in this country then I may be able to help you, though I make no promises. If you're abroad, you're on your own."

She picked up her teacup, looked at it and again put it down untasted.

"Why me?"

"I've been observing you for some time. You're good. You have strength of character. You could have gone far except …"

"I don't tolerate nonsense, particularly from my superiors."

"That's one way of putting it. You're an independent spirit but one with very specialist skills. You don't fit comfortably into a formal organisation. I think you'll be more effective leading a small team and I hope the jobs you take on will satisfy your sense of justice."

"Oh, I have a sense of justice, do I?"

"Oh, yes, you do. Otherwise, you'd simply have reported

your senior officer for inappropriate behaviour rather than making sure, in your own inimitable way, that he's unlikely to ever try bullying a junior officer's wife again."

"He was abusing his power. He deserved it."

"Of course. But your ... shall we say, *solution* showed a lot of imagination."

"I rather think he might describe it rather differently."

"Indeed he might." He took another sip of his tea, carefully replaced the cup in the saucer and looked her straight in the eye. "Now I'd like to come back to Perry Cracken for a moment."

"Now there's a surprise."

"You said you thought he was ... what was the expression you used?"

"I said I thought he was probably a very naughty boy but I don't know whose naughty boy."

"You're right. He belongs to whoever pays him. He's what you might call a freelance courier and information dealer. He'll carry anything for anyone so long as the price is right."

"So the flash drive I liberated—"

"Was his current bargaining tool. How he acquired that list we don't know, but we do know he has a nose for information and is pretty astute at judging its value. We also know that he'd offered it to both the CIA and to the Russians."

"And the CIA decided to shortcut the bargaining process."

"It would seem so."

"Well done me. I pissed off the CIA, the Russians and an American drugs ring all in one evening."

"You did."

"Ah, well. Can't be friends with everyone."

"You didn't endear yourself to Perry either."

She grinned. "Oh, I don't know so much."

The man was embarrassed. "I wasn't talking about that. I

54

meant after he discovered the USB drive was missing. Your intervention with the CIA got him out of trouble but then you dumped him right back in it by passing the information onto the British who weren't even in the bidding war. Also, a man like Perry lives by his reputation for reliability. You dented it."

"Because he couldn't deliver?"

"Not entirely. The thing about Perry Cracken is that he not only has a knack for ferreting out stuff that people would rather stayed unferreted, but he also has a phenomenal memory."

"You're not telling me he had the contents of that flash drive in his head."

"Not all of it, but enough to be useful. What he didn't have was the proof that it was accurate. That was the real value of the USB drive."

"So I pissed him off too."

"I would think so, but what I need to know is how you would react if you ran into him again."

"Is that likely?"

The man hesitated. "Who knows? Though if you did he could be a useful source of information. But actually it was a more general point I wanted to explore. Suppose you were on a job for us and you ... that is ... came across someone who ... well, what I mean is ..." He broke off, embarrassed.

"What would I do if one of the baddies turned out to be a dish, would I leap straight into bed with him?"

The man flushed. "Well, you could put it like that ..."

"Don't worry. It's not something I make a habit of. The job will always come first, as it did that time with Perry, as it happens."

He nodded. "I needed to ask because, if you take on this job, you'll have to be ready for any eventualities."

"I see that." She thought for a moment then said, "When do you want an answer to the larger question?"

"I want your initial response now. In my experience first instincts are usually the most reliable."

She half smiled. "And you know what I'm going to say, don't you?"

"I think so. But this isn't something to take on lightly."

"You think I'll say 'yes' because anything is better than sitting round all day wondering how to fill the hours between breakfast and bedtime."

"I can imagine how frustrating you find that but I think you'll say 'yes' because of your inherent sense of justice."

She took another look at her teacup and again rejected it. Then she raised her gaze and looked the man straight in the eye.

"Is this an official government thing?"

There was a long pause before he answered. "No, not even slightly. Governments, very nearly *all* governments, whether right or left, are not to be relied on or trusted. Their only true interest is getting re-elected, keeping their noses in the trough and protecting their friends. Justice does not figure in their thinking."

"Bit harsh."

"Maybe, and also something of a generalisation. However, at the highest levels there does seem to be an increasing tendency for personal influence to triumph over all other principles. You probably read about the Warrender business."

She thought for a moment. "Is that the industrialist guy? The bloke who won a public money contract to build social housing but instead he built a raft of luxury homes which he sold for a fortune?"

"Yes, and was never charged. If you or I had done that we'd have gone to jail, but Mr Warrender contributes large sums of money to whichever party's in power so no action was taken. It was all described as a misunderstanding."

"And that offends you?"

"I would hope it offends anyone with any sense of right and wrong which, in my view excludes most senior politicians."

"Don't pull your punches, do you."

"However, there are still a few people who think independently about what's good for society in general. The proposal I've just put to you comes from a group of such people, influential people in public and business life from right across the political spectrum, people who realise that sometimes the law and justice might not be the same thing."

"All men?"

"Most certainly not. But there are no politicians among them."

There was a long pause, then she said, "Are you sure this isn't just dangerous arrogance?"

For the first time the man looked disconcerted. "No, it's not. It would be if a few individuals decided to act in spite of the law, but that's not what we want. As I explained, there's a long chain to pass through before any action is taken and any project can be abandoned at any stage."

"So if you ask me – or me and my team – to do something we feel is wrong ..."

"Then you don't do it. You're not joining a disciplined service. We cannot order you, as I explained, only give you the facts and let you decide."

She stood up abruptly, walked across to the window and stood looking out on the London street. The man said nothing, he finished his tea and then sat, waiting.

After a few minutes she turned away from the window and faced him. "Okay, I'm willing to give it a go on the understanding that I can quit at any time."

"Understood."

"And when I say 'quit', I mean just stop working and walk away. Not 'retired' by a secret hit squad."

The man smiled. "This isn't the Mafia. You can leave at any time."

"Okay, so what happens now?"

"You go away and recruit the team you want. I'm sure you've made a number of useful contacts over the years."

"One or two, here and there, yes."

"When you have your team in place, you and I will meet again. I'll give you a number where you can contact me."

"Okay." She paused. "You said no names. Just work names."

"Yes."

"So do you have a work name?"

"I do. I am known as Forseti."

"Ah, the law speaker and God of Justice in Norse mythology."

"You're well informed."

"And the work names of my team?"

"That's for you to decide."

"Depending on who I recruit."

"Precisely."

"Okay. But you're recruiting me so have you chosen my work name?"

"Yes, I have. You will be The Hunter."

MUSWELL HILL

LATER THAT DAY, after she had shoved a frozen pizza into the microwave, she sat down and began making notes of the range of skills she would need to recruit. Her flat was simple and comfortable, a place of refuge where she could shut the door on the outside world.

Broadly speaking, she thought, there were two main areas she needed to cover – action and support – though in a small team there was bound to be overlap.

Action. She would need a natural problem solver. Working in the grey areas that Forseti had outlined, problems would obviously arise and a lateral thinker with lots of contacts and knowledge, to say nothing of the ability to improvise, would be invaluable.

Then there was the question of weapons. She knew that a level of violence, either faced or delivered, was inevitable and all her experience had taught her to be prepared for the worst-case scenario. Following the same line of thought, a bit of strong arm muscle on the team would be a good idea.

As far as support went she would need someone technical. This was a digital age where more was done in cyber space than in the real world. There was also the question of organising secure communications.

Then she would need an efficient manager, someone who could manipulate money across the world, make it all look legit, be able to move funds when required and source any back-up resources they might need.

Brain power, lateral thinking, technical know-how, admin control and physical strength. That should do it, she thought.

She finished the pizza, poured herself a large Laphroaig, lay back in her armchair and let her thoughts drift. Although she had played it cool with Forseti, inwardly she was excited by the challenge he'd given her. Her approach to any task had never been conventional and now for the first time that lack of convention was being encouraged, not criticised.

The Hunter. She savoured the name. If she was the Hunter then, by god, she would hunt, but first she needed to recruit her team. She had never kept written records but her memory was better than any filing cabinet. Methodically she ran backwards over the years, bringing back to mind the various people she had met.

By the following morning she had two pages of scribbled names. In the cold light of day she removed several of them but there was one particular person who kept coming back into her mind. It was a long time since they'd last met but, unless he'd changed a lot, his skills would be invaluable. She made a couple of calls to old contacts and before long she had tracked him down to an address near Bakewell in the Derbyshire Peaks.

BAKEWELL

THE OLD STONE cottage had once been the gatehouse of a large estate. It wasn't very big but he didn't need a lot of room, he was quite a small man and in any case he was no stranger to living in a confined space. He had just finished his bread and cheese lunch when there was a knock at the door.

Visitors were rare up here so he was very cautious, but when he opened the door he was amazed.

"Good god, where on earth did you spring from?"

"London, if you want to be literal about it."

"Don't matter, come in, come in. It's wonderful to see you."

She stepped into the room and glanced about her. It was small but comfortable. There was a log burning stove on one wall, a bookcase on another. A green waxed jacket was draped over the back of a chair and binoculars were lying on the table. The whole atmosphere was one of relaxation and peace.

"Take a pew. I'll make some tea."

He moved a pile of papers onto the floor and she sat down on an upright chair at the table. He made the tea quickly and efficiently and brought it across to her, together with a plate of chocolate bourbons.

For a moment they just looked at each other and then she said, "Well, this is all very nice. How you doing?"

"I'm doing fine. Largely thanks to you."

She shook her head. "Nothing to do with me. All I did was point you in the right direction."

"Oh, sure. And how many other cons do you visit in prison after making sure they're banged up?"

"Not many."

"So why me?"

"Don't know. You deserved to go to jail but I thought you were worth more than that. Just needed a bit of push in the right direction."

"D'you remember what you said to me?"

"Not specifically."

"You said, 'Don't waste your time while you're in here. You're far too bright to spend the rest of your time going in and out of prison. You're still young enough to find something that makes you glad to wake up in the morning, something that will absorb all your energy'."

"I said all that?"

"More or less."

"And did you find it?"

"I did. Wildlife, conservation, animals, birds, all the beautiful things around us. I began to study for a qualification while I was inside. When I was released I became a volunteer with a Wildlife Trust, you even gave me a reference, remember?"

"Well, now you come to mention it …"

"What was so great was you told them about my convictions but said all I needed was a chance. They gave me that chance and I've never looked back."

"I'm glad."

"How about you? The buzz was you left the police."

"Yes."

"So what you doing now?"

She paused. "Before I tell you that, can I ask, do you still have all the … what shall we say … manipulative skills that first got you into trouble?"

"You could say that. But all strictly legit these days. You wouldn't believe how easy it is to play the system and still stay within the law. The Wildlife Trust thinks I'm Christmas come early. I can always find a way through the red tape or access supplies they're struggling to find. That sort of stuff."

"Good. That's what I hoped. So, what am I doing now? Well, I've been offered a job, an unusual job. I need to put a small team together and you were the first person I thought of."

His face clouded for a moment. "That's very kind but I really like what I'm doing now. I wouldn't want to give it up."

"You won't have to. This job is not full time. It carries a financial retainer with it and occasionally we'll get together as a team and carry out a specific task. After that we go back to whatever else we were doing."

"Is it legal?"

"Not even slightly, but we do have high level approval."

"That sounds like classic double talk."

She grinned and after a moment he grinned back. "Okay, tell me more."

She outlined the conversation she'd had with the man in the Willesden house, holding nothing back.

When she had finished he nodded. "Interesting idea. I can see why it would appeal to you, but why me?"

"Because you're a problem solver and a lateral thinker. We're going to face situations which will need unconventional solutions. With you on the team I'm confident we'll always find a way through."

"Flattery will get you everywhere."

"And I'm pretty sure you still have a wide range of contacts that wouldn't be available to someone like me."

"I probably do." He paused, looking at her, sizing her up. "Okay, just for you I'll give it a go, on the understanding I can shove off at any time if I get uncomfortable about what we're doing."

"Fine by me. I made the same deal."

"Do I have to meet your boss guy?"

"Definitely not. He won't know any of you other than me. No names, just titles, that's what he said. You're going to be The Fixer."

"The Fixer? I like it." He glanced across at her, mischief in his eyes. "What's your title?"

She met his gaze. "I'm The Hunter."

BEAMINSTER

THE WOMAN WAS savagely attacking a rose bush with pruning shears, probably killing it off completely, she thought ruefully. She pulled yet another thorn out of her anorak sleeve and wondered if it was worth the effort of getting the car out and going down to the library before it closed. The evenings were especially lonely here, she had never read so many books in her life, but reading was better than anything the television had to offer.

When she'd been forced to leave the job she enjoyed, she had chosen isolation and retreated to this cottage where she could lick her wounds in private. However, she had found it difficult to settle and resented this lonely, inactive life that had been forced upon her. The sense of betrayal had never gone away and, although she knew it was eating her up, she seemed powerless to do anything about it.

As she wrenched her jacket free from the rose bush yet again she saw a car pull into the layby on the other side of the lane. She watched as someone got out and headed towards the cottage.

As she got closer the visitor called out. "Hallo, been a long time."

At first she couldn't believe it. "Oh, my god. It is you, isn't it?"

"It certainly is."

"Well, this is amazing. How did you find me? Why did you find me? No, look, leave that for the moment. Come on in. I'll make some tea."

Inwardly the Hunter sighed. So far this job seemed to involve endless tea but she said nothing and followed the woman into the cottage. It seemed comfortable enough, but impersonal as though the occupant was only camping there.

The tea appeared in big pint mugs accompanied by a plate of digestive biscuits. There was a pause as they sipped and nibbled then the woman said, "It's great to see you but I'm guessing this isn't a casual visit."

"Astute as ever."

"Okay, what is it?"

"I've come to offer you a job."

"Then the answer's yes."

"Don't you want to know what sort of job?"

"Well, unless it's washing up in a pizza restaurant it has to be better than sitting round here all day, attacking the garden and reading crap."

"Oh, I think you'll find it more interesting than that."

"Go on then."

"First, do you still do any shooting?"

The woman opposite her became more wary. "The occasional pheasant or rabbit. Why do you ask?"

"So you have a shotgun. Any other weapons?"

The atmosphere had grown decidedly cooler. "I don't think I want to answer that."

"Okay, then. Do you still do any work for The Firm?"

There was a silence in the cottage, then after a moment the woman said, "I definitely don't want to answer that."

"I understand. My information is that they retired you after that incident in Poland."

No response.

"An unnecessary retirement, since it was subsequently discovered that it was a low level British diplomat who

66

betrayed your agents, not you."

Still silence.

"I understand this must be very painful for you. I don't want to open old wounds but before we go any further I have to know if you're still in contact with your old employers."

Eyeball met eyeball. Eventually the woman said, "No. No more contact and not likely to be."

"Good. Then you're just the person we need."

"We?"

"I need to form a team …" And she proceeded to tell the woman the same story she'd told the Fixer.

As she spoke the woman's eyes never left her face. "Are you serious? You're really going to do this?"

"I am."

"Why me?"

"I need people I can trust. Specifically in your case I need someone who knows about weapons, how to use them, where to source them. Someone with initiative, but still a good team member. I instinctively thought of you. Anyway, you're the only person I've ever met who was a better shot than me."

For a moment the Hunter thought the woman might give way to emotion but she got herself under control. After a moment she spoke. "You said 'someone you could trust'."

"Yes."

"You would trust me?"

"With my life." And it may come to that she thought to herself.

There was another silence then suddenly the woman stood up. Surprised, the Hunter did the same. She thought, but was never sure, that there might have been a tear in the corner of the woman's eye.

"So?" she asked tentatively.

The woman straightened her sweater and ran a hand

down her jeans, instinctively tidying herself up. She gave a grim smile and held out her hand. "I'm with you. I can't think of anything else I'd rather do."

"That's great."

"So what happens now?"

"I have others to see but when we have a full team I'll get in touch so we can meet and sort out the practical matters."

"Right." She glanced down at the mugs on the table. "Oh, to hell with this. What say we have a proper drink? I'm afraid I don't have any Laphroaig ..."

"Good memory."

"But I do have a bottle of Talisker."

She turned to leave the room, then paused. "You don't know what this means to me, to have something positive to do and" – she paused for a moment – "to be trusted again. I'll get the glasses."

When she returned, bottle and two tumblers in hand, she said, "You said we would only use work names ..."

"Yes."

"What will mine be?"

The Hunter smiled. "What else? You'll be the Armourer."

CAMBRIDGE

S HE KNEW EXACTLY where to go for the next person she wanted and she found him in a comfortable apartment block on the edge of Cambridge. When he opened the door she saw he was wearing a sweatshirt with the logo:

What part of $f(x)=x2+7x+10f(x)=x2+7x+10$
don't you understand?

At first he wasn't too keen to let her in, but finally, somewhat reluctantly, he relented. He clearly lived on the ground floor but he took her up to his workshop on the floor above, a large room packed with a mass of technical and IT equipment. He removed a pile of manuals from a chair and pushed it towards her. He remained standing.

"You're wasting your time. I'm completely legit now."

"I know you are and anyway I'm not with the police anymore."

He relaxed slightly. "So what do you want?"

"Before I answer that, I need to know if you're still as good, technically, as you were back in your hacking days?"

His face lit up. "Oh, better. Much better." He gestured to the racks of equipment and computer monitors in every corner of the room. "Going legit and starting this consultancy was the best thing I ever did. I make good money which means I can afford any bit of equipment I need. It's like Christmas every day."

"Good for you. Right then, the reason for my visit. I'm

building a team and I need someone with your expertise."

"What sort of team?"

So again she ran through the story, laying emphasis on the kind of technical skills that would be required. When she had finished she said, "So what do you think? Are you up for this?"

He hesitated. "I don't want to let my consultancy work go."

"You won't have to. We just need you to be available when we've got a job on."

"I've never really worked as part of a team. I find other people ... difficult."

"I appreciate that, but you have knowledge and skills that none of the rest of us have. That will earn you respect."

He gave a shy smile. "Well, if you put it like that ..."

"And for a lot of the time you will be able to work alone. We'll have team meetings, of course, when we discuss what needs to be done, but then we each get on with our own bit."

"It certainly sounds like a challenge." He let his glance drift round the room. "You probably don't know what most of this stuff is."

"No idea."

"You'd surprised what can be done with the right kit and a bit of technical skill."

"That's why we need you."

There was another pause, then he nodded. "Okay, if you're sure it's me you want ..."

"I'm sure."

"Then I'll give it a whirl. When do we start?"

"As soon as I have a full team. Now all we need is a work name for you. I'm the Hunter, so what are we going to call you? Any ideas?"

He thought for a moment and then said, "I'll be

the Python."

"Why Python?"

He blinked as though surprised that an explanation was necessary. "Python is an interpreted, high-level, general-purpose programming language. One of several I use, but given the kind of work that you've just outlined to me, it sounds like the right sort of name, don't you think?"

"I do. Welcome to the team, Python."

MUSWELL HILL

BACK HOME SHE lay in her armchair, her feet propped up on the coffee table and reviewed progress. She now had a team of four but there were still two areas to cover. Muscle and admin. She picked up her list of names but none of them seemed to fit the bill.

She put the list aside and tried to think it through logically. First, what did she need muscle for. Not as a strike force, she and the Armourer could provide that. So it if wasn't the main strike force then what was it. It had to be defence. Someone who could provide protection while the others were doing whatever it was they were doing.

Protection. Of course. Personal protection. She knew all about that and the people who were good at it. Once she'd reached that conclusion the answer was obvious. Another search on the computer and she found the person she wanted was living in the Barbican.

THE BARBICAN

THE SOUND OF the door buzzer startled him. He never had visitors here. He pressed the intercom button and said a curt, "Yes?"

When he heard who was downstairs he could hardly believe his ears but hit the release button instantly.

He opened the door and they just stood and looked at each other for a moment. Then she stepped forward and, rather awkwardly, they shook hands.

"Well, well, look what the cat's brought in."

She smiled, the wry smile that he remembered so well. "You finally retired then."

"Not of choice. The company seemed to think I was heading towards my thump by date."

"And are you?"

He just looked at her and they both laughed.

"No more than you, I suspect."

They moved through into the rather spartan living room. Very few personal belongings were on view but everything there was neatly arranged.

"So what have you been up to?" he asked.

"Oh, you know, this and that."

"Last time I saw you was on that Spanish job."

"When we ended up knocking hell out of three CIA men."

"And you had a fling with the American we rescued."

"A very brief fling. Just the one night. And it did show a decent return."

"It certainly did. I guess a lot of bad guys took you off their Christmas card list after that." He looked at her for a moment. "You were good. I never really understood why you left IGS."

"Personal reasons."

He looked at her but her face remained blank.

"Fair enough." He gestured to a chair. "Anyway, take the weight off and tell me to what do I owe the honour?"

"Do you fancy going back to work?"

She saw the gleam in his eye before he casually said, "Might do. What d'you have in mind?"

This time the story was shorter. They shared the same language, the same experience and he could fill in the gaps for himself.

"So what's my role?" he asked as she finished talking.

"You're in then?"

"What do you think? Unemployment's over-rated, believe me."

"Okay, no real specific role, just an active part of the team. Thinking muscle, how does that sound."

He chuckled. "I like it."

"Seriously, I need someone I can rely on to watch my back."

"I can do that."

"I know."

"So when do we start?"

"Soon. I need to find one more person and then we'll get the whole team together."

"More muscle?"

"On the contrary. I need a good admin bod, someone to take care of the money, run the back office, resource management, you know."

"Sure." He looked thoughtful. "I may know just the

person. Used to do creative accounting and stuff for the Firm."

"I don't want any involvement with the Firm. We have to be completely independent."

"Relax. He's long gone from them."

"Why?"

"The old story. New faces at the top. Old faces further down the line don't fit. Bit like you and me."

"Sounds promising."

"I'll give you his details. He's got an office in Swindon."

"I could go down there tomorrow."

"Okay. I'll give him a call, tell him you're coming, otherwise you might not even get past the door."

"Thanks. Oh, you're going to need a work name. Any ideas?"

He thought for a moment. "How about The Defender?"

SWINDON

SHE NEVER KNEW what the Defender had said to the man in the office in Swindon but this was the shortest recruitment conversation yet.

At first sight he looked an unlikely prospect, dark suit, white shirt, silk tie, but she trusted the Defender and she'd also done some homework of her own. She gave a brief outline of the purpose of the team and he nodded.

"I understand. You need someone to maintain the base camp, as it were, make sure the finances run smoothly and deal with any admin problems that arise."

"Exactly."

"Well, that's not a problem. I'm not a field man, of course – you appreciate that."

Inwardly she smiled but kept a straight face. "Of course, though you have been active in the field from time to time, so I'm told. I gather there was a very interesting incident involving a crocodile in the Tiergarten Schönbrunnhe zoo in Vienna many years ago."

There was a long silence and then he said, "Who told you that?"

"No matter. You ran a very successful operation and the loss of one of his legs didn't prevent a very naughty international banker from going to jail."

"That life was a long time ago. I was younger then."

"Yes, and I appreciate you'd prefer a background role these days."

He sighed. "Let's stop fencing with each other. What you're working round to asking is can I pull my weight in other areas if necessary."

"Exactly."

For the first time he smiled. "I think the answer's 'Yes'."

"I think so too. Now you appreciate the need for complete confidentiality? Everything we discuss, everything we do, must be kept entirely within the team. Not even the person who recruited me will know about the rest of you."

"Fine by me. You said we'll all use worknames."

"Yes. I'm going to call you The Housekeeper."

Her team was complete.

TEWKESBURY

THEY MET IN a hotel conference centre just off the M5 near Tewkesbury. The Fixer had booked them in for two days as a staff training day for a small company specialising in bespoke life insurance.

"Good security," he said, "nothing bores people more than insurance, especially life insurance. If anyone asks – they won't, but if they do – just say we sell individual life insurance for the over 60s. And say it in a flat monotone. It's a dead cert anyone hearing that will run like hell."

The first evening they all had dinner together. It was an interesting meal as they met each other for the first time and began feeling their way towards forming a team relationship. Only the Python seemed slightly wary and hardly spoke at all.

The following morning they convened their first meeting and the Hunter sat at the head of the table.

"Welcome," she said, "you all know why we're here. At the moment we're simply six individuals. The purpose of the next two days is to change that so we become a cohesive team. You've each been picked for a particular set of skills or knowledge so as a first step I suggest we go round the table, introduce ourselves – work names only – and say briefly what each of us brings to the party."

The Armourer raised her hand. "Is the idea we only ever use our work names even when we're alone?"

"Yes. Get into the habit now. We don't want any slip ups. The time may come when our anonymity is a lifesaver.

I presume you all followed instructions and booked in here under another name."

Nods all round the table and the Defender grinned. "Granny sucking eggs."

The next hour was interesting and to her relief she saw them begin to relax. The Fixer's unconventional sense of humour helped and at one stage even the Housekeeper cracked a small joke.

They broke for coffee and comfort and then she said, "Okay, let's move on to practical matters."

"Have we been given a task yet?" asked the Armourer.

"Yes, we have. Something relatively low key for us to cut our teeth on. At least that's what Forseti says."

"Pompous name," muttered the Fixer.

"Maybe, but he's the reason we're all here. I'll tell you about the job later but first we need to sort out some practical stuff."

"Bank accounts," said the Housekeeper.

"Of course." She turned to the Python. "Can you set up an encrypted email address so Forseti can send the necessary information to Housekeeper."

His face brightened as he found himself on familiar territory. "Will do."

"And on that subject," said the Housekeeper, "I will need receipts and lists of any expenses you incur."

The Defender groaned and the Housekeeper smiled. "Don't panic, they don't have to be accurate, in fact they don't even have to be true. All I need is some raw material so I can spin a web of accounts."

"What happens if we have to go abroad?" asked the Fixer, "you know, passports, stuff like that?"

"Leave that to me," said the Housekeeper. "I'll set up some new identities complete with passports, visas and so on, plus a bit of back story."

The Hunter nodded. "Good idea. Go for the full monty. Driving licences, credit cards, insurances, perhaps some membership cards, all the stuff people carry with them."

"Sure. I think I'll create six identities for each of us. Give ourselves some wriggle room. I'll need photos from all of you."

"Fair enough. We'll leave that with you then." The Hunter glanced round the table. "Now then, communications. It's vital we can always stay in touch with each other, even though we're pretty widely spread geographically."

After a few moments the Python said, rather tentatively, "I've been thinking about that. It shouldn't be too difficult. I can organise a unique mobile phone for each of us."

"What makes them unique?" asked the Armourer.

"They'll be modified. They'll each have two SIM cards. The first will be a regular one, the second one can only be accessed via the first card using a secure password. All our contact details will be on the second SIM, together with a series of codes. I can set up a group code which will send an individual beep to all the phones and means 'get in touch'. I'll also arrange an emergency code. This can be used for the whole group or just to one individual and will mean 'I need help now'. I can add other instant message codes as and when required."

The Hunter smiled to herself. Clearly the Python was revelling in his new role. Aloud she said, "Sounds good. How long will that take?"

"I should be able to have those ready in about a week."

There was a short silence round the table and then the Housekeeper said, "You can do that, can you?"

"Of course," replied the Python looking surprised.

The Housekeeper raised an eyebrow. "I'm beginning to

see how this team will work."

The Python flushed with pleasure.

"Good," said the Hunter, "now then, weapons."

She turned to the Armourer. "Not sure what we might need at this stage but I assume you can source most things for us."

The Armourer nodded. "Should think so. Specialist stuff might take a little longer but I don't see a problem." She paused for a moment. "Not yet anyway."

"Good." The Hunter glanced round the table. "I presume some of you have a personal weapon?"

The Armourer and the Defender both nodded. The Fixer, the Python and the Housekeeper shook their heads.

The Fixer looked worried. "I'm none too keen on guns. I've never carried one and don't really want to."

"I understand. Shouldn't be a problem. You're not on this team for your sharp-shooting skills." She looked at the Housekeeper. "I appreciate you don't have your own weapon these days but I suspect you can still remember what to do with one."

"I think I could manage."

"Good." The Hunter sat back in her chair. "Well now. I have no idea how this enterprise will work out but hopefully we'll be able to do a bit of good. We all know there's often a gap between the Law and Justice. Let's see if we can close that gap a little."

Heads nodded.

"Right then, let's have some lunch."

"Oh, yes, please," said the Housekeeper, "these chairs are bloody uncomfortable."

"Yes, they are rather." The Hunter stood up and stretched. "Okay, let's eat and then this afternoon I'll tell you about the first job we've been offered."

AN ANONYMOUS ROOM SOMEWHERE IN LONDON

THE MAN SITTING at the desk, whose workname was Odin, looked up as Forseti entered the room. He raised an eyebrow.

Forseti said, "Just to let you know the Hunter's team is now in place."

"Good. Do you have confidence in them?"

"I have confidence in the person I chose as the Hunter. I therefore have confidence in the team the Hunter has chosen, even though I don't know who they are."

"And I don't even know who the Hunter is."

"No, as we agreed, all set up on a need-to-know basis."

"I suppose you're right."

"I am. I've also offered them their first assignment."

"Already?"

"The Hunter made a very valid point. They can't do any practical training if they don't know what they're training for."

"Fair enough. How long do you think it will be before we can let them loose on the American?"

"That'll be quite a while. We need them to settle down so I'm giving them something simpler and nearer to home to begin with."

"A few small jobs to get them ready for the big one?"

"Well, yes, but as we discussed, all jobs worth doing."

"Okay, so what did you give them?"

"Rackham and Pately."

"Ah. Good idea. How d'you think they'll deal with that situation?"

"Haven't a clue. We'll probably never know."

TEWKESBURY

A S THEY WALKED back along the corridor to the meeting room after lunch, the Housekeeper caught up with the Hunter.

"I spoke to someone on Reception about those awful chairs in our room. Explained how uncomfortable they were to sit in for any length of time, asked if they had any better ones."

"And?"

"No go. *'Aym sorry, sir, the chairs go with the room. There is nothing aye can do about it.'* Bloody jobsworth."

However, when they reached the meeting room they found that the hard upright chairs had been replaced by comfortable ones with soft seats and padded arms.

"That's more like it," said the Housekeeper. He glanced at the Hunter. "How the hell did you fix that?."

"I didn't."

"Well, who did then?"

The Hunter glanced round the table and her eyes came to rest on the Fixer who just gave a faint smile.

"No idea," she said, "now let's get on."

They settled down and the Hunter noticed with pleasure that the atmosphere round the table was already quite relaxed.

"There's a decent sized swimming pool here," said the Armourer, "think I'll give that a go when we finish today."

"There's a good gym too," added the Defender, "if anyone fancies a workout later."

The Python shuddered. "Not for me," he said.

The Fixer looked at him. "Come on, chum. You could always do it in byte sized chunks."

The Python clearly didn't get the joke. "I'll stick with computers, thank you. I'm not convinced that exercise is healthy."

"No spirit of adventure," said the Fixer, but he was grinning and after a moment the Python grinned back.

"Focus, people," said the Hunter. "As I said this morning we've been offered our first job. I'll outline the situation to you and then we need to decide if we're willing to go ahead."

"Do we have a choice?" asked the Housekeeper.

"Yes, we do. That's the arrangement. If the job has come this far down the line then it's considered worth doing, but we only go ahead if we agree the cause is right."

The Hunter sat back in her chair and glanced round her team. "Okay, so here's the situation. Our targets are two men, Kyle Rackham and Ron Pately. They come from Deptford and a few months ago they attacked a security van in Peckham but they botched the job completely. They managed to surprise the guards but the alarm was raised and they had to flee before they got any cash. Unfortunately, as they sped away they hit a child on a zebra crossing. The child later died in hospital."

"Bastards."

"However, while making their escape they'd taken off their hoods and when they hit the kid their faces were uncovered. An Asian shopkeeper, Ahmed Patel, saw both men very clearly and was able to give a good description to the police."

"Good for him."

"Well, actually it wasn't good for him. Rackham and Pately were known to the police and were quickly arrested. Mr Patel picked Rackham out at an ID parade, but wasn't sure about Pately. In spite of that they were both charged but when they appeared in the magistrates court, Pately was freed on bail although Rackham was remanded in custody."

The Fixer sighed. "Don't tell me. Mr Patel had a couple of visitors and suddenly wasn't quite so sure what he'd seen."

"Precisely."

The Housekeeper leaned forward. "So what happened to Rackham and Pately?"

"The CPS decided to push ahead with the trial but with no witnesses willing to testify the pair were acquitted. They left the court to cheers from family members shouting '*Victory for British Justice. Police fit up fails again*'. That sort of stuff."

"British Justice, my arse," muttered the Fixer.

"Quite. So, this is the situation. We know they committed the attempted robbery. We know they killed the kid, and we know they got away with it through intimidation. Unfortunately, there's nothing more the law can do except wait for them to do something else and hope to get lucky next time."

There was a long silence. Then the Python said, "Is this the kind of thing the suits had in mind when they set up this team?"

"Yes. This one's on a small scale maybe, but, yes, I think it is. It's quite clear to me that justice has not been served in this instance, but the final decision lies with us. Are we going to take this on?"

After a moment the Armourer said, "Would anyone else like to come for a swim later?"

"Oh, for heaven's sake, can we just deal with the question?"

The Armourer smiled. "But there isn't really a question, is there? Of course, we're going to take it on. Otherwise what's the point of us being here?"

The Hunter glanced round the table as the others all nodded. "Right then, that's settled. The next thing is, what are we going to do about it?"

There was a moment's silence then the Fixer said, "Let's see if I've got this right. These toe rags think they've got away with it and they're even boasting about it."

"Yes."

"So, our job's to show them they got that wrong. Maybe make them suffer a little while we're about it."

"Something like that."

"Then I've got an idea, boss."

"Don't call me boss … What sort of idea?"

"Okay boss, point noted. We take them out of their comfort zone. We'll need a motorhome, an RV as the Yanks call them. Has to be a big one."

"Give me the spec and I'll sort that out," said the Housekeeper.

"Okey doke. It'll need a bit of conversion work but I can fix that."

"If we're getting a vehicle, it will need registering," said the Python. "I guess it needs to be untraceable."

"Naturally."

"I'll buy it through a cut out," said the Housekeeper, "and create an identity for its owner."

"And I'll sort out online registration," said the Python. "We can make sure it has a good history which won't be traceable to us."

"Good stuff. Next we need a nice lonely place somewhere abroad, but not too far, say a couple of days' drive."

"Leave that to me," said the Defender.

"You've got it. And finally we'll need some, well, let's call them medical supplies."

"Depends what you want," said the Armourer, "but I can probably take care of that."

"Okey doke. I'll give you a list."

The Hunter intervened. "Okay, so that's your nuts and bolts. Now tell us what we need them for."

The Fixer smiled. "I think you're gonna like this," he said.

THE FIRST HORNETS

KYLE RACKHAM LEFT the video arcade well pumped up. He loved the feeling of power when he killed something – electronically, that is. He'd sometimes wondered if he could actually kill someone in real life but so far he'd never had to try. His reputation for violence meant that he was rarely, if ever, challenged. He'd already forgotten the kid on the zebra crossing.

He felt good tonight. Bag of chips, then home, maybe surf a few porn sites on the internet. As he approached his car, he saw that it seemed to be sitting at an odd angle and to his fury he realised he had a puncture. Cursing, he went round to the boot to get his tools but as he lifted the lid he felt his arms gripped tightly on each side.

"Hey, what the fuck's going on?"

There was no reply, but as he started to struggle a damp pad was pressed over his mouth and nose. He was briefly aware of a rather sweet smell but after that he had no recollection of a van drawing up or being bundled into the back of it. He was away with the fairies.

LATER THE SAME EVENING Ron Pately left the Horse and Hounds and headed for home. As he turned the corner into the High Street, he saw a beggar sitting in a shop doorway.

"Spare a few pence, guv," the man whined.

Ron loathed beggars, dregs of society he called them, so he moved towards the figure intending to give him a quick kick in the ribs but as he got closer the beggar's hand came out from under the blanket and Ron was hit full in the face with a mace spray.

He staggered back screaming and suddenly found his arms gripped tight and before he knew what was happening he too felt a damp pad against his face and the world seemed to fade away.

IN A RENTED GARAGE on the edge of Croydon the Hunter regarded the two unconscious bodies.

"How long will they be out?"

The Armourer did a quick calculation. "Probably not much longer, hard to say exactly."

"When should we give them the injections?"

"Now would be good while the chloroform's still working. If I give them a large dose then we can get them into the compartments in the camper and head for Dover. I'll stay in the back with them but I think the one injection should see us well into France."

The Channel crossing was uneventful, they were waved through French Customs, and took the A16 towards Boulogne. Eventually they turned off the main road and found a lonely spot in a belt of trees. The Defender got out first and made his way back to the side of the road where he could see in both directions. The Hunter got out of the driving seat and she and the Fixer went through into the main cabin to join the Armourer.

"We'd better get them out now if we want to keep them alive," said the Armourer.

Between them they lifted the cushion off one of the divan seats and pulled Ron Pately out of the cavity below it. His wrists were handcuffed behind him and his ankles were also cuffed.

They dumped him unceremoniously on the floor and then extracted Kyle Rackham from the other divan. There was a separate bedroom compartment in the motor home and the two prisoners were carried into it, laid on the beds and then strapped down with webbing belts. The windows in this part of the van had been blacked out.

It was twenty minutes later when they began to stir and before long they were completely conscious and started straining at their bonds. As they began to swear, the Hunter, wearing a black hood, leant forward and smacked each of them round the face.

"Be quiet and listen."

"What's going on?"

"Who the fuck are you?"

"We are the deliverers of justice."

"What fucking justice? What you on about?"

"We're here to deliver justice on behalf of the little girl you killed and the shopkeeper you threatened."

"Get stuffed. That wasn't us. We was found innocent."

"No, not innocent, just not enough evidence to convict you. But we know you did the robbery and killed the little girl so now you will suffer."

"You fucking cow, you don't know who you're dealing with. Once I'm free I'll sort you, whoever you are."

"Who said you were ever going to be free?"

Silence. Then, "Where are we?"

"Doesn't matter. Now we're going to give you both some water. We don't want you to die just yet."

"Are you the filth?"

"Don't be stupid. They couldn't do this. We can. You may be beyond the law, Mr Rackham, but you are not beyond justice."

"How much do you want to let us go?"

"Forget it, sunshine. This isn't about money."

The motorhome continued its journey south. Before long they had to stop again and put gags on their two prisoners, the volume and language had become unbearable. That night they camped in a forest clearing somewhere to the south-east of Bordeaux. They made themselves a simple meal, which they shared with the prisoners who by now had become a lot less vocal.

The Defender, wearing his black hood, hobbled the prisoners' ankles and one at a time took them for a short walk to keep their muscles working. It was painful for them but any complaints were muffled by the gag which had been replaced when they had finished eating. By now they were both very subdued.

The Hunter split the team into two watches – two slept on the sofa beds while the other two kept watch. At 3.00am they changed places. By 7.00 the next morning they were on the road again, heading south-east.

They crossed the Pyrenees on a narrow winding road over the Col de St. Martin. The Fixer was driving with the Defender sitting beside him giving directions. About half an hour later, when they were well into Spain, the Defender said, "Turn left here."

The Fixer swung the camper van onto a single-track road heading up a narrow valley. Seven or eight miles further on they passed through a tiny community and a few miles beyond that, at a gesture from the Defender, they turned left again, climbing into the hills.

The final turn took them up a rutted track, round several corners until they reached a small clearing where the Defender called a halt.

"This is the place."

The Hunter climbed down first and looked about her.

"Seems lonely enough."

"It's lonely all right. You could fire off a brass canon here and no one could hear you."

"Fine. Let's get on with it then."

They put on their black hoods, then between them pulled Pately and Rackham out of the van and removed their blindfolds. They were very stiff from having spent so long in cramped positions and they could hardly walk. The Defender led the way and the Armourer prodded the two men along the track that led into the trees for about a mile by which time they were half sobbing as they stumbled along.

At last the Defender was satisfied. "This'll do." They dumped Pately and Rackham on the ground back to back. By now they were quivering with fear and Pately had wet himself.

"What you gonna do?"

"Are you gonna kill us?"

It was the Hunter who spoke. "No, we're not going to kill you. We're just going to leave you here. We'll untie your ankles before we go and we'll leave a small backpack nearby with some water and biscuits. If you manage to free yourselves and find the bag that should keep you alive while you decide what to do next."

"I'm gonna kill you for this when I find you."

"Good luck with the finding bit."

"Who the hell are you?"

"I am the Hunter. You may have escaped the law, Mister Rackham but you haven't escaped justice. And let me give you fair warning. If you manage to get home, which is by no means guaranteed, then any attempt on your part to exact revenge will be dealt with. You don't know us, but we know you and we'll be watching. If you hurt anyone again then you will die. Got that?"

"What d'you mean, manage to get home? Where the hell are we?"

"All I'll say is you're no longer in the UK. You're in a very lonely place. You have no money, no passports and, I suspect, you don't speak the local language. It's going to be a challenge, Mister Pately, one which you may or may not win."

"You can't just leave us here."

"Why not? Goodbye."

"Nah, hang on—"

But that last cry fell on deaf ears. The Hunter, the Fixer, the Defender and the Armourer walked away down the track and the forest fell silent again.

BY MID-MORNING THE NEXT day the camper van had reached the outskirts of Rouen. They found their way to the station and there the Fixer and the Armourer left to catch a train for Dieppe and the ferry to Newhaven.

The Defender and the Hunter continued further north to take the Calais to Dover crossing.

Sitting in the train, the Armourer said, "D'you think Rackham and his mate will make it back to England?"

"Doubt it," said the Fixer.

"I'd love to see their first encounter with any of the locals."

"That's the bugger with these capers, you never get to see the fun bit."

"They could still spin a sob story. If they can get to a British consul they could be repatriated."

"Maybe."

"You don't seem too concerned."

"I'm not. Let's say they manage to free themselves and make contact with the locals. How they gonna make themselves understood? It'll be pretty impossible so almost certainly the police will get involved."

"So?"

"And the police are likely to be very interested in the stash of coke sewn into their belts. I changed them over while they were unconscious and popped a bit more coke into the bag we left for them for good measure."

"Cocaine? You didn't."

"Oh, yes, I did," said the Fixer.

AN ANONYMOUS ROOM SOMEWHERE IN LONDON

FORSETI TAPPED ON the door, opened it and walked straight in. Odin looked up from his desk.

"Progress?"

"Probably. Rackham and Pately seem to have disappeared from their usual haunts."

"Has it been reported?"

"Not yet, but unless they turn up soon it probably will be."

"And do you think they will turn up soon?"

"I think it highly unlikely."

Odin thought for a moment. "Okay, let's wait and see what happens. I'm assuming this is the Hunter's team at work."

"Almost certainly."

"Wonder what they've done with them."

VARIOUS LOCATIONS

CAMBRIDGE

THE PYTHON SAT AMONGST his array of technical equipment and ran his hands lovingly over a keyboard. He felt a great sense of satisfaction. He was really enjoying the technical work he was doing for the Hunter's team. At last, he felt he was being useful rather than just helping pompous business people unravel their software cock-ups.

MUSWELL HILL

THE HUNTER BOUGHT A new bottle of Laphroaig on her way home, had one small glass then went to bed and slept for twelve hours, smiling in her sleep.

THE BARBICAN

THE DEFENDER CLOSED THE door of his flat behind him. He was tired, but not over-tired. It was good to be working with the Hunter again and tomorrow he would resume his sessions in the gym.

BAKEWELL

WHEN HE ARRIVED BACK at his cottage the Fixer spent the evening drawing up a list of outstanding things he needed to do for his Wildlife Trust. He also began to seriously think about his dream – to move somewhere even wilder and set up his own wildlife guiding business.

BEAMINSTER

THE ARMOURER STOPPED AT the library on her way home and picked up some more undemanding reading material. From experience she knew that putting her mind into neutral was the best way to re-charge her batteries so she'd be ready for the next challenge. She felt happier than she had done for a long time. It was good to be working again.

SWINDON

THE HOUSEKEEPER RECEIVED THE encrypted report from the Hunter and began moving money around the various accounts he had set up. All their expenses and payments were shown, just not quite as they had actually happened. He also made a few other transactions to keep all the accounts visibly alive and working.

AN ANONYMOUS ROOM SOMEWHERE IN LONDON

FORSETI GAVE HIS usual tap on the door before walking straight in.

"You wanted to see me?"

"Yes." Odin waved him to a chair then picked up a sheet of paper. "Following on from our conversation… what, about three weeks ago… remember, the Hunter's first job."

"Yes."

"The Spanish authorities have been in touch with the Foreign Office."

"The Spanish?"

"Yes. They apparently have two foreigners in custody – English by all accounts. They were found wandering in a remote forest somewhere in the Pyrenees, half starved, freezing cold and babbling about being kidnapped."

"Do we know who they are?"

"I think it's probably safe to say we do, but the Spanish don't. The two men have no passports, no papers, no identification of any kind. According to the Spanish they speak a kind of '*fruity English*'." Odin looked puzzled for a moment. "What do you suppose '*fruity English*' is?"

Forseti kept his face straight. "Probably a broad south London accent, if you want my guess."

"Ah. So you agree that they might be Pately and Rackham?"

"Seems likely. Dumped in the Pyrenees, eh? Well, we

wanted the Hunter's team to be imaginative. That pair must have had one hell of a time."

"Still having it. Apparently they were both carrying a significant amount of cocaine. They denied all knowledge of it of course."

"I daresay they did. Ironic that this is the one time they may have been telling the truth."

"The point is, what do we do now?"

"I suggest we do nothing in a hurry. They'll tell the Spanish authorities who they are. The Spanish won't believe them and will ask us about them. We can prevaricate for quite a long time."

Odin smiled. "Indeed we can. The Foreign Office is very good at prevaricating."

"Well, the Hunter has clearly meted out just the kind of punishment we had in mind. Be a pity to bring it to an end too quickly."

"I agree." Odin scribbled a brief note on the bottom of the sheet of paper and tossed it into his tray.

"Now then. The Hunter. Do you have another job for that team?"

"I do have something in mind."

"But still not the American?"

"No. As you know that's an extremely complex situation. It's obviously one for the Hunter eventually, but I'd rather give them a bit more of a run first."

"If you say so. What did you have in mind?"

"I was looking over our initial list of possible targets and there was one in particular that caught my eye. Kenneth Bowman."

"Ah, the arsonist."

"Not in the eyes of the law."

"Of course not. But we all know what really happened.

That's why he's on that list."

"Of course, but the law will never be able to touch him—"

"— but the Hunter might. Okay, Forseti, let them loose again."

MINSMERE

THE TEAM MET in the café at the RSPB Bird Reserve at Minsmere in Suffolk. The Fixer went to get the drinks as they settled themselves round one of the outside tables in the sun.

The Armourer was frankly puzzled. "Why we meeting here?" she asked.

"It was Fixer's idea," said the Hunter, "Good security – never meet together at the same place twice and this isn't the first place one would think of to hold a clandestine meeting. Glad to see you all brought some binoculars."

"I had to borrow a pair," said the Housekeeper. "I've never done anything like this before."

"Time you gave it a spin then," said the Fixer putting the tray down on the table. "Do you good to get out onto a bit of heathland once in a while."

The Housekeeper and the Python exchanged glances.

"Let's come to order," said the Hunter. "Congratulations everyone. As far as we know our first job went well."

"Has there been any feedback?" asked the Python.

"No, and there won't be. That's the point. We need to stay as anonymous as possible and that means keeping our distance."

The others nodded.

"However," the Hunter went on, "I think we can assume that Forseti and the people behind him are happy with the outcome as we've been offered another job. As before, I'll outline the situation and then we can decide whether we're willing to go ahead."

"There's a goldfinch over there on that bird feeder," said the Fixer.

The Hunter threw him a bleak stare.

"Okay, okay, just keeping up the cover. Sorry, boss."

"Don't call me boss."

The Fixer just grinned.

"Right then. Here's the situation. There's a man called Kenneth Bowman. Runs a construction company – BLB – stands for Bowman Luxury Buildings so I'm told."

"Houses?"

"Houses, offices, anything that can show a quick profit. He specialises in buying up pieces of land and holding onto them until he can either sell them on or get planning permission to build."

"Fair enough. So where do we come in?"

"Some of the land he buys isn't always spare, if you see what I mean."

There was silence round the table for a moment then the Housekeeper said, "Do you mean pressure is brought to bear to make people sell?"

"Sometimes. Other times he takes a short cut and just burns down properties on the land he wants to acquire."

"Seriously?"

"Seriously. We know of at least four confirmed instances where reluctant to sell owners have been unlucky with fire."

"But no doubt Mr Bowman is miles away at the time."

"Of course. Alibis coming out of each ear."

"And no one's done anything?"

"The first three – that is, of those we know about – are still ongoing, unsolved cases but the last one is a bit different."

"How?"

"It was a row of half a dozen old cottages standing between a derelict petrol station and a plot that used to be allotments before the local council sold them off a year ago."

"And bought presumably by Mr Bowman."

"Good. You have been listening."

"And presumably Bowman also owns the garage site," said the Defender.

"Of course. And he obviously wanted the cottages but three sets of occupants refused to sell."

"Hence the fire."

"Hence the fire. Unfortunately, the people who actually did the deed were told the properties were vacant and didn't check to make sure."

"Anyone killed?"

"Fortunately no. But a woman and two children were very badly burned. One of the arsonists – a guy called Keith Billhook – was so upset that kids had been harmed, he went to the police."

"And they did what?"

"They arrested Billhook, obviously, and based on his evidence they also arrested Bowman."

"Don't tell me. He had a cast iron alibi and an expensive brief," said the Fixer.

"Yup. Never charged, and his company was able to pick up the remains of the cottages for a song. Billhook, of course, went to jail."

There was silence round the table for a moment then the Defender said, "So I presume Bowman's our target."

"Our proposed target, yes. What do we think?"

There was a pause, then the Python said, "Seems to fit the bill."

The Hunter glanced round the table. "Anyone else?" She looked across at the Fixer.

104

"Well, Python's right, does seem to fit the bill ..."

"But?"

"But I'd like to have a bit of a poke around. From what you say this Bowman guy is a nasty bit of work, but we don't really have any hard and fast facts ..."

"There's the evidence of Keith Billhook."

"Sure, but he might just be a disgruntled employee trying to get his own back."

"So what do you want to do?"

"I'd like to dig about a bit. I want to know more about Mr Bowman, the other fires, the guys who work for him – all that stuff. I think we need more gen before we go rushing in."

"I agree," said the Armourer. "We have to be certain."

"Take your point," said the Defender and the Python and Housekeeper both nodded.

"So where do you want to start?" asked the Hunter.

"Well, I need to have a nose around on the ground but it's also worth having a gander at the official stuff." The Fixer glanced across at the Python. "Can you get copies of Bowmans accounts, tax returns and all that stuff?"

"I should think so, so long as you don't ask how."

"Once you've got them, I'll check them over," said the Housekeeper.

"Okay," said the Hunter, "you go and have your nose around, Fixer." She turned to the Armourer. "Meanwhile lets you and I see what else we can turn up. I suggest we all meet again in, say, a fortnight. Everyone happy with that?"

"Where shall we meet and will I still need these binoculars?" asked the Housekeeper.

The Fixer laughed. "Don't worry about the bins," he said, "I'll sort out a new meeting place and let you all know."

"That's settled then. I'll tell Forseti what we've decided."

AN ANONYMOUS ROOM SOMEWHERE IN LONDON

FORSETI PUT HIS head round Odin's door. "Got a minute?"

"What's up?"

"Been an interesting development with the Hunter."

"Are they going ahead with the Bowman job?"

"Probably. But not immediately. Apparently some of them want to do some investigating of their own before accepting the job. They have no doubt that arson is involved but they want to be certain that it's actually down to Bowman."

"Do they indeed. What's your take on that?"

Forseti pulled a chair forward and sat down. "Actually, I think it's brilliant. It shows the system is working. I remember Hunter asking me at the beginning if they were just a hit squad. I said no and this means they've taken me at my word."

"What if they turn the job down?"

"Then they turn it down, that was always the deal. We wanted them to be an independent arm of justice. Admittedly a rather unusual arm, but unless everyone is satisfied of guilt then no action should be taken."

"I'm perfectly satisfied already."

"So am I, but we're not the ones instigating action. I think this shows a great sense of responsibility."

Odin leaned back in his chair. "Yes, all right, I can see that. What conclusion do you thinking they'll come to?"

"I'm pretty sure it'll be the same as us. But it will be their conclusion, not ours."

"So we just wait."

"Yes. We wait."

MEMBURY
SERVICES ON
THE M4

ONE BY ONE they drifted into the main complex at the Membury services and gathered round a table. They all had coffee and the Python also had a large slice of chocolate cake which occasioned some rude comments.

"Never the same place twice," murmured the Armourer glancing round at all the other tables.

"Less conspicuous meeting in a crowd," said the Fixer.

"Okay," said the Hunter, "what have we learned?"

"If I were the Revenue, I'd like a reason to turn his accounts over," said the Housekeeper. "They're all a bit too neat, too much movement from one area to another. Never a good sign. I should know. I do enough of it myself."

"Are the Revenue interested?"

"No way to tell, but probably not. An investigation needs a trigger, something to make them think that all is not as it should be. I didn't find anything like that. It's just an instinct."

"Which isn't proof," said the Hunter.

"True," said the Fixer, "but now I've had a shifty I'm pretty sure Bowman's guilty as charged, or rather not charged. I've had a natter to a few people who've worked for him and he's definitely not squeaky clean."

"Proof?"

"Nothing you could take to the Old Bill but then there wouldn't be, would there? However, I've had a chat with a few of me old mates. One guy reckoned Bowman's been doing this for years. He reckons the 'lucky accidents' that Bowman's profited from run well into double figures."

"I spoke to a guy who refused to play ball with him," said the Armourer. "He says when he refused to carry out one of these attacks, he was suddenly out of work, his car was vandalised and he was 'encouraged' to leave the area."

"Did he go to the police?" asked the Python.

The Armourer looked at him. "What do you think?" she said.

There was silence for a moment then the Python said, "How on earth do you find these people?"

The Armourer said nothing. The Defender put a hand on the Python's shoulder. "That's the sort of question we don't ask each other," he said gently. "We all have our various sources but they're not for sharing."

The Python coloured slightly. "Of course. Sorry."

"Anything else?" asked the Hunter.

"Circumstantial," said the Fixer, "but a couple of days before each incident Bowman books himself and his wife into an hotel or a country club miles away where they join in every activity on offer."

"Creating an alibi."

"Sure

"So your verdict is?"

"Guilty as hell, but not provable of course."

The Hunter glanced round the table. "Are we all convinced?" Everyone nodded. "Fine, so we go ahead."

"How do we go about it?" asked the Armourer

"Well," said the Hunter, "as it happens Fixer and I have a suggestion to make. The only snag is we can't do anything until August."

"Why August?"

"Because that's when Bowman and his missus shove off to their house in the Dordogne for a month which means the Esher house is empty," said the Fixer.

"Don't tell me, we're going to burn it down." said the Defender.

"Tempting, but a bit crude. We can be more imaginative than that."

"Oh, yes," said the Fixer, "but there's quite a lot of prep involved. So I've roughed out a list of things what need doing."

AN ANONYMOUS ROOM SOMEWHERE IN LONDON

"**A**UGUST?" SAID ODIN.

"August," confirmed Forseti.

"Why August? That's two months away."

"I didn't ask. Not our business. That's the whole point of this exercise."

"Well yes, but if they're willing to do the job I can't see why they can't get on with it."

"They'll have their reasons."

"I suppose. So we just wait ... again."

Forseti smiled. "We do, but I suspect it will be worth it."

PALACE PIER, BRIGHTON

I T WAS THE end of July and the Palm Court Restaurant on Brighton's Palace Pier was crowded, just the way the Fixer liked it. The team had come together to discuss the final plans for the Bowman job which was scheduled for the first week of August.

"Bowman and his wife pushed off to the Dordogne yesterday," said the Fixer, "so the house is empty apart from the cleaner. She comes in twice a week, sorts the post and so on. There's also a gardener who comes in each Friday."

"I've dealt with the cleaner," said the Python. "She'll get an email tomorrow, apparently from Mrs Bowman, giving her the month off on full pay. Says she'll be in touch again when they get back in early September."

"The gardener doesn't seem to have an email address," said the Housekeeper, "but he'll get a letter in the next couple of days telling him not come again until September as they're having some work done on the house which might disturb the garden."

"Good," said the Fixer, "I've got the 'For Sale' board ready to go up tomorrow."

"Any risk of one of the neighbours seeing it and letting Bowman know?"

"They might see it, but I doubt they'll do anything. They keep themselves to themselves on them estates and anyway Bowman's not the most popular of neighbours. He's had barneys with several of them over the years, noise, hedges, that sort of thing."

"What company name's on the For Sale board?"

"Red Hot Properties," said the Fixer with a straight face, "and if anyone rings the phone number—"

"— they get through to a dedicated phone," said the Python, "with a recorded message inviting them to leave name and number and someone will call them back."

"Burglar alarm?"

"In hand," said the Hunter. "That will be taken care of tomorrow."

The Fixer gave a slight smile.

"What else? Ah, yes. Bowman's insurance company?"

"Identified," said the Python. "By the way I have to say these sausages are pretty good."

"So's the Fisherman's Pie," said the Housekeeper then, responding to a bleak stare from the Hunter, he hastily added, "I've drafted the letter to the insurance people, I've prepared samples of Bowman's notepaper and I also have a copy of his signature. I'll get the letter away tomorrow."

"Good." She turned to the Fixer. "And you've found a removal company."

"Yeah," said the Fixer. "Well, I call it a 'removal company'. It's actually a few mates with a couple of big vans."

"Low risk?"

"Very low. They owe me. Won't be a problem. They're only doing the first stage anyway."

The Armourer swallowed her last piece of calamari. "Storage is all organised," she said, "it's a two stage move. The first place is on the edge of Cardiff. I thought that'd be remote enough from Esher but handy for motorway access. So Fixer's guys take the stuff there and then two days later I've arranged another transport company to take the lot up to a storage facility near Newark. I reckon that should cover our trail nicely."

"Good," said the Hunter. "So the big event is booked for the day after tomorrow."

"Will you need me?" asked the Python.

"No. Four of us can handle it."

"I'll be there with the removal boys," said the Fixer. "Hunter and Defender will be there as the apparent owners. I wasn't entirely honest with the guys with the van. I let them believe that the owners are doing a moonlight flit."

"From Esher?" said the Housekeeper raising an eyebrow.

"You'd be surprised," said the Fixer, "anyway that's all they needed to know …"

"Armourer will be in the area but not visible," said the Hunter. "Her job is to keep a watching brief and act as trouble shooter if necessary."

She glanced round the table. "Now if you've all finished stuffing yourselves I suggest we wrap this up."

"Dessert?" said the Python hopefully.

"No. Buy yourself an ice cream on the way back to the station."

A POSH HOUSING ESTATE NEAR ESHER

I T WAS 2ND September. Kenneth Bowman and his wife, Cynthia, came off the overnight ferry from Caen to Portsmouth and headed for the A3. Just over an hour later they turned off towards Esher and their home.

As they turned into the drive, Cynthia said, "That's odd. There's no sign of Mrs Ormison's car. She was meant to be here today with milk and stuff for us. Wonder where she is."

"Probably still at the shops. Come on – let's get the car unpacked."

He opened the boot while Cynthia went into the house but then suddenly he heard her scream. He dropped the case he was carrying and ran after her, only to stop short in amazement. The hall was completely bare. No furniture, no pictures, nothing. Cynthia was in the living room.

"Everything's gone. We must have had burglars. There's nothing left at all."

Kenneth was stunned. She was right, the room had been stripped bare. As they went through the house they found every room was the same. Not a single one of their possessions remained. Carpets, crockery, clothing, all gone. Even the fitted appliances in the kitchen had vanished.

"I don't understand," he said, "why would burglars take everything and what about the alarm?"

"It was properly set. I had to disarm it when I came in. I

don't understand."

"I'll check the garage."

He went out into the garden, looked in the garage and looked in the two sheds but they had also been stripped bare. There was nothing left except a few oil stains on the garage floor.

He was starting to get an uncomfortable feeling about this business when he heard another scream from Cynthia.

"Kenneth, kitchen, now."

He rushed across to the kitchen to find her holding a big white envelope in her hand.

"I found this, addressed to both of us, with these photos, look."

She held out a batch of glossy prints. Kenneth took them. The pictures showed all their furniture and possessions in a number of piles on what appeared to be the floor of a large warehouse. Another picture was obviously in a field where there was a large bonfire and, to his horror, Kenneth recognised his antique desk in the centre of the flames. Draped across it were the remains of some of Cynthia's clothes. The printed note with the pictures simply said.

"All your belongings will be burned over the next few days. We're sorry you won't be able to see your life go up in flames."

"Who's done this?" Cynthia demanded.

"I don't know."

She looked at him suspiciously. "Why would anyone break in, steal everything and then burn it. Doesn't make sense."

"No idea," said Kenneth, but deep down he thought he had a very good idea indeed.

He rang the police – reluctantly, but Cynthia insisted. They came, were incredulous that the whole house had been stripped. In spite of Bowman's protests, Cynthia showed them the photos and the note. A detective constable looked at them, then looked at Bowman. "Have you had a dispute with anyone lately, sir? Received any threats?"

"Of course not."

The man gave him a long look. "Well, then, it's certainly unusual."

The police spoke to the neighbours and learned that shortly after the Bowmans had left for their holiday home a '*For Sale*' board had gone up outside and a few days later a removal firm arrived. The Bowmans were not popular and it all seemed perfectly normal, so no one had taken any notice.

Cynthia finally got Mrs Ormison on the phone. "Why on earth didn't you report that the house had been burgled?"

"Well, I didn't know, did I? You told me not to come in while you were away."

"I did no such thing."

"Yes, you did. You sent me an email."

"Of course I didn't, you stupid woman. If you'd done your job properly this wouldn't have happened."

"You've no call to talk to me like that. You can keep your bloody job and I'm glad you've been burgled." And Mrs Ormison slammed the phone down leaving Cynthia fuming.

The Bowmans booked themselves into the Bear Hotel in Esher and Kenneth rang his insurance company. When he finally put the phone down he had gone white.

"What is it?" asked Cynthia. "Are they being difficult? Let me guess, they're trying to claim we forgot to set the alarm before we went away. All the same, bloody insurance companies."

"We're not insured."

"What do you mean, we're not insured? Did you forget to pay the premium?"

"Oh, no, I paid the premium all right, but apparently I wrote to them at the beginning of August saying we were moving and would they cancel the insurance policy with immediate effect."

"What the hell did you do that for?"

Kenneth finally lost his rag. "I didn't do it, you stupid cow. Can't you see, we've been set up, taken for a ride."

There was a long pause and then Cynthia said, "You've been up to your old tricks again, haven't you? This is a revenge job. That's why they've taken everything and why it's all been burnt."

AN ANONYMOUS ROOM SOMEWHERE IN LONDON

A WEEK OR SO later Forseti entered Odin's office. Odin waved a sheet of paper at him.

"This is a report from the Surrey police. Apparently they were called to Kenneth Bowman's house to find it had been stripped bare?"

"I did hear something of the sort."

"They were a bit suspicious. Burglary is one thing but stripping a house completely is another. They suspect some kind of insurance scam."

"Except that Bowman didn't have any insurance."

"Oh, come on, he must have done."

"Well, yes, he did, but apparently he wrote and cancelled it about the time they went on holiday."

Odin gave a snort which might have been suppressed laughter. "I suppose we have the Hunter to thank for this."

"Of course. And there's more."

"Tell me."

"The only thing left in the house was a set of photos showing all their possessions in piles and one pile had been set on fire."

"What did the police make of that?"

"I suspect they thought it confirmed the insurance scam theory. Bowman would have made the link immediately of course."

"And there's nothing left at all?"

"Well, there's Cynthia."

"Mrs. Bowman? What about her?"

"She's left. Left Bowman. Apparently they had a stand up row in a pub in Esher. She accused him of fraud, arson and god knows what. I don't give that marriage much of a chance, especially as all their money was in accounts in her name. Tax reasons, I suppose. Anyway with her spitting nails, I think our Ken might be up the spout."

"That won't keep me awake at night." Odin thought for a moment. "Did the Hunter really burn all their stuff?"

"No, just the one piece plus a few of Cynthia's clothes. Pity really, it was rather a nice old desk but they had to destroy something recognisable to make the whole thing credible."

"What will happen to the rest?"

"I am told it will be auctioned and the proceeds will go to charity."

"Why not back into our kitty?"

"I did tentatively suggest that but was told that the Hunter's team are an instrument of justice not a revenue income stream. I decided to accept that."

After a moment Odin nodded. "So what next? Are they ready for the American yet?"

"I don't think so. I'd still like to leave it a bit longer before we tackle that can of worms."

"Reasons?"

"The Hunter's team has made a good start but I'd prefer them to have more experience of working together. The American job is not going to be easy and if it goes belly up we could lose them all."

Odin sighed. "I suppose you're right. So you want them to deal with some of the… shall we say, less controversial targets first."

"Yes. I have a list of suggestions here. I thought we might go over them together."

A FEW MONTHS IN WHICH SOME NAUGHTY PEOPLE GET THEIR COMEUPPANCE

THE HUNTER AND her team had always expected interesting challenges and they were not disappointed.

Over the next few months, the Hunter had a number of meetings with Forseti in a variety of venues which included a ladies exotic underwear shop, a room in Smithfield market with carcasses hanging around them, the basement of a drinking club, the store room of a launderette in Camden and once going round and round on the London Eye.

On each occasion she was offered refreshment – tea, coffee, doughnuts, biscuits, once a set of beautifully cut triangular sandwiches. In the case of the London Eye it was a flask of hot chocolate.

How Forseti chose the meeting places she never discovered, but in a way they were matched by the Fixer's selection of venues for the team's briefing meetings. He had a wicked sense of humour and so they found themselves gathering in places like the tearoom of a children's petting zoo, an evening excursion with dinner on a railway preservation line, a geology museum in Scarborough and a second hand bookshop in Wales.

The range of assignments they were offered varied widely. To an outsider there was nothing to link them together but Forseti knew the background to each one and the imaginative outcomes made him very content.

A corrupt Catholic bishop was arrested in a raid on a Soho strip joint one night and found to have a large quantity of heroin in his possession.

The British directors of a chemical plant in Indonesia who denied responsibility after an explosion suddenly found that all their assets, which they had thought were safe in off-shore tax havens, had mysteriously been syphoned away.

An Estate Manager and Gamekeeper, who were routinely poisoning birds of prey on a grouse shooting estate in Scotland, abruptly found that they were an embarrassment to their benefactor, an upstanding member of the House of Lords, when photographs showing their actions were sent to all media outlets.

There was a tabloid journalist who hacked into the mobile phones of a family who had recently lost a teenage daughter in a hit and run. He transcribed their conversations and published them under the heading *Family Grief Knows No Bounds* which caused them great distress. A few weeks later, rival tabloids published an exposé of his attempts to seduce the wives of several of his colleagues, including his editor, claiming all costs on expenses. Suddenly he was an ex-journalist.

When hundreds of homes in the north of England were badly flooded following a series of violent storms, a government minister was quoted as saying, *"It's just one of those things. They're probably people of low worth anyway."* A few months later he came back home after a week in London to find his house full of water. All the doors and windows had been sealed and all the taps had been turned on and left running.

The Hunter's team also turned down two assignments during this period. The first concerned a long distance lorry driver who'd been caught smuggling wild animals and several tonnes of ivory. The team did some investigating of their own and came to the conclusion the driver was acting under duress.

A whistle blower who accused the building company she worked for of cutting corners was found dead, apparently from an overdose. The circumstances surrounding her death were far from clear and the Hunter's team came to the conclusion that the case against her employer was not totally reliable. As the Hunter told Forseti, "We have to be absolutely certain and in this case we're not, so we're exercising our right not to act."

THE HUNTER UNKNOWINGLY CASTS HER BREAD UPON THE WATERS

THEN THERE WAS the time when they were investigating a group of high profile people who were thought to be running a modern slavery ring. Their enquiries led them to a large detached house in Hackney and the Hunter decided that they should have a closer look. It was to become one of those jobs where Forseti would only receive a carefully edited report afterwards.

She took the Defender and the Fixer with her and in the small hours of the morning the Fixer neutralised the alarm, eased open the back door and they passed into the silent house. The downstairs rooms were all empty so they made their way up to the first floor.

There were three bedrooms on this floor, all with external locks on the doors. The Fixer made short work of them and when they went in they found piles of discarded personal possessions, together with a number of passports and other documents, presumably confiscated from their victims.

Suddenly they heard footsteps coming down from the second floor and someone went into the bathroom across the landing. After a few moments the toilet was flushed but when the man emerged he found himself in the iron grip of the Defender. The Fixer, who appeared to be a walking burglary supply shop, produced a roll of gaffer tape from his backpack so they gagged the man, bound his wrists, then crept silently up the stairs to the floor above.

The first room was empty but the bed had been slept in. Across the landing there was another room and here there was a man asleep so it was not difficult to secure him in the same way.

"Don't touch anything," said the Hunter, "we'll photograph everything then tip off the police. They can deal with this."

"Are we sure there's no one else here?"

"Don't think so. We've checked the whole house."

"Not quite. I think there might be a cellar."

There was a cellar and on its walls was a line of ring bolts with chains through them. Fastened to one of them was a girl of around 16 or 17. She was terrified and pleaded with them in Spanish to let her go. Both the Hunter and the Defender spoke reasonable Spanish and eventually they managed to get her to understand that they were here to rescue her. The Fixer rummaged around in his bag again and produced a small hacksaw so the Defender could cut her free.

"Now what?" said the Defender.

The Hunter was very angry. "This girl's not staying in this house a moment longer."

The Defender nodded. "I agree, but if we're going to pass this place onto the police then technically we're tampering with the evidence."

"Sod that. This girl, this child, deserves better than having to kick around in some police station. God knows what would happen to her then."

"They'd probably charge her with prostitution and deport her," muttered the Fixer, whose view of the police was instinctively biased.

"This is risking exposure," cautioned the Defender. Then

he saw the look the Hunter shot him and held up his hands. "I just feel it needs to be said. We're meant to be invisible. This action leaves traces."

The Hunter made a decision. "She's coming with us. We'll bring those two guys down here and cuff them to the water pipes. Then we'll leave it a day or two before tipping off the police, but first let's make sure this girl is returned to wherever she's meant to be."

In the end the Hunter booked a room for herself and the girl in a small hotel in Bloomsbury and began the task of assuring her she was now safe. It took a long time but when she had calmed down, the Hunter learned her name was Sabela and she came from Cariño in north-west Spain. She had come to London three months ago to attend an English language course, she had gone to a party, been given too much to drink and when she woke up she was in the cellar where they had found her.

"When was this?" asked the Hunter.

The girl didn't know. She thought perhaps four or five days ago. It had been hard to tell in the dark of the cellar. She understood that they sold people into work – immigrants, homeless, anyone without a safety net.

Sabela wanted to call her father. The Hunter assumed he was in Spain but after Sabela had spoken to him she said that her father was in London and was coming to get her.

There was something in the way she spoke about her father that put the Hunter's instincts on full alert. A couple of hours later there was a knock at the hotel room door and when she opened it she was thrust violently back into the room, grabbed round the neck and a knife put to her throat. It was only when Sabela screamed, "Papa, no," that the pressure on her neck was eased. She gasped for breath as she found herself facing a heavily built man and, behind him, two other men also carrying wicked looking knives.

Sabela rushed into her father's arms, letting out a torrent of Spanish. He listened as he gently stroked her hair and then turned to the Hunter.

"I am Xabier Carrasco. I am sorry for our greeting." He nodded to his two men who relaxed a little. "My daughter, she has been lost for several days. I not know what we find when we come here."

The Hunter massaged her throat and smiled sweetly. "I do understand. I was not sure either."

She nodded towards the door.

The three Spaniards turned to see the Defender behind them and the Armourer in the bathroom doorway, both holding automatic rifles.

For a moment Señor Carrasco tensed and then suddenly he burst out laughing. "Comprendo. You rescue my daughter, but no policia."

"No, no policia."

"You are bad persons?" Then he winced as Sabela pummelled him furiously.

"No, no son malos. Ellos me salvaron."

Carrasco held up his hands in mock surrender. "Lo siento, not bad." He paused and thought for a moment. "You not law persons?"

The Hunter smiled. "No, we are not the law. We're simply people who believe in justice."

The Armourer and the Defender lowed their guns making it clear they were not a threat. Everyone relaxed.

"I am glad we were able to help your daughter, Señor Carrasco. I imagine she'll want to go home now."

Señor Carrasco nodded. "My name, it is Xabier," he said, "you are now friend of my family."

"Oh, right, thank you."

"Please, what is your name?"

"Just call me the Hunter." She fumbled for the Spanish word. "La Cazadora."

"Ah, La Cazadora. Comprendo. Gracias, now we go home." There was a brief exchange in Spanish between Sabela and her father then Xabier turned back to the Hunter.

"Cazadora, there is problem. The men who take my daughter, also take her pasaporte."

"Ah."

"So now we must need la policia, si?"

The Hunter thought fast. "Can you wait another day?"

"Why we wait?"

"If you wait I will get you a passport for your daughter."

There was a long pause and then a big grin spread across Xabier's face. "Aha, I think you are a little bit bad, no?"

The Hunter shrugged and Xabier went on, "We will wait and we thank you."

"Okay." The Hunter turned to the Defender. "Can you get onto Housekeeper and get that fixed."

"Sure."

"Right then, that'll be sorted. We'll meet here again tomorrow, yes?"

"Bueno." There was a pause, then Xabier enfolded the Hunter in an embrace, kissing her on both cheeks. "You good person, Cazadora. You good friend to Sabela. You need help from Xabier some time, you call. I come."

"Oh, er … thank you."

Later that day the Defender said to the Hunter. "What kind of business do you suppose that Carrasco guy is in?"

"I think it's best we don't ask. Probably just as well he wasn't with us in Hackney."

"Yes … The girl knows where that house was though."

The Hunter acted on that note of warning but the police

moved too slowly. Two days later there was a report in the press that two bodies had been recovered from a fire that had destroyed a house in Hackney, and she wondered again about the true occupation of Señor Carrasco.

AN ANONYMOUS ROOM SOMEWHERE IN LONDON

IT WAS ABOUT a year after the Hunter's team had first started work when Forseti decided the moment had come for the job they had planned for her all along.

He asked for a special meeting with Odin who greeted him warmly. "Am I right in thinking you're finally going to let the Hunter loose on the American?"

"Yes."

"And about time too, if you don't mind my saying so."

"I do mind actually. There was never any hurry, other than our own impatience. Waiting this long has achieved two things. First we've proved that the Hunter's team can function extremely efficiently."

"And second?"

"By now the American will think we've forgotten him or at least given up. That means the Hunter's job will be fractionally easier."

Odin thought for a moment then said, "I understand the reasoning. I hope you're right. So are we clear about the result we want?"

"In an ideal world we would want Hoskins back in the UK to put him on trial."

"That wouldn't go down well with the American authorities."

"No, it wouldn't. Of course, once we've got him we could

insist on a trial, we have the evidence, but it would depend on our politicians standing firm against American pressure."

"Which is unlikely."

"Very unlikely."

"We're too squeamish. If the positions were reversed the Americans would just snatch our guy as soon as he set foot outside British soil and dump him in Guantanamo Bay or whatever their equivalent is this week."

Forseti smiled. "I've been thinking about that. Maybe we need to arrange our own Guantanamo Bay. There's plenty of lonely islands off the Scottish coast. A few special forces guys to take care of him. No one need ever know."

"You're serious?"

"Perfectly. Of course there is still the easier option?"

"We've been over that. If we simply kill him in the States it will just go down as another unsolved murder and they have more of those a day than we have in a year."

"Agreed. So we grab him and make him sweat a little?"

"I want him back in the UK, Forseti. Even if we can't publicly admit we've got him, I want it known in places where it matters that the arm of British justice is a long one."

SOHO

THIS TIME THE address she was given turned out to be a leather goods shop in one of the alleys off Rupert Street. No one acknowledged her as she walked into the shop, pushed her way through racks of somewhat unusual clothing, and made her way into the back room. As usual there were two chairs and a small table. Forseti was sitting in one of the chairs and on the table was a bottle of Laphroaig and two glasses. She smiled faintly and sat down.

"So, this is the moment when you give us the biggie."

"The biggie?"

"Well, we've done a good few jobs now and so far in our briefing meetings I've been offered tea, samosas, doughnuts and so on. Now there's a bottle of Laphroaig. The conclusion is obvious."

Forseti smiled, then leaned forward, opened the bottle and poured two small measures. "Cheers."

"Slàinte."

"Your team has performed well. You've done what we hoped you'd do when you were recruited so …"

"So now you think we're ready for the big one, the one you really wanted us for all along."

"You're right, of course, but this one is a real challenge."

The basic story was very simple. Frank Hoskins, an American living in London, ran the UK end of an extensive drugs ring. After a couple of years of very hard work, the Drugs Squad finally managed to get enough evidence to arrest him but when they went to his house in Essex they met serious opposition. They put the doors in and poured into the house but the occupants fought back. By the time the drugs gang were in custody, three of them were seriously injured and one police officer was dead from a knife wound in the chest.

The other bad news was that Frank Hoskins himself and two of his associates were not there.

An all ports warning went out for them but Hoskins had his own boat at Maldon on the Essex coast and before the net could close he was on the continent and on a flight to the States.

Once the British authorities discovered where he was they applied to the USA for his extradition. It was refused. The view was that the accusations of drug dealing against Hoskins would not stand up to scrutiny in the American courts and therefore he could not be extradited.

"So that's the current position," said Forseti. "While the Americans refuse to play ball we have a stalemate."

"How long ago was all this?"

"Oh, well over two years. But until now there's been nothing we could do. We have reason to believe that the FBI don't entirely buy the upright citizen and benefactor role, but Hoskins has high level protection. There are rumours that a very powerful Senator has a financial interest in his business."

There was silence for a moment, then the Hunter said, "What do you want us to do?"

"Well, we'd like him back in the UK. We would like to make sure that justice is done, not the least for the family of the police officer who was murdered."

There was another long silence. Then the Hunter leaned forward and poured herself another drop of Laphroaig.

"When you first recruited me you said we weren't an

assassination squad."

"And you're not."

"No. However …" she paused again and took another drink. "To remove an American citizen from America and bring him back to the UK is a big ask."

"I know."

"We can give it a go but if it all went belly up there'd be diplomatic hell to pay."

"If the Americans believed this was an official operation, yes."

"But we're deniable." Forseti said nothing and after a moment she went on. "It'd be much simpler just to stalk him and shoot him – that should be possible."

"I'm sure it would be. However, the downside is his death would not be linked to the crimes he's committed in this country. You could argue that he'd been punished but is it justice? Is it your kind of justice?"

The Hunter glanced round the room and said, half to herself. "I hate places with no windows."

Forseti made no response and after a moment she said, "For an operation like this, the first stage would have to be to get him to Canada."

"Not exactly British jurisdiction these days, but, yes, the situation would be, shall we say, easier to manage if Hoskins were in Canada."

"Okay, let's suppose we manage to get him back to the UK and he appears in a British court, the Americans aren't going to like that."

"I didn't say anything about a British court."

"Ah."

"As you pointed out, Hunter, the whole operation needs to be deniable. Hoskins will be imprisoned but without the formality of a court hearing. We won't even admit we have him."

"Interesting."

"Think of it as 'Rendition', a process the Americans themselves invented."

"And where is our Guantanamo Bay?"

"You don't need to know that. Your job is to get him back here. We'll do the rest"

"And I thought I was ruthless."

"We're merely taking a leaf out of the American's own book."

"They may not see it that way."

"I am sure they won't."

There was a pause then the Hunter said, "I understand why you don't just want him killed – and I agree with that. Of course we'll give it a go but there's a dozen things that could go wrong and I can't guarantee bringing him back alive."

"Well, we'd prefer him alive but I appreciate what you're saying. The important thing is for him to know why this is happening to him. Later, whatever the outcome, we can let it be known that there's no safe haven for people who murder British police officers."

The Hunter looked at him for a moment then drained her glass and put it back on the table.

"Right then, well, in that case we'd better get on with it."

PETERBOROUGH

THIS TIME THE team met in a conference centre not far from Peterborough. They were booked in as the marketing team for Pannout, a specialised saucepan manufacturer. The Fixer's sense of humour was inexhaustible.

They listened in silence as the Hunter outlined the brief they had been given. When she finished and sat back in her chair there was a kind of collective sigh.

It was the Armourer who finally spoke. "So this is what we've effectively been in training for."

"So it would seem."

The Fixer said, "This one won't be a doddle and could be dangerous."

"Yes, it could." There was another pause, then the Hunter added. "We can always say no, that was the deal."

Another silence and then the Defender said, "Surely the criteria isn't the potential danger but whether this case falls within our original remit – to effect justice where the law can't act."

No one spoke for a moment then the Armourer said, "I think this is exactly the kind of thing we were recruited for."

Nods all round the table. "Sure," said the Fixer, "but how the hell we going to do it?"

"Pity we can't just shoot him. That'd be very straightforward."

"My first thought too, but we've been over that."

"Justice, not simply revenge."

"Precisely."

"First things first," said the Fixer, "where does Hoskins live?"

"He has a house on the Tiburon peninsula in California."

"I know it," said the Housekeeper, "the other side of the bay from San Francisco. Posh area."

"We need to do a recce," said the Armourer, "I think a couple of us should go over and sus the place out. I'm happy to do that."

The Hunter nodded. "I agree." She turned to the Housekeeper. "How well do you know San Francisco?"

"Very well. I lived there for five years."

"Then why don't you go with the Armourer. Local knowledge could be useful."

"Fine by me."

"In that case I suggest we travel as a married couple," said the Armourer, "less conspicuous."

"Also fine by me."

"Don't get any ideas."

"Wouldn't dream of it. Anyway you're too young for me."

"Cheeky sod."

"How soon can you leave?" asked the Hunter.

"Pretty quickly. I can adapt a couple of our standby passports. I just need to sort the ESTAs."

"In the meantime," said the Defender, "I suggest we do some scenario projections."

"Some what?" asked the Python.

"Sorry. Professional jargon. It's an operational planning structure. You set out the aim you want to achieve, the facilities you'll need to achieve it, plus the things that could go wrong or prevent you achieving your aim and what you might do to counteract them."

"Fine," said the Hunter, "Now I suggest we break for

the day, mull over all this stuff and we'll meet again in the morning. Obviously, until we have more information from the recce on Hoskin's place a lot of it will be guess work, but we can still make a start on the Defender's scenario projections."

THE FOLLOWING DAY WHEN they reassembled the Fixer kicked off the discussion.

"I reckon this is a three stage job," he said. "First we need to – well, shall we say – collect Mr Hoskins; second we need to get him out of the States; and third bring him back to the UK."

"Can't do much about the first until Housekeeper and Armourer report back."

"No, but I've been thinking about ways of getting this guy over the Canadian border."

"And ...?"

"I've had an idea but I'll have to go to Canada to sort it out and I'll need to buy a small truck over there." He turned to the Housekeeper. "Can you set me up with a Canadian identity, passport, driving licence, the lot?"

"Sure. What you thinking?"

"Well, if my idea checks out then at some stage I'll have to drive the truck across the Canadian border into the US. I've been told it's easier to do that if you're a Canadian citizen."

The Hunter looked round the table. "Right then, so Armourer and Housekeeper will do the recce and Fixer will explore ways of getting Hoskins into Canada. So for the moment that just leaves stage three. How do we get him out of Canada and back to the UK?"

The Fixer shook his head. "That one's a bugger. You can't just waltz into an airport with an unconscious drugs baron under one arm and check him in as hold luggage."

"Nice idea, but no, don't think that would work." The Hunter thought for a moment. "Frankly I don't think we're going to crack this one on our own. I'd better have another word with Forseti."

There was a pause and then the Python said, "About this recce, if Armourer and Housekeeper are going to San Francisco to suss out Hoskin's pad, I presume they'll be watching the house, noting who comes and goes, what security arrangements they have and so on."

"Yes, and also checking to see if Hoskins is actually there at the moment."

"Well, this is much more your area than mine, but I don't think you can just park yourself on a deckchair in front of his house with a clipboard on your knee, can you?"

"Hardly," said the Armourer, smiling.

"And I guess even a covert observation is risky if it's done too much and too often. Particularly as it seems he likes to have a highly trained, heavily armed security team close to hand. Am I right?"

"Yes ..."

"Then I have a suggestion that would keep you well out of sight but still provide us with plenty of information."

The Armourer was no longer smiling. "That would be very useful. What do you have in mind?"

"Well ..." said the Python, "what I thought was this ..."

SAN FRANCISCO

FIVE DAYS LATER the Armourer and the Housekeeper flew into San Francisco and checked into a hotel in North Beach. The following morning they hired a car, drove over the Golden Gate Bridge and out onto the Tiburon peninsular.

It didn't take them long to identify the house where Frank Hoskins lived and then they scouted round for a good observation point. They found one on a headland looking out over San Francisco Bay from where they could see the entrance to the Hoskins house through binoculars.

Various vehicles came and went in the course of the next few hours. Each time they stopped at the gate, someone came forward and presumably had a brief conversation before the gate was finally opened and the vehicle drove in or out.

"They're pretty security conscious," said the Armourer.

"And that's just in the daytime," said the Housekeeper. "I wonder what happens at night."

"We'd best find out."

They didn't stay long in case they became too conspicuous but that night after dinner they went back. The Housekeeper was driving and when they approached their observation point he pulled over and let the Armourer out.

"How long do you think you'll need?"

"No idea. I'll text you when I've had enough."

The car drove away and the Armourer climbed cautiously up to the place where they had been that morning. She found a piece of undergrowth and wriggled into it until she was pretty well concealed. She had a set of night glasses and trained them on Hoskins' gateway.

There were lights on in the house but no activity outside. After about half an hour she saw the lights of a vehicle approaching along the road below. As it got to the gate of Hoskin's house, it flashed its lights and stopped. A few moments later the whole gateway area was lit by huge arc lamps and two men appeared carrying large guns. The Armourer thought they were probably Heckler & Kochs, but it wasn't easy to see.

This time the conversation went on longer until finally two men got out of the car and were let into the grounds through a small gate to one side. The main gate stayed firmly shut and the whole area was brightly lit. An hour later the two men appeared again, were let out through the side gate and they left in the waiting car. Once they had gone the floodlights were extinguished.

"Definitely security conscious," muttered the Armourer to herself.

The following day the Armourer drove to the airport to collect the Python who had flown to Dallas and taken an internal flight from there. By the time they got back to the hotel the Housekeeper had prepared a list of stores which sold electronic equipment. The Hunter had suggested it would be easier to buy what they needed on the spot, rather than try to import it in their luggage, so the Python spent the rest of the day shopping.

By the following morning he had assembled three motion-activated cameras originally designed to monitor wildlife. They all had a solar cell to keep them fully charged, a SIM card connected to cloud storage and a large internal memory card as a backup.

That night they drove back to the Tiburon peninsular

and managed to position the cameras so they could see the gateway of Hoskins' house from two angles. The third camera was equipped with a telephoto lens and was trained on the front door of the house.

Once they were satisfied the system was fully functional the Armourer and the Housekeeper flew back to London while the Python stayed on in case of any technical problems. He had his laptop so he hunkered down in his hotel room and continued to run his UK business as normal while they waited for something to happen.

WEYMOUTH

THE HUNTER RENTED an Airbnb in a back street in Weymouth and they set up their monitoring station there. She was not unaware of the incongruity of sitting in a room with floral wallpaper and pictures of various cute animals while watching the front gate of an American drugs baron on a computer monitor.

Working shifts they viewed the feeds from the observation cameras and before long they had developed a healthy respect for those police officers who had to spend hours and hours viewing CCTV footage after a crime. Boring didn't even begin to cover it. The only comfort was that Weymouth was living up to the reputation of English seaside resorts. Outside it was pouring with rain but they were snug indoors.

Time passed very slowly. During the day there was quite a lot of coming and going at Hoskins' house and they made a note of all the registration plates of vehicles that passed through the gate. The night was a different matter. There were often visitors but they rarely stayed beyond midnight. As the Armourer had noted on her recce, the main gate was never opened after dark, visitors came and went through a little side gate.

One morning when the Hunter was watching the screens she suddenly stiffened. A man climbed out of a car by the gate and, although she only had a back view, for a moment she thought there was something familiar about him. He spoke briefly to one of the guards who shook his head so the man climbed back into his car and drove off. The Hunter was slightly uneasy but no matter how often she replayed the clip, she couldn't identify him.

Two weeks passed and the knowledge gained – apart from a long list of licence plates – was nil. They did not even know if Hoskins was in residence. Then one Sunday afternoon a large utility vehicle appeared on camera. It stopped at the gate and a man got out. The Housekeeper was on duty and he saw that it was definitely Hoskins. He exchanged a few words with one of the guards, then the gate opened, Hoskins got back into his vehicle and drove up to the house.

That sighting gave them a boost of confidence. At least they now knew Hoskins was there, but as the week dragged on with no further sightings, boredom set in again. The Hunter shortened the length of each viewing duty. She knew how easy it was to lose concentration when nothing happened day after day.

Then finally about a fortnight later on a Friday night there was a change. Just after midnight a car was seen coming down the drive from the house. The gate opened but the normal arc lights did not come on. The car passed through, the gate swung shut behind it and the car headed away up the road. Around five in the morning while it was still dark the same car appeared, the gate opened, the car turned in and vanished up the drive.

A few days later the Fixer returned from Canada and reported that his plan should definitely work. He'd purchased a van and everything was in hand and ready to go. His news was welcome and so was he. They gave him a cup of tea and then he was set to work to take his turn monitoring the screens.

"Should have stayed in Canada," he grumbled.

Another week passed, and then on the following Friday

just after midnight the car appeared again, the gate opened, the arc lights stayed off and the car vanished up the road.

"We need more information about this," said the Armourer.

The Hunter contacted the Python and that night he visited the motion cameras and made some adjustments to one of them so it focused on a tighter area. Then he repositioned it to pick up the windscreen of the car as it passed through the gate.

The following Friday just after midnight the anonymous car appeared again and this time the adjusted camera caught a close up of the driver.

"It's Hoskins himself," said the Housekeeper, "and he's on his own."

"But where's he going?" asked the Armourer.

"A drugs pick up?"

"Maybe. But why's he alone? Surely, he'd take some muscle along on a drugs deal."

"Could Python follow him, d'you think?"

"No way," said the Hunter, "it's not his skill. Let's face it, it'd be difficult enough for one of us to do it unobserved."

"Well, let's see if he's got any ideas."

They set up another encrypted conference call and put the problem to the Python.

"There's a simple technical solution," said the Python. "We put a tracker on the car."

"How?"

"No idea."

"It could be done," said the Defender, thoughtfully, "when he comes out of his gate he turns to go up to the 101 to get onto the bridge. Yes?"

"Maybe he's not going into San Francisco."

"Maybe not, but he has to go up to the 101 wherever

146

he's going."

"Okay, so what's the idea?"

"Suppose a couple of us are standing by and as he approaches that sharp bend just after he's left his house, a car pulls across in front of him as though by accident."

"Yes?

"Well then, while that's being untangled with hosts of apologies from the drunk driver, the other person can slip a magnetic tracker up inside his wheel arch."

"I can fix the tracker," said the Python, "but I don't fancy driving the ambush car."

"No sweat. I'll do that," said the Defender. "You get the stuff you need and I'll join you as soon as I can get a flight."

SAN FRANCISCO

BY THE TIME the Defender arrived in San Francisco the Python had the kit all ready. They went out to Hoskin's house that night and the next as a precaution, but they didn't expect that the mystery car would appear until Friday.

They were right. The third night was a Friday and the Defender's plan worked like a dream. Hoskin's car was not stopped for long, just enough time for him to swear at the drunk who had nearly hit him and then he was gone again with a tracking device on board.

The Defender picked up the Python and they set out to follow the car. The signal took them over the Golden Gate bridge and down into San Francisco. They followed Hoskins along Columbus Avenue then he turned off into a maze of side streets in China Town, finally parking in an old car lot behind a Chinese supermarket.

On this occasion they were too late to see where Hoskins had gone so they had to contain their impatience for another week. The following Friday the Defender was in position behind the supermarket and followed Hoskins to an apartment building nearby. The next day he visited the building and that evening he told the others what he had found.

"I'm pretty certain it's a knocking shop. I don't think this is a drugs deal. I think our Mr Hoskins is just partial to a bit of extra-curricular nooky."

WEYMOUTH

BACK IN THE monitoring station there was an air of satisfaction.

"Right," said the Hunter, "we're making progress. We know Hoskins is in residence, we know his security is pretty tight ..."

"Apart from his weakness for a bit of how's your father with a local lady," said the Fixer.

"We don't know it's a female," said the Defender who was on the encrypted link from San Francisco.

"I'd put money on it."

"So would I, but assumptions are dangerous."

"The point is," said the Hunter, "that we now know where he can be found without protection around him. So that's where we snatch him."

"Bang on," said the Fixer, "Grab him, bung him a quick dose of the ether bunny, shove the old needle in his arm and bingo."

The Armourer looked pained. "Ether bunny?" she said but the Fixer just grinned.

"That'll be fine," said Hunter, stifling a giggle. She turned to the Armourer. "Can you sort out the supplies as you did before?"

"Sure."

"Now once we've got him we need to move fast." She turned to the Fixer. "Is the truck ready to go?"

"All set. It's all kitted out, registered to me under my

Canadian identity and sitting in a lock-up on the edge of Vancouver."

"Okay, so when we're ready to move you and Armourer fly to Vancouver, collect the truck and head for San Francisco. We'll need to find somewhere to park it until we've got Hoskins."

"I'll sort that out," said the Housekeeper.

"Thanks. We'll need to rent a vehicle to do the snatch, I suggest an SUV, but we'll also need another one. Once we've grabbed Hoskins we'll switch vehicles before heading for wherever the truck's parked."

"I'll take care of all that," said the Defender.

"I've had another idea," said the Python.

"Go ahead."

"I'll book three flights from San Francisco in Hoskins' name for the day after the snatch. One to, say, Mexico City, one to Panama and one to … I don't know … Buenos Aires maybe. I'll pay for them with his credit card and we'll leave the booking confirmations in his car. That should confuse anyone who tries to find him."

"You'll use his own credit card?"

"Yes, of course."

"How?"

The Python looked puzzled. "Well, I hacked into his bank accounts long ago and cloned all his cards. I thought they might be useful."

The Hunter took a deep breath. "Fine. Okay, one last question, do we wait for him to finish and exit the building or do we gatecrash his love nest?"

"He'd be at more of a disadvantage if we catch him in the act."

"True, but then we've got the problem of the lady …"

"Assuming it is a lady …"

"Yes, yes, you know what I mean. Either way we'd have two bodies to deal with, not just one. And we have no quarrel with her."

"In that case I suggest we lift him as he comes out the building."

"That's best," said the Fixer, "he'll probably be knackered by then anyway."

"Right," said the Hunter, "so that's the snatch organised. And Fixer's got the Canadian border crossing sorted."

"What about Stage Three?" asked the Armourer. "Getting him back to the UK?"

"I've talked to Forseti," said the Hunter, "and he accepts we can't really do that ourselves. We've come up with a solution but it is going to need very careful timing."

"How careful?"

"Forseti will organise a training flight for the Special Air Services, give them a chance to test new navigational equipment, something like that."

"Ye–es …"

"Once we're ready to go, they'll fly to Ottawa, then onto Vancouver. From there they'll head home but on the way they'll touch down at a Canadian air base near Edmonton. They'll say it's for a bit of extra practice and to pick up one of their guys who's been on leave in Alberta. It will need very careful timing but we can hand Hoskins over to them and they'll bring him home."

"Bloody hell."

"The thing is, we must get the timing right. Those guys can't hang around Edmonton for too long. So let's get on with the preparations."

SAN FRANCISCO DAWN

THREE WEEKS LATER they were ready to go. The Canadian truck from Vancouver was parked in a service area off Interstate 5 to the north of Sacramento. The Housekeeper was sitting in a rented station wagon in a parking lot on the road to the airport and the Python was in his hotel room monitoring their communications.

Half past four in the morning. It was beginning to get light but a heavy mist lay over the whole bay area. The Defender had rented a black SUV which was now parked near to Hoskin's own car in the deserted lot in Chinatown. The Fixer had picked the lock on Hoskins' car and had placed an airline reservation for Mexico City in his glove compartment. Everything seemed to be going smoothly but the Defender was uneasy. Driving down into Chinatown he had pulled off to the side and stopped for a moment.

"Something wrong?" asked the Hunter.

The Defender peered through the back window. "Probably not. Just for a moment I thought we were being followed. Can't see anything. Probably mistaken."

The rest of the journey passed without incident and now the Armourer and the Fixer were hunkered down in the front seats, out of sight but ready to go at a moment's notice. The Defender and the Hunter were watching the door of the apartment block.

Right on cue Hoskins emerged from the building. The Defender blipped his phone once and the Armourer started her engine. As Hoskins approached his car, the Defender gripped him from behind, the Fixer smacked the chloroform pad over his mouth and they bundled him into the back seat of the SUV. The Defender went in after him, the Fixer got into the front seat, but as the Hunter moved to join them it all went wrong.

Two men suddenly appeared on the far side of the parking lot, a shot was fired and the back window of the SUV shattered. At the same time someone slammed into the Hunter, dragging both her arms into a painful bear hug. As the Armourer began to drive forward there was another shot and the two strangers flung themselves at the vehicle which began to slow. The Hunter saw the back door swing open and realised the Defender was trying to come to her aid.

"No," she yelled, "Go, go, go."

The Armourer flung the car into reverse and roared backwards knocking down one of the men as she did so, then shifted gear and vanished down the side street with one back door still swinging open.

The arms securing the Hunter tightened. In front of her one of the other men got groggily to his feet, the other lay very still – the Armourer had driven right over him.

The man in front of her shook his head, looked around, realised the car had gone and swore violently. He came up to the Hunter and slapped her face twice.

"Where they go? Tell us, or you die."

"Get stuffed."

He regarded her for a moment then said, "Maybe you not die yet. Maybe we try little persuasion first." He jerked his head. "Bring her along."

The man who was holding her started to drag her backwards. She fought every inch of the way but then suddenly there was another shot. A look of surprise came

153

over the man in front of her as he slowly collapsed onto his knees and then fell face down in the dirt. At the same time the pressure holding her was eased, there was a brief scuffle, a grunt and she was free. She span round and found herself looking into a familiar face.

"Perry?" she said in disbelief.

"My turn to help you," said Perry Cracken.

THE STREETS OF SAN FRANCISCO

TWO STREETS AWAY as they were approaching Columbus Avenue the Defender said, "Stop the car."

The Armourer pulled into the kerb and the Defender got out. "I'm going back for Hunter. Fixer, you get in the back with chummy and the two of you head for the car switch. Forget me, just follow the plan. Hunter and I will join you later."

And with that he vanished into the mist.

SAN FRANCISCO DAWN

THE HUNTER COULD hardly believe her eyes. "Where the hell did you come from?"

Perry shook his head. "No matter, not now. We need to get out of here." And he indicated the three bodies, two dead, one unconscious.

She followed his gaze. "I hope it's not the bloody CIA again."

"Wish they were. These guys are Russians."

"Russians?"

"Yeah. Come on, we need to move. I don't want to be — ugh."

He broke off choking as an arm came out of the shadows and a sharp blade was pressed against his throat.

"One move and you're dead," said the Defender.

Perry gurgled wildly and the Hunter stepped forward and tapped the Defender on his arm. "Thanks for the support and all that, but he's on our side." And she indicated the three bodies on the ground.

The Defender looked unconvinced but lowered the knife slightly. "You all right, Hunter?"

"I'm fine, but only thanks to Perry here. He shot one of them and biffed the other."

"Perry … ? Perry? Not the guy from …?"

"Yeah. Look, we need to get out of here. Where are the others?"

"On plan."

"Good." She turned to Perry. "We need to talk. Where do you suggest?"

Perry scowled at the Defender. "There's an all-night diner out on Route 1."

"Great. I could kill a coffee. Do you have a car?"

"Next block," he said rubbing his throat.

"Then let's go."

THE STREETS OF SAN FRANCISCO

THE ARMOURER SWUNG the SUV onto Route 101 and headed towards the airport.

"Everything okay back there?" She called over her shoulder.

"He's had the needle and he's sleeping like a baby," said the Fixer, then added. "What we going to do about Hunter and Defender?"

"Nothing. They'll take care of themselves. We have our own job to do."

"Bit heartless."

"No, it's discipline. Team discipline." Then under her breath she muttered. "Doesn't mean I have to like it though."

They drove in silence for a few minutes, then the Fixer said, "What about those bullet holes in the back window?"

"Not a problem. We'll dump this car when we switch vehicles."

Twenty minutes later they pulled off into the parking lot where the Housekeeper was waiting for them. He spotted the bullet holes immediately.

"Trouble?"

"Just a bit."

"Where are the others?"

"No idea. Come on, we need to get chummy sorted."

Together they lugged the inert body of Hoskins out of the SUV and into the back of the station wagon. The Fixer and the Housekeeper got in beside him while the Armourer moved the SUV into the darkest corner of the parking lot.

She wiped down the door handles and steering wheel, then got into the driving seat of the station wagon and headed back towards San Francisco and the Oakland Bay Bridge.

CONVERSATION
OVER COFFEE

A S THEY SAT over mugs of coffee served by a yawning waitress, the Defender was still more than a little suspicious. The Hunter looked closely at Perry Cracken.

"You haven't changed much."

"Nor have you. Still in the same line of work?"

"Similar, not the same."

"Still got the same friend, I see."

"Yes. Defender, you remember Perry Cracken."

"I do."

"Defender? I'm guessing that's not what his mom christened him."

"No."

"And he called you 'Hunter'. Would that be Mrs. Hunter by any chance."

"No. More of a job description than a name."

The Defender leaned forward. "Look, chum, thanks for stepping in back there but I'd like to know why you were there at all."

The Hunter had a sudden flashback to the surveillance pictures in Weymouth. "You've been hanging around outside Hoskins's house, haven't you?"

"How d'you figure that?"

"No matter, but I'm right, aren't I?" Perry said nothing and the Hunter went on. "Let me ask you the same question. Are you still in the same line of business?"

Perry still said nothing and the Defender broke in. "What

line of business was he in?"

"Freelance courier. Information trading. Carry anything for anyone so long as the price was right."

"And last time we met you screwed me proper, in more ways than one."

"And you lied to me. You weren't attacked by Basque terrorists, were you?"

"I had one hell of a few months after you walked off with that flash drive."

"I bet you did. You seem to have survived though."

"Yeah, because I'm good. I managed to persuade my client I was done over by the British Secret Service. I presume that's what you were."

"Actually, no. Not then and not now."

"Shit."

"Okay, Perry, enough small talk. What's your connection with Hoskins and why do you say those guys back there were Russians?"

"I don't like this, none of it. I think we're all in deep shit."

"You might be," said the Defender. "I don't think we are."

"You guys have snatched Hoskins, haven't you?"

The Hunter and the Defender were silent and Perry sighed. "I saw what happened. Your pals have got him, so I guess my chances of doing a deal with him are gone."

Silence.

Perry looked from one to the other. "Talk about a rock and a hard place. Look, I have information. Sensitive information. I was trying to set up a deal with Hoskins but then the Russians got to hear about it."

"What sort of information?"

"Let's just say it implicates a couple of very senior people in the American government in rather dubious activities."

"Why did Hoskins want it?"

"He wanted to suppress it. The Americans were protecting his drug business. Well, frankly I think they were controlling the whole damn rodeo."

"You're saying that Hoskins' drug activities involve senior members of the American government?"

"Sure, no surprise there."

"Okay, then. So what about the Russians? What's their interest?"

"Their interest is more, well, let's say, aggressive."

"In what way?"

"Jeez, do you need everything laid on the line? Hoskins wanted to stop this information going public, the Russians wanted to make sure it did go public, embarrass the Americans, then take over the operation themselves."

"And where do you fit in?"

"I've got the information. Phone tap recordings, emails, photos of meetings, the whole nine yards."

The Defender leaned forward. "Have you indeed and where did you get them, can I ask?"

"No, you can't. But they're genuine."

"So you're playing off one side against the other?"

"Well, I was, but I rather think you guys have just screwed that up."

"Still the same old Perry."

"Still the same old lady, but you're not getting a second crack at my soap."

The Hunter smiled across the table at him. "Come on, Perry, why were you down in Chinatown tonight? I'm glad you were, of course, but it wasn't chance, was it?"

"I just wanted to talk to him, Hoskins. Trying to get through the security at his bloody house is hard work and then I thought, even if I got in, it might be even harder to get out again. I figured it wasn't a good place to drive a hard bargain."

"Why here?"

"I'd heard Hoskins liked a bit of naughty and I figured he wouldn't go hunting it in daylight so I staked out his place and followed him down here one night. I came back a couple of nights ago to have a looksee at the place and spotted you."

"Me?"

"Yeah. Bit of a shock to be honest, but I figured you weren't here for fun so I followed you when you left, checked your vehicle, and then picked you up tonight. Hadn't cottoned the Ruskies were following me through."

"And then it all got pretty crowded. So what happens now, Perry?"

"Guess I'm screwed, unless Hoskins is likely to reappear once you guys have finished with him."

"Unlikely."

"I'm in deep crap then. The Russians ain't gonna be too happy I shot one of their guys."

He leaned forward and looked at each of them in turn. "Are you sure you're not British agents?"

"Quite sure."

The Hunter was watching Perry closely. "But we do have connections if there's something you want to share."

"Well, I'm gonna need to find another market. D'you figure the Brits will pay for this stuff?"

"Depends what you've got."

"I've got heaps. Did you know Hoskins ran the UK end of this drugs ring for a while?"

The Hunter smiled faintly and Perry put up his hand. "Okay, okay, sure you know. But do you know the name of the British cop who was protecting him?"

"No. No, we don't."

"Well, I do. And I've also got some scuttlebutt about who's controlling him in the UK, nothing certain, senior cop maybe. I can let you have all that. So, do we have a deal?"

" Maybe. Could be interesting. I'll need to check, but just at the moment we're rather busy."

"For crying out loud… See, so long as I'm the only guy with this information then my life's on the line. Once I've passed it on I can drop our of sight for a while, especially if I've been paid for it."

"Okay, Perry, I'll ask, but our guys are going to want to evaluate it before paying up."

"No way, José. I'm not that dumb."

"Well, you can't expect them to buy sight unseen."

There was silence for a moment. Perry looked from one to the other then he said, "Okay, here's the deal. I'll give you a list of the stuff I have, but without the proof and without the name of the Brit. You talk to your guys and see if they're interested. If so, we'll see if we can work something out."

"Do you have that information with you?"

"No."

"When can we have it?"

"Tomorrow. Give me your cell number and we'll fix a handover."

The Defender shook his head. "No, you give us your number. We'll call you tomorrow and take it from there."

Perry looked at him for a moment then pulled out a piece of paper and scribbled on it.

"Thank you. Now I think it's time we were going."

"Want me to drop you off somewhere?"

"Thanks, but no thanks. I'll just nip out and call a cab."

The Defender put Perry's number in his pocket, stood up and walked out of the diner.

The Hunter and Perry looked at each other.

"You still look great," he said.

"Thank you … You're not so bad yourself."

"I enjoyed that night in Spain, apart from the final outcome."

She leaned across the table. "So did I. If circumstances had been different … well … you know."

"Yeah … It was a chance encounter, wasn't it? You didn't set me up or anything."

"Complete chance."

"Only I've sometimes wondered if it was just a professional thing."

"It wasn't just a professional thing, Perry, at least not at the beginning. Trouble was, I just didn't believe the Basque terrorist bit and that made me suspicious."

"I'll remember that for next time."

"There won't be a next time. At least not with me."

"Well, we'll have to see about that, Hunter Lady."

"Don't call me that. It's patronising."

"Well, I've gotta call you something. You are a Hunter and you are a lady."

In spite of herself she laughed. "You're incorrigible." She thought for a moment. "Okay then, if I'm Hunter Lady you can be Yankee Boy."

Perry looked a bit taken aback. "Okay, I guess."

The Defender reappeared. "Cab's on its way."

"Okay, so call me tomorrow, yeah?" I don't want to go to the Ruskies but a guy's got to earn a living."

"We'll call you."

There was the sound of a horn outside and the Defender and the Hunter got to their feet. Perry lounged back in his seat smiling. "So long again, Hunter Lady, hasta luego."

"See you, Yankee Boy."

They went out and climbed into the cab. "San Regis Hotel," said the Defender.

As the cab pulled away the Hunter said, "What if he tries

to follow us."

"Not a chance. I nicked his car keys while he was eyeing you up. I've left him a note in his pickup telling him where they are but it'll take him a while to find them."

"Good thinking."

"So what's this 'Yankee Boy stuff?"

"Work name for him. Good security."

"I'm not sure this is a good idea. You're adding an unnecessary complication to an active operation."

"Listen, Forseti knows about Perry. He once told me he's a good contact, the kind of guy who's likely to have stuff that'll be useful. I think this is well worth a punt."

"If you say so."

"So now we need some more wheels and then join the others up at …"

She broke off. The Defender had suddenly stiffened and was frantically patting all his pockets.

"What is it?"

"I've cocked up," he said, "now we've really got a problem."

SOUTH OF SACRAMENTO

THE STATION WAGON came off Interstate 5, into the service area and pulled up beside the Canadian truck. The Housekeeper hadn't seen it before and raised an eyebrow at the sight of the logo on the side – *Logan's Travelling Waxwork Exhibition* painted in kaleidoscopic colours.

The Armourer switched off the engine with a sigh of relief.

"So far, so good. How's our lad doing?"

The Housekeeper felt his pulse. "Seems okay. D'you think we should give him another shot?"

"Let's wait till we've got him in the truck. Fixer, if you get it open, Housekeeper and I will bring him across."

"Okay, won't be a—" He suddenly broke off. "Oh, my god."

"What is it?"

"I don't have the keys. I gave them to Defender for safe keeping."

"You're kidding?"

"Nope."

"Oh, shit."

At that moment the Armourer's cell phone rang.

"Armourer, this is Hunter. We've got a problem."

"Yeah, I know. You've got the keys to the truck."

"That's the problem. We haven't. Defender left them in the glove box of the SUV. Did you find them when you cleaned the car?"

"Never looked in there. Didn't think we'd used it."

"Damn. Any chance you can hotwire the truck."

"Not a good idea. I don't want to risk being spotted trying to hijack a Canadian truck, especially not when we've got our man here with us."

"Take your point. We'll have to get those keys then. Defender and I will go back but we'll need to get a set of wheels."

The Python had been listening in. "I've still got my rental car," he said, "but it's due back today."

"Sod that," said the Hunter. "Let's get going. Armourer ..."

"Yeah?"

"Can you keep chummy safe until we can get to you?"

"We'll have to, but I'm not staying here. We'll get back on the road and wait to hear from you."

"Right. Python, bring your car keys down to your hotel lobby. We'll meet you there."

"There is just one thing ..."

"What?"

"I don't like big cars. My rental is a Fiat 500."

There was a pause and then the Defender said, "Well, it's all we've got."

They heard him sigh. "Sorry Hunter, you'd better drive. If I try and use the pedals in a car that small I'll get toothmarks in my knees."

THE ARMOURER, THE FIXER and the Housekeeper held a quick conference.

"Don't think it's safe to stay here," said the Armourer, "we don't know how long they're going to be."

"In that case," said the Housekeeper, "I suggest we carry on up the interstate, then turn off at Williams for Yuba City, from there turn south again and re-join I-5 at Woodland. We can keep going round that circuit for as long as we need but we'll never be too far away from here."

"What are you? Some sort of mobile USA road atlas?"

"Told you I lived round here for years. You get to know a place."

"You sure do. Okay, but let's give chummy another shot before we go. Don't want him coming round while we're on the move."

They wrapped a rug around Hoskins so it looked as though he were sleeping on the back seat and the Armourer turned the station wagon onto I-5 North.

THE STREETS OF SAN FRANCISCO – AGAIN

B ACK IN SAN FRANCISCO the Hunter and the Defender were approaching the parking lot where the SUV had been abandoned.

"Almost there," said the Defender, desperately trying to stretch his legs. "I think it's opposite that furniture showroom."

"Got it."

They turned into the parking lot and headed towards the back where the Armourer said she had left the vehicle. At that moment they saw a black SUV coming straight towards them.

"That's our car," said the Defender, "it's being nicked."

Without any hesitation the Hunter swung the Fiat hard against the front wing of the SUV throwing it off course. As the cars collided the Defender was already out of their vehicle hauling a young man out from the SUV driver's seat. As the Hunter followed him another guy came out of the passenger seat clutching a long knife.

He made a lunge at the Hunter who simply side stepped, let the man's momentum carry him past her, then gave him a vicious chop on the neck. He went down screaming. She turned to see the Defender with his foot on the neck of the driver who was also vocally indicating his displeasure.

"Well, we timed that right," she said.

"Yup." He gestured down at the two men. "What we

going to do with them?"

For once the Hunter let her irritation show. "We don't have time for this crap. Finish them off, dump them in the back of this car and leave it."

"What the fuck," came a muffled cry from under the Defender's foot. "You can't just waste us, man."

The Defender looked down at him. "Oh, yes, we could, very easily, but we're not going to." He turned to the Hunter. "You know we can't do that. That's not what we do."

"No, I know. It's just that—"

"— it's one thing after another ... Sure." He thought for a moment. "Well, we can't take them with us, so we have to leave them here. Do we have any cord?"

"Don't know. Fixer put a bag of stuff in the back – 'in case we need it' as he put it."

"Go and have a look. I'll watch these guys."

The Hunter went to the back of the SUV, found the bag and opened in. There wasn't any cord but there was a reel of gaffer tape. As she took it out of the bag she heard another scream and ran back to the front of the vehicle.

"Everything all right?"

"Sure. Your guy tried to get up and go for me so I kicked him in the face. You might just move that knife out of range."

"This is getting messy," said the Hunter grimly as they taped the wrists of the two men behind their back and bundled them into the back of the SUV. Then the Hunter drove it back to the far end of the lot while the Defender examined the Fiat. It had a badly dented wing where they'd rammed the SUV but was still drivable. The SUV was also looking the worse for wear with a damaged wing to add to the bullet holes in the back window.

The Hunter opened the glove box and, to her relief, there were the keys to the Canadian truck. They used a bit more of the gaffer tape to gag the two men, then they locked the SUV and threw the key into the undergrowth.

A few minutes later they were driving north again on 101 heading back the way they had come.

AN UNWANTED ROAD TRIP

THE ARMOURER HAD always thought that driving the long straight roads of America was seriously dull at the best of times but when there was no specific purpose other than to kill time, it was even worse. She hated any form of inactivity and was getting seriously bored as they drove through Yuba City for the second time. Then suddenly she felt an unnatural vibration through the steering wheel.

"Sod it, we've got a flat." She managed to pull off on the side of the road just outside the gates to a cemetery. "Great timing," she thought, "a puncture, a public road and an unconscious drug baron on the back seat."

"Not our day, is it?" muttered the Fixer. The Housekeeper just sighed, open the trunk and pulled out the spare wheel and the jack. The Armourer and the Fixer also got out and the Fixer bent down to help the Housekeeper who was struggling with the wheel nuts.

While they were working a passing car stopped and the driver got out. "Hi, you folks got a problem? Anything I can do to help?"

"Thanks, but we're fine," said the Armourer.

"Say, you're British, aren't you? Can't mistake that accent. My ma – that's Dad's first wife – she came from England, some little village called Man-chester. Think that was it."

"When was that?" asked the Armourer politely.

"Oh, way back, 1947 I guess. She was a GI bride you know."

"Did she ever go back to … Man-chester?"

"Naw, never did. Always wanted to, you know, see the place she was born one last time. Never made it, cancer got her."

"Oh, I am sorry."

"Sure, but maybe just as well. Things and places are never quite how you remember them, are they?"

"I think she might have noticed a few changes in Man-chester."

"Sure. I mean this place" – he waved his arms expansively – "is nothing like it was when I was a kid growing up."

"You mean the cemetery is new?"

"What?" His brow furrowed. "Oh, I see, you're kidding me. No, I meant the whole town, the cemetery's been here for ever." He grinned and for a moment the Armourer thought he was going to dig her in the ribs. "The cemetery's the dead center of town, get it? Dead center." And he gave a big laugh.

"Ah, yes, dead centre. Good one."

"Now then, let's see if we can't get you folks sorted out." He peered into the car. "Be easier to jack her up if your friend got out too."

"No, he can't. He's not well. It's best he just gets some sleep."

"Oh, okay."

"Not a problem anyway," said the Fixer getting to his feet. "It's all done and dusted."

"Well, that's just fine. Say, can I buy you folks a cup of coffee?"

"That's very kind," said the Armourer, "but we're in a bit of a rush actually. Need to get … our friend … back home, into bed, you know."

"Sure. Cool. Well, it's been real nice meeting you. Now when you get home you say hi to little old Man-chester for my old ma, won't you?"

"We certainly will. Nice meeting you. Goodbye."

They all got back into the station wagon, waved to the man with the Manchester mum and drove off.

There was silence for a moment, then the Fixer said, "I reckon I feel about ten years older than I did when I got up this morning."

SOUTH OF SACRAMENTO

TWO HOURS LATER the Defender parked the battered Fiat beside the Canadian truck in the service area on I-5. Fifteen minutes later the others arrived in the station wagon. While the Armourer kept watch, the Fixer opened up the truck and he and the Defender shifted Hoskins into the back of it.

The Defender was quite surprised when he saw inside the truck. "What the hell you got in there? You been raiding museums or something?"

"Kind of. You're looking at all the paraphernalia of a travelling waxwork exhibition. Stall, models, flags, sound system for backing music. We travel the country visiting fairs, exhibitions and so on."

"Oh, you do, do you?"

"Well, up to a point. The point being that's the answer we'll give when we get stopped at the border."

The Hunter was talking to the Armourer. "You okay?"

"I'm fine. You ever been to Yuba City?"

"Don't think so."

"Well, don't bother. Once is once too often and I've now been three times and I haven't even had any breakfast yet."

"Well, we can soon put that right."

They left the Defender in the truck with Hoskins and the others went across to the diner in the service area. With a coffee inside her the Armourer began to relax again.

"So what's the next stage? Are we heading straight for the border?"

"It's not quite as straightforward as that. I've told Python to hire a decent sized car and meet us out here and then we can plan the next stage. While we're waiting for him, let's sort out chummy."

Back at the truck. Hoskins had come round but he still looked pretty groggy. The Defender stood behind him with the Fixer off to one side. The Hunter sat on a crate just in front of him. There was a low light inside the truck as the doors were all closed.

"Can you hear me, Mister Hoskins?"

"I hear you."

"Good."

"What gives?"

"You're going on a journey. I hope you'll survive it but just in case you don't, I want you to know what's happening to you and why."

"My guys are going to chew you up when I get out of here. You don't know what you're tangling with, lady."

"Oh, I think I do. And your guys, as you call them, won't worry for a while yet. By the time they do you'll be safely in the UK."

"What the hell's all this about?"

"We know all about the drugs operation in London, Mister Hoskins. Some of your colleagues in that enterprise are currently serving long jail sentences, one of them for murder. A policemen was killed in the raid on your house."

"You can't pin that on me."

"Well, we can actually. We have all the proof we need and if you'd stayed around, you'd have been charged with murder as well."

"Bullshit. The Brits can't touch me. I have protection in

high places, lady. No way am I gonna get extradited."

The Hunter smiled sweetly. "Actually, Mr Hoskins, you're in the process of being extradited right now. Or, as you Americans call it, you're undergoing rendition."

"Crap. You're bluffing."

"You're on your way to Canada. From there you'll be flown back to the UK and then you'll just disappear."

"I've got friends in the Senate. They're never going to stand for this."

"There's nothing they can do. Officially, the British will deny knowing anything about you."

There was a long silence. Then Hoskins said, "Suppose I believe all this bullshit, are you just going to bump me off?"

"Oh, no. That would be too easy. If we'd wanted you dead we'd have killed you last night. No, you're going to have a long, long time to brood over what you've done. You're going to spend the rest of your life in a British version of Guantanamo Bay."

"Who the hell are you?"

"They call me The Hunter and I've been hunting you, Mister Hoskins."

"How much?"

"What for?"

"To let me go. Whatever your client is paying, I'll double it."

"I'm not getting paid for this, well, apart from expenses of course, which, frankly, is just as well. We do seem to be getting through rather a lot of vehicles."

"You expect me to believe that?"

"I don't care one way or the other. This isn't about money, it's about justice. A word that I suspect isn't in your vocabulary."

Hoskins glared at her. "Think you're so smart, doncha?

But the Senator's got the measure of you Brits. There are plans for your country you know nothing about, lady."

"What sort of plans?"

Hoskins laughed. "You'll find out but one day soon you'll wish you'd never been born."

The Hunter sighed. "You wouldn't believe how often I've heard that but, as you can see, I'm not quite dead yet."

Suddenly she'd had enough. She stood up. "We won't meet again, Mister Hoskins. Enjoy the British Guantanamo. My guess would be it's going to be a lot colder than the American version."

She turned to the Fixer. "Get Armourer in here and put him under again. We need to get going."

"No—oo." Hoskins started to struggle but the Defender held him a grip of iron.

The Hunter left the truck and walked over to the station wagon. A few moments later the Fixer joined her.

"He's out for the count again."

"Good. As soon as Python arrives you need to get on the road."

"Sure ... What was all that about?"

"Fulfilling our brief. If anything goes wrong along the way, kill him. I'll tell Armourer the same. There's no way back for him, but if we do have to waste him then I wanted him to know why."

There was a long pause then the Fixer said, "I can see why they picked you for this job." Another pause, then. "I don't think I could just kill someone like that, right out of the blue."

"I hope you won't have to. Don't worry, I appreciate it's not something you've ever had to do. If it becomes necessary Armourer will do it."

The Fixer nodded and the Hunter went on, "But you do see why it might be necessary, don't you?"

The Fixer nodded again. "You're the boss."

"Don't call me that. Now, let's get ready for the next stage."

Fifteen minutes later The Defender found the Hunter sitting on a low wall on the edge of the service area.

"You okay?"

"Yeah. Bit tired."

"Not surprising. We were all up early."

"True, but it's not just that."

"It's those two guys in the SUV, isn't it?"

"Yes. I could have done it, you know. I could have blown them away. I was just so …"

"Focused?"

"Maybe. Angry, perhaps. Everything had gone to plan then one small thing …"

"My small thing."

She shrugged. "The point is that our timetable was up the spout and then suddenly these two … no-hopers … were threatening everything. If we'd lost those keys …"

"I know. But that's not the answer."

The Hunter was silent for a moment. Then she said, "No, but it's going to happen sometime, isn't it? If we go on doing these kind of jobs then sooner or later someone's going to get killed. It could even be one of us."

"I know."

"We've already acquired a couple of dead Russians. Who knows what might spin off from that."

The Defender suddenly stood up. "Look, there's no point in dwelling on this stuff. We all knew what we were taking on when we agreed to be part of this team. You're a good leader, Hunter, concentrate on that. Forget what might have happened back there."

"Lecture over?"

"Sure."

"Then let's move on."

BY THE TIME THE Python arrived, rather self-consciously driving a Toyota RAV, the Hunter had herself in hand again.

"Right then, here's what we're going to do."

The Defender and the Armourer exchanged glances.

"Fixer and Armourer, you're heading for the Canadian border in the truck."

"I'll make Hoskins up to look like a waxwork of Boris Karloff," said the Fixer. "The border guys will almost certainly want to see in the truck but so long as Hoskins is still knocked out, he'll just look like another model."

"Great. Are you still planning to use the border crossing at Osoyoos?"

"I think so. I can say I'm heading for Banff to put on a show there and it's not a bad run from there up to Edmonton."

"Okay, so, Housekeeper and Python, you'll follow the truck in the RAV. Now, Fixer, once you're over the Canadian border send a text to that number I gave you. That'll tell the SAS guys where you are and they can plan their take off time accordingly to rendezvous with you at Edmonton. So, any questions?"

"And where will you be in all this?" asked the Armourer.

"Ah, well, something's cropped up. There's someone I have to meet before I can join you."

The Armourer was not satisfied. "What sort of someone?"

The Hunter sighed. "Well, it's like this ..." and she filled them in on Perry Cracken and his background.

The listened in silence but when she'd finished the Housekeeper said, "I'm not sure this is a good idea."

"I'm certain it isn't," said the Armourer.

"I appreciate your concern," said the Hunter, "but I think

181

it's what Forseti would want. This guy could turn out to be very useful to us."

"Could be a double cross," said the Fixer.

"Yes, of course it could. That's why the Defender's coming with me."

They all looked at the Defender who shrugged. "I'm not happy either but she's going to do it so we just need to make sure it doesn't go wrong."

"Right. That's settled," said the Hunter.

Half an hour later when the Defender came back from the diner, the Hunter beckoned him out of earshot of the others.

"I've spoken to Perry, we've agreed a meeting place for tomorrow but he says I have to go alone."

"No way."

"Thought you'd say that."

"It's a trap, it has to be."

"Quite possibly, so we have to decide how to play this."

"Where's the meet?"

"A place called Point Reyes National Seashore. It's some kind of nature reserve on the coast north of San Francisco."

"Lonely?"

"I guess so. He said to go to a town called Inverness and head for the Point Reyes lighthouse. Five or six miles down that road there's a ruined barn opposite a track. I'm to take that track down towards a sea inlet where there's an old cabin on the beach used by fishermen in season."

"And that's where he wants to meet?"

"Yup."

"When?"

"Six a.m. Tomorrow."

"Don't like it."

"Nor do I, but if we get going now we'll have time to recce it before the meet tomorrow."

"You still want to go ahead?"

"Yes."

"Then we'd better get cracking."

POINT REYES NATIONAL SEASHORE

JUST BEFORE SIX the following morning the Hunter drove slowly down a sandy track towards the sea. The sky was beginning to lighten in the east as she spotted the isolated fishermen's cabin that Perry had described. She parked the station wagon, got out of the car and began to walk towards it.

When she was a few yards away the cabin door opened and Perry appeared.

"Morning, Hunter Lady."

"Hallo to you too."

"You alone?"

"As agreed." And she held her arms out wide.

"Good."

"So what have you got for me, Perry?"

Perry Cracken sighed. "Not what you were expecting, Hunter Lady. I'm very sorry but things have changed."

As he spoke two more figures appeared in the cabin doorway, each carrying a gun.

"Oh, Perry, you lied to me."

"Hey, look, sorry, okay? This ain't my fault."

As he spoke one of the men stepped forward and put his gun against Perry's head.

"Cracken's not gonna sell to you, lady. He found another customer."

184

"Let me guess, would this be a certain Senator?"

"None of your business."

"If you say so. But if you're only here to tell me there's no deal, what's the point of meeting?"

One of the men sniggered. "I guess that's you. You're the point."

"Really."

"Yeah. Well, more like Hoskins. You hand him over to us nice and peaceful and no one need get hurt."

"Don't listen to them, Hunter Lady. They're going to ... ugh—"

Perry fell to the ground as one of men hit him hard on the side of his head with his gun.

"Shut up, punk. Okay, lady, where's Hoskins?"

"No idea. Why ask me?"

"Don't give me that crap. You guys lifted him the other night and before you do the innocent stare bit, we know he ain't in Mexico City."

"Are you sure?"

"Yup. There's a contract out on him down there. That's the last place he'd go.

Ooops, thought the Hunter, *good idea, wrong destination.*

Aloud she said, "Can't help you, chum. Hoskins is halfway to the UK by now. He's been a very naughty boy, you know, and the Brits have quite a score to settle with him."

One of the men stepped forward. "Let's quit this bullshit. Hoskins sure ain't going to the UK. You're going to hand him over to us, yeah? Or do we have to encourage you a little?"

"I'd really rather you didn't do that. Oh, look ..." She flung her hand up in the air. "Hey, there's a turkey vulture up there."

Neither of the men moved. "You don't fool us that way, lady, do you think we're stupid?"

"No," said the Hunter calmly, "I think you're dead."

As she spoke two shots rang out. The man who'd been holding Perry spun round and fell to the ground like an amateur extra in a western. The other man fell to his knees, cradling his shoulder where the bullet had hit him. Quick as a flash Perry rolled sideways and grabbed the man's gun.

From the dunes behind the cabin the Defender appeared carrying a rifle.

"You see, Perry," said the Hunter, "I lied as well."

Perry had just began to get to his feet when they heard the roar of a high powered motorbike. The Hunter half turned as the Defender yelled. "Hunter, get down."

Instinct kicked in. She dropped to the ground and rolled sideways as a motorcycle came roaring across the dunes, the driver crouched low over the handlebars, his passenger spraying the ground with an automatic weapon. The Defender had also gone flat but before he could reach for his rifle there were two more shots. The driver and the marksman went flying off the motorbike which then span in a circle and collapsed into a sand dune. The two riders lay very still.

The Hunter got to her feet, brushing the sand off her clothes.

"We're going to have to ask Forseti for a clothing allowance at this rate."

"I guess that was the Senator's back-up team?" said the Defender.

She looked at him. "I know you're good but that wasn't you who shot them, was it?"

"Nope, that was our back-up team."

"Armourer?"

"Yup."

"And what the hell is Armourer doing here when she should be miles away by now?"

"You could say, saving your arse. Well, mine as well, I suppose."

The Hunter sighed. "Well, let's see what the damage is."

The two riders from the motorbike were dead and so was one of the men who'd been holding Perry. The other man was moaning to himself, clutching his shoulder which was bleeding profusely.

"I said we'd have a stiff or two before we were done," said the Defender.

The Armourer appeared with a high velocity rifle under her arm. The Hunter looked at her for a moment. "I suppose I should say thank you."

"You're welcome, boss."

"Don't call me that."

The Defender intervened. "She's here at my suggestion. I wasn't at all happy about this set up. Reckoned we might need some reserve fire power."

"Did you indeed, and how did she get here?"

"In the RAV."

"I see. And the ... other vehicle?"

"On its way as planned with a crew of three."

"So you disobeyed my orders?"

"Sure we did. We're a team. We look out for each other. Anyway orders are made for the obedience of fools and the guidance of wise men."

In spite of herself the Hunter laughed. "You're crazy."

"You're all crazy if you ask me," said Perry.

The Hunter gathered herself together. "Right, we need to get out of here. What d'you think we should do with them?" And she gestured towards the bodies.

"Drag them inside the cabin. Could be days before they're found."

"What about this guy?" The Defender gestured towards

the wounded man.

"Shoot him," said Perry.

"No," said the Hunter, "we kill when we have to, but we don't execute people."

"Let's have a look at his shoulder," said the Armourer. She bent over the wounded man who flinched away from her.

"Good. Clean wound. Bullet went right through. I'll bandage it up, stop the bleeding and then we can leave him with the others."

"What about me?"

"You're going to have to come with us, Perry, at least for a while. Can't just leave you here."

"Why not?" asked the Defender.

"Because I say so."

"Okay, you're the—"

"Don't say it."

Perry looked from one to the other. "What if I don't want to come?"

The Defender smiled. "If you don't come with us, Perry, then we'd have to kill you and, for reasons best known to herself, Hunter's not too keen on that. Maybe it's something to do with your soap."

Perry made no further comment. The four of them, Perry helping reluctantly, dragged the three dead gunmen into the cabin. They went through their clothes and removed their cell phones and a couple of knives. Then, at the Defender's suggestion, they lashed the wounded man's feet together, bundled him in with the corpses and closed the door.

They kicked some sand over the pools of blood on the ground and then the Defender said, "We need to get rid of the hog too."

He went over to the gunmen's bike and pulled it upright. He climbed into the saddle, kick-started it, swung it round in a wide circle then opened the throttle wide. As the bike gathered speed he headed for the shoreline and in the split second before it hit the water, he flung himself clear. The bike ploughed on into the sea and vanished beneath the waves. The Defender watched it go with regret.

"No way to treat a Harley."

They collected the various weapons that were lying around then piled into the station wagon and drove to where the Armourer had parked the RAV. The Armourer and the Hunter transferred to the RAV, taking Perry with them. The Defender drove the station wagon behind them. They reached Highway 1 at Olema where the Defender drove into a campsite and dumped the station waggon.

"Another abandoned car."

"Probably just as well," said the Armourer, "we never did get that puncture fixed."

They set off, the Armourer driving with the Defender beside her. The Hunter sat in the back with Perry who was clearly uncomfortable.

"It wasn't my fault, you know, they just appeared and grabbed me."

"Did they choose that meeting place?"

"Yeah. I guess they had you figured as some dumb broad. Get you alone in a place like that and you'd be a pushover."

"Bad guess," said the Defender over his shoulder.

There was a pause and then Perry said, "What gives now?"

"Depends on you. D'you still want to deal?"

"Not a lot of choice. You've killed off all my other options."

"So what you offering?"

"For starters, this." Perry took off his shoe and then his sock and produced a sheet of paper. "Safest place to keep it," he said in answer to a raised eyebrow from the Hunter.

"What is it?"

189

"A list of all the emails and documents I have which show the Senator's involvement with Hoskins and how the Senator, and a couple of others high up in this administration, are actually funding the whole drugs racket."

"And the British guy you mentioned."

"There's stuff about Hoskins' time in London. It's clear he had protection there, some cop on his payroll, but you don't get the name until I've agreed a deal with your guys."

"They're not my guys, but I can certainly get this to them but you said there was also someone else, higher up the food chain."

"That's instinct, not knowledge. I'm pretty sure the cop wasn't acting alone but can't prove that."

"Okay. Now this …" she waved the bit of paper, "is this the only copy?"

"Yup."

"Why would you let us have the only copy?"

"Well, it's like this. I've been blessed – or cursed, depending on your point of view – with excellent powers of recall. I could recite that list to you now word for word."

"Could you indeed? Okay, if our guys are interested how do we get hold of you?"

"You've got my cell number. How do I get hold of you?"

The Hunter took out her phone. "I'm texting you a number. Call this and you reach me. Feel free to use it anytime. It's not traceable."

"No sweat." Perry took a deep breath. "Hey, I've no idea who you guys are but you're pretty smooth operators. Is Hoskins really headed for the UK?"

"Yes."

"Shit. You really are something." He looked at her for a moment. "I guess you know you've turned me into a target."

"Have we?"

"Sure. The CIA were bad enough that time in Spain but the hired muscle the Senator can call on is something else. I'm a marked man."

"You're breaking my heart," said the Defender.

"You gonna take me to the UK too?"

"Nope. We're just going to dump you somewhere. Any preference?"

Perry glanced out of the window. "You heading for Sacramento?"

"Briefly, yes. We're not stopping there."

"That's no good for me anyway. Too big. You going anywhere near Carson City?"

The Defender consulted the map. "Could do." He handed it to the Hunter. "Takes us a bit out of our way. What do you think?"

She studied the map. "I think that'll be fine. Let's do it."

"Thanks. I've got contacts there. And I'd quite like to get out of California before that guy back there wriggles loose and calls his boss."

Three hours later, the Armourer brought the car to a halt outside a casino on North Carson Street and the Hunter and Perry got out.

"Good luck, Perry. I'll give you a call once I've talked to my guys."-

"Got time for one last coffee, Hunter Lady?"

The Hunter looked at him for a moment then said, "Okay, why not?" She turned to the Defender. "Give me half an hour. I'll call when I'm ready."

"This is a bad idea."

"No it isn't. Go and find yourself an ice cream. I'll call you."

THE DINER WAS PRETTY FULL but they managed to find

a table in a corner.

"This isn't just 'one last coffee', is it?"

"Quick as ever, Hunter Lady. No, it ain't. I've got a proposition I'd kinda like to put to you."

"A Spain type proposition?"

"I wish. No, this is more in the way of business."

"Go on."

"I don't know who you guys are or who you work for, but I've seen the way you operate and I guess I can trust you." He paused. "Trust don't come naturally to guys like me."

"I'm sure not, so why?"

"Hey, no idea. Instinct maybe. That, and what you said back on the beach."

"What did I say?"

"You said '*We kill when we have to, but we don't execute people*'. That changed things. Most guys I know would just have shot that hood and not thought anything of it."

"I'm not most guys."

"You're telling me."

"What's your proposition?"

"I've never trusted anyone before. Don't know if this will work."

"What's your proposition, Perry?"

"Well, I get to know a lot of stuff, sensitive stuff."

"So I gathered."

"Sometimes I can sell it on, sometimes I can't. Sometimes just knowing it puts me in danger." She stayed silent so he carried on. "As I said, I'm gonna be a marked man now. I'm tired of hawking information round people who'd be quite happy to see me dead so long as they got what they want."

"The proposition?"

"I'm ready to settle for one regular market. Suppose we stay in touch, I share information with you. Okay? As I get to

192

know stuff, I pass it on. That'd be good for me. Sharing it gets me a tiny bit of insurance."

"What about payment?"

"Well, now, I guess that's where the trust bit comes in. If I get anything for you, I want paying. A guy's got to earn a living."

"If your information is good then I think I might be able to arrange for you to be paid."

"I guess I have to trust you. So what do you think?"

She did not respond but looked straight at him. He met her gaze and his eyes did not drop. After a moment she said, "I regret what I did to you in Spain. But it's only fair to tell you that I'd do it again. The job always comes first."

"Always?"

"Always. In a parallel universe you and I might have had something going, but that kind of life's not for people like us."

There was a long pause, then he said, "No, I guess not."

"So if that's understood, I accept your proposition. Whenever you have something to tell me, I'll listen. What I do with that information is my decision. If it's useful, I'll do my best to make sure you'll get paid. Okay?"

Perry took a deep breath. "Okay."

There was a pause then she said, "Was there something specific you had in mind?"

"Not sure. There's some scuttlebutt going around. High level rumblings. I know there's always yatter about government corruption but this feels a bit different. Might involve the Russians. Don't like the sound of it but don't have any hard and fast info as yet."

"Well, let me know if you hear anything definite. Were you serious about your memory skills?"

"Yup, mixed blessing. Can be a bummer, you can't forget

something you know."

"No, I see that. You can burn a bit of paper, wipe a computer file but you can't erase a memory."

"Well, you can, but it's kinda permanent."

She stood up. "I've got to be going. That number I gave you is a dedicated number. Reaches no one but me and no one else will ever use it. Been good to see you again, Perry. I guess the score's two-one now, yeah?"

Ten minutes later she was back in the RAV and they were heading north towards Reno.

SOMEWHERE IN OREGON

IT WAS A LONG, long day. Late that afternoon they stopped for a comfort break and while the Armourer was inside a roadside café, the Defender, leaning casually against the side of the RAV, said, "You keen on this Perry guy?"

"Not keen exactly, but I do have a bit of a soft spot."

"Dangerous in our line of work."

"Don't worry. It won't compromise anything."

"He's a mercenary, Hunter. No matter how tasty you think he is, he'd still sell his grandmother's teeth to the highest bidder."

"I know, but he could be useful."

"Maybe. D'you think Forseti and his chums will do a deal with him?"

"I think they might. Why?"

"Just wondered if this might be useful," and he produced a USB flash drive from his pocket.

"Where'd you get that?"

"Cracken's pocket. Saw he kept patting it, reckoned he was checking it was safe. Bumped into him as he got out the RAV and ... liberated it ... is that what you say?"

"You're a devious bastard, aren't you?"

"Takes one to know one."

"What's on it?"

The Defender shrugged. "No idea, but maybe Forseti and his chums won't need to do a deal with him. All the stuff he's offering could be on that stick."

THE CANADIAN
BORDER

THE TRUCK WITH HOSKINS on board had passed
through Oroville and was only a few miles from the
Canadian border when the Fixer pulled off to the side and
stopped the engine. He went round to the back and opened
the door. The Housekeeper peered at him over a waxwork
model of Buffalo Bill.

"Anything wrong?"

"No. How you doing in here?"

"All fine. He's sleeping the sleep of the—"

"— unjust?"

The Housekeeper laughed and the Fixer went on, "Okay,
let's arrange him at the bottom of the pile of dummies."

"Need to make sure he can still breathe."

"Sure, but we don't want him too near the top of the pile."

"Should I come into the cab for the border crossing?"

"Yep, wouldn't look right if you was in the back."

They sorted out the dummies and the other equipment
then they all climbed into the cab. The Fixer turned to the
Python. "You got that bit of gubbins I asked for?"

"Of course."

"Sure it'll work?"

"Of course it will work."

"Okay, but we only get one crack at this."

"It'll work."

"Good."

They sat there for a few minutes and then the Housekeeper

said, "Are we going or what?"

"Wait a bit. I'm hoping we'll get lucky."

A number of vehicles passed them, a few private cars, several trucks. Suddenly the Fixer leaned forward and started the engine. "Here, we go."

A large artic roared past them, weaving slightly as it went, and the Fixer pulled out and hung on his tail.

"Don't get too close. I think that guy's drunk."

"Hope so," said the Fixer and the other two looked at him.

They approached the border post and joined the queue. The US border guard glanced at their passports, asked where they had come from then waved them through. The Fixer turned to the Python.

"Activate your little toy when you hear me say 'Fragile'."

Ahead of them the artic with the drunk driver weaved its way towards the Canadian border post and they pulled in behind him.

A border guard appeared at their window. "Where you come from?"

"San Francisco."

"Where you headed?"

"Banff. We've got a show there in a couple of days' time."

"How many guns you carrying?"

"None," said the Fixer with a straight face.

"Open up, please."

"Sure." The Fixer climbed out of the cab and glanced towards the other truck. "Say I think that driver's drunk."

The guard followed his gaze. "Could be."

"He was certainly weaving about a bit when we were behind him back there."

They reached the back of the truck and the Fixer opened the doors. The guard peered in. "What the hell's all this stuff?"

"It's the equipment for our show. We run a travelling

197

waxwork exhibition, stall, models, flags, sound system for backing music. We travel the country visiting fairs, exhibitions and so on. We did show in Marin County a few days ago and now we're heading for Banff."

"Let's have a look." The guard heaved himself up into the back of the truck and the Fixer followed him.

"Please be careful, some of this stuff's fragile."

The guard started to poke around and then suddenly outside there was a huge cacophony of horns, hooters and car alarms followed by a lot of shouting and commotion. The guard jumped down from the truck. "What's going on?"

"I think that drunk driver's causing a problem."

"Oh, shit. Okay guys, on your way. Have a good show."

"Thank you."

The Fixer got back in the cab, pulled carefully round the artic where the driver was trying vainly to punch a border guard and headed into Canada.

Once they were out of sight of the border post the Housekeeper said cautiously, "You didn't actually plan that, did you?"

"Not entirely, it was luck, but there was always a good chance. While I was buying this truck I was tipped off that some of these long distance drivers get bored and have a drink on the job. I hoped we might meet one and we did. Makes a good diversion, especially when Python's little toy set off all the horns and car alarms."

"Told you it would work," said the Python.

The Housekeeper shook his head. "I can see why they call you the Fixer."

SOMEWHERE SOUTH OF THE CANADIAN BORDER

WAY TO THE SOUTH the RAV had just entered Washington State when the Hunter's phone buzzed. The Armourer was driving with the Defender beside her. The Hunter had been stretched out on the back seat trying to catch up on her sleep but when she heard the phone she was immediately awake.

From the front seat the others couldn't really hear the conversation but they did hear her say a very loud "Oh, shit."

A few moments later the Hunter ended the call and leaned forward. "Can you find somewhere to pull over. We need to talk."

A few minutes later the Armourer spotted a rough track leading off to the right and turned into it.

"What's up?" asked the Defender.

"That was a message from Forseti. The Canadians are being difficult."

"How difficult."

"They're not going to let Fixer's truck onto the air base. They say only security-cleared service personnel can enter."

"Bugger."

"Exactly."

"Do you suppose Fixer's called the aircraft yet."

"I imagine so."

"I'll call him and check."

The Defender spoke briefly to the Fixer then turned to the others. "They're well into Canada already. Should be in Edmonton by around 8.00 am."

"Okay, so how we going to play this?"

"Can someone from the air crew come off base and collect Hoskins?"

"Even if they could, Hoskins isn't security cleared personnel either. And the Canadians might just wonder why he's handcuffed and drugged."

The Armourer laughed. "They could just tell them he's drunk."

There was a pause and then the Defender said, "Do you know, that might just work."

"What would?"

He turned to the Hunter. "You said, it was our guys from the SAS who are doing the pick-up, yes?"

"Yes."

"Do you know the name of the SAS officer back in London who fixed this for us?

"No, but I can ask. Why?"

"Ask. We may just hit lucky."

The Hunter got back on the phone and a few minutes later she scribbled a name on a piece of paper and handed it to the Defender. "Any good?"

"Oh, yes. Can you get a contact number for him?"

The Hunter turned back to her phone and after a moment said, "No, they won't let us have a number but if we have a good reason they'll get him to call us."

"We have good reason. Get them to tell him that Frisky has a problem and needs his help urgently. Give them my mobile."

The Hunter relayed all that, ended the call and turned back to the Defender. "Well, Frisky … are you going to explain?"

"No, but we've struck lucky. Pingo and I go back a long way and he owes me one."

"Pingo?"

"Don't ask." At that moment his phone rang. "Look, I'll take this outside if you don't mind. This won't be a conversation for sharing."

The Defender got out of the car and walked a little way down the track. The Armourer and the Hunter looked at each other and the Armourer gave a wry grin.

Twenty minutes passed and then the Defender came back and got into the car.

"Okay, all sorted. Let's go. I'll fill you in on the way and then we need to brief Fixer."

STURGEON COUNTY, ALBERTA

THE TRAVELLING WAXWORKS show truck was parked on an old industrial site about two miles from the Canadian Air Base near Edmonton. They'd only been there twenty minutes or so when a Canadian Air Force jeep appeared with three men in it, all dressed in combat fatigues.

One of them got out and came across to the truck. His voice was unmistakably that of a British officer. "Morning. I'm the captain in command of this unit. I've been told no names. Is one of you Mr. F?"

The Fixer nodded. "That's me."

"Gather we've got a body to collect."

"Yes. Have you brought—?"

"— suitable clothes? Sure. Sergeant, bring the kit, will you." He turned back to the Fixer. "I imagine our man's in the back of your truck."

"He is."

"I'm told he's been a bad lad."

"If you call running an international drugs ring and being responsible for the murder of a British policeman 'bad', then you're right."

The captain didn't bat an eyelid. "Thought it must be something like that. Okay, let's get him sorted. We're in a bit of a rush, the locals aren't too keen on us being here."

The Housekeeper opened the back of the truck and they all climbed in. The captain glanced round him with interest but his only comment was, "You see something new every day in this job."

Hoskins was still drugged and it was only a matter of moments for them to strip him and dress him in the combat gear the British soldiers had brought with them. Then the Fixer took two bottles of whiskey and poured them liberally over Hoskins. The soldiers watched with regret.

"Waste of good scotch," said the sergeant sadly.

The Fixer patted him on the shoulder. "Don't worry, mate, it's not scotch, it's Canadian Club."

"Still a waste. Never mind, it'll do the job."

The carried Hoskins cross to the Canadian jeep and propped him up in the back with a soldier on either side of him.

"I hope this is going to work," said the Fixer.

"No sweat, chum. The Canadians think we've come to arrest one of our guys who overstayed his leave and is wandering around roaring drunk. They'll be so glad to see us back and on our way that they'll never notice it's the Sergeant here doing the drunken singing, not chummy. He'll be very convincing. Had a lot of practice, haven't you, Sergeant?"

The Sergeant grinned.

"Right then. Time to go. Get this bastard back home."

The captain climbed back into the jeep and it roared off towards the air base.

The Fixer took out his phone and sent a text. "The parcel is on its way."

Three hours later the Fixer dropped the Python and the Housekeeper at Calgary airport and then headed for Vancouver to dump the truck and make his way home from there.

When the Hunter received the Fixer's text, they altered direction, crossed the Canadian border at Morgan and headed for Winnipeg dropping the Armourer off at Regina on the way.

One by one, and by a variety of different routes, the team made their way home. The job was done.

NATURAL HISTORY MUSEUM

S HE THOUGHT SHE could no longer be amazed by the various meeting places that Forseti chose but the Natural History Museum came as a real surprise. She presented herself at the front desk, giving the name she'd been asked to use, and was guided down to the basement. She was led along a corridor, stepping cautiously round a set of giant Elk antlers, until they reached a door labelled 'Storeroom 1001'. Her guide opened it, said, "Your visitor is here, sir" then ushered her in.

The room was crammed with all kinds of artefacts. There were a couple of large bones propped against one wall, there were storage drawers below a glass cabinet which seemed to be full of rocks and on a shelf to her right was a fragment of jawbone containing the most ferocious looking teeth she had ever seen. In the middle of all this were two upright chairs and a small table with a bottle and glasses. Forseti got his feet as she came in.

"Welcome and congratulations."

She shrugged herself out of her waterproof jacket and shook the rain off it.

"Where the hell are we?"

"In one of the museum storerooms. They have far too many objects to put on public display. There are dozens of rooms like this."

"It's all a bit weird." She gestured to the set of teeth which were even more alarming up close. "Whose are those?"

"Those are the teeth of a Velociraptor. Impressive, aren't

they? Around seventy million years ago it was a rather efficient carnivore."

"I wouldn't want to meet it on a dark night."

"I don't think you'd really want to meet it at all. Anyway, take a seat."

She moved forward and sat down gingerly. Forseti took the other chair and reached for the bottle. "Drink?"

"Still Laphroaig I see. Is this a celebration or are you buttering me up for another job?"

"Let's just say it's an acknowledgement of a job well done." He poured a couple of small measures and handed a glass to her. "You did very well. Getting Hoskins back here was a great achievement."

"It was a team effort."

"Of course."

"Sorry we needed to call in some help for the last stage but we couldn't come up with any way to get him out of Canada."

"Don't worry. Pity the Canadians proved a bit sticky at the end."

"No problem. We coped."

"Yes. I'm still not entirely sure how."

"I'm not sure myself. Probably best not to ask."

"Anyway, I'm told the lads who delivered our Mr Hoskins were highly amused, especially when they were told his backstory."

"And he's now safe and sound?"

"Very safe, not so sure about sound. When they landed at … well, that doesn't matter … Hoskins tried to make a run for it. Not a good idea with gentlemen like that."

"No." She paused. "There was just one thing…"

"Yes."

"At my last meeting with Hoskins he said *'The Senator's got the measure of you Brits. One day soon you'll wish you'd never been born'*. At the time I took this as an empty threat but thought I should pass it on."

Forseti sat very still. "And those were his exact words?"

"As far as I can remember, yes."

There was a long silence and then Forseti said, "Thank you, Hunter."

"So what happens now?"

"Your job is finished."

"I meant repercussions. How are the Americans reacting?"

"Ah, repercussions. Yes, I was coming to that."

"Let me guess. Official complaints to the Foreign Office, publicly denied, privately two fingers to you, chum."

"Well, I suppose you could put it like that." Forseti paused and cleared his throat. "There is one slight complication. It seems the Russians aren't happy that two of their people were killed in San Francisco."

"Don't suppose they were."

"Unfortunately, they appear to know there was some kind of unofficial unit responsible for those deaths and their leader is called The Hunter. I understand they've put a contract out on you."

"Good luck with that. They'd need to find me first."

"And there's more. This information is apparently also known to Senator Beckford."

"Beckford? I presume he's the Senator who was running the Hoskins operation behind the scenes?"

"That is so. I'm very much afraid your cover is blown."

The Hunter thought for a moment. "Don't see how. They don't know my real name."

"True, but by now there are a lot of nasty people out there who are aware that someone called 'The Hunter' is responsible for their downfall."

"I guess so. But they're not going to look me up in Yellow

Pages, are they?"

"No, but I do wonder if perhaps Perry Cracken's been a touch indiscreet."

For a moment she paused. She'd given Forseti a very brief explanation when she'd handed over Perry's USB flash drive and said she was hopeful there'd be more information coming from the same source. When she'd mentioned Perry's name Forseti had given a slight smile but said nothing. Now he sat watching her and she had to say something.

"Perry? Unlikely. Anyway, he doesn't know who I am either. By the way, was the content of that flash drive useful?"

"Oh, yes, well, up to a point. Added a bit more detail to the written notes he gave you. Nothing we can prove but some very useful intelligence, especially about Senator Beckford. I gather the CIA have had their eye on him for some time but he's virtually untouchable."

"Did the flash drive have the name of the British police officer who was protecting Hoskins' drugs ring?"

"It did. A sergeant in the drugs squad. He's been unobtrusively side lined and is under observation. However, we have no idea who else might be involved, always assuming Cracken was right about someone higher up also being on the take."

"Perry might find out some more about that."

"Yes, he might. I'm rather glad he's taken a shine to you. He could be very useful in the future."

"So you want me to stay in touch with him?"

"I think it would be a useful information channel. But I'm concerned that the Russians know about you."

"All they know is there's a 'unit', nice word, by the way, with a leader called The Hunter."

"You're happy to go on?"

"Do you have something else in mind?"

"Well, as it happens …"

She laughed. "You're a cunning old fox, aren't you?"

"Well, there is something else that would seem appropriate for your team. I don't have all the necessary information yet but the thing is, it involves the Russians so I'm not sure it's a good idea."

"Why not?"

"I'm thinking of you. It might be best not to tweak the tiger's tail."

"Does this tail need tweaking?"

"Well, yes, I think it probably does."

"Then let's tweak. We have a licence to tweak."

"I thought you might say that. Okay, this is the situation. There's a Russian businessman in London who appears to be controlling and financing a network that is bringing people into the UK, not to settle here like asylum seekers, but to be used as cheap labour, modern slavery effectively. The few we've picked up have fake visas, good fakes I might add, but are clearly living in horrendous conditions."

"Who's organising this?"

"Well, it's not the Russian government but that doesn't mean much. There are a lot of very powerful oligarchs in Russia today, not all of them too bothered about the law. A profitable business supplying people in the UK who want cheap labour for only a one-off payment."

"Can't you just expel this guy?"

"We could, yes, but that won't touch the people who run the operation and anyway he'd just get replaced by someone else."

"So officially you can't do anything?"

"Officially, no. Unofficially—"

"— unofficially you're talking to me. If we deal with him then it'll be completely deniable and no one except us – and you – would know what had happened."

"Precisely."

The Hunter put her glass down on the table. "How are they getting these workers into the country?"

"I don't have the full picture yet, probably be a couple of weeks before I can brief you properly. I just needed to know if it would be something you would consider."

"Of course. No problem. Let the tweaking begin."

AN ANONYMOUS ROOM SOMEWHERE IN LONDON

ODIN WAS IN a cheerful mood. "Well, the American operation was certainly a success. Well done." He paused. "So that's that. I guess we can disband the Hunter's team now."

"Why on earth would we do that?"

"Well, we don't have any further use for them, do we? It was Hoskins we really wanted them for. The rest was just practice."

"I don't agree. Their brief was to mete out justice where the law couldn't act. There's plenty of things for them to do yet."

"You may be right, Forseti, but there'll always be cases of injustice. We can't deal with them all."

Forseti kept his temper with difficulty. "That's no argument for not dealing with some of them. I think we may yet find further use for the Hunter's team. I'm pretty concerned about this situation which seems to be developing between Washington and Moscow."

"Oh, come on, that's something completely different."

"I disagree. I'm going to keep Hunter's team in place and in fact I plan to let them have a crack at this slave trade immigration business."

"And you still think it's the Russians running that?"

"It's a Russian, that's for sure. Don't know who's behind it."

Odin sighed. "It's only a handful of people. Is it really worth the bother?"

Forseti kept his temper with difficulty. "Yes, I think it is."

"And you think the Hunter's team can handle it?"

"I'm sure they can."

"But how?"

"No idea. I don't know and I don't want to know."

Odin sighed. "Well, I can see you're set on this. Okay, go ahead but for God's sake be careful."

MUSWELL HILL

A FEW DAYS LATER the Hunter had a call from Perry Cracken.

"Hi there, Hunter Lady."

"Hi yourself, Yankee Boy."

"Didn't expect me to call, did you. Reckoned I was just spinning you a load of bullshit."

"No, not really. I just wasn't expecting it quite so soon."

"Even though you guys lifted another of my flash drives? That big pal of yours would make a great dipper. It was him took it, wasn't it?"

"I didn't know about that till later. Anyway all that info will be locked up in that memory of yours, won't it?"

"Not the point. It was sneaky, but, hey, over and done with. Was the stuff useful?"

"I'm told so."

"Good, and …"

"I'm organising payment for you. Just let me know where you want it sent."

"Good girl …"

"Perry. Let's get one thing straight. 'Girl' is not acceptable."

"Sorry. Force of habit, Hunter Lady, but I do have something for you."

"What?"

"Not on an open cell phone. We need a secure way of communicating if our exchange deal is going to work. Can you fix that?"

"I'm sure I can. Leave it with me."

The Hunter contacted the Python and explained what was required. "If I'm right, this guy could be a good source of information but we have to know it's secure. What do you suggest?"

The Python thought for a moment. "I think we need to set up a Casanova System."

"A what?"

"It's like email, only with cut outs. I'll set it up on a secure server with an access key for your guy. Basically, it's end-to-end encryption. You send messages through an app. Not WhatsApp but similar. Bit like the old scrambler telephones in old spy movies."

"And you can guarantee this is absolutely secure."

There was a pause, then the Python said, "Nothing can ever be 'absolute' in the cyber world, Hunter, but this is as good as it gets. Probably best never to use real names in the messages though."

"Fair enough. Oh, why's the system called 'Casanova'?"

"Dunno. Think he might have been a spy or something as well as a bit of a lad."

"Hmm. Well, I don't think I'll tell my guy what it's called. Don't want him getting any ideas."

A FEW DAYS LATER the Hunter received her first Casanova message from Perry.

"Hi, you there, Hunter Lady?"

"I'm here, Yankee Boy."

"Okey-doke. Well, here goes. There's a guy, Don Palamino, works out of Chicago, has a deal going with a guy in London someplace for shipping out-of-date pharma products though London to Africa."

"Name of London guy?"

"Not known, but it's a small shipping company, C&G Transport. No address but it's in a place called Shore Ditch. Does that make sense?"

"It does. Thanks, Yankee Boy. We'll check this out."

The Hunter sat back and thought. She had no way of confirming this information but it was definitely worth passing on so she sent an email to Forseti. She had a brief acknowledgement but no more.

Two days later another Casanova message arrived. "Did you pass on that info, Hunter Lady?"

"I did."

"Well, just had a tip-off there's a consignment arriving in Shore Ditch next Thursday night."

She passed on this information too, again had a brief acknowledgement but nothing further.

Ten days later Forseti called her for another meeting.

KENSINGTON

THIS TIME THE meeting was in an old fashioned, luxury English restaurant in Kensington, all red velvet and shaded table lamps. She was shown up to a private dining room on the first floor by a gentleman in a very smart dinner jacket who kept a perfectly straight face as he led her to the room. Inside a table was laid for two, wall-to-wall cutlery, white napkins, sparkling crystal glassware, the lot.

Forseti rose to greet her as she was ushered in and the door closed discretely behind her.

She glanced around. "Well, this is an improvement on doughnuts."

"Indeed it is. I felt you had earned a good dinner after all this time."

He waved her to a seat and she sat down. "You do realise that everyone down there will think that you're a dirty old man entertaining his mistress."

"They can think what they like."

"So are you ready to let us loose on the Russian?"

He raised a hand. "May I suggest that we leave business until after we've eaten. Don't want to spoil our enjoyment of the food, do we?"

"Heaven forfend."

Some fifty minutes later when the coffee had been served and the door was finally shut firmly behind the waiter, she leaned forward.

"So, the Russian."

"First, the tip-off about C&G Transport. Thanks to the information you sent, the consignment was intercepted and there are several gentlemen in custody."

"Good."

"It looks as though Mr Cracken is going to be a useful contact so please stay in touch."

"So, the Russian?"

"Ah, yes, the Russian. Well, we know quite a bit more about him now."

"Does he have a name?"-

"Dmitri Balakirev. We've traced his business connections to a trawler fleet registered to one of the Baltic ports. We've got satellite images of these trawlers making contact with small camps on the Russian coast, where they pick up quite a lot of people. A motley crowd, including women and they all have some baggage with them. We don't think this is an official Russian operation but effectively these trawlers are being used as modern slave ships and I'd guess a lot of blind eyes are being turned. When the trawlers have a full cargo they set out, ostensibly on a fishing trip in the North Sea, then when they're close enough to our coast they land these people on the beach."

"How?"

"We think they're met by a landing party with dinghies. It's hard to be certain but all the intel suggests that once ashore these people are taken to secure accommodation and then gradually farmed out to people who buy them for slave labour."

"And you think that if we can … let's say … discourage Dmitri, that this traffic will stop?"

Forseti sighed. "That might be too much to hope for. But we need to make it clear we know what's happening and that there'll be unofficial reprisals if it continues."

"And by unofficial, you mean my team. What sort of reprisals? I hope you're not going to ask us to kill Dmitri. I said at the beginning I wouldn't be part of an assassination squad."

"The Russians probably think you are."

"That's their problem. Okay, some of their guys were killed when they gate-crashed our San Francisco operation but not all of them. We also killed three Americans at Point Reyes, but one lived. We could have wiped him out too."

"May I ask why you didn't."

"Those who died were killed while we were protecting ourselves. Once we were secure there was no further need. We may kill, but we don't execute."

"The Russians might not appreciate such a fine distinction."

The Hunter shrugged and Forseti went on, "We've been talking about Russians in general but our information suggests there's one specific Russian we need to be aware of."

"Name?"

"Not known. He's a shadowy figure but he's definitely a powerful man. We think he is aware of you so you need to be aware of him."

"And you think it's this guy who's running Dmitri?"

"It seems likely, that's all I can say."

"So if we give Dmitri a hard time Mr X is not going to be a happy bunny."

"You could say that."

"That's not going to stop us though, is it?"

Forseti poured himself another coffee and gestured towards her with the cafetière but she shook her head.

"No, it's not going to stop us, but we don't want you to kill Dmitri, we want you to … shall we say … discourage him from continuing. Discourage him to the point that he would not be enthusiastic about briefing a successor."

There was a pause and then she said, "Well, that would certainly be a challenge. How do we find him?"

"Well, he has a flat in Highgate but he works as a drama critic with close ties to the Russian equivalent of the Arts Council. On the surface, he's promoting opportunities to collaborate with Russia in regional arts projects so he spends most of his time touring around the UK but we think he is actually seeking places where he can house the people he's bringing in. We want him stopped, Hunter, so please talk to your team and let me know your decision."

"I will." She got to her feet. "Thanks for dinner. Do you think that Mr Starched Shirt downstairs could order me a taxi?"

YORK

AS USUAL SHE had left the meeting arrangements to the Fixer and this time he chose the family café in the National Railway Museum in York. Through excited chatter about 4-6-2 bogie wheels and the strengths of the *Mallard* over *The Battle of Britain* class locomotives, the Hunter outlined the task they had been offered.

When she'd finished there was silence for a moment then the Armourer said, "Picking up Dmitri should be easy enough, it's what we do with him when we've got him, that's the question."

"It's not just Dmitri," said the Fixer, "we need to deal with the trawler traffic too."

"Dmitri must know about the trawlers," said the Housekeeper. "Presumably he has to organise the reception committee."

The Armourer nodded. "So we need to pick up Dmitri and persuade him to let us know when the next landing is due."

There was silence for a moment as the team considered the reality of this operation in human terms. Then the Defender said, "I think Dmitri needs to experience some of this for himself, don't you?"

"Nice idea, but how?"

The Fixer looked thoughtful. "It might be possible." He turned to the Housekeeper. "Could you lay your hands on a decent sea-going boat, motor yacht maybe, that we can hire, borrow or steal for a week or so?"

"I'm sure I can."

"Then we'll also need an isolated house somewhere."

The Hunter broke in. "I can see where this is going but a sea going boat needs a captain and I don't want to bring in an outsider."

"No need," said the Defender. "I have an Ocean Skipper's certificate."

"Do you indeed?"

"I do. I've sailed boats from the UK down to Spain and Portugal and back and, believe me, it doesn't get much rougher than the Bay of Biscay."

"Better you than me," muttered the Python. "I get seasick standing beside a deep puddle."

They all laughed. "Don't worry, Python, boats like that don't need a large crew. We'll manage without you."

"But first we need more info about our Dmitri," said the Fixer, "you'd better leave that to me."

For the next few weeks the Fixer worked away at the kind of thing he did so well – extracting information from people without them realising it was being extracted. The Housekeeper tracked down a motor yacht which was moored in Weymouth and the Defender had a look at it.

The final part of the Fixer's research was to obtain a list of Dmitri's proposed travels. He went over this with the Hunter and they selected Cornwall for stage one of the re-education of Dmitri Balakirev. The Defender and the Armourer sailed the borrowed motor yacht round to the Helford River and the Housekeeper leased an old farmhouse in a lonely place on Bodmin moor.

Then the team was ready to go.

CORNWALL

DMITRI BALAKIREV HAD always enjoyed the plays of Shakespeare and in particular *Measure For Measure* – the betrayal and double standards in the play appealed to him. One night in May he left the Minack Theatre near Porthcurno in Cornwall where he'd been watching an amateur drama production of the play. He didn't think it was especially good though he'd been very taken with the actress playing Isabella. It was a cloudy night, though fortunately the rain had held off during the performance. The Minack Theatre, perched as it is on the side of a cliff, is not the most comfortable place in the rain.

He unlocked his car and climbed into the driving seat, already thinking of a nightcap and then a warm bed in his Penzance hotel. However before he could start the engine he felt something hard and cold pushed into the back of his neck and a voice said, "Don't make a move or you're dead."

For a moment he froze, then said, "I think you must have wrong person. I am Russian citizen."

"I don't care if you're the Queen of Sheba."

In his mirror Dmitri could see a dark figure in a balaclava in the back seat. He wriggled slightly and the gun was pressed more tightly against him.

"Sit still."

All around them car doors were slamming, people were shouting "Goodnight", cars were revving and driving away. Gradually the car park emptied and then another person, also wearing a balaclava, appeared beside the driver's door and opened it.

"Get out of the car."

It was a woman's voice but she also had a gun so Dmitri did what he was told.

"You are making mistake. I have no money."

Silence. The back door of his car was opened and he was bundled in. The man kept the gun to his head while the woman pulled his arms behind his back and he felt the click of a pair of handcuffs. Then she bent down and put a set of cuffs round his ankles before pulling a black hood tightly over his head. There was a small mouth slot so he could breathe but he could see nothing. The woman got into the driving seat, started the car and they headed down the hill into Porthcurno village.

After a moment Dmitri spoke. "Where you taking me?"

"You're going on a little sea trip for a few days, then we've arranged some accommodation for you."

"There will be repercussions for this. I told you I am Russian citizen. My government will be very angry."

"So what? We're nothing to do with any government. We simply have an aversion to people who trade in the misery of other people."

"I not know what you mean."

"Oh, I think you do, Dmitri."

There was a pause and then Dmitri said, "Are you going to kill me?"

"It's an option. Not our preferred one, but if we have to, then yes."

Dmitri went very quiet.

An hour or so later the car came to a halt and the engine was switched off. The back door was opened, the ankle cuffs removed, Dmitri was dragged out and led forward. In a few moments he felt shingle under his feet and heard the sound of waves.

"Small flight of steps now," and he felt himself guided up onto a wooden platform. He was led across this, then sensed the presence of other people.

"Good evening, Dmitri," said a woman's voice, a different woman. "Glad you could join us."

Speaking through the hood was difficult but he did his best. "Who are you people?"

"I am The Hunter."

In spite of himself Dmitri shivered. "The Hunter? I have heard of you."

"Good, then you know we are serious. My friends and I don't like you, Dmitri, we don't like what you do to desperate people. However, it's just possible you don't know how the people you traffic actually suffer, so we're going to give you a practical demonstration."

Dmitri felt himself being lifted bodily, there was some jerking and then he was set down again. He realised from the motion beneath his feet that he was on some kind of boat before he was hustled down a steep stairway into a cabin.

On shore the Defender tossed the keys of Dmitri's car to the Housekeeper. "Okay, over to you."

"Right. I'll book it in to the long stay at Bristol airport. It'll be ages before anyone finds it. Then I'll get the train back to Swindon."

"Fine. We'll give you call when we need you."

The Housekeeper drove off and the Defender turned back to the yacht. The Armourer appeared on deck.

"We've got Dmitri handcuffed down in the main cabin. All the windows are blacked out. When do you want to sail?"

"I think we'll wait till dawn. If we sail now someone will notice and ask why? Where's Fixer?"

"I'm here."

"Good. So to recap. Hunter and Armourer will come with me on the boat. You'll stay here and we'll stay in contact in case anything goes wrong. Then, once Dmitri has had his little sail we'll bring him back here and you'll meet us with a van."

"The van's all sorted. It's in a lock-up in Truro. I'll just need a couple of hours warning to fetch it here."

"No probs. Okay, let's go."

ALL AT SEA

DMITRI DID NOT ENJOY the next few days. He had never been a wonderful sailor and the hood over his head made him disorientated so that even on their trip down the river he began to feel queasy. By the time they were out in the channel he was very miserable indeed.

Two days later, they brought him up from the cabin. They removed his hood, the handcuffs were taken off his wrists but those round his ankles remained. He was lowered down into a dinghy and all day they towed the dinghy with Dmitri bouncing around in it as the wind stirred up the sea. The next day was the same and Dmitri spent another stomach-churning day in the dinghy in the Atlantic.

At one stage the Defender said, "What do we do if he gives up and jumps overboard? He can't swim with his legs handcuffed."

"He drowns," said the Hunter laconically, "but that would be his choice. We wouldn't have killed him."

The Armourer looked at her. "Something of a fine distinction, I'd have thought."

After three days in the dinghy Dmitri was in a very bad way and the Hunter decided to move on to the next stage. She went down to see him in the cabin.

"How you feeling, Dmitri?"

"I need doctor, get me doctor. I'm ill."

"We need some information first. When's the next trawler due with its human cargo? And where will they land?"

"Trawler? What trawler. Ya ne ponimayu."

"Eto nepravda, Dmitri," said the Hunter, "I think you understand perfectly. Now for the last time, when and where is the next trawler due?"

"Svoloch …"

The Hunter smiled. "Actually, no, my parents were married. So what's it to be?"

"Idi k chertu … Go to hell …"

"No need to translate. I got the gist."

Dmitri turned his back on her.

"Okay, your choice. We'll give you a few more days. See how you feel then."

Two days later Dmitri finally cracked. "Okay, okay, what you want to know?"

"The dates of the next trawler run."

"If I tell, you let me go, yes?"

"Not quite. We'll need know you're telling the truth. Once we have checked the information, you will be set free."

And so he told her.

OFF THE EAST COAST OF SCOTLAND

THE RUSSIAN TRAWLER anchored off the east coast of Scotland just over three miles offshore. The seven-man crew were well used to the process and it did not take long for the forty passengers to be brought up on deck, most of them sick and shivering.

The captain flashed a coded signal to the shore and before long a powerful dinghy arrived towing a string of smaller dinghies behind it. The man from the landing party exchanged a few words with the trawler captain then the passengers were put down into the dinghies and the little convoy set off back to the beach. It was only when they reached the shore that the leader realised the situation had changed and a different group of people were waiting for him. Within minutes he was handcuffed and being led to a police car at the top of the beach to join the other members of his landing party while a group of immigration officers were helping the bewildered and frightened people ashore.

Back on the trawler, the captain had begun to take the ship back out to sea and the crew had retired to the main cabin and opened a bottle. They did not hear the soft swish of a RIB approaching from the seaward side. The first they knew was the appearance of three masked figures holding guns who appeared at the door of the cabin.

"Nikto ne dvigayetsya," said the Hunter but in spite of

that one crew member made a lunge for his gun and went down screaming as the Defender hit him full in the face with the butt of his automatic rifle.

After that there was no resistance. The crew were all disarmed, and the Armourer stood guard while the Defender took the wheel and headed the trawler out into the North Sea.

When they were about eight miles offshore he stopped the engines again and the crew were brought up on deck. The Hunter and the Armourer lowered one of the trawler's life rafts into the water and the Russian crew were helped down onto it.

Their captain said, "Who are you? Why you do this?"

"I am the Hunter. Remember the name. We are outside the law but we work for justice. What you do is evil and if we catch you again you will die. Vi ponimayete?"

The crew watched from the life raft as the Hunter and the Armourer got into their RIB followed a few minutes later by the Defender. The RIB started up and circled the trawler and then the Russian crew heard the unmistakable sound of the bilge alarm. The sea cocks on the trawler had been opened. Twenty minutes later the trawler was well down in the water and within an hour it had vanished beneath the waves.

Just over three weeks later another Russian trawler appeared off the Scottish coast somewhere south of Aberdeen. Once again the dinghies went out to the ship but this time when they got back to the beach they were met by a platoon of the Special Forces Support Group. In the short battle that followed two Russians were killed but their captives were freed. On board the trawler, the crew were captured, set adrift and had to watch as their vessel quickly sank out of sight.

Ten days later the third trawler was due, but this time no vessel arrived so the Hunter decided it was time to dump Dmitri.

THE DEFENDER AND THE Armourer collected him from the lonely house on Bodmin Moor where the Housekeeper had been holding him. Dmitri was sullen and subdued but still had some spark left in him. As they were loading him into the van he spat at the Hunter's feet.

"Ty suka ... I will laugh the last. You think this stop here? Niet. One day you and I, we meet again with shoe on other foot."

The Hunter smiled. "I've heard it all before but I'm not quite dead yet."

They took Dmitri back to the boat at Helford. Two days later they were off the southern coast of Ireland near Baltimore and later that night Dmitri was landed on a lonely beach not far from Mizen Head. They left him with plenty of water, some biscuits and chocolate bars but no personal possessions and no form of identification. Then they sailed away.

MUSWELL HILL

A FEW DAYS LATER, back in her flat and trying to relax for the first time in weeks, the Hunter received another Casanova message from Perry Cracken.

"Hey, Hunter Lady, you still there? Still alive?"

She laughed to herself and tapped out a reply. "Yes to both, Yankee Boy."

"Do you wanna make some friends in Europe?"

"What's all this about?"

"There's a large shipment of arms going out next week, Baltimore to Antwerp. Final destination, somewhere in Afghanistan."

"What sort of arms?"

"Handheld weapons, high velocity rifles, semi-automatics, that kinda stuff."

"Who they going to?"

"No idea, but they'll be in crates of chocolate and cocoa products. Some of the crates have been doctored, hidden compartments, yeah? Those crates have a tiny little brown coconut image stencilled on the side."

"Who's sending them?"

"Not sure. Look, I know this ain't one for you directly but if you tip off the authorities in Antwerp—"

"— then we have a favour we can call in if we need one. Thanks, Yankee Boy, I'll pass it on."

"And payment?"

"Look, we'll warn Antwerp, if they make a hit, then you'll

get paid."

There was a pause before his reply came. "You can be a hard bitch, Hunter Lady."

"That's why I'm still alive."

"Yeah. Well, try and stay that way. I need to warn you."

"Warn me?"

"Our friends in the American drugs ring are pretty angry. They were all set up to piggyback on some human trafficking operation run by the Russian mafia to carry their drugs on the same trips. That was about to start happening, but word on the street is that a couple of the Russian operations recently went belly up big time, so the deal's been called off. Wouldn't be anything to do with you, would it?"

"No comment."

"Be careful, Hunter Lady, be very careful. The Russians are very angry and the stateside guy we both know about is even angrier. The Americans have put a contract out on you."

"They'll have to get in the queue. Do they know who I am?"

"They know they're after the Hunter and they're very persistent. I'm just warning you. Walk carefully."

AN ANONYMOUS ROOM SOMEWHERE IN LONDON

IT WAS NOT a comfortable meeting.

"We must definitely close down The Hunter's team," said Odin, "we have no further use for them."

"That would be crazy, they're an invaluable resource. This recent Russian trawler operation was disgusting. Aren't you glad that's stopped?"

"It may not be stopped. It may only be interrupted."

"Doesn't that strengthen the argument for keeping them?"

"So what do I tell the Foreign Office if the Russians make a formal complaint?"

"Tell them nothing, but there won't be any formal complaint. The whole operation was illegal, and I doubt it was anything the Russian government wants to claim credit for directly."

Odin was silent.

Forseti went on, "The very reason we asked the Hunter's team to deal with this was to keep it unofficial. The Foreign Office know nothing about it."

"Well, even if you're right why not suggest the Hunter takes a break. Tell him he's earned it."

Forseti smiled to himself but all he said was, "I'll try, but I'm not hopeful."

"Sounds like you have something else in mind for them."

"As it happens, no, not at the moment. But it's comforting

to know they're there, especially if these rumours about the American drug gangs and the Russian mafia forming some kind of alliance turn out to be true. We may need all the help on offer."

"Oh, come on, you can't really believe that guff. It can't possibly be a serious threat."

"I hope you're right. I used to think the same, but then we started hearing about this memory drug thing, this Mayoquoid."

"Yes, I've heard about that. But what's that got to do with us?"

"No idea. Maybe just a red herring, but it's starting to bother me. Don't know why but instinct tells me there's something nasty in the woodshed over there."

"Woodshed? What woodshed?"

"Never mind, doesn't matter. All I'm saying is that we need to keep our ears and eyes open."

HOLBORN

THE HUNTER'S NEXT meeting with Forseti took place in the basement room of a bakery in Holborn. This time the refreshments on offer were currant buns and a cup of tea, a fact which amused the Hunter when she saw them but she said nothing.

Forseti on the other hand said quite a lot. "Well, you have been busy, haven't you?"

"Isn't that what you wanted?"

"We wanted you to discourage Dmitri. Make him see the error of his ways. Now he seems to have vanished. I don't want any details but it would be useful to know if he's still alive?"

"As far as I know. After a fashion."

"After a …" Forseti swallowed. "Well, then, is he likely to reappear at some point?"

"Probably. But I think you'll find his enthusiasm has gone. Apart from possibly wanting to kill me," she added.

Forseti was silent for a moment and then said, "And where is Dmitri now?"

"At this precise moment, no idea. All I'll say is we deposited him – alive – on a foreign shore. He was not wearing his own clothes and had no form of identification on him. His flat in Highgate has also been emptied of all traces of personal possessions and we have destroyed his passport, driving licence, credit cards and so on. He is effectively a non-person."

"You don't do things by halves, do you?"

"If you do things by halves then, by definition, that means that half the job may not get done. If we take something on, we complete it."

"Can I ask what happened to two Russian trawlers?"

"Sure, we dismantled them and turned them into garden ornaments. Fixer thinks we should try flogging them down Camden market."

Forseti looked at her then suddenly started to laugh. "You're incorrigible, Hunter, but this won't endear you to our Russian friend in Moscow."

"I can live with that. Do you have any more information about him?"

"It may be more of a 'they' than a 'him'. We think we've identified one person, Nikolai Lazovsky. Don't know much about him, doesn't appear to be part of the government, at least not officially, but if our information is correct he wields a lot of power behind the scenes."

"Russian Mafia?"

"Maybe, possibly, not really relevant. 'Mafia' has become a catch-all phrase for all kinds of nastiness in Russia."

"Is he the one who was running the slavery operation?"

"Seems likely, but we're not certain. However, we're also getting reports of another rather shadowy figure operating quietly in the background. No name for this one. He seems to operate below the radar, maybe working for the State but isn't part of the State, if you see what I mean. We're wondering if he's the enforcer for Lazovsky."

"And we don't know who he is?"

"No, only a workname. He's apparently known as 'Hotnik'. Funny sort of title but perhaps ..." he broke off. "Why are you laughing?"

"You don't speak Russian, do you?"

"No, but what …?"

"I suspect this guy's workname is actually 'Okhotnik'."

"Maybe. So what?"

"Well, only that *okhotnik* is the Russian for a huntsman. Maybe I have a clone in Moscow."

"Oh."

"This is starting to get interesting."

"Possibly more interesting than you think. As it happens we think you hit two targets with one shot."

"You mean the Americans and their plans to use the Russian slave operation as another route into the UK for their drugs."

"You appear to be very well informed. Would this be our Mr Cracken again?"

"Could be."

"You need to be very careful, Hunter. We know the kind of violent people Senator Beckford can call on and I have no doubt that this … this … Okhotnik … person could be equally dangerous if not more so."

"Daresay we'll cope. I'm not quite dead yet."

"And I very much hope you won't be. Your Mr Cracken does get around, doesn't he? His information about that arms shipment was right, by the way. The Belgium authorities were well pleased."

"So will he be when he gets another payment."

"I'll see to it." Forseti paused for a moment. "It may not be able to continue though. It's been suggested that we should stand your team down."

The Hunter sat back in her chair and looked at Forseti thoughtfully. "So the world has suddenly become a better place, has it? Sweetness and light. No more injustice."

"That's not what I'm saying."

"No? Then why am I thinking that for the first time you're

not being honest with me?"

"What's wrong with having a break? You've earned it."

"I don't need a break. What would I do? Take up knitting?"

In spite of himself Forseti laughed. "That I would like to see."

"Well, I wouldn't. If you're worried about the Russians, don't be."

"No, it's not the Russians. Well, actually I suppose it is the Russians, and others, but it's nothing to do with you."

The Hunter was silent and after a moment Forseti sighed. "Look, Hunter, when your team was set up I was given the task of being your manager, controller, point of contact, whatever term you want to use. Now something else has arisen which might take me away."

"What sort of something?"

"I can't discuss that."

"But you want to, don't you?"

"Look, just take a break. Forget the knitting, go and sit on a beach somewhere, Relax. Have fun. You could even …" His voice trailed off and he shook his head. "I'm wasting my breath, aren't I?"

"Of course. Look, Forseti, I have a great team. We have complementary skills, we work well together and above all we trust each other. I'm their leader but I'm also part of a larger team, your team. We couldn't have achieved anything without your support, your help and your trust. Now, you've got what sounds like a nasty problem. Okay, maybe it isn't the reason the Hunter and her team came into being, but so what? We've been successful because we're unconventional, we think laterally, we don't think '*can this be done?*'. We think '*how can we do it*'. You've supported us all this time. Now it's time to let us support you."

There was a long silence. Then Forseti said, "Quite

a speech."

"So?"

"I'm not meant to talk about this."

"But you're going to, aren't you?"

"If I share this with you, then, presumably, you'll share it with your team."

"Of course."

"Oh, to hell with it." Forseti took a deep breath. "Listen, this is not public knowledge and must never become so."

"Understood."

"For some while now it's been known in intelligence circles that there are powerful criminal elements in the States and in Russia who appear to be creating some kind of alliance."

"What kind of alliance?"

"An unholy one."

"More than just the shared use of Russian trawlers as a courier service?"

"Naturally. We all know that big business, the rich, the powerful, special interest groups, have always wielded a disproportionate influence over governments of whatever political hue. In Russia it's even easier – no theoretical democracy to act as a barrier."

"And you think this American-Russian power alliance is trying to take this a step further."

"It's a possibility, yes. I think what we might have here are two groups of powerful people in their own countries both intent on expanding their empires. My fear is that they've realised competing with each other is not profitable in the long term, whereas a strategic alliance could prove very advantageous to both groups."

"So you think the bad guys in America and in Russia may be combining with … what ultimate purpose?"

"Power. Freedom to carry out their various nefarious

activities without any serious fear of reprisals. I know it might sound crazy, but, yes, that's my suspicion."

"Where does the UK stand in this?"

Forseti gave a grim smile. "On the surface – nowhere. But, I'm wondering if certain people in this country might see profit in turning a two-way Alliance into a three-way one."

"Are you serious?"

"I don't know, Hunter, but even if it is only a faint possibility I don't think we can afford to ignore it. There are some very strange things going on at present."

"Such as?"

"The unexpected death of the union leader, Trevor Fortescue. The Tory MP, Mark Bantry, apparently driving his car off the top of a cliff. Margaret Crambling, the campaigner for press freedom who apparently fell under a bus, plus several more deaths not always reported. The common factor is that they were people with moderate views. I know they're all on record as being accidents but it's all a bit of a coincidence."

"Are you suggesting these deaths are being orchestrated?"

"There's no direct evidence of that, but I don't like coincidences."

"So you think this points to a third party? An unholy UK-Russian-American alliance."

"Not yet but I think could become so. There's still a lot of distrust between the American and the Russian groups but we suspect they're beginning to move closer, to create some kind of power base. If they do, they're bound to spread out across Europe and then it would be hard for the UK to resist, especially if there was inside help from some people in power."

"Are you sure this isn't just paranoia?"

"It's not paranoia. Part of my job is to think the unthinkable. However, instinct tells me that there is an extra factor we don't know about. Something's missing in this equation and I don't know what."

"And you're worried?"

"Yes."

"So why not let us help you."

"Can you help?"

"I don't know, but we're a very much 'off the wall' operation. Maybe just what you need."

"Well … If you did get involved it would be even less official than usual. If you hit trouble I may not be able to help."

"Let me worry about that. Now first I think we need to try and find out a bit more about what's going on under the surface as it were. Leave that to me."

"Perry Cracken?"

"Will be one starting point."

After she had gone, Forseti ate the last current bun and thought about what he had just done. It wasn't the first time he had ignored instructions and followed his instincts, but he had more confidence in the Hunter and her team than he had in many of those who were technically above him.

DIFFICULT CONVERSATIONS

BACK IN HER FLAT the Hunter decided the only way to convince Perry Cracken to help with this problem was by talking to him. She didn't feel she could be persuasive enough using an encrypted Casanova message. She was reluctant to call him on her mobile phone near her own home which would activate a local mast so she drove down to Sussex and walked out onto the top of Beachy Head.

When Perry answered he was very abrupt. "Not a good moment, buddy. Can we discuss this sales order some other time?"

Obviously he wasn't alone so she just said, "When?"

"Couple of hours," and he hung up.

There was quite a strong breeze coming off the sea and sitting on a bench looking out at the English Channel for two hours was not very tempting. Instead she drove down into Eastbourne, bought a take-away coffee and went onto the pier to play a few slot machines.

Two hours later, seven pounds the poorer but having acquired a plastic dinosaur, she was back up on Beachy Head but even then it was another thirty minutes before her phone rang.

"Couldn't talk before. I was at home and not alone. Why you calling on your cell?"

"I need your help with something really serious. I'll send you the details via the usual channel but I wanted to speak to you personally to make sure you understand just how critical this is and how your help may be vital."

"Sounds big."

"It is."

"Okay, I hear you. Send your message and I promise I'll take it seriously."

"Thank you."

There was a pause then Perry said, "As it happens this could work both ways. There's something I need to tell you and you might not believe it when I do, but trust me, I'm not kidding."

"Don't like the sound of that."

"Don't think you will, but I'm serious, so don't dismiss it, okay?"

"Okay, we'll be in touch."

Back in London she set up a Casanova link and briefly summed up the conversation she'd had with Forseti and what she wanted Perry to do. There was a delay before he replied but finally he messaged, "Well, I can give it a shot. Not something I can do in a New York minute though."

"In a what?"

"Gee, don't you Brits speak your own language. It won't be quick, okay? I know a lot of guys, but I'll have to dig. If something is going on over here then it's not gonna be posted on billboards on Fifth Avenue."

"What about the Russians?"

"Harder. I'm not flavour of the month with those guys, partly thanks to you."

"Even so ... you can try, Yankee Boy, can't you, for me."

"Can that, Hunter Lady, I ain't falling for that line."

There was a pause then another message came in. "My turn. You ain't gonna like this, Hunter Lady, but the senator's mob still have that contract out on you and they may be able to find out who you really are."

"How would they do that?"

"Well you remember when we were first setting up this deal, after Point Reyes …?"

"Sure."

"And I said I was pretty sure your bent cop wasn't acting alone but I didn't know for certain."

"I remember."

"Well, I guess I was right. The scuttlebutt is there's someone high up in UK government on the American's payroll."

"What?"

"I said you wouldn't like it."

"Name?"

"Not known, but high, very high. Hey, I wonder if this might tie in with what you're talking about?"

"How sure are you?"

"Bang on the money. No guess work, it's a safe bet. Walk carefully and trust no one, Hunter Lady. Hasta luego."

She closed Casanova, poured herself a large Laphroaig and sat down to consider all the implications. If Perry was right she could be in real danger but while 'trust no one' might be good advice, it wasn't entirely practical.

The next day she called the Python and told him what she wanted.

THE SOUTH BANK

A FEW DAYS LATER she was ready to act. She called Forseti and asked for an urgent meeting and later that day they met on a bench outside the National Theatre. Forseti apologised for the lack of refreshments.

"There wasn't time to organise anything," he said, "you made it quite clear you wanted to meet urgently."

"Yes, I did. About the matter we discussed the other day, I've been in touch with Perry Cracken. He'll give it a go but it's going to take him a while to ferret around."

"Naturally. Look, Hunter, can we dispense with the small talk. What's really on your mind?"

"Perry also told me that someone high up in the UK government is actively involved with the American drugs ring."

Forseti sat very still. Finally he said, "That is a very serious allegation. Do you have a name."

"No."

"Proof?"

"Yes, at least I think so. Earlier today I received a printout of an exchange of emails. No names were mentioned but I think there's enough detail to identify the person this end."

"Can I see these emails?"

"Eventually, of course, but not yet. I've only skim read them so far. I want to have a closer look before doing anything."

"Where is this document?"

"Safe. Literally. In my personal safe."

There was a long pause then Forseti said, "I need to see this document as soon as possible. Can we meet again tomorrow?"

The Hunter shook her head. "Not tomorrow. I have to go to Brighton. Won't be back until Thursday."

Forseti nodded. "All right, Thursday then. I'll send you the meeting place details as usual."

CAMBRIDGE

THE HUNTER DID NOT go to Brighton. She went to Cambridge and met the Python in his workshop.

"All set?"

"All set. There are four cameras in your flat, covering the entrance, the living room, your bedroom …"

"That one comes down as soon as this is all over."

"Spoilsport. The final one shows the kitchen. There are also two outside covering front and back entrances."

"And they're live now?"

"They are. You can see their output on that monitor – split screen. We just need to keep an eye on them."

"Take it in turns?"

"Sure. Do you think he'll bite?"

"I hope not. I hope I can trust him, but if I can't, I'd expect something to happen while I'm away, before I have the chance, as he thinks, to read the documents in detail."

"Okay, d'you want to take the first stint? I've got stuff to get on with."

She settled down to watch six still images of her own flat, reflecting that the writers of action thrillers rarely acknowledged the high level of boredom that so often went with the job.

Later the Python brought in a Chinese takeaway and then they split the night watch between them.

By the evening of the following day she felt she'd had enough Chicken Chow Mein to last the rest of her life but there had been no activity on any of the monitors so the Hunter felt more at ease when she received the date and time of her next meeting with Forseti.

THE OVAL

THE OVAL CRICKET GROUND with no cricket being played was a rather desolate place. When she arrived she was directed to a small meeting room in the middle of which stood a table with two large cakes on it. Forseti greeted her in his usual courteous fashion.

"I thought this was appropriate. If Bryan Johnson and John Arlott were here, I am sure they would approve. They always liked their slice of cake on TMS, didn't they?"

"I have no idea what you're talking about, but I could kill a slice of that Lemon Drizzle."

"It's yours." Forseti cut a generous slice and handed it to her. She raised her eyebrows.

"Cake forks too. How the other half live."

"Much kinder on the fingers. D'you know, I think I might just sample a piece of that chocolate gateau."

When they'd settled themselves and taken the first nibble, Forseti said, rather indistinctly, "Did you bring that email printout with you?"

The Hunter swallowed her piece of cake before replying. "No."

"Why not?"

The Hunter took another delicate bite. "Because it doesn't exist."

"Ah."

"I'm sorry, but I lied to you."

"Lied about the high level involvement?"

"No. Lied about having proof."

"I see." He took another bite of cake and delicately wiped his hands on a napkin. "So do you still believe that we have a problem?"

"I do."

"Why so confident?"

"Because I trust Perry, and I trust his sources of information. I can't see why he'd invent something like that."

"Perhaps he's been set up to pass that on. Misinformation. Set us off chasing our own tail."

"Possibly, but my instinct says unlikely."

"And you trust your instinct?"

"I do."

"Good, I trust it too."

"Yes?"

"Yes, as you know I've had my suspicions for some time but there's no proof. You'll appreciate that raising this sort of concern without a reasonable degree of certainty is not really an option."

"So you really think we have a traitor high up in the corridors of power?"

"I don't know where he or she is but, yes, I think there's someone well below the radar who's got access to intelligence and is manipulating government decisions, possibly even to the extent of neutralising any immediate opposition."

"Neutralising?"

"I told you that there've been a number of 'accidental' deaths over the last year or so. Too many for comfort, at least for those of us with a suspicious mind."

The Hunter thought about that for a moment. "Any idea who the traitor might be?"

"No. Not surprisingly, people like that stay in the very deep shadows."

"But you're certain, in your own mind?"

"I am now. If you're right and there's someone here involved in the American drugs racket then that might also explain the origins of some of the funds that have been finding their way into government or quasi-government hands."

"Bribes?"

"Not as such. More like very large donations from obscure sources. Someone in a position of power is pulling strings."

"But aren't all political parties obliged to declare where such donations come from?"

"In theory, yes, but these aren't openly made donations and the trail is well hidden."

"I see, and of course people don't hand over large amounts of money without expecting something in return."

"Precisely."

"So what are you doing about it?"

"Until now, nothing. I've had no starting point or didn't have. But now ..."

"This traitor, are we talking about an MP or senior civil servant?"

"If I'm right, then maybe neither." Forseti paused then said, "There are a handful of ... shall we say ... special advisers appointed to manage things for senior government ministers. They're privy to everything, from minor committees to the contents of top secret intelligence reports. They're unelected, rarely known to the public at large and yet they wield enormous power."

"And you think it's one of them."

"I'd bet my pension on it. Personally – and I know most of them personally, of course – I wouldn't trust any of them an inch. Power has certainly gone to the heads of two of them and all the things they say about power are true."

"Power without responsibility. How did you put it? *Laws*

catch flies but let hornets go free'?"

"Precisely."

"How many of these men … I assume they're men … are we talking about?"

"Yes, they're all men and there are four possibilities, though one is a bit of a long shot."

"But don't rule him out. Okay, so what do we do now?"

"Well, the first stage is to identify him. Could Cracken get any more information, d'you think?"

"I can ask. Can I have another bit of cake?"

"Help yourself."

While she was cutting another slice, Forseti said, "Would I be right in thinking you didn't go to Brighton on Tuesday?"

"You would be right."

"You wanted to see if anyone tried to gain access to your flat to look for the fictional email document."

"Of course."

"And when they didn't, you decided to trust me."

"I trusted you anyway, but it was a sensible precaution. I wanted that trust confirmed."

Forseti nodded then got to his feet and paced around the room. "Thank you. I'm very touched, but I haven't been entirely honest with you."

The Hunter stiffened but Forseti smiled and shook his head. "Nothing to worry about but it wasn't just chance that we chose you – that I chose you – for this job. You see, I knew your father."

"Oh."

"We were close friends. I watched you growing up and after he was killed I followed your career with great interest. Your father was a very special man. I suspected, and now I know for certain, that his daughter is also very special."

She was silent for a moment then, she said, "You knew

my Dad?"

"I did."

"Were you with him when …?"

"No. He was always what we called 'an out at front' person, much as you are. I was always the support behind the lines."

"As you are now."

"Precisely."

She thought for a moment. "I don't remember you from when I was little."

"No, you wouldn't. Your father was always determined to keep work and family life separate. He showed me photos of you, told me what you were doing, but you and I never met back then."

"Did you know my mother too?"

She thought she saw him flinch at this question. Perhaps he dreaded it. "Yes, it was a great loss when she died so young."

"I was only three."

"Cancer is very cruel."

"You helped my father get through it when she died, didn't you?"

"I hope so. It wasn't easy but friendship was more important than anything, back then. Even the job." He paused, then said gently, "You can always trust me, Diana. I will never betray you and I hope I will never let you down."

With an effort she controlled her emotions then said, "Okay, so this is another job for the Hunter. We'd better get cracking."

Forseti smiled to himself but replied formally, "Thank you, Hunter. I will send you the basic information about all these men so I think we need to give them work names."

"How about Hornets One, Two, Three and Four?"

"Very appropriate. Now would you like to take a bit more of this cake with you. I'm certainly not going to finish it all."

MUSWELL HILL

THE DISCOVERY THAT FORSETI had known her father brought back many memories but she knew she had to push them back down again, at least for the moment, and concentrate on the job in hand.

Back in her flat she sent Perry a Casanova message saying they needed to talk. It was an hour or so before he responded.

"Don't hassle me, Lady. I told you this will take time."

"Sure, but it's not just that. Your last message caused a flutter in the dovecotes over here."

"A flutter in the what?"

"Sorry. Caused consternation. Worried a few people. This high level UK guy you mentioned, we need to identify him. Do you have any more information?"

"Ah, got you. Well, yeah, there's a bit more poop."

"Poop?"

"Information. Get with it."

"Sorry. 'Poop' has rather a different meaning over here. Usually refers to dog shit. What have you got?"

"Dog shit? Gee, well I hope this is better than that. Okay, still no name, but the guy apparently went to some posh school or other. Funny name, sounds a bit like 'Heating'."

"Eton."

"Yeah, that could be it. Does that help?"

"Not much. A lot of people in high places wasted their childhood there."

"Oh, well, try this. I'm told your guy was at the Davos

summit last January. Had a meeting with one of our senior government officials."

"Any idea why they were meeting?"

"Nope. Don't think it was official but I'm still digging. I've been told a journalist may have taken a picture of them together. I'm working on that. Not optimistic. Even if it exists it was probably a sneak shot at long distance so could be a bit fuzzy."

"Well, anything you can come up with …"

"Sure. It ain't a breeze, but I'm starting to think you're right. Something is brewing. I'm getting very bad vibes."

She broke the Casanova connection and sent an email to Forseti. "Were any of the Hornets at the Davos summit last January?"

The following day she had a reply. "Both Hornet 1 and Hornet 3 were at Davos."

"Good. Our short list could be down to two."

Three days later she received a photo image from Perry but to her disappointment, it was very long distance and very out of focus. All it showed was two men standing face to face. They appeared to be shaking hands.

She didn't think it was much help but sent it to Forseti anyway. She had an acknowledgement, then heard nothing more for a week.

WEST HAM

EVENTUALLY, THE HUNTER received a text setting up a meeting, this time in a gymnasium in West Ham. The place smelled of sweat and testosterone but when she arrived the guy at the front desk was clearly expecting her.

"Storeroom," he said pointing down a corridor. She walked along the passageway, past photographs of men with what seemed to her to be highly improbably developed muscles in unlikely places.

She pushed open the door marked *Storeroom* and found Forseti sitting there with the usual two chairs and small table. On the table was a bottle of sparkling water and a box of chocolates.

He saw her look and said, "This is a good place to meet but their catering leaves a little to be desired. I thought this would be safer."

She grinned and sat down. Forseti leant forward. "First of all, congratulations. Our man is Hornet 3."

"You could work it out from that photo?"

"We could. I agree the features are very indistinct but the height gave it away. We've identified the American and we know he's six foot two. The man in that photo only just comes up to his shoulder. Therefore he is Hornet 3 – Hornet 1 is also around six foot."

"So who is Hornet 3?"

"Oliver Sanderlin. He's a kind of special adviser, mostly working with our Foreign Office, but he has a pretty large roaming brief. Have a chocolate."

"Do you want us to deal with him?"

"No, I think not, at least not yet. We need to tread carefully."

He took a sip of water and pushed the box of chocolates towards her.

She shook her head. "But he's clearly a Hornet. Are you saying he's above justice?"

"No."

"Well, it sounds like it."

"No. I suspect we will have to deal with him eventually, but my instinct tells me to hold back for the time being."

The Hunter looked at him for a moment and then leaned forward and chose a chocolate from the box. "Ah, good, a hard centre." She sucked on it for a moment then said, "So you want to play the long game."

"Yes. If I'm right and there is something brewing between the Americans and the Russians, then it's possible Sanderlin is involved."

"Didn't you say that if the Russians and Americans are up to something, then it's the bad boys doing it, not the government. Sanderlin was meeting an American government official – there can't be a connection, can there?"

"I very much hope not, but I wouldn't rule it out."

"Why?"

"I said we'd identified the American in that photo. It's Clyde Beckford."

"Beckford? The senator behind the American drugs ring."

"The very same."

"Shit."

"I agreed with the sentiment if not the vocabulary."

"Sorry, but if you're right ... God's teeth, this means your theory about the bad boys American-Russian partnership

258

could actually be true."

"It is certainly looking more likely. And there's something else. Have you ever heard of Mayoquoid?"

"No, what is it?"

"It's what they call a Neurological Active Compound, usually known as an NAC. Not surprised you haven't heard of it. It's not a treatment that is publicly available and has been rubbished by most of the scientific establishment."

"So why are we interested?"

"It was developed, discovered, not sure what the exact term is, by an Australian ethnobotanist."

"A what?"

"An ethnobotanist. Someone who studies how people from specific areas or cultures use indigenous plants. They do much of their work in the field, building relationships with local medical practitioners and studying the local plant life."

"And what does this ... this Mayoquoid do?"

"The ethnobiologist, Stewart MacQuoid, says that when this compound is prepared and treated in a particular way it can cause short term memory loss. His idea is that it could be used in operations that are likely to be traumatic so the patient will have no memory of what they have just been through. He also claims it can be used to help people get over very traumatic experiences by isolating and wiping part of the memory."

"Does it work?"

"Depends who you listen to. There's a lot of scepticism in the medical world, but MacQuoid insists it works. Apparently they've tested it on rats. The test subjects which had learned the way through a maze forgot the route after being injected with this. The effect lasts a few days and then wears off."

"Okay, but why is this a problem?"

"Of itself, it isn't. The problem is that we recently heard

that MacQuoid has been killed and all his case notes have vanished."

"Sounds extreme, even for a pharmaceutical company."

"This wasn't industrial espionage, Hunter, this was an assassination. His body was found in his home in Bowral, that's a small town in New South Wales. He'd been severely tortured."

"Ah."

"What we don't know is why someone was so keen to get their hands on that process."

"Well, it doesn't sound like a greedy pharma company."

"No, and that's not all. A few weeks ago an American researcher was found dead in his home in Paso Robles, that's in California. He'd also been tortured and all his case notes were missing."

"What was he working on?"

"A way of processing hemp to create a liquid compound that can be injected into a patient so they'll yield to hypnotism, even if they were resistant to it."

"For what purpose?"

"Well, as I'm sure you know, in spite of the popular belief, it's virtually impossible to hypnotise people against their will. Hypnosis is a state of consent and cooperation. The only control a hypnotherapist has over you is the control you allow him to have."

"Yes?"

"So that's fine if all you want to do is give up smoking, but if the subject doesn't, or can't, co-operate, hypnotherapy won't work. However, this new process can briefly override that resistance allowing treatment to take place. Its effect isn't long lasting but it could be used to help treat mentally ill patients or to help people undergo painful experiences but without feeling any pain."

"Invaluable for dentists then."

"Well, I hadn't though of it like that, but, yes, I suppose so."

"Does this compound have a name?"

"Apparently they're calling it SD77 – SD stands for Sweet Dreams, so they tell me."

"Very Californian. Okay, let me see if I've got this straight. If you used this compound on me and then suggested I should transfer the contents of my bank account to you, I might agree for the short period when I'm under the influence but when I come out of it, rationality would kick back in and I'd say, 'Not a chance, sunshine'."

"Something like that, yes. Except if I also gave you a dose of Mayoquoid, you may not even remember a word of it until it was too late."

The Hunter thought for a moment. "Yes, I see. A combination of the two could be very dangerous in the wrong hands."

"And given the level of violence used in both cases, I would say it's quite likely that the wrong hands now have this information."

"But which wrong hands?"

"Impossible to say. There were a couple of Russians in the Bowral area at the time Stewart MacQuoid was killed who were initially in the frame for the killing, but the police couldn't find any direct connection. The men protested their innocence and maintained they were researching the history of the German internees who were in a camp in that area during the First World War."

The Hunter suppressed a snort of derision. "Russian assassins buying presents in the Salisbury Cathedral gift shop."

"The similarity had occurred to me. Of course it may not be them at all. Maybe it was the Americans. They'd have been

261

less obvious."

"And the Californian researcher?"

Forseti shrugged. "Same answer. Could be the senator's guys, could be the Russians. It was violent enough for either of them, but there's no proof."

The Hunter thought for a moment. "So the only certain information we have is that the details of these two processes have been stolen."

"Yes."

"So the Russians thugs might have both, or the American drugs ring might have both, or they may have one each."

Forseti nodded. "Or a third party might have at least one of them."

"You're thinking of Harlot 3? Mr Sanderlin?"

"Maybe. But we come back to the same point – whoever has them, what do they want them for?"

"And are they working together or trying to form alliances?"

There was a short silence. Then the Hunter said, "Do you suppose that any of the players actually have a stock of one or other of these compounds or do they just have the information needed to create them?"

"Another 'don't know', but I suspect that at this stage it's the details of the process we're talking about. Manufacturing them would be the next step."

"So it all comes down to why they want them, doesn't it? Though given the nature of the people we're talking about I doubt it's altruistic."

"I'm sure it isn't, but in our work we have to expect the unexpected."

"So, if we deal with Sanderlin now, we could lose our only lead into something bigger."

"I hope I'm wrong but ..."

"Trust your instincts?"

"Yes."

The Hunter got to her feet and began to pace around the room. "Any clues?"

"None. We're hoping your Mr Cracken might have more luck."

"I can't push him again. We have to let him make his own pace."

"Of course."

"But in the meantime we could have a subtle sniff around Mr Sanderlin."

"That would be useful, but make it very subtle, Hunter. Don't go sinking his trawlers."

BRIEFINGS AND PLANS

THE TEAM MET at the Hilton Park Services on the M6 where they took their various drinks and snacks out onto the terrace in the sun.

The Python knew some of the story already so the Hunter quickly brought the others up to speed. There was silence for a moment as she finished and then the Fixer said, "Is this kosher? You reckon this government bloke's involved in some kind of dirty deal?"

"Looks that way."

"Technically Sanderlin's not in government," said the Housekeeper.

"No, but he has a lot of power and a lot of influence and if he's got links with an American crime syndicate then it can't be good news."

The Armourer brushed the last grains of doughnut sugar off her jacket. "You say Forseti thinks something's brewing internationally but he doesn't know what."

"That's about the size of it."

"But you think it might have something to do with these neurological wotsits, these compounds?"

"It's possible."

"What's your gut feeling, Hunter?"

"I think we should be taking this very seriously."

"No idea what the possible threat could be?"

"No."

The Fixer began to make notes. "Okay, so we start by

having a shifty round Mister Sanderlin. Address, domestic set up, spare time activities, all that kinda hows-your-father."

"Can we fix a phone tap?" asked the Armourer, "and maybe an email intercept."

"Won't the security services have done that?"

"No," said the Hunter, "no one apart from us, and Forseti, knows anything about this and it has to stay that way. If we're right and Sanderlin is being naughty with state secrets, then fine. If we're wrong—"

"— we're expendable," said the Fixer with a short laugh. "No dirty linen laid out in Parliament."

The Hunter turned to the Python. "Can you get access to his phone and email?"

"Probably."

"I bet his security is tighter than a duck's arse," said the Fixer.

"Maybe, but even a duck's arse has to open sometimes."

There was a ripple of laughter round the table and the Hunter said, "Okay, Python, once we've got the basic information give it your best shot. As for the intel gathering, Fixer, over to you. Let us know if you need any help."

"There's just one thing," said the Defender.

"What?"

"We have that distant photo of Sanderlin and the Senator together, thanks to Cracken's contacts."

"So?"

"But for that meeting they took advantage of the Davros summit where they were both entitled to be. However, they can't do that very often so how do they stay in touch?"

There was a moment's silence, then the Hunter said, "They can't, not regularly so ..."

"So they must each use an intermediary. We need to find them too."

The Hunter sighed. "Right, plenty to be getting on with then."

BY CHANCE, BACK IN London the Hunter received another Casanova message from Perry.

"There's a guy called Burke on the staff of Senator Beckford. Officially on his office staff that is – but word on the street is that he's Beckford's enforcer behind the scenes. Nasty piece of work. You wouldn't trust him further than you could pitch a plastic horseshoe in a high wind."

The Hunter had never considered pitching a plastic horseshoe – or any other kind of horseshoe for that matter – in any sort of weather, but Perry's meaning was clear.

"This Burke's been having regular meetings with a Brit. My source said he thought it was someone official acting as a spokesman for the British Government but I kinda got doubts about that."

"Why?"

"There's places you hold official meetings and places you don't. Back street saloons in Brooklyn, pool halls in New Jersey are definitely among the 'don'ts'."

"Do we have a name for the Brit?"

"Nope, but you're right. It's a cinch something's going on. And there's more. Burke's been seen down at Coney Island quite a lot recently."

"Holding an ice cream and sliding down the helter-skelter."

"I guess not, but these days Coney Island is best known for its large Russian-speaking community."

"Ah."

"I know I keep saying this, but you gotta be careful, Hunter Lady. Word is Burke's a real fruitcake, gets a lot of pleasure from hurting people."

"I'll bear that in mind. Now I've got something for you." And she told him about her conversation with Forseti and the two compounds Mayoquoid and SD77.

"And you want me to dig around, yeah?"

"That's the idea."

It's not possible to sigh in an email but she could imagine his expression.

"Okay, I'll give it a shot? You're really making me earn my corn, yeah?"

"Hint taken. I'll arrange a new corn shipment asap. Okay?"

POKING ABOUT

THE FIXER SPENT a couple of weeks getting to know Oliver Sanderlin even though Sanderlin himself was not aware of it. It didn't take him long to discover that Sanderlin lived in Chelsea and once that that was established, he and Armourer kept the house under observation. It soon became apparent that Sanderlin lived alone, although there appeared to be a woman who went in twice a week.

"Presumably she takes care of all the domestic stuff," he said to the Armourer.

"Gender type-casting," muttered the Armourer.

Meanwhile the Housekeeper set out to explore Sanderlin's work pattern. He was well suited to this task as he was able to move around in social circles where the Fixer would have stood out like a sore thumb. He soon discovered that Sanderlin's main work was with the Foreign Office but he also had a small office suite on the first floor in a building in Tothill Street.

"Sanderlin is a curious man," the Housekeeper said in his report to the Hunter. "Wherever he's working, he arrives early and leaves late. I managed to attend a couple of drinks events where he was socialising with some very influential people, and I had the impression that he's someone who talks little and listens a lot."

"Does he appear to be popular?"

"Not easy to tell but I suspect not. Smiles if he has to, but never with his eyes."

Once they'd confirmed Sanderlin's address and workplace, the Python set to work in the back alleys of cyberspace where he was so much at home. He established there were two landlines in the Tothill Street office but they were hardly ever used. He identified two mobile signals from inside the building and three sources of emails, all encrypted. He told the team that he could probably crack them but it wouldn't be quick.

"How about the Chelsea house?"

"One landline. As far as I can work out it's only used by the lady wot does," he glanced sideways at the Armourer, "to place grocery orders."

Between them, the Fixer and the Housekeeper identified a smart restaurant in South Kensington which appeared to be Sanderlin's favourite. Sanderlin always arrived at the same time, ate alone and afterwards would go straight home. One evening the Housekeeper and the Hunter booked a table there for dinner and were struck by the care and attention that Sanderlin received from the staff.

The Armourer, putting her prejudices to one side, re-established contact with a few of her old colleagues at MI6. In general conversation she heard no specific mention of Sanderlin apart from one, now retired, SIS officer.

"I knew Sanderlin," he said, "cold fish. Never put a foot wrong. Squeaky clean." He paused. "Too clean for my liking but that's just instinct. No one else was ever interested in him."

The Fixer had switched his attention away from the Chelsea house to the South Kensington restaurant. After several evenings of watching people eat a full meal while he was munching on a sandwich he was getting very bored but he knew the value of patience and finally it was rewarded.

One evening, undistinguishable from any other except by

the persistent drizzle, Sanderlin emerged from the restaurant but instead of heading home as usual he was picked up by a black Mercedes. The Fixer followed it to an address in Hampstead where Sanderlin stayed for a couple of hours before the Mercedes drove him back to Chelsea and dropped him off a few streets away from his house.

This opened up a new line of enquiry so the Fixer went back to work. He soon identified the owner of the Hampstead house as a Damian Rackenford and confirmed that the mysterious Mercedes was registered to the same name.

By haunting the local shops and pubs and chatting with various people he met, the Fixer learned that Damian Rackenford appeared to be some kind of businessman.

"Dunno what he does," said one old boy in the pub on the corner, "but he's away a lot, abroad, so I'm told. Oh, yeah, thankee, I will have another half."

The Fixer conferred with the Housekeeper and they each went to work in their own spheres of influence and before long they knew a lot about Mr Rackenford. It was time to brief the team.

THE HOUSEKEEPER KICKED OFF. "Our Damian seems to be a bit of a smoothie. He used to hold a senior management position with Rokesby Pharmaceuticals but they gave him the boot. He was suspected of doing some dodgy under-the-counter deals with a rival firm – based, believe it or not, in the USA. Nothing proved but …"

"He jumped before he was pushed."

"Looks that way."

"Where'd he jump to?"

"Well, after leaving Rokesby he set up a marketing company specialising in medical supplies. He's often in the States, in theory to make distribution deals but …"

"Who knows."

"Precisely. Oh, and another interesting thing, he also visits Moscow a lot."

"Does he indeed." The Hunter looked round the table. "Well, what do we reckon? Could Damian be the link between our Hornet and the Senator via this Burke guy that Perry told me about?"

"Could be."

"And I guess it's possible that he's also the link between Sanderlin and whichever Russian baddie is involved in all this."

"Worth exploring."

"Okay, let's sum up. What do we have so far?"

The Housekeeper had been collating the information as it came in so he kicked off.

"Right, so we know Sanderlin is a power behind the Foreign Office throne. From his general behaviour it looks as though he's cultivating the appearance of a rather dull private life. We now know he has links with a dodgy character who in turn has links with the American pharmaceutical industry – possibly meeting the senator's enforcer, this Burke bloke – and possibly meeting up with the Russians as well, though we don't know who. However, this does suggest a direct link between the Foreign Office and two other powers. A link which the Foreign Office might not be aware of."

The Hunter cut in. "So that's what we know. What don't we know?"

"We don't know for certain what the connection between Sanderlin and Damian Rackenford is, we don't know for certain that it's the American Burke that Rackenford is meeting, we don't know anything about the Russians that either Rackenford or Burke are meeting. We don't know for certain that there's a connection between the murder of the scientists behind these two neurological active compounds and the Americans or the Russians."

The Defender said, "Let's do some scenario projections."

"Oh, God," said the Python, "here we go again."

Everyone laughed and the Defender went on, "Let's assume that Forseti's instincts are right and that something big is going on at a high level between the senator's group of criminal Americans and a Russian mafia group. Are we assuming that our Hornet, Sanderlin, is also part of this conspiracy?"

"On the face of it, it definitely seems possible."

"But we have no idea what they're planning or where the theft of these two chemical processes fits in?"

"No idea. It's all speculation."

"So what do we do?"

"We wait. We keep an eye on Sanderlin and Rackienford and wait for something to happen. I don't see we have any choice."

CASANOVA CALLING

ANOTHER DAY, ANOTHER Casanova session with Perry.

"Found your Brit yet?"

"Possibly. Still checking."

"Well, I've got some more poop on Burke for you. He goes to the UK a lot. When he's in London he's based at the American embassy and stays at a hotel near the Hyde Park."

"Okay."

"But there's also a house, a big house, somewhere in a place called Hampshire. Is that a town you know?"

"Not a town. It's a county."

"Cool. Say, we have a state called New Hampshire, that's a coincidence, ain't it?"

"Probably not."

"Anyway, I'm told this is a real smart place, own grounds, fancy porch, windows with arches on top, maids' rooms in the attic, that kind of stuff."

"What about it?"

"Well, on paper it seems to belong to the American embassy but the scuttlebutt is it's for the sole use of Senator Beckford when he goes to the UK. No one else at the embassy ever seems to use it."

"So?"

"But the Senator never goes to the UK. I reckon it's really for this guy, Burke. God knows what he gets up to there but I guess it'd be worth taking a look."

"Well, we can try, but Hampshire's a big place. Do you know where it is exactly."

"Nope."

"Ah, well. Any news on those two compounds?

"Nope, but I've got the name of a guy who swings both ways, if you see what I mean. Trying to set up a meet with him. Might get some poop there."

"Great. Go for it, Yankee Boy."

MORE POKING ABOUT

PROGRESS WAS SLOW. The Python managed to intercept the mobile phone calls and emails from Sanderlin's office in Tothill Street but there was nothing significant.

The Armourer checked on the woman who went to Sanderlin's house twice a week but, as expected, she was just his cleaner. Nothing suspicious about her.

The Fixer was very frustrated. Talking to the Hunter he said, "I've reached a dead end, unless I break into Rackenford's place and have a shifty."

"Could you do that without him knowing someone's been in?"

"Possibly, couldn't guarantee it."

"Then, no, not at this stage."

The only bit of progress at this time was that the Housekeeper, using his contacts at the American embassy, managed to identify the Hampshire house that Perry Cracken had mentioned. It was an old manor house not far from Stockbridge so he paid it a quick visit but it appeared to be unoccupied. He bought some chocolate in the village shop and casually asked about it but no one knew much except the owners occasionally held parties there.

It didn't seem like much progress for all their efforts but then suddenly everything changed.

One night, at 2.00 am, the Hunter received another Casanova message from Perry Cracken. It was very short.

"Need to meet urgently. Amsterdam. Schiphol. Thursday. 1600."

The Hunter tried to contact him but there was no response so on Thursday morning she flew to Schiphol.

OCEAN CITY – NEW JERSEY

PERRY CRACKEN HAD always lived life on the edge. Working for anyone, trusted by no-one, his was a lonely existence. He owned a small single storey town house in Ocean City but more often than not he was on the move, gathering information, meeting potential clients and always making sure that his trail was well covered.

It was on one of his brief visits home that he met Irina in a bar. She was arguing with the barman and kept waving a bundle of papers under this nose.

"Lady, I'm not interested in those. Now you gonna pay for your drinks or not?"

"No money. These papers, very valuable. Worth many dollars."

"Not to me they're not. I want cash or I call the cops."

Sensing an opportunity, Perry stepped forward. "Hey, give the kid a break. I'll settle her bill. How much is it?"

"Thirty bucks."

"Yeah, and the rest. Here's twenty – bet that covers it."

"Okay, smart guy."

Perry turned to Irina. "Come on, let's get outa here."

She followed him into the street. "Thank you. You want papers?" She thrust the bundle of papers towards him.

"Maybe. Look, where you staying?"

Irina shrugged. "Nowhere. They throw me out when I have no more money."

"Well, you can't sleep on the sidewalk. You'd better come

back with me."

She shook her head. "No, don't do that."

Perry sighed. "I'm not asking you to. I'm offering you somewhere to sleep. You're free to go at any time but you're going to need some money."

"I sell these." She waved the bundle of papers at him.

"What are they?"

"Very important. Very valuable."

"Okay, I'll have a look at them. Now are you coming or aren't you?"

She came. He showed her to the spare bedroom. Then he sat down to examine the bundle of papers.

Most of it was jibber-jabber as far as he was concerned but the summary paragraphs at the end made him sit up in alarm. At first glance it looked as though he may have stumbled across some of the material that the Hunter had asked him to explore.

The following day he began trawling his extensive network of contacts and the more he learned, the worse it got. The final nail in coffin came from one of his anonymous sources in Washington DC. He'd never known this man's name and he'd never seen his face but he knew he was very close to the seat of power. This man's information had always been totally reliable so what Perry learned there scared the hell out of him.

Perry was a realist and he knew that the information he now had was a complete game-changer so he wasn't surprised when he had a sudden phone call saying: "Perry, they're coming for you. Go now." He had long ago prepared an emergency escape plan so within twenty minutes he was in the car and driving towards New York. He abandoned the car there, took the train to Boston then flew to Calgary in Canada. From there he sent a message to the Hunter and bought a ticket to Schiphol.

SCHIPHOL

THEY MET ON the main concourse opposite a shop that sold a selection of Dutch cheeses. Perry was very agitated.

"We've got big problems, Hunter Lady."

"Okay, but why we meeting here?"

"It's on my way."

"On your way to where?"

"Don't know yet, and sure is best you don't know."

"What's so urgent."

"You've really dumped me in the shit, Hunter Lady."

"I have?"

"Just a little bit of information, you said. Who meets who, Russian baddies, American gangsters, what they up to?"

"Yes, okay."

"You didn't say anything about international conspiracies, nothing about laying my life on the line."

"Perry, calm down. Just tell me what's happened."

"Look, I trade information, okay? People tell me things, I pick up stuff, I sell it on."

"So what's changed?"

"The stakes, Hunter Lady. Thanks to you I now know stuff I wish I didn't, and there's some nasty people out there wish I didn't too."

"Perry, what the hell are you talking about?"

"I can't unknow this so I'm gonna tell you. You ain't gonna want to know it either, but maybe you can do something about it. I can't. I know I can't, so I'm out of here."

"Tell me what?"

"You're not gonna believe this."

She was getting impatient. "Okay, so I won't believe it and I'm not going to like it, just get on with it, will you."

"Right, well this compound doo-dah you told me about, the short term memory loss one …"

"Mayoquoid?"

"Yeah, whatever, and the other one, SD77, yes?"

"What about them? They don't seem particular dangerous."

"Not individually, no, and anyway I'm told the effects are only short term. But what no one has said is, if you stick 'em together it's a whole new ballgame."

"What sort of ballgame?"

"Look, my technical understanding of this is pretty much nada but as far as I can make out it's possible to manufacture this Mayo whatsit and the SD77 and then combine them – chemically, I mean – into a new compound. I'm told that gets you something much more long lasting. You could give a guy a dose of this stuff then tell him to go out and kill his own Grandma and he'd do it, right? He wouldn't even know it was his Grandma. But in any case he would *never* remember and he would never stop doing what he was told."

"Jesus."

"Don't think he's gonna help.

"How do we know it works?"

"The guys I've been talking to seem to think it will and if they're right then it's dynamite. They're calling it 'Minnie Ha-Ha'."

The Hunter thought for a moment. "So who has it? This … Minnie Ha-Ha?"

"No one yet, but they're all after it."

"Who's 'they'?"

"The usual suspects. Senator Beckford's goons, a bunch

of Russians. Rumour has it the CIA are probably lurking somewhere in the background too."

"A whole bunch of Hornets in fact."

"Come again?"

"No matter. So the next question, why do they want it?"

"The usual – power and profit. Look let's go back a step. In the States we've got a number of organised crime syndicates. Right?"

"Right."

"This is all a bit murky, I couldn't ask too many direct questions but back home we've been seeing an unusual coming together of the big players, unusual alliances. I've also been told something similar is happening in Russia."

The Hunter froze. This sounded like a confirmation of Forseti's fears.

Perry went on. "Seems crazy to me but if Minnie Ha-Ha does work as they say, then it'd be a very powerful weapon. Look, suppose Senator Beckford got it and managed to use it on someone he knew closely, a buddy like, I don't know, someone in government, maybe even the President, then effectively Beckford would be the one in power. The elected government would just be puppets, they could be controlled to do all sorts of stuff and no matter how bad it was they'd think they were doing the right thing."

"Come on, how could they do that? Run round the Senate sticking needles into people's arms?"

"Wouldn't have to. As I understand it Minnie Ha-Ha can be produced as a spray. So, for example, if they put it into the air conditioning system on Capitol Hill then anyone in the building at the time would be affected. Then the bad guys could set their own agenda."

"Where do the Russians fit into this?"

"Well, they don't necessarily have to worry about

controlling their government, they get a pretty free rein as it is, but it still comes down to power and profit and I don't like the idea of them having access to Minnie Ha-Ha. This stuff could be very, very dangerous."

There was a long silence as the Hunter tried to take all this information on board.

After a moment Perry said tentatively. "There's another complication and this you won't like."

The Hunter sighed. "I don't like any of it but go on."

"My source says the Brits are definitely involved in this."

"The Brits?"

"Not officially, obviously, but there seems to be some guy behind the scenes who's in regular touch with Beckford and also one of the Russian big boys. Hey, maybe this Brit is the guy who was meeting Beckford at the Davos summit."

"Sanderlin?"

"Don't know his name but there is definitely a triumvirate controlling this thing, an American, a Russian and a Brit. In fact, I get the impression that it's the Brit's who's holding the balance. No matter what nefarious transactions they are planning, it's still hard for an American to trust a Russian and vice-versa."

"This gets more fantastic by the minute. Why would any of them trust Sanderlin?"

"No one trusts anyone, Hunter Lady, but if either of the others thinks the Brit favours their side then that puts him in a very powerful position."

The Hunter shook her head. "I'm struggling with this but let's look at the facts. Do we know who currently has the information, formula, whatever you call it, to manufacture these two compounds?"

"This is where it gets complicated. Can't really get any straight answers but as far as I can make out, Beckford's goons got hold of one of these compounds or rather the process of how to manufacture it, but they can't do anything with it, at least not yet. We're talking street fighters, not scientists. You can't just go into your local drug store and say 'make this up for me, guys'."

"What about the Russians?"

"Well, if they do have the other process they'll probably just grab some poor sod and lock him up until he's done what they want. But my guess it that your Brit has the information for at least one of them. That's what's giving him the casting vote."

"So, am I right in thinking that, as far as we know, neither side have physically manufactured these compounds yet?"

"Don't think so."

"But even if they did, you're implying that they'd need to come together at some stage to combine both processes to manufacture this Minnie Ha-Ha thing?"

"Yeah, well, that's the good news."

"Tell me. I could do with some good news."

"Well, it seems the process to obtain Minnie Ha-Ha is very involved and complicated and takes a long while. First you have to manufacture a sizeable quantity of the Mayo doo-dah, then you have to manufacture the Sweet Dreams stuff. Only when you have large quantities of both can you begin the complicated process of combining them. So, as I say, it ain't quick, but the fact it's remotely possible scares the shit out of me."

"This information on how to manufacture Mayo and SD77, do we know in what form it exists?"

"Hard to say. Paranoia rules. It'll be closely guarded, that's for sure. It's not a case of doing a quick Google and it hasn't been published by some lab tech in New Scientist. So, maybe they're on a memory card or even just a printed paper copy.

You can't hack a page of print and the fewer the copies, the tighter the security. Fine, so long as it's you who has the copy."

"Yeah, okay. So one group or another needs to get their hands on both the original processes to make these compounds before they can start to combine them and produce this ... this Minnie Ha-Ha thing."

"That's about it."

"But even then, whoever gets hold of both of them, that's not enough. They'll still need the third formula, process, call it what you will, that shows them how to combine the two."

"Yup."

"So who has that bit of information? Do we know?"

Perry swallowed. "Yes, we do. It's me."

A SERVICE FLAT SOMEWHERE IN LONDON

FORSETI SAT IN the living room of his London flat feeling very alone. The feeling that something was wrong wouldn't leave him and he was too old in the game to dismiss such feelings out of hand.

He'd decided not to tell Odin that he'd let the Hunter loose on Sanderlin. He wasn't sure why, but the 'need to know' principle was very strong in him. Time enough to mention it if and when there was some hard and fast information to share.

There was a time, many years ago, when he'd not been so circumspect and deep in his heart he had always wondered if it had been betrayal from inside that had led to the death of the Hunter's father. Not many people had known about the mission but anyone of them might have passed it on, either to the other side, or just to a colleague. It didn't even have to be deliberate, one casual unguarded mention could be all that was needed.

He remembered the old saying that a secret is something you only tell one person at a time and these days he was far more cautious. But caution could only be taken so far. Sometimes you just had to take a risk, trust someone and hope for the best.

He had total trust in the Hunter but had moments of anxiety for her as well.

SCHIPHOL

THE HUNTER LOOKED at Perry in disbelief. "You've got this formula?"

"Yup, well, not on me. But I know where it is. No one else does."

"How the hell do you come to have it?"

Perry looked embarrassed. "Well, there's this broad. A Russian. Met her in this bar one night. She was in a bad way, frightened and broke, so I kinda ..."

"Took her under your wing."

"Sure, why not. I paid her bar bill, she offered me this bunch of papers. I thought it might be something I could sell on so I took them."

"This girl, was she some kind of expert?"

"Jeez, no. Great kid, but not that bright. Thing is, she'd been the mistress of this Russian scientist guy. She was a bit vague but it seemed he had samples of both compounds, Mayo and SD77."

"How the hell had he got those?"

"No idea, but apparently scientists are a kind of international club. Maybe he knew the two guys and they'd sent him their stuff, all I know is that he had them. Irina said he wasn't too interested at first but then he began to do some experiments of his own. His idea was to try and refine the two processes, make them more effective. Well, he did that all right."

"So what happened?"

"When he realised what his combined process actually did he got a bit nervous. He tried to contact the guys who'd sent him this information, only to discover they were both dead. At this point he panicked but by then the information about his discovery had leaked. He saw which way the wind was blowing so gave Irina all his papers and told her to vamoose. She made it to the States and ended up in Ocean City."

"What happened to him?"

"No idea. Probably—" Perry drew a finger across his throat.

"And she gave you his papers?"

"She didn't really know what she had, but it was her only asset and she was broke."

"So what did you do?"

"Read them, or tried to. Couldn't understand most of it but the summary at the end made me think. Seemed like the kind of stuff you'd been asking about so I talked to a few people. That's when I learned stuff I wish I'd never known."

"Okay, so what happened then?"

"I was frightened, don't mind admitting it. I knew this was red hot. Then I got word they were coming for me so I got the hell out, sent you a message and here I am."

"What about the girl – Irina?"

"No idea."

"So you abandoned her."

Perry looked away and the Hunter went on, "Okay, so who knows you've got this information?"

"Everyone, I guess. The Senator's guys, the Russians, probably your Brit, maybe the CIA and your Intelligence people too."

"Christ, Perry, you do live dangerously, don't you?"

"Not of choice. That's why I'm disappearing."

"They'll trace you. Airline schedules are easy to access."

"I'm not travelling by air, not now I'm in Europe. In a few minutes I'll rent a car and disappear. I'm not using my own name."

"Look, Perry, this drug, this Minnie Ha-Ha thing, is lethal. It would be catastrophic if anyone, anyone at all, ever got their hands on it."

"Yeah, I know."

"So if you've got the only copy of the formula why don't we just destroy it?"

"Can't do that. I need the insurance. If any of these guys find me my life's not worth a hill o' beans. But they want that formula and they know if they kill me they'll lose one chance of getting it."

"One chance? Who else has this?"

Perry swallowed again. "You do. At least that's what they think. That's why I needed to warn you. They'll be coming after me and they'll be coming after the Hunter too."

"Jesus, Perry, you mean you've dumped me in it."

"I'm sorry, Hunter Lady, I'm really sorry, but I can't fight these people. I have to vanish. There's already a hit out on you so what's the difference."

"Thanks for that."

"Look, I figured you stand more chance of sorting this mess out, you and those guys you work with. You're a team, you've got resources, you can handle this, I can't."

"Looks like we're going to have to. So where is the formula for this combined process? Is it safe?"

"As safe as I can make it. It's lodged in an encrypted storage account on a private secure Cloud."

"Which only you can access."

"Natch."

"But the bad guys think I've got access as well?"

"Yup."

"Jesus, Perry, so what do you expect me to do?"

"Get the other two formulas and destroy them. Then they've got nowhere to go. You can't combine something you don't have. This thing could be really nasty, Hunter Lady. I may be all kinds of creep but I wouldn't wish Minnie Ha-Ha on anyone."

"Where the hell do I start?"

"Ah, well, I've got one thing that might help if your techie guy can make sense of it."

"What's that?"

"Think it's a coded message from Beckford to the Russian guy. You don't need to know how I got it but if you can make sense of it, you might find a way in. It's here."

He handed her an envelope and stood up. "Time I was gone. Good luck."

He lifted a hand in farewell and vanished into the crowds on the Schiphol concourse.

WHIPSNADE ZOO

THEY MET AT the Lemur enclosure in Whipsnade Zoo. It was a sunny day but the wind was chill.

"No drinks today," said Forseti, "the tone of your message suggested something serious so I thought this would be safer."

She nodded. "Shall we walk?"

They made their way slowly up past the chimpanzees towards the giraffes while the Hunter told Forseti about her conversation with Perry Cracken.

"I was afraid of something like this," he said when she had finished. "But a lot of things now make more sense."

"The question is what do we do? What can we do?"

"I think your Mr Cracken is being extremely selfish. The sensible thing to do would be to destroy this combination formula, always assuming he really does have the only copy."

"He doesn't see it that way."

"No. So, let's think about the individual formulas. Do we know where those are?"

"Not for certain, except no one seems to have both of them."

"But Sanderlin might have one of them."

"That's the impression Perry gave me. He said that Sanderlin was 'holding the balance.'"

"Well, for the moment let's assume he's right. If we could find these formulas and destroy them, then the threat of Minnie Ha-Ha goes away. As Mr Cracken pointed out, you can't combine things you don't have."

"Suppose not."

"However, as far as the combination formula itself goes, you say the only copy is lodged on a secure Cloud somewhere and Cracken is the only person who can access it?"

"Apparently so."

"But the Russians, Americans and so on think you have access too?"

"Yes."

"And do you?"

"Of course I bloody well don't. But it doesn't make any difference, does it. They'll still come after me."

"Yes, I rather think they will, but we need to them to, don't we?"

She asked the question even though she knew the answer. "How do you mean?"

"Well, if we're going to destroy the original formulas you can't go chasing all over the States and Russia looking for the people who have them, but this way—"

"— I don't have to go looking for them. They'll come looking for me."

"Precisely."

They walked in silence for a few minutes then Forseti said, "I think the time has come to … what shall I say … explore Mr Sanderlin a little closer, especially as I've been hearing some rather disturbing rumours recently."

"And they are?"

"My information is that Sanderlin is, very subtly and behind the scenes, planting the suggestion that the UK would be better off if we came out of the United Nations."

"What."

"He's not got a lot of support – not yet – but the drip drip of lies and misinformation, exaggerated errors and so on will eventually have an effect. Of course, there have been rumblings about the oversight of the ECHR, the cost of NATO etc in the right-wing press for years, but this is different. It's coming, though not directly, from someone who has great influence with the government.

"But for us to leave the UN would be disastrous. It isn't just a political choice. It's a body that every serious sovereign nation belongs to. If we left we'd be kicked off the Security Council as well and it'd completely destroy our international credibility. What on earth would we gain?"

"Plenty, if you're Oliver Sanderlin reaching for personal power."

"Are you saying he wants to be Prime Minister?"

"Good heavens, no. He is a classic example of control from the deep shadows. No, my guess is that he wants to be Kingmaker, to control the Prime Minister and other people in power."

"Hence his interest in Minnie Ha-Ha."

"Yes, and it also explains something else. Think about it, Hunter. On the surface what do a Russian mafia boss, an American Senator who runs a drugs ring and a senior member of the British establishment have in common?"

"On the surface – nothing."

"Exactly, so this isn't a conspiracy in the normal sense of that word, but it could be an alliance. If they all wanted the same thing there could be a lot infighting but if they all had different aims then working together could be an advantage. Complementary rather than competitive."

The Hunter shook her head. "How do you know all this?"

"I don't, I'm hypothesising, but it does fit the facts we have."

"Okay, so if I buy that, what is each Hornet after?"

"Money, in whatever form it comes. And through that,

power. If you're an American senator running an international and very profitable drugs ring then, no matter how powerful you are, you always run the risk of losing everything. If you can control, not only the government but the law enforcement agencies as well, then there's nothing to stop you making a fortune."

"And the Russians?"

"More or less the same. Since the fall of the Soviet Union it's been a bit of a free-for-all over there. Climbing to the top in an underworld hierarchy is one thing, staying there is something completely different. You can't afford to relax for a moment unless, of course, you have the opposition under control."

"Okay, so what about Sanderlin?"

They'd reached the porcupine enclosure and Forseti came to a halt. For a moment he looked down at the spikey little creatures and then he sighed.

"I very much fear that Sanderlin might be one of those individuals who believes Democracy is a weakness. There have always been some people who think that they, and they alone, should have the right to make decisions that affect everybody. For example, there was a strong body of opinion in the 1930s that Hitler was a good man with the right ideas."

"But there have always been dissenting voices," said the Hunter, "extreme groups, right wing, left wing, protesters who take direct action. Gets uncomfortable at times but we've always coped."

"But what if one of those groups stopped being simply a dissenting voice and actually came to power here in the UK today …"

"Not likely."

"Not in the current system, no. But suppose Sanderlin and his supporters, and I am sure there are supporters, could control the government from behind the scenes ..."

"I see ... we're back to Minnie Ha-Ha."

"Exactly. Never underestimate the hate factor. There are always groups that are dissatisfied with the status quo. We've seen it in America, we have outbursts of it here. It's not difficult for a ruthless manipulator to tap into that."

The Hunter became business like. "Okay, so we need to make sure that no one can get their hands on Minnie Ha-Ha."

"Yes, without that I think our Hornets will lose their sting."

"Yes, but the only way to do that is to destroy the formula, except we can't because Perry has the only copy and he's disappeared."

"Agreed. So what we need to do is to find and destroy the Mayoquoid and SD77 formulas. Without them Minnie Ha-Ha can't be manufactured anyway."

"Sounds so easy when you put it like that." She thought for a moment. "Well, I guess Sanderlin is the place to start, at least he's near at hand."

Forseti said nothing. In the distance they heard the mournful howl of a wolf, an incongruous sound in the English countryside.

Finally the Hunter said, "Sorry but I do need to ask, are you certain that Sanderlin is working behind the scenes to destabilise our elected government?"

"I'm certain."

"And to do that he's conspiring with foreign forces which would appear to be enemies of this country ..."

"So it would seem."

"That makes him a traitor."

"It does indeed. But on the surface there is nothing he could be charged with and he has very powerful friends,

friends who, incidentally would not believe a word about any threat to the establishment from an American-Russian made mind-control compound of which we have no proof, no samples and no formula."

They walked in silence for a while then she said, "This is a serious threat, isn't it?"

"I think so. It's early days, it takes time to undermine democracy, but left alone I have no doubt Sanderlin will get there."

"But he won't get there overnight?"

"No … unless …" he paused, "unless he gets his hands on Minnie Ha-Ha. That could be a game changer."

"Yes, I can see that. Well, in that case we'd better make sure that he doesn't."

"Yes, and to be perfectly clear, I suspect we'll have to deal with Sanderlin at some stage but for now finding and destroying those formulas is our priority."

They reached the Meerkats enclosure and paused for a moment. Forseti pointed to one of the animals sitting up on its hind legs looking around him.

"Astute little beasts. There's always one of them on guard keeping an eye out for predators. I suggest you do the same, Hunter."

ALEXANDRA PALACE ICE RINK

THE HUNTER MET her team in the food hall of the ice rink at Alexandra Palace. The Housekeeper arrived a little late which prompted the Fixer to say, "Should have got your skates on, chum."

There were a few wry smiles round the table which soon vanished when the Hunter set out the problem they now faced.

She told them about the situation with the various formulas, Forseti's theories about Sanderlin's long term plans and the dangers posed by an alliance between Sanderlin, Beckford and Lazovsky.

"We need to find and destroy these two formulas and, if possible the Minnie Ha-Ha one as well. This isn't the purpose our team was created for, but this is an unconventional problem which needs an unconventional solution. However, if any of you feel you don't want any part of it then now's the time to say so."

"No question," said the Armourer, "of course we go for it."

"I can hardly believe what I'm hearing," said the Fixer, "but if you're right, then I agree with Armourer."

There was a series of nods round the table.

"Thank you. So now the question is, how do we proceed?"

"Well, trying to get to Beckford or Lazovsky would be damn nigh impossible," said the Defender, "the only people accessible to us are Sanderlin and Rackenford."

"We need to tread very carefully round Sanderlin," said the Hunter. "As far as the world's concerned he is a respectable member of the British Establishment."

"Just like Kim Philby was," muttered the Armourer under her breath.

"Okay," said the Fixer, "but if we assume Sanderlin's got one of these formulas, where's he likely to keep it?"

"Could be in his home," said the Housekeeper, "or maybe a safe deposit box."

"Safe deposit would be tricky to access, unless Sanderlin could be persuaded to co-operate."

"That'd be the last resort," said the Hunter.

The Housekeeper looked at the Fixer. "Could you get us inside Sanderlin's place?"

The Fixer frowned. "Probably, but I bet his home security is good. We'll have to stage it as a regular burglary."

"Not an option," said the Hunter, "if we do that and don't find the formula all we've done is alert Sanderlin to the fact that someone is sniffing around."

"So that leaves Damian Rackenford," said the Armourer. "We know he and Sanderlin are in regular contact and we're pretty sure he's Sanderlin's link with the Senator and the Russian."

"Would Sanderlin trust Rackenford enough to let him take charge of the formula?"

"Maybe not, but we might learn something from him and we have to start somewhere."

"Worth a try." The Hunter turned to the Fixer. "What about Rackenford's place?"

"Should be able to get in," said the Fixer, "Though again, as I said last time this came up, I can't promise I wouldn't leave some trace, but I guess with Rackenford that's less critical.

The thing is I don't know what I'm looking for?"

"Anything relating to Sanderlin or Beckford or Lazovsky for that matter. One of the formulas would be nice but in any case, you know, just have a poke around. Any kind of lead would be useful."

"Well, okay, but I wouldn't know a formula if it sat up and played a trumpet at me."

"Well, it's going to be chemically based, so it will probably be a string of lots of capital letters some small letters and some even smaller figures. Something like this." She grabbed a piece of paper and scribbled on it.

The Fixer peered at it doubtfully. "Okay, if you say so."

"I do. Now whether it's on paper or a digital file, it will most likely be secreted away somewhere, it's not going to be in a photo frame on the mantlepiece."

"Oh, I don't know," said the Defender, "it would probably be safer there than anywhere else."

There were smiles round the table and the Fixer said, "Okay, so I need to allow time for a thorough search but I won't overlook the mantlepiece."

"Leave that with you then. Do you want anyone to come with you?"

The Fixer shook his head. "No. I'll be better on me own."

The Defender leaned forward. "Okay, that's fine as far as it goes. Maybe Fixer will find something, maybe he won't, but even if he does we have to assume it's unlikely that there'll be a direct link to Sanderlin."

"So what d you suggest?"

"I think we need to provoke some action, cause some panic, that's when people start making mistakes ."

"True," said the Hunter, "but how do we do that?"

The Defender scratched his head. "Well, we know they think the Hunter has the Minnie Ha-Ha formula so let's give

Sanderlin the Hunter."

"Thanks very much."

The Defender smiled. "Not literally, but suppose Sanderlin thought Perry Cracken was meeting with the Americans to do a deal over the Minnie Ha-Ha formula, deliberately cutting out both him and the Russians. He wouldn't like that, would he?"

"No, but what's he going to do? He doesn't have a group of paid thugs he can send in."

"I know what I'd do," said the Armourer. "If it were me and I thought the American drugs gang was double-crossing me, I'd tip off the Russians. They'd have the manpower to intervene."

"Good thinking," said the Defender, "and if he thought he'd been betrayed he might well let some info slip to the CIA as well."

"What about our intelligence service."

The Housekeeper shook his head. "No, he wouldn't want any official British involvement. My guess is he'd want the others to fight it out between them leaving him free to pick up the pieces."

"So," said the Defender, "we plant the information about this double cross with Sanderlin and then we let the Americans know that Perry wants to contact them to arrange a deal but he insists he'll only meet them in that Hampshire house the Americans have."

"Why do we need the Americans?" asked the Python.

"We want to sow a bit of discord between allies. Once the info is planted we can sit back and watch who does what to whom."

"So how do we get the information to him and to the Americans?"

"Forseti can arrange that," said the Hunter.

"Going to be an interesting meeting," said the Armourer, "pity we can't actually take part."

The Hunter glanced at the Armourer and realised she wasn't joking. "Okay, let's get going. Housekeeper, will you draft something that Forseti can plant with Sanderlin?"

"Sure."

"And Fixer, you'll give Rackenford's pad the once over. If you find nothing there we'll have to think again."

"The only thing that bothers me," said the Defender, "is that we're using you as bait."

"What else can we do? Anyway, they don't know who I am."

The Python took a last bite of his scone, licked his fingers and said, "I've been thinking …"

Five pairs of eyes turned and looked at him and he went on. "You said that Cracken has parked this drug information on an encrypted server which only he can access."

"That's right, but he's told them I can too."

"Which you can't. But you could do, after a fashion."

"How d'you mean?" asked the Armourer.

"Well, I could set up an encrypted cloud storage area with various layers. We could invent some kind of formula, break it into sections so that each layer is accessed a section at a time. Then if we were ever up against it we could give them the first access code, then the second one and so on."

"How would that help?" asked the Housekeeper.

The Python spread his hands wide. "In the long term it wouldn't, but it might buy us some time. Worth doing, you think?"

"Definitely," said the Hunter, "set it up?"

When the meeting came to an end the Fixer announced that he was going to rent a pair of skates and give the ice rink a go.

"I've spent a lot of my life skating on thin ice," he explained, "thought I'd try some thick ice for a change."

MUSWELL HILL

THE FOLLOWING MORNING there was a ring at the Hunter's doorbell and she found the Armourer and the Defender on the doorstep.

"We need to talk to you," said the Armourer.

"Well, in that case you'd better come in."

The Defender came straight to the point.

"We're not happy about the position you're in. You've been made a target and these guys don't mess around."

"Name of the game."

"Sure, but you don't have to face it alone. You're going to have some company for a while, twenty-four-seven."

"You're planning to move in with me?"

"We'll take it in turns, but, yes."

"Do I have a say in this?"

"Nope."

The Armourer smiled. "I've got the first shift. I've got my bag in the car and I did some shopping on the way here."

The Hunter looked from one to the other of them. "You're a conniving pair of buggers," she said, "but thank you."

The Armourer and the Defender nodded. Their intentions were good, their idea was sound. The trouble was they had chosen to protect the wrong person.

HAMPSTEAD

IN THE WEEK that followed, Python set up his counterfeit formula and gave them all the access codes to the encrypted site.

The Armourer and the Defender made sure the Hunter was never left alone and, to her surprise, the Defender turned out to be a very good cook.

The Hunter set up a meeting with Forseti, gave him the text of the message they had concocted and Forseti said he'd make sure it reached Sanderlin and somehow also pass it on to the Americans. Unseen by Forseti, the Defender, the Armourer and the Housekeeper formed a protective barrier around their meeting place.

The Fixer visited a safe deposit box in a bank in Sheffield and withdrew a small attaché case which contained his old housebreaking tools. He also did a recce of Rackenford's house in Hampstead and laid his plans. By the end of the week he was ready to go.

The Fixer made his entry into Rackenford's house through the back door at 2.00 in the morning. The burglar alarm was a piece of cake.

He passed through the kitchen and paused in the hall to listen. Everything was silent so he began to explore. The first door on the left led into a large room, clearly a living room with a dining annex off to one side. As a wink to the Defender, he had a look at the mantelpiece but the only photo there was a framed picture of a 1934 BMW 303 Sport Roadster with

Rackenford standing beside it, his hand caressing the bonnet. The Fixer knew nothing about classic cars but the caption at the bottom of the photo said *1934 BMW 303 Sport Roadster*, which didn't leave much room for doubt. Even so he carefully took the back off the frame but there was nothing there.

There was a single shelf of books which he flicked through but there was nothing inside them. The only cupboard held glasses and crockery. Nothing down the back of the sofa or chairs and the floor was polished wood so no carpets to hide things under.

He moved across the hallway into a room which was clearly a study where the most prominent piece of furniture was a large antique desk. All the drawers were locked but that didn't delay him for long. He quickly skimmed through the contents but there was nothing there remotely like a formula. However, the Fixer knew a lot about old desks so he fiddled around at the back of the drawers then suddenly a hidden compartment slid open and inside he found a sheet of paper.

At first he thought he'd found one of the formulas. The paper had a series of rectangles and inside each one an apparently random selection of letters and figures. The Fixer had no idea what any of this meant, but it didn't look anything like the scribble that the Hunter had shown him. However, he reasoned if it had been hidden away it must be important so he took a photo of it on his phone and emailed it to the Hunter and the Python. Then, as a precaution, he deleted the photo from his phone, replaced the paper in the hidden drawer and closed it up.

The desk offered nothing else of interest so he explored the rest of the room. It didn't take him long to find the safe. It was behind a fire screen in what had once been an ornate fireplace. He had a bit of a struggle with it but eventually got it open only to find it was empty. There was no other obvious hiding place in that room so he moved back to the hall.

He thought briefly about going through the kitchen in detail but he found the idea of poking around in sugar canisters or tins of cocoa looking for a secret formula rather depressing so he decided to try the bedrooms first.

He moved silently up the stairs to the landing where he was faced with three doors and another flight of stairs which led on upwards. He chose a door at random, eased it open and cautiously stepped inside.

The caution was unnecessary. The body lying on the floor would never pose a threat to anyone again. In spite of the terrible injuries across his face the Fixer recognised Damian Rackenford immediately. He was naked and lying in a large pool of blood. There were numerous knife marks all across his body but the most horrifying thing was the severed arm lying neatly by his side.

With an effort, the Fixer controlled the feeling of nausea that rose in his throat. He backed out the room and, although he'd been wearing gloves all the time, carefully wiped the door handle. He no longer cared if the formula was hidden in this house or not. He wanted out of there.

He let himself cautiously out of the back door and clambered back over the fence at the end of the garden but as his feet touched the ground the other side, he was slammed back against the wall and he felt a gun against his head. Then an American voice said:

"Well, howdy, Hunter, nice to meet you."

MUSWELL HILL

WHEN THE ARMOURER arrived at the Muswell Hill flat to relieve the Defender she walked straight into a problem.

"We think Fixer may have gone missing."

"Why?"

"He should have reported in by now. He'd planned to be out of Rackenford's place long before dawn."

"And no word?"

"Nothing, and his phone is dead, not even any voicemail."

"When did you last hear from him?"

"The middle of the night. He emailed me with some stuff he'd found in a hidden drawer in Rackenford's desk."

"The formula?"

"No. No idea what it is. Looked complete gibberish to me. Presumably some kind of code. He sent it to Python too."

"Didn't Cracken give you something like that? Something he got from Beckford?"

"He did. That was gibberish too. Let's hope Python can make some sense of it all."

"Let's try Fixer again."

The Hunter accessed the encrypted SIM card on her phone, and pressed the contact name. Nothing.

"Something's happened. We need to find him."

She punched another number and when the Python answered she told him what was going on and asked him to try and trace the Fixer's phone.

HANCOCK HOUSE

THE FIXER OPENED his eyes cautiously. His head hurt like hell but he wasn't aware of any other injury, except he could not move. He was very firmly tied to what seemed to be a large wooden chair. His legs were strapped to the chair's legs. His arms were also strapped down and he was held firmly round the waist by a belt.

He tried to move but it was a very heavy chair and it wouldn't budge. He looked around him. The room seemed to have stone walls, no windows, just dim light from a bulb hanging from the ceiling. Two of the walls were lined with racks and there was a large wooden door in another wall. After a moment he realised he was in an old wine cellar.

As his mind cleared, the events of the night before came back to him. For once he had been extremely careless. He remembered the gun at his head, then being hustled towards a car and he remembered breaking free and making a bid for escape before something heavy hit him on the back of the head.

He tested his bonds again but there was no give anywhere. There was no point in wasting his strength so he tried to relax. Was there anyone around, he wondered, or had he just been left here to die. He decided to try and find out.

He shouted, "Hallo, anybody there?"

At first there was no response so he shouted again. Then he heard the heavy creak of a door and a man of about fifty dressed in a smart suit, white shirt with neat tie came in.

"So, you're awake." The voice was American, he thought from the East coast somewhere but he couldn't be sure. The Fixer decided to try the innocence card.

"What the hell's going on? Who are you and why am I tied up like this?"

The man smiled. It wasn't a nice smile. "It won't wash, Hunter," he said. "Guess you're busted."

"My name's not Hunter."

"Sure, but your real name don't matter. You are the Hunter. You and your guys have caused us a lot of grief."

"What the hell you on about?"

"Cut the bullshit. We've wanted to meet you for some while."

The Fixer realised the time for bluffing was over and he might as well go onto the attack.

"Did Senator Beckford send you?"

The man was clearly surprised. "How do you know about the Senator?"

"Oh, get real, sunshine, the world and his wife knows about him. The CIA, the FBI, the British, the Russians. Even the Chinese have got a dossier on the Senator."

"How would you know that?"

"I've seen it, "said the Fixer, always a fluent liar, "in fact we've been working very closely with the Chinese. I reckon your Senator's days are numbered. The Chinese want his business and what the Chinese want, they usually get."

"You're bluffing."

"You'll find out."

The man recovered himself. "Well, whatever, it'll be too late for you, Hunter. Maybe we can use you to cut a deal. There's a lot of people want what you know."

"And what is it I know?"

"You know I know what you know."

"Hey, that's quite good. Like tongue twisters, do you?"

The man regarded him for a moment then said, "There's a couple of reasons why we're pleased to have you as our … guest. We want information and we want revenge."

"Why revenge? It's pointless, hard to achieve and gains you bugger all."

"Listen, buster. You bastards have caused us a real mess of problems, you've killed some of our guys, damaged our business, upset our partners and for what? What have any of you got out of this … this … interference?"

The Fixer treated him to an innocent smile. "Satisfaction, perhaps."

"You won't be laughing soon. Life's going to get very unpleasant for you, Hunter. Worse than you could ever imagine. And that's the bit I enjoy."

His eyes glinted, obviously savouring the thought. "You know, I'd be kind of interested to know what you reckon would be the worst possible thing that could happen to you?"

The Fixer thought for a minute then said, "The worst possible thing?"

"Yeah."

"Well, that would have to be when your finger goes through the lavatory paper when you're cleaning yourself up."

There was a long pause, then the man said, "I've never appreciated British humour."

"I reckon you could drop the word 'British' from that sentence, chum, and it'd still be bang on the nail."

"Okay, smart guy, here's the deal. You tell us what we want to know and you will die quickly."

"And if I don't?"

"Then you will die slowly and painfully."

"I presume the 'die' bit isn't negotiable."

"Nope."

309

"Not much of a deal then, is it?"

"It's the best on offer."

"Okay … What d'you want to know?"

"We have the formula for the SD77 hypnosis drug and we also have the Mayoquoid formula. Now we want to know how to combine the two. We know that bastard Cracken gave you the details of that process."

"I think you're bluffing, pal. You don't have both formulas. You may have one of them but I reckon you were looking for the other in Rackenford's place."

"How d'you know we didn't find it?"

"If you had you'd've been out of there like shit off a shovel, not hanging around to see who else came looking."

"Okay, maybe, we don't have the Mayoquoid formula yet but it's only a matter of time. Then all we'll need is the combination process and that's where you're going to help us."

"Don't look at me. I haven't got it."

"But you know where it is."

"Maybe."

"I suggest you turn 'maybe' into 'yes' if you know what's good for you."

"What'd be good for me is to stay alive but if that's not an option why should I bother?"

"There are ways and ways of dying, Hunter, and we have some very imaginative ones."

"I bet you do. I saw what remained of Rackenford."

"Stupid limey. Refused to cooperate, even after considerable persuasion."

"Maybe he didn't have what you wanted."

"He was the Brit's poodle and we're meant to be working with the Brit so if he had the other formula he only had to say so. Anyway, don't matter, it was fun working him over."

The man's tone was cold and matter of fact. The Fixer swallowed. "Okay, you want the combination process, what else?"

"We want Perry Cracken. Revenge is sweet, Hunter, whatever you may think."

"Cracken? Sorry, no idea. When I last heard he was somewhere in Europe but I guess that's not much help."

"No, it isn't." The man eyed the Fixer thoughtfully for a moment. "Okay, moving on, we want Frank Hoskins released. We know you guys kidnapped him illegally."

In spite of the situation the Fixer had to smile. "Illegally. I like that."

"You will set Hoskins free and deliver him to the American embassy."

"No can do, chum. We don't have him. We handed him over to the British authorities."

"That's a lie. The embassy made enquiries and we have an information source in your government. There's no record of his capture."

"Don't suppose there is. Do you Yanks publish a list of people held in Guantanamo Bay?"

There was a long pause and then the man said, "That's bullshit. The Brits don't do stuff like that."

"Oh, yes, they do. But our Guantanamo is a lot colder than yours."

"I think you're bluffing but we'll park that for the moment. Here's an easier one. I want the names of the rest of your team and where to find them."

"Now why's that? So you can offer them life membership in a Country Club in Washington?"

The man just smiled. Not a nice smile.

"Okay. Mr Burke, I'll give your requests some thought."

There was a long silence. Then the man said, "How do

311

you know my name?"

"You're not very clued up, are you? You're as well-known as Senator Beckford. You're employed at the Pentagon, that's your public face, but you also run a number of nefarious activities on behalf of the senator, not the least being the drugs ring with Hoskins."

"How many people know this?"

"Enough."

There was a long silence and then Burke said very gently. "I will give you one hour to think about my demands, Hunter. If you don't choose to co-operate then the process to kill you slowly and painfully will begin."

In spite of his bravado the Fixer felt far from confident. He knew the real Hunter and the team would be moving heaven and earth to find him and he had to hang on as long as possible to give them a chance.

MUSWELL HILL

THE HOUSEKEEPER HAD joined the others at the Muswell Hill flat when the Python called from Cambridge.

"I've got him, or at least I've got the location of his phone."

"Where is he?"

"Hampshire, not far from Stockbridge."

"Hampshire?" said the Defender "Oh, hell, what's the betting he's in the Senator's house."

They looked at each other.

"Well, that complicates things," said the Housekeeper, "we've just set that place up for a serious confrontation. If Fixer is there he could get caught in the crossfire."

"Worse than that," said the Hunter, "we know that house is used by that Burke guy and Fixer says he's a real sadist. Don't like thinking of Fixer in his hands."

"Then we'd better get to him pretty sharpish," said the Armourer. "Come on. Let's get cracking."

The Python had another thought. "I could monitor Fixer's phone in case anyone tries to access that Cloud we set up."

"Good idea. Stay in touch."

HANCOCK HOUSE

AN HOUR LATER the door to the wine cellar creaked open again and Burke came in. "Well, Hunter, had time to consider?"

The Fixer drew a breath. "Bring me Sanderlin. I'll pass on the access information to him, but not to you. You can sit in, if you like, if he'll let you."

There was a long pause then Burke said, "I don't know anyone called Sanderlin."

"Bullshit. He's the Brit you were talking about, your inside man at the top of the British establishment. He's the guy Rackenford was working for."

"You have a lot of dangerous knowledge, Hunter."

"Bring Sanderlin here. I know where the combined formula is stored but I haven't tried to access it so I don't know if it will work. I need Sanderlin to do it."

"What d'you mean, you can't access it? Where is it?"

"It's in an encrypted vault on the Cloud. Cracken reckoned it would be safe there, no bit of paper to steal or get lost, just electronic access when it was needed. He made Sanderlin the key."

"What sort of key?"

"There is a piece of personal information about Sanderlin that is needed to unlock access. And don't look at me, I know the question, but not the answer."

"So you're saying that you know enough, but not too much? How convenient."

"Sure, but as your Founding Father, Benny Franklin, said, *'An investment in knowledge always pays the best interest'.*"

"I see. Well, if you want quotations how about Shakespeare, *'A little knowledge is a dangerous thing'.*"

"Good try. The actual quote is *'A little learning is a dangerous thing'*, and it was Alexander Pope not Shakespeare, but, hey, we'll let that pass."

Burke whipped out a long knife from a sheath on his belt and, stepping forwards, held it against the Fixer's neck.

"I would really like to kill you now."

"I'm sure you would, but then you'd lose all chance of getting hold of that formula, wouldn't you."

There was a pause, then Burke lowered the knife. "We seem to have reached an impasse."

"Easily solved. Just get Sanderlin here. Then you can cut me off at the impasse, as you might say."

"I do not find you funny."

"You're not the first to say that," said the Fixer sadly, "and one tries so hard."

Burke slid the knife back into its sheath and turned to the door. "I'll see what I can do. See you later. Don't go anywhere, will you."

IT WAS NEARLY THREE hours before Burke returned, this time accompanied by two men carrying a pile of equipment. It had not been a pleasant three hours for the Fixer but he managed to present a stoical face to the man in front of him.

"Do come in. Sanderlin on his way, is he?"

Burke gave his snake-oil salesman smile. "Sorry to disappoint you, Hunter, but Mister Sanderlin will not be joining us. As it happens we no longer need him."

"Found your missing formula, have you?"

"Well, I guess so. I have some good news, maybe more

315

for me than you. I gave your cell phone to some of our techie guys and they've found the access code to a very interesting looking cloud storage area. They're working on it now."

The Fixer let his face fall as though in disappointment but behind the mask he was blessing the foresight and the technical skill of the Python.

"Once we've broken into that you'll be expendable, but we still want to know the names of the rest of your team."

"Go to hell."

"Oh, and I have some more bad news for you." Burke was smiling broadly so it was fairly clear the 'bad' bit didn't apply to himself.

"Don't tell me, *'Moronic American'* came in last in the 3.30 at Newmarket."

"Always the comic, Hunter, well, see if this makes you laugh." He left a dramatic pause and then said, "We've just heard your friend, Perry Cracken, is dead."

As the Fixer had never met Perry Cracken he wasn't too deeply disturbed by the news, though he thought the Hunter might be. Aloud he said, "So he didn't take kindly to your persuasion techniques either. What did you do to him?"

Burke's face opened wide in innocence. "We did nothing. His car went off the road somewhere in the Alps."

"So you got your revenge after all."

"Sadly, no, it really was an accident. Pity, I'd like to have got hold of him and watched him suffer. But hey, I don't suppose he enjoyed plummeting off a sheer drop down a mountain. The car caught fire when it hit the bottom, by the way, so maybe I can feel satisfied after all."

"You're a sadistic bastard, aren't you?"

"You flatter me. Now we have a special little surprise prepared for you. Revenge is sweet, as I've mentioned before."

The Fixer stayed silent.

"Let me explain what's going to happen while these guys are setting up the stuff. See this large candle? It burns down quite slowly and we'll attach a slow fuse about halfway down, the sort of fuse they used for setting off canons in the old days. Eventually the candle flame will set light to the fuse which will then begin to burn along its length. The burn time is about ten minutes and when the fuse gets to the end it sets a small oil lamp alight. This lamp heats a strip of metal which will eventually bend in the heat and make contact with another metal strip to complete an electrical circuit."

While Burke was speaking one of the men was setting up the fuses while the other was connecting a long hose to the edge of the kitchen sink.

"Before all this begins we'll soak your legs with petrol which will add a little excitement. The electrical connection will start an electric pump which will pump water from the sink into that pipe. The sink of course will be full of water with the tap left running so it's constantly replenished. Oh, I forgot to mention, the end of that pipe will be taped into your mouth so once the pump starts you will slowly drown from the inside, unless of course the candle has set light to the petrol by then. Death by drowning or fire who can guess which?"

By now the Fixer was terrified but with a huge effort of will he managed to keep his face impassive.

"Ingenious, eh. I do so enjoy watching prolonged agony. It's great fun – for me that is, probably less so for you."

Behind him the two men were methodically going about their preparations.

The Fixer decided that if he was going down, then he'd go down in style. "You must have had a very sad childhood. Did your mother have an affair with an alligator, is that where you came from?"

317

He could see the hatred on Burke's face but the man's smile did not waver. The Fixer had never really understood the phrase 'he spoke through gritted teeth' but he was now being presented with a practical example.

"It's time to choose, Hunter. Give me the names of the rest of your team and I'll kill you cleanly."

"Okay, if you insist. Get your pencil ready. The names are Doc, Grumpy, Happy, Sleepy, Dopey, Bashful and Sneezy."

There was a long pause and then Burke's horrible smile became even wider.

"You just can't resist it, can you? Well, buddy, we'll see if you're still laughing when that candle begins to burn."

He turned to the two men. "Everything ready?"

"Sure, boss. Light the candle and the whole caboodle kicks into action."

"Great. So get him strapped into the hose."

The men approached the Fixer who tried to struggle but he was tied too tightly. One of the men forced his mouth open, the other inserted the end of the hose through his teeth. While he held it in place the other one taped it down onto the Fixer's mouth and strapped it right round the back of his head.

"Make sure the nose is clear," said Burke, "he must be able to breathe." He smiled at the Fixer. "We won't do the petrol yet, this is just by way of a rehearsal, Hunter. I want you to experience the maximum misery possible, much worse than weak bathroom tissue."

The Fixer glared at him.

"Once my guys have broken your little code and we've got the combination formula, we'll do this again only then we'll take it to the wire."

The men finished their work and Burke waved them towards the door. "Right, you can get out. Tell them I don't want any interruptions while I play with my little toy." And Burke gently patted the Fixer's head.

The door closed behind them and Burke regarded the Fixer thoughtfully. "You puzzle me, Hunter. I can't figure out what drives you. Guess it must be the dough, usually is, but somehow that don't feel quite right here."

Not surprisingly the Fixer said nothing. A mouth taped up with a hose between the teeth is not a great aid to conversation.

"Well, I guess it's not important any more. Once my tech team have cracked that access code we'll have everything we need."

He walked over to the candle and took out a cigarette lighter.

"You know, the best thing about killing a guy this way is the time it takes. The slow burn of the candle, the slow burn of the fuse and all the time the guy is sitting there, helpless, watching death creep inevitably towards him. I can't tell you how much pleasure it gives me to watch that."

He flicked the lighter, held the flame out towards the candle and watched it begin to burn.

"I've been looking forward to this all day. I never reckoned you'd play ball, British stiff upper lip and all that, but I did kind of think your guys might have tried to find you. Guess they're not up to the job, eh?"

He was interrupted by the creak of the door opening and Burke swung round angrily. "I said no interruptions. What the hell is it?"

"Not so much what, as who." Standing in the doorway was a woman who smiled gently as she stepped further into the room.

"Who the hell are you?"

"They call me The Hunter."

"You're crazy, this is the Hunter."

"Not so, but he is a valuable member of my team so I've come to collect him."

Burke laughed out loud. "You can't be the Hunter. You're a woman."

"That's a non sequitur."

"Call it what you like, you stupid bitch. You alone?"

"Of course." And she held her hands out wide to show she was unarmed.

"Then you're even dumber than most Brits." He took a step towards her and produced the long knife from his belt. "I think there's a bit more fun to be had here. You can watch your buddy die and then we can arrange something similar for you. What d'you say to that?"

"I think you've been reading too many trashy thrillers."

"Okay, bitch, how would you kill a guy?"

"Like this." As she spoke another figure appeared behind her, fired a single shot and Burke fell to the floor. The Hunter came forward and stepped over his dead body. "So much quicker, you see, and far more effective. No fancy bits and pieces to go wrong. Oh, I lied by the way. I'm not alone."

Behind her the Armourer came into the room. The Hunter went straight over to the Fixer, snuffed out the candle then began untying him. As the hose came out of his mouth he choked and the Armourer went across to the sink and fetched a glass of water.

He took a long drink then said, "You don't know how glad I am to see you."

"I can guess."

"Where are the others?"

"Defender's keeping guard at the top of the cellar steps, Housekeeper's keeping watch outside. Python's not with us but he's the one who found you. He'd apparently installed a tracker app in all our phones."

"That guy's brilliant. His decoy idea of Cracken's cloud definitely bought me time."

"I presume this is Burke. Did he tell you if he's got the formulas?"

The Fixer stood up, swaying a little as life came back into his stiff limbs. "Not sure. I think he's got one of them and he implied Sanderlin had the other."

The Hunter knelt down beside Burke's body and went rapidly through his pockets. "Nothing here, just his wallet. We'll keep that – something for the Python to nose through – but let's get rid of him."

"Burn him. There's some petrol in that container over there that was intended for me."

The Armourer, ever practical, lugged Burke's body over to the petrol container and draped him across it. She glanced around, saw some of the fuse hose on the floor, cut off a short length and tucked the end of it under Burke's body. She stood back to admire her work and nodded to herself in satisfaction.

The Fixer looked around him. "Where exactly are we, by the way?"

"This is Hancock House. The old manor house, technically owned by the American embassy, you remember, Cracken told us about it."

She broke off as the Defender appeared in the doorway. "We've got to get moving. There's a lot of activity in the main hall and Housekeeper's just texted to say there are various groups of people arriving outside. I reckon this could be the confrontation we'd planned but we didn't plan to be part of it. We need to get out."

The Armourer picked up Burke's lighter from the floor and lit the end of the fuse. Then they left the wine cellar, the Defender leading the way. The Hunter was helping the Fixer who was still a bit shaky.

They caught up with the Defender as he was eying a narrow flight of wooden stairs. Elsewhere in the house there was a muffled crash and the sound of voices.

The Defender said quietly, "The stairs at the end of this passage lead up to the main house. Don't think we want to go that way. Let's try these." And he pointed to a narrow set of steps winding up into the dark.

A COUNTRY LANE

THE HOUSEKEEPER WAS BALANCING in the branches of an oak tree almost directly opposite the gate to Hancock House. His knees were aching and there was a sharp twig digging into the small of his back.

I'm getting too old for these capers, he thought, *I don't bend like I used to.*

It had been very quiet after the Hunter, the Armourer and the Defender had headed into the grounds. It was almost dark by now but he had a set of night glasses with him and a few minutes ago he'd seen two large cars appear further down the lane. They stopped and half a dozen men got out and walked purposefully towards the house, all carrying weapons. That was when he sent the text to the Defender.

Five minutes later he saw a people carrier approaching from the other direction. That also stopped short of the gates and another group of men emerged. He sent another text.

There was obviously serious trouble brewing inside Hancock House.

After a moment's thought he climbed down from the tree, checked his gun was safe in its shoulder holster, then avoiding the gate, climbed the wall and staying in the shadows headed towards the house so he would be available for backup if he was required.

He was pretty sure he would be.

THE FIREFIGHT

THE BACK STEPS led them up into the kitchen area where they paused briefly. They could hear a murmur of voices the other side of a green baize door, so the Defender silently indicated another staircase heading upwards.

This took them into a passage which they followed to a door at the end. The Defender eased it open and they found themselves on a gallery that ran around two sides of the main hall. Cautiously, he peered over the balustrade.

Below them, in the hall, were several men dressed in casual jeans and roll necks. There were several guns in evidence and a heated discussion was going on with a lot of angry arm waving.

Suddenly the main door to the hall burst open and another group of men poured in, all cradling semi-automatic weapons in their arms. One of them, clearly an American, yelled, "Don't anybody move."

Even as the home team, as it were, swung round to face this threat, yet another group appeared at the opposite end of the hall, also carrying a ferocious set of weapons. Their leader yelled, "Seychas vse na polu", but as the Hunter was the only one to know it meant "Everyone on the floor, now", it was not surprising that the command was not obeyed.

The home team had used the distraction of the Russians' arrival to grab their own weapons so now there was a triangular stand-off, none of them knowing which of the other groups posed the biggest threat.

"Time we were out of here," muttered the Defender but suddenly they became aware of the smell of smoke and saw flames licking under one of the doors. At that moment another man appeared in the doorway from the kitchen and yelled: "Fire!"

He clearly meant this as a warning that the house was alight but the three groups involved in the stand-off took him literally. There was a burst of gunfire from all sides and then the smoke was spreading and people were running and falling all over the place.

"Shit," said the Defender, "we need to go back."

They turned to do so, the Hunter in the lead, but then suddenly there was a man in front of them holding a very large handgun.

"Drop your weapons. No one's going anywhere."

"Oh, goodness gracious me," said the Hunter theatrically, "what kind of weapon do you call that?"

"Colt Python, 357 Magnum calibre revolver," muttered the Armourer automatically.

The man switched his gaze to the Armourer and in that moment the Hunter acted. She leapt forward, grabbed the man's gun arm and forced it upwards. The revolver went off, severely reducing the quality of the carved ceiling rose directly above. In the same movement she pulled the man towards her, swung him around, then picked him up bodily and threw him over the gallery balustrade.

The Defender smiled faintly but the Fixer watched open-mouthed. "Remind me never to ask you for a date."

There was the sound of footsteps on the back stairs so the Armourer edged round the Hunter, slammed the gallery door shut and rammed home the bolts.

"That's torn it," said the Defender. He glanced down into the hall. "This won't be fun but we're going to have to make a run for it. Okay, we'll go straight down that main staircase, then split up and head for the nearest exit. Keep your head down and we'll re-group in the garden."

He let the way towards the stairs with the Armourer following him but at that moment one of the Russians glanced up and saw them. "Opasnost!" he yelled and fired a spray of bullets at them. His yell had given them time throw themselves flat, all except the Armourer who coolly put two bullets into the Russian's forehead.

"Danger's about right," muttered the Hunter as she ran down the stairs after the others.

Then they were down on the ground floor with carnage all about them. The Fixer was halfway across the room when he was hit by a flying chair which knocked him to the ground. He heard a crack as his elbow hit the floor then someone grabbed him and hauled him upright. He felt dizzy but he recognised the Housekeeper who was dragging him towards an open window.

"Out you go," and the Housekeeper picked him up bodily and threw him through the window. He screamed as he landed on his injured arm but then the Housekeeper was beside him, helping him to his feet and half dragging him towards a line of trees.

Back in the room the Defender had a stranglehold round one of the Russians and was using him as a shield as he headed for the door. The Hunter started to follow but suddenly there was another man in her path, his gun pointing straight at her.

She leapt forward, grabbed the gun and used it to pull him towards her. He was caught by surprise but before he could react she spun him round and applied a chin lock. She heard a click as his neck broke so she dropped him, grabbed his weapon and headed after the Defender.

She saw another man fire at the Defender but he hit the

Russian. The man fired again but this time his gun clicked on an empty magazine. Then he was spinning away, running fast but with the Defender hard on his heels. She heard someone screaming in Russian and a bullet thudded into the wall beside her. As she dropped to the floor, another man burst through the door so she came out of her roll and fired. He fell, but then a shape appeared at a window and as she got to her feet she saw something thrown into the room.

Shit, that's a grenade, she thought but at that moment something hit her in the shoulder and she fell down again. The next moment the grenade went off and she was sent flying across the room as the ceiling came down in a pile of debris.

She must have briefly lost consciousness but clearly not for long. She was dimly aware of another, louder explosion and the next thing she knew she was being dragged across the room by one leg. She tried to reach her gun but it had disappeared but then she heard the Defender say. "We've got to get out. The place is on fire," and she realised that it was him who was dragging her.

"I'm okay," but she wasn't. Her knees were weak and when she tried to stand she fell down again. "You go on, I'll be fine."

"Bollocks." The Defender dragged her up and half carried her as they staggered towards the aperture where the door had been. Somehow they made it out into the open air. It was dark by now but the garden was lit by the rapidly spreading fire.

She tried to say "Put me down. They'll see us in the light of the flames ..." but the words would not come. Then suddenly the Armourer was there, a semi-automatic rifle in her arms.

She said, "Get her clear. I'll take care of this."

The last thing she heard before she lost consciousness again was the clatter of automatic fire and distant screams.

TIME TO REGROUP

THE HOUSEKEEPER REACHED the wall that surrounded the garden and with some difficulty helped the Fixer over it. By now the Fixer was in a lot of pain but they managed to make their way to where their vehicle had been hidden down a track. A few moments later the Defender arrived, out of breath but with the Hunter in his arms. She was just starting to regain consciousness.

"Is she hurt?"

"Yup. Got a bullet in her shoulder. And her leg's bleeding too. I need some bandages now."

The Housekeeper dug into the boot of the car for their emergency kit. He found dressings and bandages and handed them to the Defender.

"Thanks, once we've stopped the bleeding we need to get her somewhere safe. Get all of us somewhere safe come to that. Any ideas?"

"No, I think we need some back-up."

The Hunter was struggling to speak but she managed to say, "Call Forseti, use my phone."

The Defender took the Hunter's phone, handed it to the Housekeeper then began wrapping a bandage round the Hunter's shoulder.

"How bad is it?"

"Could be worse. You stopped one in your shoulder and I think the bullet's still in there so we need to get it sorted. There's also a flesh wound on your leg but that's not serious."

The blood was still seeping through the shoulder bandage so the Defender strapped another dressing on top of that. He hoped that would do. They didn't carry a full hospital with them.

The Hunter struggled with the pain but managed to say, "Is everyone safe?"

The Defender glanced round and saw the Fixer lying on the ground. He bent over him. "Fixer, you hurt?"

"My arm. Think it's broken."

"No bleeding."

"No."

"Okay. Hang on."

He turned back to the Hunter. "Fixer's arm's broken but I think the rest of us are okay," but even as he spoke the Defender realised the Armourer was missing.

"Hang on, where's Armourer?"

"I'm here," and the Armourer emerged from the trees, a semi-automatic rifle cradled in her arms. "Well, that was a bit lively, wasn't it?"

The Defender gave a short laugh. "You could say that." Then he noticed that there was blood dripping from the Armourer's right hand. "Are you hurt?"

She glanced down at her hand. "This? No, not really. A silly little man tried to take my gun away, so I hit him."

The Housekeeper ended his phone conversation and came towards them. "Okay, Forseti's getting it all fixed. There's a safe house that the Firm uses just the other side of Winchester at New Arlesford. He's getting that open for us and organising a doctor as well."

The Defender tightened the last bandage round the Hunter's shoulder. "That should hold it. Right, let's get going."

DAMAGE LIMITATION

LESS THAN AN HOUR later the Hunter was tucked up in a warm bed with a doctor probing as gently as she could into the shoulder wound. The doctor was a woman and even through her pain, the Hunter appreciated the sensitivity of Forseti.

Downstairs the rest of the team was having a discussion. The Fixer sat to one side, his arm cradled in a rough sling. The Armourer had a bandage around her knuckles.

"We have to disappear," said the Armourer, "Hunter's in good hands now and I gather Forseti is on the way. We really don't need to meet him."

The Defender turned to the Housekeeper. "Can you take care of Fixer. He needs to have that arm fixed – if you'll pardon the pun – and that cut on his head could do with some attention."

"Sure. We'll get well clear of here and then find a Casualty department."

"Okay, guys, on your way."

There was a pause, then the Armourer said, "You coming too?"

"No, I'm not leaving Hunter. I'll catch up with you in the next day or two."

"But …"

The Defender touched the Armourer gently on the shoulder. "You've more than done your bit. This doesn't need both of us. I'll stay in touch. Okay?"

There was a long pause. The Armourer looked at him, then said, "Okay." She turned to the others. "Come on, let's get moving."

The Defender watched them go, then lay back in the chair and closed his eyes.

CODES IN CAMBRIDGE

SITTING IN HIS WORKSHOP in Cambridge, the Python was struggling to unravel the information the Fixer had found in Rackenford's desk. It was a series of letters and numbers laid out in eight separate blocks which on the surface had nothing in common with each other. When the Hunter first sent it to him, he'd welcomed the challenge. He was conscious he was the least physical member of the team but he knew that when it came to technology he was a match for anyone, so initially he'd approached this task with enthusiasm. However, by now he was getting very frustrated indeed.

He turned back to the sheet of paper that Perry Cracken had given the Hunter. He was working on the assumption that both these messages were linked to the various people in this international conspiracy but it was certainly no ordinary code, even if the two messages were actually using the same system.

He laid the messages side by side. The Rackenford material was laid out in eight separate blocks while the Beckford material was just one long block of letters and numbers, apparently divided up randomly. There was no obvious similarity between them and yet he could sense that they had something in common. He ran his finger over the Rackenford blocks as though their meaning could be picked up by touch. If Rackenford had valued this information enough to hide it away then it was clearly significant. Perhaps it wasn't a message, perhaps it was a coded clue to the code itself. Now there was a thought.

As well as his own highly developed skill, the Python had several technical apps – some of them legal – designed to unravel encrypted messages, but nothing was working.

He took a break, had a doughnut and a cup of tea, then sat down to think the whole thing through from the first principles. The Rackenford material had to be a list but for what purpose? A contact list maybe but why would that be needed amongst people who all knew each other? Then a thought struck him. The Hunter's team all knew each other too, but he had set up a 'below the radar' network through the second SIM card in each phone to allow safe and confidential communications. Suppose something like that was in operation here.

He selected another decryption tool and ran one set of letters and numbers. Nothing. Whatever coding they were using was either extremely sophisticated or … another thought struck him … it was so ancient that no one would think it was still in use.

The Python did not have a large library but he'd always been interested in the history of computing. It took him several hours but he finally found what he was looking for in a very detailed – and to most people as dull as ditch water – book about the history of computer programming at Bletchley Park back in the 1940s.

He looked at it in disbelief. They couldn't be using that, could they? He closed the encryption software, loaded a maths program, then took one of the Rackenford strings and fed it through. The result was exactly what he had guessed. Someone had used a very ancient mathematical technique to hide a modern encryption system. He mentally took his hat off to whoever had come up with that idea but now he had broken through the outer defence he knew he'd be able to break into the complete system. It would just take a bit of time.

He opened a new packet of doughnuts.

THE HUNTER'S DEATHBED

WHEN FORSETI ARRIVED at the safe house he was met by the resident caretakers, an ex-marine sergeant, and his wife.

"All's well, sir. You've just missed the doctor but the lady's been patched up. Everything seems to be under control."

"Thank you."

"There's just one thing."

"What's that?"

"The lady isn't alone."

As Forseti turned towards the house a tall man appeared in the doorway. For a moment they regarded each other. Then the man spoke.

"I guess you must be Forseti."

"And I imagine you're 'The Defender'."

"Indeed I am. Sorry to break cover, as it were, but there was no way I could leave her alone like this."

"I understand. How is she?"

"Bruised and battered. She took a bullet in the shoulder. The doctor's dealt with that. There was also a flesh wound on her leg but that's pretty minor."

"What happened?"

"Bunch of thugs working for that American senator captured one of our team. We traced him and went to get him back but unfortunately they were holding him at the place where we'd set up the confrontation operation."

Forsetti nodded.

"Then two other lots of baddies arrived and everything kicked off just as we had hoped it would. The only thing was, we hadn't intended to be part of it."

"But you were."

"We certainly were. It was quite a party."

"So I gather." Forseti thought back to the report he had seen before he left to come down here. The Hampshire police were going crazy. They had a number of dead bodies, some clearly foreign, lots more people injured and a house burned to the ground. They were starting a clean-up operation but soon they'd be looking for answers and Forseti was determined they wouldn't get them.

"Anyone else in your team hurt?"

"Not seriously. Couple of minor things. Fixer, that's the guy they captured, he's got a broken arm and a nasty scalp wound. They'd given him a pretty rough time."

"Where are the others now?"

"Gone."

"I understand. Now I need to see the Hunter." He anticipated the next question. "Alone first. But don't go away. We have to decide what happens next and you'll be involved in that."

"Fair enough. She's in the room on the right at the top of the stairs."

Lying in bed the Hunter heard a tap on the door and Forseti came into the room. He came across to the bed and peered down at her anxiously.

"Are you all right?"

"I think so. Not sure."

"You've been knocked about a bit but your ... erm ... colleague ... assures me you're fine."

"Feel responsible, do you?"

336

"Well, yes, of course."

"No need. We knew what we were taking on."

Forseti gave a half laugh and the Hunter looked up quickly.

"Let me guess, that's the kind of thing my father would have said."

"It's what he did say when I tried to persuade him not to go on that final job."

"You tried to stop him?"

"I did."

"Why?"

"I don't know. Instinct possibly. I was uneasy. Nothing definite, nothing certain. I was just …"

"Uneasy."

"Yes. I wished afterwards I'd been firmer."

"Was it your decision?"

"No, it wasn't, but …"

"There you are then. Not your fault." There was a pause, then she said, "Did you know where he was going?"

"Yes."

"Abroad?"

"Yes."

"Where?"

"It doesn't matter, not now."

"It matters to me."

"No, it doesn't. It's irrelevant. All you need know is he did a good job, as usual, and he managed to get the information back to us before he was …"

"Captured?"

"Shot. At least it was quick. If they'd taken him alive he'd have had a very nasty time."

The Hunter thought for a moment then she said, "You think he was betrayed, don't you?"

"It's possible, I don't know. But even if he was I've never

been able to decide if it was deliberate or just someone being careless."

The Hunter lay back on her pillow. "Ah, well. No need for you to feel guilty about me, but it was kind of you to come."

"Kind?" Forseti gave a grunt. "Well, maybe, but also practical. There's something we need to organise and organise now."

"Can't it wait?"

"No, it can't. But I think your Defender should be in on this. Can I ask him to come up?"

"Sure."

When the Defender joined them Forseti said, "Now listen carefully. There's going to be a lot of fallout from today's events so it's important we make our plans first."

"What plans?"

"What happens next. It's been mayhem today. I'm not sure exactly who's been doing what to who but—"

The Defender interrupted him. "I can tell you. This American guy, Burke, was the front guy for Senator Beckford, did all his dirty work. They got hold of the Fixer thinking he was the Hunter and tried to persuade him to give them the Minnie Ha-Ha combination process."

"Which he didn't do."

"He didn't have it."

"And Burke?"

"Killed, while we were rescuing Fixer. It was after that, when we were trying to get away, that we ran into the firefight. I tell you, it was like the Hampshire version of the O.K. Corral in there. Mayhem's putting it lightly."

"Hang on", said the Hunter, "What happened to Burke's wallet?"

"The Armourer has it. No formula in it, just a few more sheets of obscure jargon. She'll pass it on to Python."

338

Forseti said, "Do you know who else was involved in this firefight?"

"Not for certain. The people in the house were definitely the Senator's men. One of the new lot were definitely Russians, don't know about the second bunch, Americans I think but don't know who."

"They were CIA, which is going to be tricky when we start adding up the bodies."

"Sure, but I don't see what else we could have done."

"No." Forseti turned back to the Hunter. "Well, I think I need to take some responsibility for this. You asked me to let it slip to Sanderlin that Perry Cracken and the Americans were planning a meeting to do a private deal over Minnie Ha-Ha."

"Yes."

"So that's what I did. I thought it was a good plan. I thought the ripples from their confrontation would be interesting. What I didn't know is that it would turn out to be more of a tidal wave than ripples and that you and your team would be in the front line when they all met"

"Well, we shouldn't have been."

"No, but you were. When we originally planned for them to come after you I wasn't expecting anything like this."

"Nor was I."

"You were lucky today, but there are a lot of dead and damaged bodies lying around."

In spite of herself the Hunter gave a weak grin as she remembered the Armourer pushing past her with an automatic weapon in her hand.

"I don't have the full tally yet but we have at least one CIA man, three Russians and a collection of what I can only assume are Burke's American hitmen, all dead, to say nothing of the walking – or not walking – wounded."

The Defender spoke again. "There's one other thing. Fixer said that while he was a prisoner, Burke told him that Perry Cracken is dead."

"Oh, no …"

"I'm sorry, Hunter, but apparently his car went off the road in the Alps somewhere. There doesn't seem to be any doubt."

She lay there for a moment trying to absorb the news. Perry was dead. They had only spent one night together and she had never expected to repeat it. Even so, she still felt a strange sense of sadness.

"It's very regrettable, Hunter." Forseti laid a brief hand on her arm but then sat back. "But in a sense it makes our next move easier."

"How?"

"We need to regroup. Today's been bad, but the problems haven't gone away. Now, more than ever, you're a prime target. With Perry Cracken dead they'll come after you much harder, as far as they're concerned you're now the only route to this combination process."

"But I don't know how to access it."

"No, but they don't know that, so that's why you're going to die too."

"What?"

"Only as far as our friends are concerned. If they think you're dead they won't come after you."

"I see. However, I should warn you, if you're planning to smother me with a pillow then don't try it while he's around." And she nodded towards the Defender who grinned.

"Knowing you as I do, I wouldn't try it even if he wasn't around."

"So how do we work this?"

"I'll take care of the mis-information, but you need to

stand your team down. No one knows who they are. Not even me – well, apart from him of course ..." and he nodded back towards the Defender. "There's nothing more you can do at the moment anyway. You're the one in danger so you're the one who's going to be dead."

"I understand what you're saying but the job's not done. We haven't found either formula."

"Fixer said that Burke told him Sanderlin almost certainly has one of them," said the Defender."

"Did he? Well, in that case we need to carry on." She tried to sit up but Forseti laid a hand on her good shoulder and made her lie down again.

"No, you don't. If Perry Cracken is truly dead then the information about the combination process has died with him. Without that, the basic formulas are useless."

"But suppose Perry wasn't entirely honest with me. Suppose someone else does have access to the details of that process. What then?"

Forseti sat very still. Then he said, "In that case, my lady, the bright day is done and we are for the dark."

"And then there's Sanderlin. What about him? Does he go scot-free?"

"For the moment, yes. His plans are long term. Nothing's going to happen quickly."

The Hunter closed her eyes. "So this is the end?"

Forseti looked at her for a moment and then shook his head. "Oh, no, I don't think so." He glanced across at the Defender. "I think we all know this is a long way from being over. The threat hasn't gone away, merely been delayed. Your time will come again, Hunter, we just need to make sure you're alive when it does."

"What do you want me to do?"

"Die and disappear, in that order. Seriously, meet with

341

your team but be careful. Tell them to resume their normal lives, then you go to ground but stay alert. You will be needed again, I'm certain of it. It may be a month from now, it may be a year, but we all know the play's not over, this is just the interval."

And that was that ...

... until six months later when a couple of Russian hoods came to the Hunter's door looking for Perry Cracken.

PART 3

NOW

PICKING UP FROM THE CLAPHAM CARNAGE

IT WAS TIME to leave – or rather abandon – the Clapham house. They handcuffed the SIS men but left them on the living room floor. The Hunter knew that this place would be crawling with people before long so they could sort it all out.

She took a last look round then turned to the Defender. "I presume you came in a car."

"Yes."

"Then let's take yours. They might have details of mine."

"Fine but …"

"What?"

"Nice jumper. Impressive reindeer."

"Incongruous, isn't it."

"Sure, but you might want to change it before we go. Rudolph's just a bit conspicuous."

AN ANONYMOUS ROOM SOMEWHERE IN LONDON

A VERY ANGRY FORSETI didn't bother to knock, he just kicked the door open and went straight in. Odin looked up from his desk in feigned surprise.

"Well?"

"What the hell's going on? I've just learned the Hunter's been re-activated."

"So?"

"Why? What for?"

"To find Perry Cracken. It appears he isn't dead after all."

That brought Forseti up short. "How do you know?"

"Doesn't matter. I know, and if Cracken's alive that means—"

"— the Minnie Ha-Ha risk is back on the agenda."

"Exactly. You appreciate that if Cracken really is alive it's vital we get to him before any of the opposition do."

"But why involve the Hunter?"

"We had no choice. Cracken got in touch with us looking for a deal. Why after all this time I don't know, he wasn't very forthcoming."

"Even so."

"But he was cagey, very cagey. Wouldn't agree to meet us, it had to be the Hunter. He gave us a cryptic message to pass on. Made no sense to us so we sent a couple of our guys to ... tickle the Hunter's interest, you might say."

"You sent two people from the Firm after the Hunter?"

"In a manner of speaking. They thought they'd been sent to bring him in. In fact we wanted them to pass on this message."

"You idiot, she might have killed them."

"She?"

Forseti sighed. "Yes. The Hunter is a woman."

"A woman? Well, you might have told me."

"What purpose would that have served?"

"I don't like being kept in the dark."

"It's the world we work in. How did they know where to find the Hunter?"

Odin gave a thin smile. "Oh, you know, these things get around."

"You bastard. You realise you've put the Hunter's life in danger. There's a lot of people out there who'd like to see her dead. Until now they thought she was dead. If our people know where she is, then the others won't be far behind."

Odin's smile became even thinner. "They were in front of us, actually. We currently have two Russians, one dead, one wounded; two badly damaged CIA men; and two dead unidentified. Plus our two men who are unharmed but deeply embarrassed. I think we can safely say the Hunter can look after herself."

In spite of everything Forseti felt a moment of pride. "She's still fully functional then."

"It would appear so. Of course, the Hunter didn't operate alone, did she?"

"No."

"So do you think there's a chance she might re-activate that team?"

"Almost certainly and, regretfully, I think you may be right about Cracken. They were a formidable force and if anyone can find him – assuming he really is still alive – then I reckon they can."

"Good, well now the Hunter's flushed out into the open we won't lose him, sorry, her again. Before their … shall we say, unfortunate confrontation … our chaps put a tracking device on her vehicle. If she goes looking for Cracken then we'll be with her all the way."

Forseti kept his face impassive. To himself he thought, *Good luck with that. She wasn't born yesterday, chum.*

Odin was saying, "The question is, how co-operative will Cracken be when we get hold of him. We really need that formula."

"Why do we need it? Surely the best thing would be to destroy it."

"Destroy it? Why on earth would we do that? In the right hands it's a very powerful weapon."

Forseti had grave doubts about what constituted the 'right hands' but all he said was, "It's not something we would ever use, is it? I mean it's insane."

"No, no, of course not. It would be a deterrent, that's all, a deterrent. If the opposition knew we'd got it and could use it if their government's policies and ours didn't align …" he tailed off.

"Ah, yes, a deterrent, of course."

"So stay in touch with the Hunter, Forseti. I've put two teams onto watching that Clapham house. Her vehicle is still there so she won't be far away and when she makes a move they'll be on her tail."

RUSTINGTON

CONVERSATION IN THE CAR was minimal. The Hunter simply said, "Head out of London on the A24 and keep going." Then she lay back in her seat and closed her eyes.

Action again. Part of her welcomed it, part of her hoped they were still up to the work. They'd been inactive for over six months now and their final battle had taken a huge toll. Unconsciously she rubbed her left shoulder where she'd been shot in the firefight at Hancock House.

She began listing things that had to be done. She'd already sent the warning message to the team to stand by so the next thing was to talk to Forseti. Except … She had thought he was the only one who knew where she had been living but a whole bunch of baddies had managed to find her. Could she trust him?

Then a conversation she'd once had with him came back to her, the time when he had told her he had known her father. The only time he had used her real name.

"You can always trust me, Diana," he had said, "I will never betray you and I hope I will never let you down."

In her world, where 'trust' was rare, you had to make a judgement about people otherwise it would be impossible to operate. She trusted her team and she trusted Forseti. There was no other way forward.

Beyond that she had to find Perry and then … well, that was the difficult bit, what would happen when she found him?

They had left London behind and were approaching Horsham before she spoke again.

"We've been set up, haven't we?"

"Probably."

"For all that lot to find me they must have had a tip off."

"Some kind of tip off, yes, but from what you said back there, they weren't expecting the Hunter."

"No, they were all looking for Perry Cracken. Do you think it is possible he's still alive?"

"Well, if he is then a lot of shit could hit the fan."

"Yes." She paused. "I really thought he was dead, you know."

"A lot of people thought you were dead."

"But those guys from the Firm were looking for the Hunter, not Perry. They seemed to think I'd know where he was."

"And do you?"

"No, of course not."

"But you said there was some kind of message."

"Yes. Clearly meant nothing to them."

"But it did to you?"

"I think so."

"Then I'd say the situation's pretty clear. If Cracken is still alive the whole Minnie-Ha-Ha thing is back on the agenda. Lots of people want him and that formula, but no one knows where he is."

"So we're the last resort. Those last guys thought they were sent to bring me in, but they weren't. They were sent to wake us up and let us loose again."

"And no doubt we're going to oblige."

"Oh, yes, I think so."

"Fine, but where are we actually heading now?"

"Oh, yes, sorry. We're going to one of my safe houses.

Give us a chance to re-group, arrange a meeting with the others, get our breath back. It's been a busy morning."

At Findon they turned right through a valley in the South Downs and soon they were driving through Angmering and into Rustington. As they entered a world of endless bungalows the Defender glanced across at her.

"This doesn't seem a very likely place to have a safe house."

"That's why it's safe."

"Looks more like the Costa Geriatrica," he muttered.

They stopped outside a bungalow which looked exactly like all the others in the road. As they got out of the car, a man in the next garden cutting the lawn, called out, "Good afternoon, Mrs. Witherinshaw. How you doing?"

"Fine, thank you," called the Hunter and producing a key she opened the front door.

"Mrs Witherinshaw?"

She shrugged. "There's a coffee machine in the kitchen, coffee in the cupboard above. Get a pot going, would you while I turn the hot water on. I've not been here for a few weeks."

They drank their coffee sitting in a small conservatory overlooking the garden. Silence for a while, then the Hunter said, "So, as we're obviously back in business, we need to set up a team meeting."

"I'll give Fixer a call in a minute. Get him to arrange another insurance sales training day."

She smiled, remembering their first ever meeting as a team. "I think we were only an insurance company once, weren't we?"

"Probably. I rather lost track."

"Okay, so what else?"

The Defender thought for a moment. "Well, I need to get back to London. I'm going to need a change of clothes apart from anything else."

"Oh, I don't know. That tracksuit is quite chic really."

"The appeal might wear off after a couple of days. For both of us."

"Okay, how does this sound? Stay here tonight. I think we're safe for the moment but—"

"— best to be sure. Incidentally what you going to do about wheels?"

She smiled. "Spare car in the garage here. It's called planning."

The Defender grinned. "Okay, so when do you want to hold this meeting?"

"In about three days time. I need to talk to Forseti?"

"Can you trust him?"

"I have to," she said simply, "there's nowhere else to go."

RICHMOND PARK

THEY MET ON a bench near the Isabella Plantation. It was a dreich kind of day, low cloud with a hint of moisture in the air though it wasn't actually raining. Not far away a small group of fallow deer stood disconsolately under some dripping trees.

Forseti sat huddled in a large raincoat with the collar turned up. The weather seemed to reflect his mood.

Finally, he spoke. "I am so sorry."

"What for?"

"You were betrayed."

"Maybe, but not by you."

"Even so."

"Look, what's done, is done and if Perry really is still alive then we need to find him and find him quickly."

"Agreed. But how?"

"That message he sent, those two plonkers from the Firm thought it was rubbish. I don't."

"You know where he is?"

"I know where he's been and if I'm right then that's the place to start."

He nodded, then said, "I don't know who to trust anymore."

She winced, remembering her own train of thought.

An aircraft thundered overhead on its way into Heathrow. When the rumble had died away, Forseti said, "Don't you think it's interesting that your first callers were all looking for Cracken. It was only the Brits who were looking for the Hunter."

"Yes, they were obviously briefed, leaving aside the wrong sex bit – but the others were just following a rumour."

"Exactly, and that rumour must have been set running deliberately. The point is why."

"And who."

"Yes. That's the bit that bothers me."

"Could it be Sanderlin?"

"I doubt it very much. He has no reason to believe we know anything about him."

"You've not mentioned our suspicions about him to anyone else."

"I have not. Not even my own chain of command knows about this line of investigation. As things currently stand no one would believe me."

There was a pause. Then she said, "

"You once told me that Sanderlin's plans were long term, is that term getting shorter?"

"Almost certainly. As I said once before, you can't make a puppet out of your leader overnight but left alone I have no doubt the Sanderlin point of view will prevail. There won't be any opposition as no one will realise opposition is needed until it's too late."

"And you still think that's his aim?"

"I do."

"But we still can't prove that he's a traitor?"

"We can't prove it, but there's very little doubt. We tried to unravel the flow of drugs money, both from the States and from Russia. We know where the trail begins and we're pretty sure some of the large amounts of funding to extreme groups come from that source, but if we're right, and Sanderlin's got access to the flow of drugs money, then the route it takes is still a mystery."

"So there's no conclusive proof?"

"None that would stand up in court."

"Does it have to stand up in court?"

"I'm starting to wonder, but that's a big step."

Briefly the sun came out. The deer moved slowly and sedately out of the cover of the trees and began cropping the grass. Forseti reached down into the bag at his feet and produced a flask.

"I made us some coffee."

"Great."

They drank in silence for a moment then Forseti said, "We seem to be back to the point we left six months go. The Minnie Ha-Ha formula has re-emerged and the Unholy Trinity is still active."

"Senator Beckford, the Russian Lazovsky and Sanderlin."

"Yes. If any of them manage to acquire Minnie Ha-Ha, then God help us all. Frankly, Hunter, I think those three men present a huge threat to our whole way of life. Their respective aims might be different but the effect on ordinary people worldwide would be catastrophic."

The Hunter thought for a moment. "You still think the Minnie Ha-Ha threat is a private enterprise one, not a government one."

"That's my view, yes."

"So if they were all, what shall we say, neutralised, then all this nonsense would end?"

"I believe it would. Those three are powerful forces but if you take away the engine, then the machine stops."

"Then that's what we have to do. Remove or neutralise Beckford, Lazovsky and Sanderlin and make sure that no one can ever access Minnie-Ha-Ha.

Forseti turned towards her and touched her arm. "Hunter,

this is all getting out of hand. We're a long way from your original brief and this is not an assignment I can give you."

She smiled and gently removed his hand. "I understand."

"It won't make any difference though, will it? You'll do what you want to do."

"No, we'll do what has to be done." She paused. "Let me ask you something. If my father were still alive and sitting here today, what would he do?"

There was a long, long silence. The sky darkened again and there were a few spots of rain.

Finally, Forseti sighed. "If your father were sitting here now, in this situation, I think he'd have said something like 'Well, I think it's time we went and got the bastards'."

"Fair enough. So is anyone else going to sort out this mess?"

"Not in the current climate. I think we're going to hell in a handcart."

"There you are then. So, I'm with Dad. It's time we went and got the bastards."

A flight of ring-necked parakeets squawked overhead looking as incongruous as ever in a south London setting.

"Just one thing …"

"Yes?"

"You once said to me that you were willing to kill, but not execute."

She was silent.

"I know it's tempting, Hunter, for the greater good and so on, but please think long and hard before you do anything like that. A straight assassination of any of these men could have the opposite effect. Sanderlin's death would no doubt delay things but wouldn't necessarily stop them. It might even give them a boost."

"Create a martyr, you mean."

"Yes."

She drained her coffee and watched the deer who were getting restless. Finally one of them began to move and the others followed. The herd instinct. She understood it but had never felt comfortable being part of it.

"Let's start with the basics. We need to find a way to publicly discredit Sanderlin."

Forseti said nothing and after a moment she went on. "It won't be easy and it'll be much harder in the case of Beckford and Lazovsky, especially Lazovsky. I'm not sure it's possible to discredit a Russian mafia chief."

Another plane roared overhead and broke her reverie.

"Needs a lot more thought, but first off we need to find Perry and discover what he's up to."

"And when you find him?"

"Don't know. I don't know what he wants or why he's got in touch again."

They sat in silence for a moment then Forseti said, "I could never stop your father from doing what he believed had to be done and I know I'm not going to stop you."

She smiled faintly.

"So I'm not going to say 'Be careful' because that would be silly. But I'll give you a word of warning. Beckford and Lazovsky are very dangerous people but don't ignore dangers nearer home."

She glanced at him sharply. "What makes you say that?"

"Instinct. Sometimes focusing on the obvious danger lets something less obvious slip under your guard."

His eyes met hers and after a moment she looked away. "I'll bear that in mind."

"Good. I wish it could be different but ..." Forseti fumbled in his overcoat pocket and produced a hip flash. "In the circumstances, let's give the coffee a boost and make a toast."

He poured two measures into the coffee cups and then raised his own. "Here's to the resurrected Hunter and may she have good hunting."

WISLEY RHS GARDENS

TWO DAYS LATER the Hunter's team assembled in the café at the RHS gardens at Wisley near Guildford. The first twenty minutes or so involved coffee, cake and some inconsequential chat which the Hunter encouraged, knowing it would help relax colleagues who hadn't seen each other for some time.

Once they'd settled down the Hunter summarised what had happened in the Clapham house. When she'd finished there was a short silence, then the Fixer said, "Well, you did have a busy morning, didn't you."

When the laughter had died down the Housekeeper said, "So you think we're being deliberately provoked to find Perry Cracken before anyone else does?"

"Yes."

"And you reckon the Firm are hoping to get to Cracken through you?"

"Looks that way?"

"What does Forseti have to say about this?"

"He feels we've been betrayed, but doesn't know who by."

There was a short silence as that idea sunk in, then the Python said, "Does anyone want that last doughnut?"

There were smiles all round the table and the Defender pushed the plate towards him. "All yours."

"So what's our first step?" asked the Armourer.

"The first step is to find Cracken. His message was '*The parakeets are still squawking but without any passion*'. I think he's referring to a small town on the north Spanish coast where Defender and I dropped him after our first encounter many years ago. And no comments about the passion bit, thank you."

The Defender smiled to himself. Aloud he said, "So that's where we'll start."

"Do we all go?" asked the Armourer.

"No, Just me and Defender. Don't know what we're going to find. May not be Cracken himself but if I'm right there'll be something there for us."

"I've been thinking," said the Fixer, "let's suppose you do find Cracken, talk some sense into him and destroy any access to this formula thingummy. Sweet, up to a point, but the main problem still remains, don't it?"

"Does it?" asked the Python.

The Housekeeper nodded. "Of course. We know that Sanderlin, the American senator and this Lazovsky guy all have their own power-seeking agendas. That danger's not going to go away. Minnie Ha-Ha would help them achieve their goals quicker but even without it people like that will always be a threat."

"Okay," said the Python, "but what can we do about it?"

The Hunter said nothing but there was the ghost of a smile on the Defender's face.

"We remove them," said the Armourer matter-of-factly.

The Python was aghast. "Remove them? How? You can't just pop over the Atlantic and knock off an American senator and what about the Russian? You'd never get anywhere near him."

"I didn't say it'd be easy."

"And we've always said we weren't assassins," remarked the Housekeeper.

The Fixer had been gazing dreamily out of the window.

"Just an idea," he said, "but wouldn't it be neat if we could fix for the American and the Russian to bump each other off."

"How the hell would we do that?"

"Dunno, but it might be possible. That'd be rough justice in action, wouldn't it?"

"The problem with Sanderlin," said the Defender, "is that no one in authority is likely to believe anything bad about him."

The Python was still worried. "Are we really talking about killing a member of the British government?"

"Sanderlin's not a member of the British government, he's a traitor, pursuing a private agenda to damage this country for his own ends."

"Okay, but even so."

"I agree," said the Hunter, "we can't just kill him. He has to be publicly discredited."

"That's a challenge," said the Housekeeper.

The Hunter had a sudden thought. "Python, back in the day when we were still active, you were on the verge of cracking Sanderlin's communication network. How's that going."

"It's done. I got full access a few months ago. I've been keeping an eye on it but there's been very little activity."

"They're being cautious," said the Defender. "Judging by the attacks on Hunter's house, I reckon they're all trying to steal a march on each other."

"One thing that might help," said the Python. "I said I can monitor the communications between these guys …"

"Yes?"

"I could also put our own messages into their system."

There was silence around the table then the Hunter said, "Do you mean you could send one of them a message which appeared to come from one of the others?"

"Sure, and then I can intercept the reply so the apparent sender doesn't become aware of what is going on."

"Wow," said the Armourer.

"I wish I'd known you when I was active in the field," said the Housekeeper.

"It's not that difficult. They're using encrypted messaging, rather like the Casanova system we set up for Perry Cracken, only theirs isn't so good. It was a puzzle at first, but once I'd worked out the underlying scheme I broke into it pretty easily. Now all their stuff gets diverted to me before being bounced back to them. But I'm also controlling the bounce back so I can add stuff, suppress stuff, do what I like really."

The Hunter came to a decision. "Okay, this could be a powerful tool for us so while Defender and I go to Spain, I want you guys to get together. Python, show them how all this works. Armourer, Housekeeper, analyse all the messages that have passed between our three Hornets. If we're going to add any messages of our own we need to use the right idioms. Fixer, can you go on digging around. We need every scrap of information about Sanderlin we can get hold of. If we're going to find a way of publicly discrediting him we'll only get one shot at it."

NORTHERN SPAIN

THE HUNTER AND the Defender took the Eurostar to Brussels where they hired a car and drove to Bern. At Bern they handed in the hire car and took the train to Lyon. There they hired another car, headed for the Spanish border then drove west out along the coast road towards Bilbao and Santander.

They had passed through San Sebastian before the Defender finally asked the obvious question. "I've not said anything until now, but how sure are you we'll find Cracken at this hotel?"

"I'm not sure, I can't be, but his message clearly related to that night we first met him so it has to be the place to start. When we thought he was dead we closed down Casanova so I guess this was the only way he had to get in touch. It was clever, really, when you think about it, an apparently random phrase which would mean nothing to anyone except me."

"Suppose we do find him. What do you think he wants?"

"He'll want a trade, that's what Perry does," she said firmly. "Specifically though, I don't know. More to the point, why has he suddenly reappeared?"

They were passing through a small resort town when suddenly their conversation was interrupted by a blast of loud music. Looking ahead, they saw a procession coming towards them along the seafront. In the lead was a group of five men with trombones and trumpets and a drum. Then came a camel ridden by a woman in a very flamboyant costume and behind her were two more camels, a string of brightly coloured caravans, a troop of horses and then a number of other wagons.

"Wouldn't see that in Clapham," said the Hunter.

"It's one of those travelling fairs. You find them all over southern Europe."

The noise gradually died away as they left the town and resumed their conversation.

"The real question is, has Perry come to life again by choice or necessity?"

"Maybe he's run out of money and needs to do a deal."

"Or maybe his cover's been blown and he needs protection."

"If so, why you?"

"Where else can he go? Everyone else wants to torture him then kill him."

"And what do we want?"

"All we want is to neutralise the Minnie Ha-Ha formula once and for all."

"I agree. But I'm sure you've realised the information about Minnie Ha-Ha will never be entirely safe until Cracken's dead. How do you feel about that?"

There was a long pause, then the Hunter said, "If that turns out to be necessary then so be it."

The Defender looked at her for a moment then returned his attention to the road ahead. "Ah, looks like we're here."

While they were signing the hotel register the Hunter contrived to look over the list of other guests, mostly Spanish names and certainly no Perry Cracken. She hadn't expected there would be.

The Hunter had managed to arrange to have the same room that she'd shared with Perry all those years ago. She'd had half an idea that he might have left a message for her there but in spite of a careful search she found nothing.

The following morning she stood at the window and remembered the last time she'd been there. The view was unchanged, the hotel garden, a circular rose bed, a green hedge and beyond that the sea. Parakeets still squeaked and squawked in the trees outside, it still presented a picture of peace.

The day passed very slowly. Not knowing what else to do she decided she had to stay in the vicinity of the hotel so spent most of the day in the garden. The Defender was very patient but towards the end of the afternoon he finally asked how long they were going to wait. She replied she didn't know.

THAT EVENING AS THEY sat on the terrace with a glass of wine the hotel receptionist emerged from the building, glanced around and then came across to where they were sitting.

"Perdóneme señora, but a message has been received, I think for you."

"Who's it from?"

The woman glanced down at the envelope she held in her hand. "It says '*English Lady from Yankee Boy.*' Is that right?"

"That's right, and it is for me. Gracias."

The Hunter slit open the envelope and drew out a note. She read it then handed it to the Defender. "*Good to see you, Hunter Lady. Long time since Schiphol. If you're willing to meet me again then stand up now, walk round the table once and then sit down.*"

The Hunter glanced round the garden but could see no one watching. Nevertheless she stood up, walked round the table as instructed then sat down.

The Defender gave a wry smile. "Game playing."

"Well, he can obviously see us."

"If it is him."

"It's him. That's why he mentions Schiphol."

"So what do we do now?"

"We wait. Nothing else we can do."

By the time they went into dinner there had been no further message but when they went upstairs the Hunter found another note had been pushed under her door. This one read.

"Tomorrow night. Nine o'clock. Playa de Ondarrina."

She went and knocked on the Defender's door and showed him the note. He read it then said, "What you going to do?"

"Well, go, of course."

"There's a surprise."

"So tomorrow we need to find out where the Playa Ondarrina is. And I think we should have a quick recce. Remember Point Reyes?"

The Defender sighed. "Oh, yes, I remember Point Reyes."

The next day they borrowed a map from the hotel and found the Playa Ondarrina about two miles away. It was a tiny sandy beach with low cliffs either end. There was a rough track running down from the eastern end which skirted a group of rocks before disgorging onto the sand. At the other end of the beach the track picked up again, winding up into the trees. From the marks in the sand it looked as though it was a regular route for tractors.

At five to nine that evening the Hunter and the Defender were standing in the shelter of the rocks at the eastern end of the beach. The night was silent. After a few moments the Hunter said, "I think it's up to us to start the ball rolling. You stay here."

The Defender nodded and the Hunter stepped out into the open and walked towards the middle of the beach, well aware she was an easy target for a sniper. Two minutes, which seemed like two hours, passed and then, in the gathering dusk, a figure appeared from the other direction.

The Hunter took a few steps forward and called, "Perry?"

"Hi, Hunter Lady. So you came."

"Of course I came."

They moved tentatively towards each other. She said, "I thought you were dead."

"They told me you were dead too."

"Bit of an exaggeration all round then."

"Yup." He paused then said, "Hunter Lady, I'm in trouble."

"I guessed that much."

"Can I trust you?"

"You can trust me personally, Perry, but beyond that I can't promise."

"Guess that'll have to do."

She took another step forward but at that moment a group of four men appeared out of the shadows at the far end of the beach.

She said quietly. "Perry, we've got company."

Perry swung round and then slumped. "Oh, shit."

An American voice called, "Nobody move. Keep calm, and no one'll get hurt."

Perry turned back to the Hunter. "Hey, Hunter Lady, I'm sorry, I didn't know ..."

She ignored him and called into the dusk. "Who are you and what do you want?"

"We want you, Hunter, you and Mister Cracken here. You've been very troublesome but now it's our turn to call the shots."

"I said, who are you?"

A man stepped forward and approached them, a gun in his hand. "Not important, but if you're smart you'll tell your friend behind you to join us, keeping his hands where we can see them."

There was a pause and then she heard the Defender move up behind her and could sense his frustration.

"That's cool. Now I think it'd be a real good idea for you all to lay face down on the sand. Okay?"

The Hunter didn't move. "Didn't you hear me? I said, who are you?"

"No matter. Get this, lady, we want that Minnie Ha-Ha formula. If you have it on you then just hand it over and we'll be gone."

"We don't have it with us and anyway do I look stupid? Once you've got that formula we're toast."

"Okay, so I lied. I'm in charge, so my privilege. The only question is, do you die sooner or later, quickly or slowly."

The Hunter laughed and the man looked surprised. "Little boys playing games. I haven't lasted this long by being scared of a bunch of two-bit gangsters."

"Listen, don't push your luck …" the man took a step forward but that moment they were all startled by a loud blast on a trumpet, a drumming of hooves and a shrill female voice yelling, "Yee-hah!"

The man spun round as a group of three camels, followed by a string of riders on horses, came hurtling down the track. As the cavalry charge crashed into the group on the sand, there was another "Yee-hah" and another blast of the trumpet. The rider of the leading camel leaned down and lifted the Hunter bodily up onto the camel's back.

Clinging tightly to the back of the rider's shirt against the jolting motion of the camel, the Hunter twisted to peer back through the gloom. She saw that the Defender had been pulled up onto another camel, with Perry being hauled onto the third. There were a number of wild shots but by now the horsemen were amongst the Americans, flaying them with their whips, then suddenly the whole troop was galloping like mad up the track on the far side of the cove.

At the top of the cliff the group of riders slowed and the rider on the Hunter's camel turned and smiled at her. Suddenly the Hunter realised it was the woman she'd seen riding a camel in the fairground procession earlier in the day.

"Who the hell are you?"

"No matter for now. We must go."

"They'll have cars, vehicles, they'll be after us."

"They have cars with sand in gas tank. Not going anywhere."

"Am I a prisoner?"

"No." She turned and called across to the Defender who was fumbling inside his jacket. "Do not be silly man. You are with friends."

The Hunter caught the Defender's eye and he shrugged as if to say. "Don't think we have any choice."

As though reading his mind the woman said, "Now we ride."

The Hunter shifted herself trying to find a more comfortable way of sitting on the camel but came to the conclusion that wasn't possible so gave herself up to the inevitable.

CONVERSATION IN A CARAVAN

HALF AN HOUR LATER, during which time the Hunter came to the conclusion that camels could never be described as First Class travel, they reached the fairground campsite.

She had to be helped down from the camel as she was now very stiff. The three of them were taken into one of the larger caravans where they were given hot, bitter coffee and large brandies. The Hunter and Defender were still very much on the alert though there was no sense of immediate danger. Perry just sat there looking bemused.

After a while he roused himself enough to say to the Hunter. "Did you fix all this?"

"No, she did not fix." A curtain was pushed aside and the woman came in. She had a brightly coloured shawl round her shoulders and her hair was tied up in a red bandana.

"We have followed you for long time, Mister Cracken. We did not want wrong people to find you."

"I think wrong people already have."

"No, my friend. You are safe now." She looked across at the Hunter. "And we also want to meet your friends."

The Hunter regarded her coolly. "So now you've met us. What happens now?"

"You are the one they call 'Hunter'." It was a statement, not a question.

"I am. And who are you?"

"I am known as 'Okhotnik'." Beside her the Hunter felt

the Defender stiffen but the woman went on. "I know you speak Russian so you understand I am also 'Hunter'."

"So you're working for Nikolai Lazovsky."

The woman's eyes flashed. "Never. That pig. He is not true Russian. He is gangster. One day I kill him. I look forward to that very much."

The Defender and the Hunter exchanged glances then the Defender said, "Are you saying we're on the same side?"

Okhotnik smiled. "Hard to believe, yes? But not all Russians are mafia. My friends and I, we fight for good society."

"Good luck with that in Russia," muttered the Defender but Okhotnik turned on him.

"Do not be patronising person. Is UK any better? Useless politicians, all real decisions made by big business and tabloid newspapers?"

"She has a point," said the Hunter and then, to try and smooth things down she said, "You have very good English."

"I have degree from Oxford. International studies. You speak good Russian also."

The Hunter just smiled.

The Defender said, "Okay, I'm sorry, but can we get back to the matter in hand." He turned to Perry. "What made you stop being dead, Cracken? And why d'you get in touch with Hunter?"

"Had no choice. I was spotted and I knew my cover was blown."

"How d'you mean, spotted?"

"You probably heard about my crash in the Alps. Well, that was a set-up."

"Obviously."

"I went to ground in a little place near Como but then one day I was in Milan and one of Beckford's guys spotted

373

me. After that I knew it was only a matter of time."

The Hunter chipped in. "So what do you want from us, Perry?"

"Protection. I figured if the Americans and Russians were arguing over who controlled what, then the Brits might like a trump card." He saw the expression on the Hunter's face and said, "That's not gonna work, is it?"

"Not with our current government, no. They can't be trusted an inch."

"I'm fucked then."

Okhotnik said, "You were always fucked. From moment you stole that dangerous process you were fucked."

"I didn't steal it. Irina gave it to me."

"Irina, yes. We know about Irina."

The Defender looked at Okhotnik. "Is that why you've been following Cracken? Because you want that process?"

"No, we do not want it. We want to destroy it. We thought you were dead, Mister Cracken—"

"So did we," muttered the Defender.

"— but when we learn you are alive we have to act."

"How did you find him? Come to that, how did the Americans find him?"

Okhotnik made a dismissive gesture with her hand. "Mister Cracken is not really very clever."

"Now just a danged minute—"

"Men escaping should not call girlfriends on cell phone. Everyone hear that call. Tracing you not difficult."

The Hunter choked back a snort of disbelief. "Perry, you didn't?"

"No … well, she called me …"

"But you gave her your number?"

"She was all alone. She was desperate. She's a nice kid. I couldn't just dump her."

374

"Especially not after nicking the only asset she had." The Defender was contemptuous.

Okhotnik said, "We knew Irina was in America. We do not think she understood what professor Kollerov gave her, only that his papers were valuable. We are trying to find her when we learn Mister Cracken is still alive and in Spain so we come here."

"Okay, but those Americans on the beach tonight, who were they? CIA?"

"Maybe, maybe not. Maybe gangsters. No matter. Not good either way."

"But how did they knew Perry was here?"

"I think Irina tell them. May not want to, but no choice."

Perry said, "You're saying they've got Irina."

"Irina is dead."

"Dead?"

"Yes. American people want you. They thought she knew where to find you. Tried to persuade her to tell them. Too enthusiastic."

"Oh, Jeez."

The Hunter said, "Is there any more coffee?"

Okhotnik smiled and called, "Nikita …"

A young man appeared with a coffee pot in his hand and refilled their mugs.

"Spasibo," said the Hunter and Nikita smiled.

"Na zdorovie."

The Defender had not entirely relaxed. He glanced round the caravan. Perry Cracken was slumped in one corner. Nikita had perched himself on a stool by the door but in the middle of the room the two Hunters sat facing each other.

"What I don't understand," said the Hunter, "is why you didn't just pick up Perry here if all you wanted was the Minnie Ha-Ha process."

"Because we want more than that but we need help. Mister Cracken was waiting for someone. I thought you were that someone and I wanted to meet you also."

"Did you, indeed."

"And you came, but I had bad feeling about your meeting with Mister Cracken."

"Just as well you did, but what's all this fairground business?"

"To say nothing of all that 'Yee ha' stuff," said the Defender, "it's like some kind of bad movie."

Okhotnik looked surprised. "We watch movies too. Buffalo Bill movies. Always he yell 'Yee ha' when he charge."

The Hunter stifled a grin. "That might just be for the movies," she said diplomatically.

"Don't remember General Custer on a camel," muttered the Defender.

"Yes, and why camels?" asked the Hunter.

"This is Russian fair," said Okhotnik with a shrug. "It was circus, but circus not popular any more. When we decide to wait for you, my friends and I join up with the fair people. Good – what is word? – cover."

"Blew you cover tonight though, didn't you?"

"It was necessary. If we just come on our legs then no surprise, maybe we have a gun fight, people hurt. Camel charge provide shock factor. Russians on horses with whips are easy match for Americans."

"The last of the Cossacks," said the Defender.

"My ancestors are Cossacks. Many years ago we fight Napoleon. He try to take our country from outside. Today we fight Lazovsky who wants to take the world from inside."

There was silence for a moment, then the Hunter said, "Why did you want to meet me?"

For a moment Okhotnik almost looked shy. "We are same

type of person, we want same things."

"What things?"

"Peace and honour in our countries. My friends and I liked very much what you did to Lazovsky's ships. He was very angry."

"Oh … Right … Thank you."

"But we both know that is only small victory. You cut off leg but heart is still beating. We must stop heart."

"Ambitious," said the Defender and Okhotnik swung round to face him.

"Ambitious, yes, but necessary. So also is this Beckford American. These two men are great danger to us all."

"Do you have a plan?"

"Niet. We know what must be done but we cannot do this alone. We need help. That's why I meet you."

The Hunter nodded. She'd seen that coming some time back. "I'll need to consult my team back in the UK."

"Konechno."

"Apart from Beckford and Lazovsky we have a problem of our own back home."

"Ah, yes, Mister Sanderlin. Never smiles. Hides in shadows. Do not trust him."

"We don't."

Okhotnik turned to Perry. "So, now Mister Cracken. What do we do about this formula?"

"I'm not doing anything about it. It's all I've got to bargain with."

"But it must be destroyed."

"Over my dead body."

Okhotnik looked as though she thought that could be arranged but the Defender broke in. "Just a minute, I think we're going to need Perry."

A slight smile touched the Hunter's lips as the Defender

went on speaking directly to Okhotnik. "Just for the moment suppose we work together on a plan to remove Beckford and Lazovsky, they're not going to be easy targets, neither of them."

"That is so, but must be done."

"I agree. We agree, in fact we'd already started talking about it. Yes?"

The Hunter nodded.

"Thing is, it'd be very difficult for us to get to either of those gentlemen on their home ground so we need to find a way to draw them out into the open. We need to persuade them to come to us."

"Ya ponimayu. I understand."

"Well, I reckon you're three steers short of a rodeo," said Perry, "how the hell d'you think you can do that?"

There was a long silence as three pairs of eyes looked at him and then the penny dropped. "Oh, no, you're not using me as bait."

CAMBRIDGE

SITTING IN THE PYTHON'S workshop in Cambridge the Armourer, the Fixer and the Housekeeper were listening as the Python tried to explain the complexities of the communication system between Beckford, Lazovsky and Sanderlin.

After a few minutes the Armourer stopped him. "Look, I trust you totally but I don't understand a word you're saying. All we need to know is, does it work?"

The Python looked hurt. "Of course it works."

"So messages sent by any one of those three—"

"— or anyone else on their network," added the Housekeeper.

"— comes to you then you can decide whether to send it on intact, send it on with changes, or not to send it on at all."

"Yes."

"And they won't be aware of this happening?"

"No."

"Amazing."

"Not really. When you apply the binomial coefficients to an algorithmic system, then what you get is—"

"— an excellent way of feeding in our own misinformation," said the Housekeeper, cutting off another unintelligible explanation.

"So now we need to think how to use this to our advantage," said the Armourer. "I wonder if we could concoct a message to persuade Beckford and Lazovsky to meet face to face?"

"For what purpose?"

"So they can bump each other off," said the Fixer, "you remember I suggested that but we didn't know how to do it?"

"But why would they want to meet in person and why would they want to kill each other anyway?"

The Housekeeper said, "Thinking aloud here, but suppose they didn't know they were going to meet until they actually did. Remember our original plan for Sanderlin?"

"Come again."

"If the American, for example, thought there was a chance of putting one over on the Russian."

"Then he might take the risk, especially if he thought the Russian was trying to double cross him."

"Greed," said the Armourer, "offer him something he can't resist. Then offer the other bloke the same thing."

The Python sat back in his chair. "I'm starting to lose the plot. But if you think it can be done, just draft your messages and I'll slip them into the system."

"What sort of something would tempt them out of their home territory?" asked the Fixer, "and where would we want them to go?"

The Armourer shrugged. "At the moment I don't know, but I'm sure that's the way to do it."

CONVERSATION IN A CARAVAN

THE ATMOSPHERE IN the caravan was tense. Perry was pressed back against the wall as though hoping he could disappear through it. The Hunter tried to calm him down.

"Not bait, Perry, but if the other side know we've got you, then they're going to come looking."

"That's what scares the shit out of me."

"But they don't have to find you. All we want to do is lure them out of their territory into ours."

"And where is 'ours'? I just want to know so I can be as far away from it as possible."

"That's one of the things we need to work out." She turned to Okhotnik. "This is going to take a bit of planning. Defender and I need to go back to the UK but we can't take Perry with us."

Perry brightened up. "It's cool. I'll just vamoose."

"Not possible," said Okhotnik, "they will find you. That would not be nice."

"Can you keep him here, in the fair?"

Okhotnik shook her head. "No, not safe, not for him, not for us. We must go too. We cannot stay here now. It will take those Americans time to find us, but they will come."

There was silence for a moment then the Defender said, "How about this? You go back to the UK, Hunter, talk to the others, I stay here and take care of Cracken."

Perry looked less than enthusiastic at this thought.

Okhotnik shook her head. "There is still problem. We

wish to keep Mister Cracken with us but where to go? No safe place anywhere."

The Hunter thought for a moment, then said, "I may just have an idea."

She took out her phone and opened the contacts list. She nodded to herself and then peered more closely at the screen and frowned.

"Dead as a dodo. Is there anywhere nearby where I can get a mobile signal?"

Okhotnik spoke to Nikita in Russian and when he replied she turned back to the Hunter.

"Best place is—"

"— in the village by the café, yes, I got that. Defender, keep an eye on Perry, will you? I need to make a call." She smiled at Okhotnik. "I won't be long, but do you have something more comfortable than a camel that I can use?"

CALLING IN
THE CAVALRY

NIKITA DROVE HER down to the village in a battered Seat. By now it was late and there were very few signs of life other than the murmur of voices coming from the bar. Certainly no sign that any pursuit had tracked them this far.

They parked on the other side of the square. "Stay here," she said to Nikita and, although he looked doubtful, he nodded. She walked across to a bench under the trees where she found there was a perfectly good mobile signal. She checked her contacts list again and pressed the button.

The number rang for a long time but finally it was answered and gruff voice said, "Si?"

"Es ese señor Carrasco?"

"Quién quiere saber?"

The Hunter switched into English. "This is the Hunter, señor Carrasco, la Cazadora. We met in London with your daughter, Sabela, some while ago. I hope she is safe and happy. I arranged a new passport for her last time we met. Did it work well?"

There was a pause and then suddenly there was a huge roar of laughter. "Señora Hunter, la Cazadora. Si, the passaporte work very well. And Sabela, she very happy."

"Good. Señor, when we met in London you said if I ever needed help then I could call you and you would come."

"I say that. It is true. You good friend to Sabela. You are in London? What help you need from Xabier?"

"I'm not in London, I'm in Spain."

"Eres de verdad?" There was a short pause then he said, "I think you are being a little bit bad again, no. Where are you?"

She gave him the name of the village.

"I know this place. One hour and a half. I will arrive. Wait." And the line went dead.

She walked back to the car and told Nikita that an old friend was coming to meet her but it would take a while for him to get here. At her suggestion he went across to the bar and came back with a couple of beers which they drank sitting on the bench under the trees.

They heard no engines, no sound of anyone approaching, but it was less than ninety minutes later when a dark figure appeared in the shadows on the edge of the square and voice called softly, "Señora Cazadora."

"I am here."

There was a pause, then the voice said, "You not alone."

"This is my friend." To Nikita she said quietly, "Say nothing, leave all the talking to me."

He nodded.

The shadow moved closer until she could make out the figure of Xabier Carrasco.

She said, "Es un placer volver a verlo, señor."

His face broke into a big grin and, coming forward, he seized her by the shoulders and planted a huge kiss on each cheek.

"It is also pleasure for me, Cazadora."

Out of the corner of her eye she saw Nikita glancing nervously round the square and when she followed his gaze she noticed several other dark shadows in the gloom.

Xabier smiled. "Seguro, Cazadora. In English you say … insurance, si? I do not know your problem, so I am careful."

"Of course." She turned to Nikita. "Go and sit in the car while I talk to Xabier."

He scuttled away and Xabier sat down on the bench beside her. "So, you have trouble, yes?"

"No, not yet. But I could have, which is why I'm asking for your help."

She told him the story as quickly and as concisely as she could. By the time she had finished his face was grim.

"What you want from me, Cazadora?"

"I need you to keep Perry for me. Keep him safe. Not as a prisoner as such, he's on our side, but he may still try to get away. That mustn't happen."

"Entiendo. This I can do."

"Thank you. I need to go back to the UK to plan the next stage."

There was a pause, then Xabier said, "This American, this Russian, they are dangerous men, yes?"

"Yes."

"So you will kill them?"

"It is possible."

"So I help with that too, yes?"

"Why would you want to do that?"

"I no like big business behaving bad in my land. Is not fair. They ignore laws they don't like. Make problems for people like me who have small business."

The Hunter blinked a bit at the logic of this argument but she recognised the offer was well meant.

"How do you think you could help, Xabier?"

"You no kill these men in America or Russia or England I think."

"Definitely not."

"So you want señor Perry for … for … cebo … what is your word?"

"Bait."

"Si. Bait. So we use señor Perry to bring these men here."

385

"Here? To Spain?"

"Si. More easy to deal here. Many lonely places. No one to hear bang bang," and he grinned widely.

"How would we persuade them to come here?"

Xabier opened his hands in the age old gesture. "I not know, Cazadora. You bring them to Spain, Xabier will make sure they stay. Okay?

The Hunter took a deep breath. "Okay."

She thought for a moment. "If we're going to do that we'll need somewhere for the American and Russian to meet, somewhere lonely."

"I will think, Cazadora. Somewhere safe for bang bang but no policía, si?"

"Something like that, Xabier. Oh, and we have some Russian friends with us, good Russians. They are also in danger can you look after them as well until I get back?"

"Si, is pleasure. I will vanish all your friends. Now let us go meet your Señor Perry."

NATIONAL GALLERY TEA ROOM

TWO DAYS LATER the Hunter met her team in the National Gallery tearoom and brought them up to date on the events in Spain.

When she had finished the Armourer said, "So what do we do now?"

"That's what we need to discuss. How have you got on?"

"It's amazing. Thanks to the Python's tech skills we can intercept and control all the messages between Sanderlin, Beckford and Lazovsky, so we're well placed for setting up a sting operation."

"We've come back to my idea, that we try and arrange things so Beckford and Lazovsky bump each other off," said the Fixer.

"Okay," said the Hunter, "we've obviously been thinking along the same lines. So, let's leave Sanderlin for the moment and concentrate on the other two. The question is, how do we bring them together?"

"And where do we bring them?"

"Oh, that'll be Spain," said the Hunter. "Xabier Carrasco is working on that for us."

"How about this," said the Housekeeper, "suppose Beckford thought that Lazovsky had Cracken and Cracken was going to give him the formula ..."

"Got you … and if Lazovsky thought the same about Beckford …?"

"Then they would each come running to prevent a double cross."

There were nods round the table but the Armourer was doubtful. "But why would they come in person? Wouldn't they just send the heavy brigade?"

There was silence for a moment then the Python leaned forward. "Listen, we know – and they know – that the Minnie Ha-Ha process is lodged on a secure server. Suppose we let slip that Cracken has locked the access to that server with three voice recognition keys, and it takes two to unlock it, his and one of theirs. That would also strengthen the idea that he's set this up so he can sell the process to the highest bidder so it looks like a double cross."

"How would he have got their voices?"

"That's simple – recordings of speeches they're made, phone calls, it wouldn't be difficult. We can let it be known that Cracken has done it as a bargaining tool and anyway if we make it seem the message has come from Sanderlin they're likely to believe it."

"But if that was the deal, wouldn't Sanderlin want to be part of it?"

"Good point," said the Housekeeper. He thought for a moment. "How about this? In our misinformation we plant the idea that Sanderlin has both the original processes, Mayo and SD77. That would mean that whoever grabs Perry for Minnie Ha-Ha will also need Sanderlin on board."

"But Sanderlin does have one of them, doesn't he?"

"We think so, yes, but not both of them. No one seems to have both."

There was silence for a moment then the Hunter said, "Let me get this straight before I lose the plot entirely. We

feed information to Lazovsky that Beckford has Perry at …
somewhere in Spain … and that he is about to do a private
deal with him. At the same time we also tell Bedford that
Lazovksy has Perry – same deal. These two bits of information
apparently come from Sanderlin who says he has both the
basic formulas."

"Therefore who ever has Perry also needs Sanderlin to
finally get hold of Minnie Ha-Ha."

"But first they each think they need to get to Perry before
the other one does and, because of the voice recognition
thing, that means a trip to Spain."

"Well, I guess that might bring them. Worth a shot."

The Defender looked round the table. "And when it's all
set up, I guess we'll be there too?"

"Most of us, yes. We have to make sure that once the
Americans and the Russians come face to face that all hell
erupts. We'll need to monitor what's going on. But hopefully
keep out of the action."

"I'd quite like to be part of the action," muttered the
Armourer.

"You still might be. Hopefully they'll start wiping each
other out but we'll be on hand to make sure the main guys
don't make it home.

"You said 'most of us' will go." The Fixer looked round the
table. "Does that mean some of us will stay here?"

"Yes," said the Hunter, "I think it makes sense to leave
someone in London in case anything needs sorting this end."

"Well, in that case," said the Fixer, "can I volunteer for
that? I've had one brush with these guys and once is enough."

"The key question is, will our Hornets actually come in
person," said the Defender.

"Who knows?" said the Armourer, "But I think the
opportunity to get the formula for Minnie Ha-Ha and then

do a deal with Sanderlin will be enough to tempt them. Greed and power are great motivators."

"Going to be a lively little meeting when they all get together, isn't it?" said the Housekeeper.

ST JAMES'S PARK

THE FOLLOWING DAY, at his request, the Hunter met Forseti in St James's Park. As she sat down on the bench beside him, a panorama of ducks, swans and moorhens spread out in front of them, the Hunter was smiling.

"Isn't this a bit of a cliché? In all the best thriller novels the spy and the handler always seem to meet here to feed the ducks and exchange covert information."

Forseti kept a straight face as he handed her a paper bag. "There you go. Brown bread only. White bread's not good for ducks."

She laughed, opened the bag, broke off some bread and tossed it to the anticipatory wildfowl.

"Okay, why did you want to meet?"

"Did you find Cracken?"

She hesitated and then said, "Yes."

He waited for a moment but when she said nothing further he said, "And is he still a danger?"

"As the moment, yes, but I think we have the situation in hand."

"Is he in the UK?"

"No."

"So he's still in Spain."

"How did you …? You worked out his message, didn't you? Cunning old sod."

"I'll take that as a compliment."

"How much do you know?"

"Not much more than that. You say you have the situation under control?"

The Hunter chose her words carefully. "We are in the process of getting the situation under control. Was that the reason you wanted to meet?"

"Partly. I also wanted to give you a warning. Things are moving faster than I expected. Word has it that our Sanderlin Hornet has managed to convince several senior government figures that Britian would be better off if we come out of the United Nations. He seems to be full of confidence and I'm getting seriously worried, Hunter."

The Hunter tore off another piece of bread and threw it into the water. A mallard headed for it but was thrust out of the way by an aggressive swan.

"If that confidence is based on his support from Senator Beckford and the Russian, Lazovsky, he may not have that for much longer."

There was a pause, then Forseti said, "You're not going to tell me what you're up to, are you?"

"It's better you don't know."

"But you think this will leave Sanderlin on his own?"

"If all goes according to plan, then, yes."

"That would be good news."

"But it doesn't sort the problem of Sanderlin himself. I assume he's still the government's blue-eyed boy?"

"Very much so. I've come to the conclusion he could probably murder his grandmother in the middle of Oxford Street and they'd still find an excuse for him."

"That's what I thought, so I suggest you start thinking about ways we could totally discredit him."

"Me? Why me?"

"I've got other fish to fry for the moment and this needs a very cunning plan."

"And you think I can come up with a cunning plan?"

"Don't be so modest. I've done my homework. Do I need to remind you about the bishop and the roulette wheel? And I'm sure you remember what happened to that Malaysian gun runner when he found a giant tortoise in his bedroom. To be honest, I'm surprised you've ever needed me at all."

Forseti smiled faintly. "One grows older, the body slows down."

"But I bet the mind doesn't. Give it some thought."

"As it happens I already have. Are you going back to Spain soon."

"Tomorrow."

"With the whole team?"

"Most of them."

"Ah. I was wondering if I could borrow one of them?"

"Which one?"

"The one you call the Fixer."

"Why?"

"Well, I do have the germ of an idea for dealing with Mister Sanderlin but I need some help."

"Well, as it happens Fixer is staying in London but what about the anonymity we agreed on back in the day?"

"I think the stakes warrant a bit of relaxation there, don't you? I've already met Defender, after all."

"True … Okay, I'll ask him and if he's willing I'll get him to call you, but the decision is his, okay?"

"Of course."

She stood up and handed him the paper bag. "Here, you can give them the rest. I need to go and pack my suntan lotion and castanets. I'll let you know when the American and the Russian are out of the equation."

CABO DE COMADREJA

THE LOCATION XABIER found for them was an old disused lighthouse standing on the Cabo de Comadreja gazing out over the Atlantic. The Hunter thought it was one of the bleakest places she had ever seen.

"Cape of the Weasel," muttered the Defender, "how appropriate."

The Faro de Comadreja had originally been manned by two keepers but had been abandoned many years ago when a new automatic lighthouse was built three miles up the coast. However, the original lighthouse building, a two storey oblong structure, was still standing. The bottom floor was a large equipment room, above that was the living accommodation for the keepers and rising above that, tall and thin, the original lighthouse itself climbed into the sky.

The Hunter set up her command base about half a mile away along the cliff edge at an old uninhabited farmhouse. The Python installed a series of small video cameras around the lighthouse, in the old equipment hall and the living accommodation, plus several more covering the approaches. Sitting in the cottage with a large screen in front of him, he could see every aspect of the building.

Access to the lighthouse was along a narrow gravel track about a mile long. Halfway down was a car park for a wildlife nature reserve. At the junction where the gravel track met a small country road was an old barn and it was here that Xabier installed his men. Broad-shouldered and silent, heavily armed and rarely smiling, they nevertheless exuded confidence and power. The Hunter thought it best not to wonder about the true nature of Xabier's business but she was glad they were on her side. Perry was with the Spaniards but he was never left alone.

Okhotnik had made it very clear this was a joint operation so she and her two companions joined the Hunter's team in the farmhouse and together they set about compiling the messages that they hoped would tempt Beckford and Lazovsky to come to Spain. The messages had to create a fine balance between using Sanderlin's style of language but at the same time making the dangled carrot very clear, together with the threat of repercussions if the other side prevailed.

They had decided that for the purpose of the sting operation they should say that Perry was being held captive by a group of Spaniards who were willing to do a deal. The final text for Beckford said:

> *Cracken held prisoner by Spanish drug smugglers. He has access to the combination process to create Minnie Ha-Ha. Details stored on a secure cloud server and can only be accessed by Cracken using voice recognition keys, his plus Lazovsky or yours. Lazovsky planning a double cross, has arranged to buy Cracken from the Spaniards. The handover will be in a disused lighthouse in north-west Spain. Cannot go myself but think you should be there to protect our interests. If Lazovsky gets there first we are finished.*

Then followed details of the location, the date and the time of the theoretical handover.

A similar message was prepared for Lazovsky accusing Beckford of planning the double cross. Okhotnik tweaked the Lazovsky message slightly and Perry did the same for the Beckford message. Then they were handed over to the Python to be coded. Once that was done they were fed into the communication system and the team sat back to await the response.

BERWICK MARKET

THE FIXER HAD AGREED to talk to Forseti and they met in a coffee shop in Berwick Market. Initially they were slightly cautious with each other and there was a lot of inconsequential chat about the different street markets in various parts of London and the increasing number of coffee options apparently designed to bewilder people who just wanted a straight white. Finally, Forseti approached the main purpose of the meeting.

"When the Hunter first accepted the assignment we gave her, I know you were one of the first people she recruited."

The Fixer smiled faintly.

"She gave me no information about any of you, and I didn't want to know, but having seen the results your team has achieved over the past couple of years, I've formed some opinions of my own."

"Have you now."

"The Hunter put together a brilliant team and I know that you, in particular, have a wide range of skills. Now am I right in thinking that one of these skills would be your various contacts in … shall we say … some unorthodox areas of society."

The Fixer leaned back in his chair. "Are you asking if I know people who've had the pleasure of being guests of Her Majesty?"

"Well, that's one way of putting it."

"As good a way as any." He paused, took a sip of his

macchiato and wrinkled his noise. "Reckon I'd still prefer a Nescafé."

Forseti smiled and the Fixer went on. "The answer's probably 'yes', but depends on what you need?"

"I need a good forger."

"Banknotes, documents or pictures?"

"Documents."

The Fixer thought for a moment. "Reckon I could sort that, but I'd want to know more about what you've got in mind."

"Of course. Okay, this is what I'm thinking ..."

CABO DE COMADREJA

THE HUNTER WAS by no means certain that the bait would be taken. If she'd been offered such a deal she'd be a lot more suspicious about why she had to come in person. On reflection the whole plot seemed full of holes but she didn't have any better ideas so she waited in hope.

And the replies, when they came, justified that hope and confirmed the Armourer's cynical assessment that greed and power are great motivators. Both Lazovsky and Beckford acknowledged the information and said they would be making the necessary arrangements.

Okhotnik talked to her contacts in Russia and announced that almost certainly Lazovsky would arrive by sea. There was no way they could discover the American plans but Perry was certain they'd come by land.

"My guess is Beckford will contrive a duty trip to Spain then disappear for a day or two to meet up with his heavy mob."

The Armourer gave a grim smile. "This is going to be fun. Both groups will arrive at the lighthouse expecting to meet a group of Spaniards and Perry but instead they meet each other. I sense a nice bit of mayhem."

Perry shook his head. "I'm still worried Beckford might escape. You know what firefights are like. I'm guessing there'll be lots of injured, lots of dead, but no guarantee we'll get the guys we want."

"We will if I've got anything to do with it," said the

Armourer grimly, but Perry was not convinced.

"I want that bastard dead, no maybes, no probables, just certain. Dead certain," he added with unconscious irony.

"Beckford? Specifically?"

The Armourer looked puzzled but the Hunter suddenly clicked. "It's Irina, isn't it?" she said. "You were fond of her?"

"Well, yeah, I guess. She was a sweet kid, she didn't deserve to die. I want that bastard to pay for that."

The Hunter said, "We'll take care of him, Perry, but you leave it to us. Okay?"

THE TIME PASSED SLOWLY but eventually the 'Day of Action' as the Armourer kept calling it, arrived. They did a final check of all the electronic equipment and ran over their plans for monitoring the arrival of the two parties and then all they could do was wait.

Then, in the middle of the afternoon the Hunter had a call from Xabier.

"Cazadora, I so sorry, but Mister Perry, he is gone."

"What do you mean, gone?"

"Desaparecido. Escaped. Not know how."

"Jesus, Xabier, this isn't good news."

"We look for him but not know where to look." He paused then added. "He has taken gun."

"But how did—" She broke off. No point in an inquest. Perry had gone. She just hoped he wasn't going to do anything stupid.

DUSK ON THE CABO De Comadreja. If the various parties followed what they believed to be Oliver Sanderlin's instructions, then the Russians would arrive first. And they did.

The Hunter and Okhotnik lay in the grass on the headland

400

the other side of the bay watching a trawler arrive off shore. By now dusk was falling on the land but there was still light out at sea. The trawler anchored and shortly afterwards three RIBs were launched. They landed on the beach, about a dozen men clambered out, then pulled one of the RIBs in close so that the last person on board could step straight onto dry land.

Okhotnik had night glasses up to her eyes and she let out a hiss of breath.

"Lazovsky. So he has come."

"And doesn't intend to get his feet wet apparently."

"Is very tempting to shoot him now."

"You hate him that much?"

"Of course. That man kill my sister."

"Really? He killed her personally?"

"There was protest rally. My sister was there. Lazovsky and his ... his ..."

"Thugs?"

"Da, thugs. They fire on crowd. Many dead. My sister dead."

"How do you know it was him who shot her?"

"He gave order to fire. Who knows which bullet killed her? No matter. He=responsible."

The two women watched as the RIBs were dragged along the surf and finally secured to the rocks at the end of the bay. One man stayed with them, the others fanned out as Lazovsky, closely flanked by four men, began to climb up the cliff path towards the lighthouse.

The Hunter had her night glasses focused on the beach watching the Defender creeping down the line of rocks towards the RIBs. She saw him come up behind the Russian guard and she sensed, rather than heard, the force involved as the Defender chopped him across the neck and laid him flat on the ground. Then the Defender methodically worked his way along the side of each RIB, stabbing a hole into each air compartment as he did so. Just as he finished the Hunter saw, to her horror, the Russian stagger to his feet and launch himself at the Defender. The two men rocked backwards and forwards, locked together, but finally the Russian sagged down at the Defender's feet. Through her glasses the Hunter could see the hilt of the knife in the Russian's belly. The Defender stood, looking down on him then he rolled the guard underneath one of the RIBs and out of sight.

Okhotnik, who was also watching, grunted in satisfaction. "Your man is good. But why he not kill that man first thing?"

"We only kill when we have to," said the Hunter then, ignoring Okhotnik's puzzled look, she began to inch way back across the grass towards the trees.

IN THE CLIFFTOP COTTAGE, Okhotnik's partner, Nikita, was sitting next to the Python watching a video screen. They saw the Russians arrive at the lighthouse and cautiously inspect the building. One of them slipped inside and after a moment he reappeared. There was a muttered conversation and it seemed he was reporting all was clear as the others then went into the building.

The final version of the Sanderlin message had suggested to the Russians that they should occupy the first floor of the lighthouse so that when Perry and the Spaniards arrived downstairs, they could surprise them. The Python clicked a couple of buttons and they watched the Russians make their way up the stairs. The volume was turned up but there wasn't much conversation as the men spread themselves around the room.

AN HOUR LATER THE Armourer and the Housekeeper,

hidden in the undergrowth surrounding the nature reserve car park, watched the Americans arrive. There were around fifteen of them, travelling in four Land Cruisers. The Housekeeper recognised Senator Beckford in the middle of a tight group of four.

The Americans had been told the Spaniards would be waiting for them in the lighthouse with Perry, but not surprisingly they were cautious. There was a short muffled consultation and then the men split into smaller groups and began to make their way up the track.

"Let's get back to the others," said the Armourer.

The Housekeeper stood up and moved towards the path but at that moment another of Beckford's men appeared behind him from between the Land Cruisers. He saw the Housekeeper and went down in a crouch, reaching for his weapon. The Armourer lifted her gun but then realised a shot would bring the other Americans back and the whole operation would collapse. She tried to hiss a warning to the Housekeeper but he didn't hear.

For a moment she hesitated, then a figure appeared behind the American, a rifle butt rose and fell and the American lay unconscious on the ground. Xabier walked forward and looked down at his handywork. The Housekeeper swung round when he heard the noise and Xabier shook his head at him.

"Always one man stay with cars. You need be more careful, my friend."

The Armourer joined them, looking down at the unconscious man. "What we going to do with him?"

"Is no problem." Xabier clicked his fingers and two of the burly Spaniards emerged from the shadows. "We take care of him. We take care of these very nice cars also."

A LIVELY LITTLE GET TOGETHER

THE STAGE WAS SET for the confrontation. All the team gathered in the cottage where they could watch everything develop on the Python's multi-screen system.

"Just like YouTube," muttered the Defender.

"Actually, it's more like Zoom," said the Python quite seriously.

On the various cameras they watched the Americans cautiously approach the lighthouse then pause outside. Waved on by Beckford, one of the Americans sidled up the door and then suddenly kicked it open. Silence for a moment then the man yelled. "Come out, Cracken, we know you're in there."

This provoked the Russians into action and they clattered down the stairs and burst into the main room just as the Americans, guns at the ready, came rushing in through the front door.

Then the tableau froze as both sides came face to face, lined up like opposing teams in a gun-toting rugby match. The two captains, Beckford and Lazovsky, thrust their way forward to stand in front of their teams.

There was a long tension-filled silence and then Lazovsky spoke. "Dobro pozhalovat, moy drug."

One of the Americans whispered into Beckford's ear and the senator nodded. "Welcome to you too, my friend," he said.

Lazovsky ventured a thin smile. "Please not to worry. We

talk English. Is easier, I think."

"You betcha'"

"I not expect you."

"Me neither."

Another silence as the two sides regarded each other with suspicion. Then Beckford said, "So where's Cracken? I guess you've already done the deal with the Spaniards."

Lazovsky looked surprised. "Niet, we not met these Spaniards. It is you who has done deal."

"Whadda mean, we've done no deal. That's you guys, you must have Cracken."

"Niet. Mister Sanderlin, he tell us you have him."

"Now just a minute, buster. Sanderlin told us you've got him."

"Ya ne ponimayu. I no understand. You have Cracken. You try and cheat us."

Suddenly the atmosphere was a lot less friendly.

"Oh, no, it's you trying to double cross us, mister. What kind of crap deal is this?"

The men around Beckford lifted their weapons and immediately the Russians did the same.

Watching this on the screen in the cottage the Defender picked up the microphone linked to the sound system in the lighthouse. He glanced sideways at the Hunter.

"Remember how the shoot out at Hancock House started?"

She nodded and grinned. "Go for it."

The Defender clicked the microphone and yelled, "Fire."

The trigger happy gunmen in the lighthouse responded to this unseen command and all hell broke loose. One of the images on the screen in the cottage went blank as a camera in the lighthouse was hit by a stray bullet. Bodies were falling and running everywhere. Suddenly the Hunter saw a familiar figure appear at one of the window apertures, clutching an assault rifle.

"Oh shit, that's Perry. What the hell's he doing?"

As though answering her question Perry's voice rose above the hubbub. "Hey, Beckford," he yelled, "over here."

Beckford, surrounded by his men, turned to see where the voice was coming from and Perry lifted the gun and blasted him in the chest.

"That's for Irina, you bastard." As Beckford fell the Americans returned fire and the Hunter saw that Perry had been hit. He stumbled out of sight and she leapt to her feet.

"I've got to get over there. They'll massacre him."

"They'll massacre *you*," said the Defender but he followed her out of the door on the run.

The melee in the light house continued but suddenly Oknotnik stiffened. She saw a group of Russians surround one of their number and hustle him towards the door. Unnoticed by the others, Okhotnik grabbed her gun, slipped out of the cottage and headed back towards the cove. She reached the clifftop just in time to see the Russians running down the path towards the beach. They headed for the RIBs and began dragging them towards the water. There was some confusion when they found the dead guard and also realised the RIBs were damaged.

An argument broke out which made Okhotnik smile. There was just enough light for her to spot a man outlined against the sea standing to one side shouting orders while the others struggled with the boats.

Okhotnik lay down on the grass, the AK-74M assault rifle cradled in her arms. She breathed deeply once or twice, it had been a hard run along the cliff top and she needed to get her breathing under control. Then she carefully lined up the shot and pulled the trigger. The man standing aside from the others spun round then fell to the ground. She adjusted her aim and gave him several more bursts then hastily wriggled backwards as the other Russians returned fire randomly towards the cliff.

As the Hunter and the Defender approached the lighthouse they met Xabier who held out his hand to stop them.

"No go there. Not safe."

"What's going on?"

"Lots of bang bang. Is good. Some men escape to beach. We get them, yes?"

"They'll be the Russians. No rush, they can't go anywhere. What about the Americans?"

"Many dead. Some run for cars. My men deal with them. Have not seen senator man."

"He's dead. Perry killed him. I saw it all but Perry was hurt I must find him."

Xabier shrugged. "Perhaps he also dead. Where Russian mafia man?"

A voice spoke from the darkness behind them. "Lazovsky is dead. I shoot him."

The Defender looked at Okhotnik. "Good for you. What about the rest of his men?"

"Nowhere to go."

Xabier said, "I will deal."

"I don't think that's quite what—"

Ignoring him, Xabier turned and spat out a torrent of Spanish and a group of his men vanished into the darkness. Then he turned back to the others.

"We have success, yes? But now we must finish job?"

"What do you mean, finish?"

"Come quick away from here."

Xabier led them well away from the lighthouse and down the side of the cliff. The Defender was puzzled.

"Xabier, what's going on."

"Is good work, but now is important we … we … limpiar, how you say?"

"Tidy up?"

"Si. Tidy up." Xabier took out his mobile phone and made a quick call. "Please lie down, quick."

As he thrust them to the ground there was a huge explosion. Looking up the Defender could see the lighthouse collapsing and flames were already licking their way through the building.

"What the hell was that?"

Xabier held out his hands in supplication. "Little bomb. Big bang, no evidence, is good, I think."

"Bloody hell," said the Defender, "I think it's time we got out of here." He looked around. "What happened to Hunter?"

The Hunter was nowhere to be seen.

A SPANISH CLIFF TOP

THE HUNTER KNEW PERRY couldn't have headed west or she'd have seen him as she came down from the cottage so she made her way cautiously along the clifftop to the east. It didn't take her long to find him. He was huddled under a bush with blood oozing from the wounds in his legs and arms and a trickle of blood from the side of his mouth.

She knelt down beside him. "Lie still, Perry. I'll get this bandaged up and then we'll get you to a doctor."

"No, Hunter Lady, not this time. They got me in the back. Guess it's all over."

"You don't know that …"

"Sure, I do … maybe it's best."

"Best? How?"

"There ain't no written records of Minnie Ha-Ha."

"What about on the cloud?"

"No cloud…" more blood bubbled from his mouth. "I made it up …" He choked slightly and she tried to lift him.

"So Minnie Ha-Ha is out of reach?"

"Almost. It's just …"

She suddenly realised. "You memorised it, didn't you?"

Perry smiled through his pain. "Sure, so you see … so long as I'm alive the risk remains. Time to go … most … useful thing I can do."

"No."

"Yes."

The Hunter sat back on her heels. Deep down she knew

409

he was right.

"Promise me ... one thing ..."

"Of course."

"If they ever ... make the ... movie of all this ... they must use ... "*Nights ... in the ... Gardens of Spain* ... for the music."

The Hunter felt tears pricking the back of her eyes. "You stupid sod."

There was a pause as Perry was clearly struggling to breathe. Finally he managed to say. "Something else ..."

"What?"

"I'd like to go quick ... and now ... help me."

Her eyes opened wide as she took in the meaning of what he was saying.

He reached up and grasped her hand. "Make it quick, Hunter ... make it clean."

She thought. *I can't do this* ... but then the realist in her took over. *But I have to do it.*

Aloud she said, "I understand."

She eased her gun out of its shoulder holster and then leaning forward she kissed him on the lips.

"Farewell, Perry. This time it really is adios, not hasta luego."

He smiled up at her as she raised her gun but before she could pull the trigger she heard a shot and Perry went limp in her arms. She looked up to see Okhotnik standing behind her.

"You are brave woman, but is best I kill him."

"I would have ..."

"Da, I know. But now we have result and your conscience is okay."

"What about your conscience?"

"Easy for me. I not care for him like you."

Suddenly the Hunter felt very tired. Okhotnik looked down at her smiling. "We did good. Now I must leave, but first I have this for you."

"What is it?"

"I understand you like USB ... er ..." she fumbled for the word, "fleska."

"USB-fleska? Oh, you mean USB flash drive?"

"Yes, flash drive. Here. I think this will help with Mister Sanderlin."

"Sanderlin? What's on it?"

"Lazovsky's files, bank information, emails, lists of names. Much stuff."

"Where the hell did you get all that?"

Okhotnik did not answer. The Hunter had another thought.

"How long have you had this?"

"Long time ..."

"Then why—?"

"Who to trust? Always difficult. I need to know if you are someone who can ... what is English expression? Place your money with your lips."

"Put your money where your mouth is."

"Da, that is so. I learn now you are such person, so this is for you. Dosvidanya, Hunter. Poyezzhay s Bogom." And Okhotnik dropped a USB drive at the Hunter's feet before walking away along the clifftop.

The Hunter watched her go. She felt absolutely drained. She took one of Perry's hands in hers and just sat there.

And that's how the Defender and the Armourer found her ten minutes later.

JOB DONE

SHE HAD VERY LITTLE recollection of the next few hours. She had a vague memory of the Armourer sitting on the ground beside her, an arm round her shoulders while the Defender was busy on his phone. A few minutes later a jeep appeared, bouncing over the rutted path. One of Xabier's men was driving and everyone seemed to be in a hurry. Then they were roaring past the collapsed light house now burning steadily, past bodies scattered over the clip top, heading back to the farmhouse.

They only paused there long enough to load all their personal possessions into their own vehicle then they were careering down the track towards the nature reserve car park. As they reached it they heard another huge explosion and, looking back they saw the farmhouse engulfed in flames. The Defender had a quick word with one of Xabier's men and then they were gone again, the Housekeeper in the driving seat, the Armourer beside him and the Hunter in the back between the Python and the Defender. All she could remember was the Python muttering about the destruction of all his precious equipment.

ST THOMAS THE HOSPITAL GARDEN

IT WAS EIGHT AM. Big Ben was just striking the hour when she joined Forseti on a bench in the gardens of St Thomas Hospital, gazing out across the Thames to the Houses of Parliament opposite.

"It's such a nice idea, isn't it?" he said as she sat down beside him.

"What is?"

"Parliamentary democracy. The idea that everyone can have some kind of say in how their country is run, have some influence on their own lives."

"Don't you believe in it?"

"Oh, I believe in the theory and occasionally it works in practice. Never perfect, perhaps but, as they say, better than the alternatives. Then some bastard like Sanderlin comes along and corrupts the whole system."

They sat in silence for a few moments then Forseti said, "When did you get back?"

"Late last night."

"I thought so. Well, I'm sorry to drag you out so early."

"No problem."

"A little bird in Washington tells me that Senator Beckford seems to have vanished while on a trip abroad."

"Really?"

"Do you think he is likely to reappear sometime?"

The Hunter considered for a moment. "No," she said finally.

"And would it be safe to assume, even without any direct confirmation, that we could now refer to Nikolai Lazovsky in the past tense?"

"You could say that."

"So that just leaves—"

"Oliver Sanderlin. Yes. Did Fixer deliver that print out of the messages between him, Bedford and Lazovsky? There was a flash drive as well."

"There was. I was up most of the night working through them. The material on that flash drive was especially interesting. Was this another acquisition from Perry Cracken?"

"No. You could say it came from my counterpart in Moscow."

"Ah."

"There'll be no further information from Perry Cracken but the danger of Minnie Ha-Ha has been eliminated."

"Good."

The Hunter turned to face him. "When we first learned what Sanderlin was doing you said you wanted to play the long game."

"Yes. And we've played it."

"We've played it, and we now know that the truth was even worse than we'd thought."

"And sobering. That list of the people working with Sanderlin came as a real shock."

She nodded. "So what we going to do with this knowledge?"

There was a long silence then Forseti said, "What do you think would happen if we simply made this information public?"

"Disbelief. Denial. Perhaps a purge. More likely a cover-up."

"And procrastination. The arguments could rage for years

and that would benefit no one."

"So you can't just arrest him?"

"Well, we could, but it would be difficult to explain where some of the evidence comes from. If it ever reached court I rather fear a good barrister would have a field day. The only way our information would be credible to the public is if Sanderlin himself confirms it's true."

"That's what I thought but the fact is he's still a traitor."

"Yes, and a dangerous one – he's a man with access to the highest levels of government. I dread to think what strings he could pull, what leverage he could exert if he thought he was going to be exposed."

A few yards away a seagull and a blackbird squabbled over a crust of bread on the grass. The Hunter watched them.

Beside her, Forseti said, "Am I right in thinking you're still intercepting his communications?"

"We are. Why?"

"Well then, as of now he doesn't know his overseas support has gone …"

The Hunter sat very still.

After a moment, she asked, "How long before news of the Senator's death breaks in the press?"

"It won't be long, maybe a day at most."

She took a deep breath. "Then there's still just enough time to deal with Sanderlin. We have to finish what we started."

HUBRIS

OLIVER SANDERLIN SETTLED into his usual chair at his usual table in his usual restaurant with a strong inward sense of satisfaction. The latest message from Nikolai Lazovsky said Perry Cracken had been captured, a bit of persuasion had been applied – if Sanderlin had known how to laugh, he'd have laughed at this – and they now had the details of the process to combine the two original formulas to create Minnie Ha-Ha.

Sanderlin himself had the Mayoquoid formula so he felt he was in a strong bargaining position. All he needed now was to talk to Lazovsky privately. He had a great admiration for the Russian, in particular his lack of any moral inhibitions and the way he managed to manipulate the politics in his country to suit his own ends. However he had a deep loathing for the American. In his view Beckford was an uncouth thug but the money that flowed into Sanderlin's hands from the drugs operation was useful.

The waiter brought his first course and he settled to his meal.

Oliver Sanderlin thought of himself as a kingmaker. The present prime minister would never have achieved prominence off his own bat. It was Sanderlin, whispering in his ear, encouraging him to appoint other incompetents to senior government posts, men and women hungry for power, who would do anything to achieve it, which had brought the country to the state where he, Sanderlin, could virtually do anything he liked.

The sea bream was finished and was replaced by a crème brûlée with lavender shortbread. His eyes glistened.

There had been some resistance to his plans, of course, some from within the governing party, some from the opposition, some from senior members of the civil service and business leaders. He had quickly identified all the people who might threaten his long term plans and had taken steps to deal with them. Lazovsky had been very helpful there. The Russians had developed a wide range of poisons and nerve agents, some killed outright, some simply created a torpor that allowed 'accidents' to happen.

He had been very careful. All the fatal incidents had been widely spaced and had no direct connection to him. The only thorn in his flesh had been the person they called The Hunter. When he learned that the Hunter and Cracken had arranged a secret meeting with the Americans to do a deal over the combination formula, he had passed the information on to Lazovsky. That encounter had gone disastrously wrong but at least the Hunter was dead. Or so he had thought at the time, but apparently that event had been greatly exaggerated.

However he'd won in the end. Perry Cracken had apparently been captured. Then, a few days ago Lazovsky sent a message saying that Cracken had cracked, they had the combination formula and the Hunter was finally and definitely dead.

As he sat back in his chair toying with a coffee and a cognac, he felt at peace with the world. Power, even the behind the scenes power that he wielded, was like an aphrodisiac. At that moment he became aware of some kind of activity at the door of the restaurant and then suddenly there were two uniformed police offers walking towards his table.

"Excuse me, sir. Are you Mr. Oliver Sanderlin?"

"Yes, I am. What is it?"

"I'm sorry to disturb your dinner, sir, but Inspector Mellors asked us to find you. Apparently there's been an attempted break-in at your home. The Inspector would like you to come at once, sir."

"Of course, yes … I don't know … An attempted break-in you say?"

Oliver Sanderlin was an expert manipulator, an unscrupulous user of people, but he completely lacked what Forseti and the Hunter would have called 'tradecraft'. It would never have occurred to him that dining regularly in the same place could possibly be dangerous and despite his personal disregard for the law, it would also never have occurred to him to doubt the authenticity of a policeman in uniform. So without giving it any thought he allowed himself to be ushered out of the restaurant and into the waiting car.

He slid into the back seat and one of the policemen came in after him. As the car pulled away from the kerb he realised there was another person next to him and a female voice said.

"Good evening, Mr. Sanderlin. We meet at last."

A SERVICE FLAT SOMEWHERE IN LONDON

FORSETI SAT IN the living room of his London flat deep in thought. He had been very disturbed by the information the Hunter had brought back with her. He had long believed Sanderlin was a traitor, pursuing a private agenda, but now he knew it for certain and he was saddened by the list of people actively working for Sanderlin. This wasn't democracy, it was a hostile takeover.

He was completely at ease with the decision he and the Hunter had implicitly made. In another time he might have referred it upwards or at least shared it with his colleagues. Now he had chosen to do neither.

A half-remembered and probably misquoted line by Sir Walter Raleigh came into his mind.

> *And then none shall be so odious and disdained as the traitors who have sold their country to a stranger and forsaken their faith and obedience contrary to nature or religion.*

That just about summed it up for him, but there was still one loose end. He could safely leave Sanderlin to the Hunter but there was another aspect of this business that he knew he had to deal with himself. He was very conscious that he'd spent all his working life sending people like the Hunter and her father out to do the dirty work. He had always accepted the responsibility, but had never actually had to do the deed himself. Now he knew he had to act, him and no one else. He had no problem with the decision, but he regretted it was necessary.

He sighed and began to plan.

JUSTICE

THE ATMOSPHERE IN the car was tense. Sanderlin said, "What is all this? Who are you?"

"They call me the Hunter."

"The Hunter? No, you're not, the Hunter's dead …"

"Sorry to disappoint you, Mister Sanderlin, but I'm not quite dead yet." She paused for a moment. "I do seem to be saying that rather a lot lately."

"Are you responsible for this break-in at my house."

"There is no break-in, Mister Sanderlin. At least not yet, though I suppose you could argue that there will be shortly. We're on our way there now and you're going to let us in."

"You're out of your mind. Do you have any idea who I am?"

"Of course. That's the whole point."

"You'll regret this. I'll have you arrested and then make sure you just disappear."

"Ah, Sanderlin democracy in action."

"You stupid bitch. I have more power than you can ever dream of."

"I'm afraid you've got your tenses mixed."

"What?"

"You said 'have more power', It should be 'had'."

For the first time Sanderlin felt a twinge of fear.

"What do you mean?"

The car pulled into the kerb outside Sanderlin's house.

"I'll explain when we get indoors," said the Hunter. "Now

when we get out of the car you'll open the front door and once we're inside you'll switch off the alarm system."

"I'll be damned if I will."

"You'll certainly be damned if you won't, literally damned, I mean, because you'll be dead. And when that happens there's only one place you'll be going."

This was delivered in such a flat matter-of-fact tone that Sanderlin shivered.

They got out of the car, Sanderlin fumbled for his keys and once in the house he switched off the alarm system, prompted by a nudge of the Defender's knife.

The car driven by the Fixer pulled away while the Hunter, Defender and Housekeeper made their way up to Sanderlin's first floor study.

"You can't possibly get away with this."

"We can try."

"All right. How much do you want? I don't know who's paying you but I'll double it."

"Sorry, Mister Sanderlin, but this isn't about money. Now then, please open your safe."

"No."

"Have it your own way."

At a nod from the Hunter the Defender grabbed Sanderlin and held him while the Housekeeper went through his pockets and found his keys. He opened the safe and the Hunter stepped forward to examine the contents. There were details of several bank accounts, both in the UK and abroad, all of which she passed back to the Housekeeper.

There were two envelopes and a little notebook together with a pile of cash in twenty-pound notes, at a rough guess well over a thousand pounds. One envelope was very bulky and contained various photographs of some of the people on the USB flash card list, mostly showing them in less than flattering positions. Sanderlin obviously believed in insurance. She opened the smaller envelope, pulled out the contents and smiled. She could not understand all the writing on the sheets but she saw the signature at the end of it – Stewart MacQuoid.

This was the formula for Mayoquoid.

She handed it to the Housekeeper. "Burn this."

"No." Sanderlin screamed the word but the Housekeeper ignored him, took out a box of matches and set fire to the sheets. Sanderlin struggled to stop him but the Defender held him firmly.

The Hunter opened the notebook and found a series of rectangles and inside each an apparently random selection of letters and figures. She recognised it immediately.

"What's this?"

"Um … just rubbish, doodles, nothing important."

"Doodles? Interesting. Now if I were a suspicious person I might think that these are the access codes for your communication system with Senator Beckford and Nikolai Lazovsky."

Sanderlin was horrified but fought to get himself under control. "So what? Even if you were right, you'd never unravel that in a million years."

"We didn't need a million years. My colleague did it in a few days. We've been accessing your messages for weeks."

"That's not possible."

"Oh, but it is. How else could we have sent you the message that Cracken had given up the Minnie Ha-Ha formula and that the Hunter is dead?"

A terrifying thought was beginning to dawn on Sanderlin. "I don't believe it."

"It doesn't matter either way. As you can see I'm not dead, but both Lazovsky and Beckford are."

"They can't be. I had a message from Nikolai only a few hours ago and he said ….." He tailed off as he saw the Hunter's smile.

"My god, was that you?"

"Got it in one. You're finished, Mister Sanderlin. Your power grab is over. The Minnie Ha-Ha formula has been destroyed. There will be no behind the scenes control of the government. It all ends here."

"I'll deny everything. You've got no evidence. No jury will ever convict me."

"You're probably right, but it doesn't matter. You'll never see a jury."

"You can't touch me. I have the confidence of the Prime Minister. I am above the law."

"Sadly, yes, Mister Sanderlin, you probably are above the law but that doesn't matter. We're nothing to do with the law. Our concern is justice. And you're a traitor."

Sanderlin was suddenly very frightened. He had organised many violent acts but had never been faced with one directly.

"What are you going to do?"

The Hunter regarded him thoughtfully for a moment. "Well, that rather depends on you."

"I'll do anything. Anything."

"We have a list of all the messages that have passed between you, Lazovsky and Bedford over the past few months. We have a list of all the bank accounts controlled by the three of you and the names of all the people in the UK who have been supporting you. We know exactly what you had planned to do and we will make that public."

"No one will believe you."

"Not everybody, true, but enough people will. We will also let the Russians know that it was you who betrayed Lazovsky."

"But I didn't."

"They won't know that and I guess they'll come after you."

"Oh, my god."

"I don't think your life is going to worth living, Mister Sanderlin, and I think the world will be a better place without you."

"Are you going to kill me?"

The Hunter looked him straight in the eye. "What we're going to do now, Mister Sanderlin is leave you alone – here. Locked in this room, no phone, no computers."

"What?"

The Hunter offered him a folder. "And we will leave you with these documents, a record of all the information we have on you, all the correspondence between you, Lazovsky and Beckford, the names of all those in the UK who have supported you, enough to ensure you will serve a very long prison sentence …" She paused. "Always assuming a Russian hit squad doesn't get you first."

"You can't. You wouldn't."

"Oh yes we would. In fact we will. All this material will be distributed worldwide to every media outlet in a couple of days' time."

"Oh, my god."

"So, I think you have two options. Having read all this stuff you might choose to make a public confession and trust to the justice you have undermined. Alternatively there's this …" The Hunter put a small bottle on the desk. "Another option."

"I'll see you in hell, Hunter."

"I think you'll be there before me. We're going to leave you now. We'll have people outside the house and if you try and attract outside attention we'll come back and shoot you. We'll return in twenty-four hours to learn what you have decided to do. So that's it, Mister Sanderlin, have a nice day."

A FLUTTER IN THE DOVECOTES

THREE DAYS LATER Sanderlin's cleaner arrived at his house as usual. When she went into his bedroom she let out a scream that would have qualified her for the opening credits in a TV murder mystery. Sanderlin lay on the bed, arms neatly by his side and an empty bottle of pills on the table beside him. He was clearly dead.

Having got the screaming out of the way, the cleaner called the police, being careful to use her own mobile phone. She watched a lot of telly so knew all about fingerprints and DNA and wanted to make sure she wouldn't be a suspect.

However, when the police arrived they found a letter in Sanderlin's study written in his own handwriting. It read.

I have decided to take my own life rather than face the consequences of what I have done now that I know I have failed. I do not pretend to be sorry for my actions. Democracy is nothing but a dream for weak people, only the strong and powerful should have the right to make decisions and if I had been successful then I, together with others who feel the same way, would have been able to control this country and bring to it the discipline it lacks.

I have just heard that my dear friend, the Russian Nikolai Lazovsky, is dead. I have worked with him for many years and he taught me so much about how to overthrow a weak, spineless government and return power to where it rightly belongs.

Now my dream is over. I have lost the fight and as I am about to die, I will no longer protect all those who have aided me. None of them really believed in my dream, most of them supported me for personal gain, not for idealistic reasons. I owe them no loyalty.

Oliver Sanderlin

Although the police did not make this note public it somehow found its way to all the national papers, as well as Reuters, Associated Press and all leading broadcasters. Accompanying the letter was a list – also in Sanderlin's handwriting – of all those who supported what he had been trying to do. The names included twenty prominent MPs, together with several back bench MPs from all parties, half a dozen members of the House of Lords, four senior civil servants, the chairman of a major bank, the owner of a national newspaper, two high profile TV political commentators, an American TV evangelist and two Russian millionaires living in London.

Not surprisingly the press – both real investigative journalists and sensation seeking hacks – went into overdrive. As most of the British press operated on the *'Don't let the truth get in the way of a good story'* principle, and the dead can't sue for libel, the decision was taken to print Sanderlin's letter. The list of names was deemed too dangerous to publish without supporting evidence.

By lunchtime a statement, which apparently came from the Prime Minister's office, was made public and used in all the midday news bulletins. It said:

> *With great regret it appears that Oliver Sanderlin,*
> *once a trusted government adviser, has apparently*
> *been working against the interests of the British*
> *Government and its people. Mr Sanderlin has now*
> *taken his own life.*

When journalists pressed for more information the Prime Minister's spokesman declined to comment further, in fact some of the more perceptive journalists wondered if he had actually seen the statement at all before it was made public.

Speculation was rife but then the following day Reuters received a large package containing the exchange of emails, details of overseas bank accounts, draft speeches, handwritten letters and statements of support from all the names on the list, showing they were all actively involved in Sanderlin's attempt to create an absolute power base and neutralise Parliament.

With firm evidence in hand all the national press – with one exception – published the names and details of who these people were and what they'd been prepared to do. This was quickly picked up by broadcasters worldwide and went viral on social media.

The immediate result was several high profile resignations, the complete disappearance of five people, a challenge for the leadership of the governing party and a sudden rush for the services of prominent lawyers.

Basically it was turmoil.

AN ANONYMOUS ROOM SOMEWHERE IN LONDON

IT HAD BEEN a long day and it was nearly ten o'clock that evening when Forseti entered Odin's room. Odin looked up from his desk. "Well, we can't ever say life is dull, can we?"

Forseti gave a half smile. "Hardly, the press is having a field day."

"The Prime Minister's office is not happy."

"At least his name wasn't on Sanderlin's list. Suggests he's simply stupid rather than a traitor."

"Doesn't look like he'll keep his job though."

"Don't see how he can in the circumstances. Sanderlin was his appointment."

"And how about this Russian? Do we know for certain that he's dead?"

"Not officially, no, but I can assure you he is and so is the American Senator who ran the drugs ring."

"The American's dead too? Are you sure?"

"Absolutely certain. It's really good news for us, so, I thought maybe we should have a drink to celebrate."

Odin looked slightly surprised but said, "Oh, well, why not. Drinks cupboard is over there. I'll have a whisky."

As Forseti was pouring the drinks, he said casually, "You never really wanted the Hunter's team, did you? All you ever wanted was to get that American Hoskins back in the UK. I only realised why when I discovered it was you in charge of the police operation that was meant to capture him, the one that went so wrong. You thought Hoskins had made a fool of you and you couldn't allow that."

"That man deserved everything he got."

"Oh, I agree, but once the Hunter's team had got him back, you did your best to close her down. Why was that? Were you worried you'd helped create a force you couldn't control?"

"What on earth are you talking about?"

"Then when Cracken returned from the dead and got in touch, you passed on the information about the Hunter's address, putting her life at risk?"

"What if I did? It was for the greater good. The only way to find Cracken was to prod her into action, and anyway individuals don't matter."

"Oh, but they do. Without trust and loyalty we are nothing. What you hadn't bargained for was that other interested parties would also learn that Cracken had resurfaced and so suddenly there was carnage in Clapham."

"That's not my fault. That bloody woman brought it all on herself. I presume she was responsible for this fiasco."

Forseti handed a glass to Odin. "Cheers."

"Cheers."

They both drank, then Forseti said, "Why do you call it a fiasco?"

"Well, all this publicity is doing a lot of damage and I simply don't believe all that stuff about Oliver Sanderlin. I reckon that so-called confession was a forgery."

Glass in hand Forseti was wandering about the office. "You could be right, but it's irrelevant. It's all true, you know. He was planning to use Minnie Ha-Ha to make the UK government dance to his own tune."

"Nonsense, you can't believe everything you read in

the tabloids."

"I don't. But I do believe in hard evidence. As well as all the stuff that's appeared in the media we have copies of the Russian's files, we have Sanderlin's financial records showing the circuitous routes by which he received payments from the American drugs ring, together with all the messages that passed between him, Lazovsky and Beckford."

Odin was surprised. "Why haven't I seen any of this?"

"Because you were part of it. I'm not quite sure when you changed sides, Odin, though I suspect it was before the Hunter was first declared dead. What happened? Did you think that Sanderlin couldn't lose so decided you'd rather be part of the winning team?"

Odin drained his glass and banged it down on the table. "You're out of your mind. You always were fond of conspiracy theories, Forseti."

"I presume you were seduced by the power Sanderlin was wielding behind the scenes. We've all been watching law and order, to say nothing of decent, honourable behaviour, cease to exist in this country. What happened? Did you decide the fight couldn't be won and thought you'd hitch your wagon to the rising power base?"

"You're mad. I had nothing to do with Sanderlin."

"Now we both know that's not true. Your name was on his list of those actively working for him."

"No it wasn't. I saw that list."

"Ah, well, it was on the original list but I removed it. I wanted to deal with you myself."

Odin went very still. "I see."

"You're a fool, Odin. One expects dishonesty from elected politicians but people like you and I are in a position of trust. Trust that you betrayed. You once said you wanted people to know that the arm of British justice is a long one. Well, the

Hunter certainly achieved that for you."

"Interfering bitch. Never mind, doesn't matter now." Odin opened his desk drawer and produced a gun. "As for you, Forseti, you always were too clever for your own good."

Forseti inclined his head. "Maybe. So what are you going to do now?"

Odin smiled. "I'm going to kill you. I'll say it was because you came here to confess to helping Sanderlin and when I got angry you attacked me so I shot you in self-defence."

Forseti sniffed. "Good plan. Could have worked."

"What do you mean, could have?"

"Well, snag is that's not your gun, it's mine and it's not loaded."

"You're bluffing." Odin stood up to face Forseti and pulled the trigger. Click. Nothing.

Forseti stepped forward, shoved Odin back down into his chair and produced a gun from his pocket. "On the other hand this one is loaded. Your gun as it happens, I came in here earlier and switched them over."

Odin shivered as he felt the cold metal against his ear.

"You won't get away with this."

"Maybe, maybe not. I don't much care. I used your passcode to log in so officially I've never been in the building this evening. When they find you tomorrow morning they'll also find your written confession saying your were part of Sanderlin's group, all neatly written out in your own handwriting." Forseti sighed. "I probably read too many Agatha Christie novels as a child, but I am most impressed with the various skills the Hunter's team can call on."

"You're a reasonable man, Forseti, let's talk. We can work this out."

"No we can't. We used to hang traitors, Odin. Can't do that any more but you don't deserve to live. Goodbye."

Forseti pulled the trigger and Odin slumped face downwards on the desk. Forseti retrieved his own gun, carefully cleaned Odin's gun and put it into his hand. He stood back and looked down at the body.

"I'm sorry it had to come to this but it was your choice."

He took a sheet of paper out of his pocket and laid it on the desk beside Odin's head.

"There, your confession, all neat and tidy. You might even have written it yourself."

He turned to leave the room but at the door he paused. "Remember what we said when we first set up the Hunter's team? 'Laws catch flies but let hornets go free'? You might like to share that thought with Sanderlin when you get to the other side, Odin."

He went out closing the door behind him.

THE LETTER

IT WAS ANOTHER small suburban house, nondescript street, shabby wallpaper, musty smell. Forseti was still dressed in corduroy trousers and an old cardigan but instead of the teapot from their first meeting, a bottle of Laphroaig stood on the gate-legged table.

Forseti indicated the bottle. "I had thought of champagne but ..."

"As far as I'm concerned this is champagne."

They drank in silence for a few moments then Forseti said, "So we've been successful. Sanderlin is dead, his supporters exposed and the immediate danger has gone away." There was a pause and then he added. "What about the formulas?"

"He had Mayoquoid. Now destroyed. No idea about SD77 but it's not a problem on its own."

She paused for a moment then grinned. "Sanderlin's 'confession' was a touch of genius. I imagine you wrote it but do I detect the hand of Fixer as well?"

"He knows a lot of very interesting people."

"I hope you didn't write all the guff in the press. Some of that is pretty lurid. Though I did like that statement from the Prime Minister's office."

"Yes, that was very fortuitous."

"Fortuitous? That poor sod of a press person didn't know anything about it, did he?"

Forseti smiled faintly and she went on. "What I don't understand is why no one challenged it."

434

"Lesser of two evils. Better to be seen as a leader who's been betrayed rather than an incompetent idiot who either didn't know what was going on or who was prepared to turn a blind eye."

"So … it's all over."

"Yes. At least for now."

"That's cheerful."

"It's realistic. Dangers don't go away, they merely mutate but at least we've bought time for another generation."

"So what now?"

There was a pause then Forseti said, "I asked to meet you today because I have something for you."

"What sort of something?"

"A letter." Forseti opened his briefcase, produced an envelope and handed it to her.

She slit open the envelope, took out a sheet of paper and a photograph then a kind of dry sob escaped her. It was a picture of her as a toddler with her parents on either side. A photo she had never seen before.

"Where did you get this?"

"Read the letter."

She unfolded the sheet of paper, read the first line and then began to shake. Forseti leaned across the table and laid a hand on her arm. "Be strong, Diana, there's nothing to be afraid of."

She controlled herself and began reading the letter.

My darling daughter,

I am writing this in our London home looking at an old photograph of you with me and your mother. I know how much we both miss her but you are now in your mid-teens, not long now and you will be a young woman. I hope I will live long enough to see you become that young woman but with the work I do, I'm aware that may not be the case.

Even though you're still young I think you and I may be very similar. Perhaps I'm wrong but I sense in you a latent strength and a desire for justice. If you're reading this then it's because you must have achieved great things, and that makes me very proud. I'm not going to write about 'loyalty to Queen and country', such things are pretty meaningless. There is something higher than that, the pursuit of justice and defending those who cannot defend themselves. I have always believed in that and if you've been given this letter then you must not only believe it as well, but have acted on it.

Whatever happens I want you to know that I love you very much and have great faith in you. I'm going to give this letter and the photograph to a very dear friend to pass on to you if and when the time is right.

Be strong, my darling,
With all my love,
Dad

As she came to the end of the letter she began to cry softly. Forseti said nothing and after a few moments she got herself under control.

"Sorry about that."

"Don't be."

"Have you read this letter?"

Forseti looked shocked. "Of course not ... But I have a

good idea about the contents."

She sniffed, wiped her eyes and smoothed the letter back into its envelope.

"Time to move on. What happens now?"

"Well, for a start I think it's time for you to stop trying to justify yourself all the time."

"That's not what I've been doing."

"Oh, I think it is, at least partly, going right back to your army days."

She was silent and after a moment Forseti went on. "On a practical level, we don't need to kill you off again but I think your work has come to an end for the time being."

"Will we ever be needed again?"

"I don't know. There will always be injustices. Some you have to live with …"

"And some you can try and deal with."

"Something like that. But there's a lot to be said for retirement."

She gave a grim laugh. "Like last time, you mean."

"I was going to say, stay alert. We never know what the future might hold."

And that was the message she passed on to her team.

LIFE GOES ON

AS THE SUN CAME up over the hills, he watched an osprey plunge into the water and emerge with a salmon. He felt a deep sense of peace. The Fixer was home.

IT HAD TAKEN HIM over twelve hours to fix the database with the customer desperate to get back on line but he had found the glitch and dealt with it. This was his world. The Python was a happy man.

THE COTTAGE WAS THE same, nothing had changed, but now she was more at ease with herself. Knowing she was valued made all the difference. At last the Armourer was comfortable in her own skin.

HE FINALLY DECIDED TO retire and hand over his practice. However, he continued to run the network of clandestine accounts in case they were ever needed again. The Housekeeper had a tidy mind.

WITH THE CLAPHAM HOUSE no longer available, the Hunter moved into an old farmhouse in Gloucestershire. The Defender visited from time to time and they relaxed together, as only comrades who have faced danger side by side can do.

And then four months later her work phone gave a *ping*.